UNIFIED

THE LEGACY CHAPTERS

UNIFIED

Quill & Flame
PUBLISHING HOUSE

BY THOMAS BURTON

Acclaim

"*Unified* was a delightful read! The whole series gets a round of applause, and *Unified* was the perfect finale. It has been amazing to watch these characters grow and come into their own, and they will steal your heart all over again. Burton is a master of weaving themes and characters together for a satisfying and heartwarming conclusion. A must-read for fans of the series!"

—ASHLEY BUSTAMANTE, author of the Color Theory trilogy

"V. Romas Burton brings her masterful storytelling home with complex characters, Biblical themes, and drama—all while accomplishing the near impossible task of pulling together the threads of a large cast with multiple, overlapping arcs. *Unified* is a fiery conclusion to the Legacy Chapters, with a climax that will have you at the edge of your seat."

—AMBER KIRKPATRICK, award-winning author of *Unleashed* and *Until the Rising*

PRAISE FOR THE LEGACY CHAPTERS

"*Fortified* is a riveting, beautifully-written adventure full of intrigue, betrayal, strife, and one woman with enough faith and bravery in her heart to face it all." —CASEY L. BOND, author of *Where Oceans Burn*

"Burton's new book is filled with fast-paced action, her signature faith-based content with hard-hitting themes and characters you want to root for. The story of embracing faith and becoming confident in abilities and self is one that any young person will love. Humor, touching moments, wholesome friendships between young women of different backgrounds, political intrigue, and a burgeoning romance will keep you flipping pages and leave you impatient for the next book. Another fantastic tale, and one I'm eager to follow!" —C. M. BANSCHBACH, award-winning author of *The Wolf Prince*

"For fans of empowered heroines, soulful themes, and gorgeous worldbuilding reminiscent of CJ Redwine, Morgan Busse, and Mary Weber, *Fortified* is the kind of pure romantic fantasy that will leave you swooning. Get ready to meet Devora, a young woman with powers the kingdom hates in a fight for her life, and the secretive hero we've all been waiting for, Captain Blake, who helps her survive and is the most appealing sort of strong, silent, military version of Mr. Darcy type. Political intrigue, unexpected friendships, and the ending—my heart! Read and see for yourself!" —BRITTANY EDEN, author of the *Heartbooks* series

"The depth of this story just left me breathless. Action, romance, intrigue, and characters who linger long after the story is finished! I can't wait for the next installment in *The Legacy Chapters*!" — AJ SKELLY, bestselling author of *The Wolves of Rock Falls* series and *Magik Prep Academy* series

To anyone who has ever felt caged, it's time to be free.

Chapter One

Haden, Renta, Kadesh

Princess Haden rolled up the scroll she'd stolen from Maldove Palace's library and shoved it in her bag. It slid nicely alongside the other parchment she had stolen from Mother's desk. Both scrolls had been in her possession since she fled Tenton weeks ago.

Borrowed temporarily, Haden corrected, calming her jittery nerves. She was not going to make theft a habit if she could help it.

It had taken her more time than she cared to admit figuring out the different names inscribed on the royal family tree. The characters of the Tentonian language seemed to twist backward when she tried to read them. Why did the scribes insist on writing so small too? Her difficulty with reading was a fault she'd perpetually had, one Mother loved to exploit any chance she got.

Pushing thoughts of Mother from her mind, Haden watched a wooden cart filled with snorting pigs rumble by before ducking behind it and into a nearby alleyway. Pulling the cerulean scarf covering her white-blonde hair down on her forehead, the princess of Tenton made sure none of the strands could be seen. She was thankful that the vendor in Yekel who sold her the scarf didn't press her on the issue of the Seer. Haden didn't know much about Lady Devora Medee, but she knew why her mother wanted Devora, and that was enough.

Taking a breath, Haden peered out of the alleyway. The bustling streets of Renta, the capital city of Kadesh, were similar to Juro in many ways. People haggled for lower prices of goods and merchants tried to make more profit than they earned. However, while Juro, the capital of Tenton, was wrought with bitter cold, Renta was cocooned in a blanket of warmth. Haden found she enjoyed it immensely.

"All right, Haden, be brave," the princess whispered to herself as she clenched the bright scarf tight around her neck.

Blowing out a breath, she stepped forward into the bustling city of the kingdom waging war on her home.

Thankfully, bright colored clothes and scarves were fashionable in Renta. However, her shining hair was becoming bothersome to continuously keep covered. A few people glanced her way, and Haden tugged the head scarf farther down. Her once pale skin had tanned nicely on her journey from Northern Tenton to Kadesh, helping her blend in a bit more with the people around her. But when a gust of wind blew by, knocking Haden's scarf off her head, exposing her vibrant recognizable locks, she knew she had to do something.

Quickly tying the cerulean scarf around her neck, Haden tucked her chin against her chest, praying no one in Kadesh had recognized her as the princess of Tenton.

The streets of Renta buzzed with vendors haggling and bartering with their customers, and, for once, Haden was thankful for the crowded streets.

The sun was just about to hit midday when the shine of its light reflected against a shelf of colored glass bottles. Haden had always loved color and was instantly drawn to them.

"Ah, welcome my dear," the merchant with a blue turban and rotund stomach said, giving her a smile. Or at least Haden thought he smiled. It was difficult to tell based on the giant black mustache and beard covering his cheeks.

His Kadeshian accent was thick and rich, something Haden always liked about the foreign tongue. Though she would *never* say that to Mother or anyone else for that matter. Still, Mother made her learn Kadeshian because it was "good to know your enemy."

It had taken Haden longer than Mother desired, but she was now immensely grateful for the lessons.

"Are you interested in any dyes or perfumes?" the merchant asked, a gleam of mischief in his eyes.

Haden's brows shot up. If she dyed her hair, she wouldn't have to worry about anyone recognizing her as the princess of Tenton.

As she studied the shimmering bottles, another customer cut in front of her and began perusing the different products. Tall with broad shoulders, the man made it difficult for Haden to see the wares.

Frowning, she forced her way around a few other people and in front of the tall man who had blocked her view. Mother would be horrified at her manners, but Haden didn't have much time. Plus, she couldn't risk speaking with anyone more than necessary for fear of recognition.

Trying to keep her hair and face covered as much as possible, Haden asked the merchant, "Do you sell temporary hair dyes?" Her Kadeshian was a bit choppy, but it was good enough for the merchant to finish up selling something to another customer and come her way. Out of the corner of her eye, Haden noticed the tall, broad man give her a once-over before smirking and stepping aside.

The merchant laughed heartily, his stomach jiggling. "Oh yes, all the ladies desire to dye their hair these days." He then leaned forward as if telling Haden a secret. "Apparently the crown prince likes redheads."

The tall man coughed to cover up a laugh, and Haden couldn't help but notice he'd been studying the same green bottle for a long time.

Plucking an orange bottle from the shelf, the merchant held it out to Haden. "Use this and you may be the next princess of Kadesh."

Haden snorted and bit her lip to control her laughter. "No, thank you. I don't want to be the next princess of Kadesh."

She glanced around to see the same tall man hadn't left his spot and was poorly pretending to scrutinize the green bottle some more. He seemed harmless, but she couldn't be too careful of people eavesdropping.

Inching away from the man she asked, "Do you have dark-brown hair dye?"

The merchant frowned. "Of course, but isn't it every young lady's dream to be a princess?"

Haden flattened her gaze. Her life would have been a lot easier if she had been asked that question a long time ago. "Not this lady. How much for brown dye?"

The merchant studied her for a moment then gave her a price. Haden's eyes almost popped out of her head.

"That much?" she squeaked, squeezing the strap of her bag on her shoulder.

The merchant sighed. "I'm afraid so. However, my red hair dye is half off today."

Haden narrowed her gaze. *Why does this man want me to be a redhead so bad?*

"I'll be happy to assist you in purchasing your hair dye, miss," the tall man offered, making his presence known.

It wasn't odd for Haden to be the same height as most men. She had always been tall, another characteristic about her that Mother hated.

"Princesses are meant to be petite and demure," she would say, as if Haden was purposefully making her bones grow longer than

all the eligible bachelors Mother desired to match her with. But, compared to this man, she felt small and quaint.

"Um—" she began before the merchant butted in.

"Mal, if you're not here to purchase anything, you must leave." His mustache turned down as he furrowed his brows.

"I can assure you, Lazaar, I had every intention of buying some brown hair dye today," the tall man, Mal, confessed with a grin. He placed a hand on his heart and gave a winning smile. "Honest."

Lazaar, the merchant, narrowed his eyes.

Haden had lived her whole life having others speak for her and make decisions for her. Even though she found the tall man's kind eyes and grin attractive, and she felt her heart swooning over his accent, she was not going to have some stranger step in on her behalf too.

Lifting her chin, she took a step forward. "Thank you for your kindness, sir, but I can pay for the dye myself." She then turned to the merchant. "You make a tempting offer, but no thank you. I'm sure I can go somewhere else to find what I need."

As Haden started to walk away, Lazaar yelled, "Wait! I'll give you the brown dye and red dye for the same price."

Haden spun around, tired and irritated. "I don't want any red dye, just the brown and for half off of what you said." She'd been shopping for herself back home in Juro long enough to know when a merchant was being greedy.

Mal laughed as he watched the merchant stutter for a reply. Haden crossed her arms over her chest, doing her best to imitate Mother's unamused glare.

Finally, Lazaar sighed. "Fine. The brown dye for half off."

"And throw in this too," Mal said holding out the green bottle.

Haden frowned. *Who is this guy trying to mess up my haggling?* "I'm not paying for your things. Only mine."

Mal gave her a wide grin, and Haden almost took back the statement. But she ignored her thumping heart and stayed firm.

Mother always said she was too soft. Now was the time to prove her wrong.

"The green bottle is included," the merchant said with an exasperated sigh as he pushed the bottle back into Mal's hands. Grabbing a purple bottle from the shelf, he handed it to Haden. "Don't be angry at me when you don't become the next princess of Kadesh because your hair isn't red."

Haden laughed and handed him the money. "I won't. Thank you." Taking the purple bottle, she spun around, hoping to get as far away from the merchant and the stranger, Mal, as possible.

Unfortunately, getting rid of Mal wasn't as easy as she thought.

"That was some fantastic haggling," he commented, easily matching her stride.

Haden kept her eyes forward. There was somewhere she needed to be, and she wouldn't allow this stranger to follow her there.

When she didn't respond, he asked, "Why are you dying your hair?"

Haden stopped. "I don't know you and don't need to answer any of your questions. Please leave me alone."

Mal lifted his hands with palms out. "Okay, okay. I'm just curious to know the pretty girl hiding behind the blue scarf."

Haden pursed her lips. He was handsome, but she didn't have time for attractive men. And even though she planned to outright refuse him, she heard herself saying, "Maybe some other time."

As he grinned at her answer, Haden wrapped her scarf over her nose and mouth and scurried toward the nearest females-only bathhouse. The stranger wouldn't be able to follow her in there.

Hurrying up the stone steps, Haden didn't look back, praying Mal would just forget about her.

Once inside, she found a solitary bath in the back corner. Surrounded by tall columns, it was far more private than the rest of the bathing pools. Pulling her bag over her head, Haden knelt at the edge of the bath and uncorked the bottle. Even in Juro, her white-blonde hair was unique. People on the king's court always complimented her on its originality and exotic nature. Mother loved to use it as a selling point for the dukes who came to inquire about Haden's hand in marriage.

Haden shuddered at the memory of the last suitor Mother tried to foist upon her. Duke Redunt from Snoken, a small city in western Tenton. While Haden had no qualms against those from smaller cities, Duke Redunt was a buffoon who kept licking his teeth whenever he looked at her. She had made sure to act a little more aloof and oblivious during that meeting.

An earthy, musty scent filled Haden's nose as she studied the dye. Hopefully, the color would come out one day, but if not, she wouldn't be upset if she were to rid herself of the burden her "unique" hair brought her.

Cool liquid dripped down Haden's scalp as she massaged the dye into her strands. She did her best to read the instructions, but even if the Kadeshian symbols didn't flip around in her head as bad, it wasn't an easy task.

Once the bottle was empty, Haden scrubbed her dyed hands in a basin next to the bath. It came off easily, which worried her that she had wasted her coin. But as she washed the excess dye out of her hair, Haden realized the strands running through her fingers weren't brown, but blacker than midnight.

Searching around, she quickly found a shining tray holding a variety of soaps. Throwing the soaps off, she stared at her reflection in shock. She should've known the merchant was stretching the truth when she asked for brown. But as Haden stared at the dark strands, she found herself enjoying the midnight color. Now, she would be unrecognizable and could continue with her plan.

Drying her hands and hair on a towel provided by the bathhouse, Haden placed the cerulean scarf back on her head and exited the bathhouse. Another gust of wind blew by, and she allowed her new ebony locks to flow freely. Haden half expected Mal to be lurking somewhere and was annoyed with herself at the disappointment that weighed her heart at his absence.

Shaking her head, Haden pushed the handsome stranger from her mind. She didn't travel all the way from Juro to flirt. She had someone else she needed to meet.

As she hurried from the bathhouse back into the busy streets of Renta, Haden's previous fear returned. Her hair was dark and her skin tan, but she was still taller than most of the Kadeshian women. That alone made her stand out among the crowded streets. Hunching her shoulders, she kept her head down and continued toward her destination. If the scroll from the palace's library was correct, she was almost there.

After a few more twists and turns, Haden found the place she was looking for. The building was not as dilapidated as she assumed it would be. But after growing up in Maldove Palace, everything seemed less grand. Not that she minded. She always despised the gaudy gold fixtures and chilled marble that surrounded her since childhood. Everything in the palace was cold and unfeeling. Haden had always felt like she didn't belong, that she wasn't meant to be a princess.

She thought about the merchant's words again and couldn't help but laugh. So many women desired to be a princess, and she was trying to run as far from the throne as possible.

A group of women conversing in Kadeshian strolled by. A few of them cast curious glances her way but continued without asking any questions.

Haden was thankful she had decided to change her appearance, but still made sure her scarf was secured on her head before she studied the building before her. Comprised of warm red stone, the structure was tall, but not as high as Maldove Palace or the Fortress. Arched windows were carved out of the stone on the second floor, each holding billowing white curtains. The structure was simply designed but held an air of elegance.

Haden would often peer out her bedroom window and study the large stones of the Fortress. Was the prison really as horrible as the stories she'd heard? Being stuck in a large building didn't seem nearly as bad as the small cage she was confined to every evening.

Haden shook her head, pushing the thought from her mind. She needed to focus on her task.

Unbelievably, she'd made it this far. Tunri must have had His hand on her for the palace guards to not have found her by now. It had taken her a few weeks, but she had even made it to Yekel and smuggled herself into Kadesh without notice. Everything lined up perfectly. Almost *too* perfectly.

Chewing on her lip, Haden closed her eyes and knocked on the beautifully carved wooden door.

It's all going to work out. Don't panic. You made it this far without anything happening. What could possibly happen now?

But even with her self-encouragement, Haden still couldn't stop chewing her lip and tapping her toes. Thankfully, she had been wise enough to wear leather boots on her strenuous journey instead of her usual silk slippers. But even though the boots were hardier, she could see a hole beginning to form from wear and tear.

After what seemed like an eternity passed, the door swung open. A man with flawless dark skin and a white turban glared at Haden.

"Uh," she said before the man slammed the door in her face.

Shocked, Haden stood paralyzed. Was this the wrong place? Had she read the scroll wrong?

Of course, you read it wrong, little princess, Mother's condescending voice swirled in her thoughts. *You can't read, you can't write, you can't do anything right. You're a waste.*

Haden shoved the memories away. No. She knew she had read the scroll correctly. She didn't care what Mother said. It may take her longer to understand words and sentences, but she wasn't a fool. Everything in her soul told her this was the right place.

Squaring her shoulders, Haden knocked heavily on the door again.

Within a few moments, the sturdy wood flung open. The same angry man with the white turban answered again, and this time he spat a whole string of Kadeshian words at Haden. Although she had studied the tongue, the man spoke far too fast for her to understand everything. She could only assume his words were mostly unkind based on his flying hands and harsh tone.

Once he finished, Haden ran over her Kadeshian sentence in her mind before announcing, "I'm here to see Miguel Salvar."

The turban man didn't yell anymore, but his glare never wavered. Thankfully, he didn't slam the door in her face but stormed away all the same.

Excitement laced Haden's veins as she stepped over the threshold. The sweet aroma of cinnamon and cardamom danced around her nose. Haden first smelled the spices when she was captured—or rather given as bait—to the Kadeshians before the battle of Edo. Every evening the Kadeshian general, General Sage, would have his servants make him a drink with the delightful blend of spices. Haden always yearned to try it, maybe now she would.

Having no idea where the angry turban man went, Haden did her best to navigate her way to Miguel Salvar. Directions were never really her strong suit, but she was always up for an adventure, so she decided to take a right.

The twists and turns of the building reminded her of the night she fled from Maldove Palace after Captain Blake returned her to her room. Haden had remembered the captain often since leaving the palace, hoping he hadn't suffered the wrath of the queen because of her departure. She knew his heart belonged to another, but she was still worried about the curse controlling him. There was no light in his eyes, no joy. Haden often recognized the look in her own green eyes. Only those who had been cursed by the queen truly knew what a burden it was.

Haden rounded another corner, following the delicious scent. In a few more steps, she came upon an open room filled with various square tables with checkered patterns atop each one. Around each table sat three men: one on either end and a third between. As Haden studied the scene further, she discovered that the pairs of men were playing a game, and the third man was overseeing it.

Haden loved games. Often being left to her own devices, she had taught herself many board and card games. Sometimes the palace servants would play with her, but usually she would play by herself.

Haden started to observe one of the matches when the man with the white turban appeared. In a flurry of words and flailing hands, he came at her again. Haden didn't know what to do besides retreat. But as she took a step back, she bumped into a set of players, knocking over their board. Small, round pieces flew through the air as Haden toppled backward. The Kadeshian men playing the game erupted into an uproar as Haden fell on her backside.

After a few deep breaths, Haden opened her eyes to find a group of Kadeshian men glaring down at her. The men shared similar skin tones, but their clothing was a variety of bright purples, reds, and greens.

"Are you all right?" a voice beside her asked.

Haden immediately recognized the Tentonian tongue and faced the man. With sun-kissed skin and a bright-yellow turban, the middle-aged man extended his hand toward her. Relieved, Haden took the proffered hand and stood. Her cerulean scarf had fallen from her head and while her hair was now dark, she slapped the fabric around her hair out of habit.

Despite her disguise, Haden still worried that if anyone recognized her, the Kadeshians would capture her like they had before the battle of Edo. But the Kadeshian men around her only grumbled under their breath and went back to their games, except for the man who helped her.

Releasing a breath, Haden faced the man with the yellow turban, wondering where he had learned to speak Tentonian fluently.

But before she could ask, the man questioned, "Now why would the captured princess of Tenton be looking for me?"

Haden stared at the man, unsure of what to do. She never believed she'd get this far. Yet she knew she had to find Miguel Salvar. He was the one who could answer her questions and help her with her plan. He was the one who was there when she was stolen from her family. He was the only one who knew she wasn't the real princess of Tenton.

Chapter Two

Haden, Renta, Kadesh

"You know who I am?" Haden whispered, her eyes darting to the men trying to reset their pieces on the boards. Her confidence from the market only moments ago was a distant memory.

But the Kadeshian men playing their games paid them no mind.

Miguel quirked a bushy brow at her. "Why would you come all this way if you didn't believe I knew your identity?"

Haden blinked at the question, realizing Miguel was right. It was an ignorant question. She always seemed to ask the wrong questions.

Haden lowered her eyes, feeling as if she were back in Maldove Palace with Mother scolding her. "I apologize for the foolish question."

As Haden waited for the reprimand of her stupidity, Miguel surprised her by responding, "There's no such thing as a foolish question. But some are better asked in private."

He waved the angry man with the white turban over. The man glared at Haden before speaking to Miguel in Kadeshian. Haden absentmindedly tucked a few stray strands of ebony hair back inside her cerulean scarf. It was difficult not to eavesdrop as the two men argued back and forth. Instead, she studied the room around her.

The gaming room was spacious. Brightly covered rugs layered over one another across the stone floor. The tables holding the checkered boards were made of sturdy dark wood. It surprised Haden at how much color all the men wore. While the people of Juro, especially those in the king's court, wore some color, she had never seen so many beautiful shades. From bright yellow turbans to red tunics, the room was an array of beautiful and bold hues.

The men returned to their checkered boards with intense looks. It was an interesting game; one Haden had never seen before. She watched in fascination as each player placed a colored glass bead on different cross sections of the board. Some moves were met with smiles and cheers, others with groans or curses.

Just as Haden tried to figure out the rules, Miguel gently touched her arm.

"Apologies. We were trying to figure out accommodations for your stay here."

Haden faced Miguel and the angry white-turban man, who didn't seem as angry anymore but more shocked as he gawked at her.

"This is Amir," Miguel continued, motioning to the still gawking man. "He has been a friend to me ever since I came to Kadesh many years ago."

Haden wasn't sure how to address Amir, so she simply nodded her head in acknowledgment while Amir stared.

Miguel gently nudged his friend. "Amir, if you could be so kind as to lead us to the rooms for rent?"

Amir snapped out of his daze, mumbled something in Kadeshian then hurried out of the game room. Miguel motioned to Haden and the two quickly followed Amir.

After a few steps of silence, Haden whispered to Miguel, "Why did he stare at me like that?"

Haden had been groomed since a young age to endure the gawking of strangers, but it still made her uneasy.

"Smile and wave, my dear," Mother would always say. "Your beauty is a tool that I will help you use to your advantage."

Haden never understood what her mother meant until she was sixteen summers. Then things changed. Apparently, Haden was not only meant to be beautiful but to have the gift of tinkering, as well. Haden had never heard of tinkering and didn't really know what it or any other gift was. But when her sixteenth birthday came two years ago and Haden remained giftless, Mother changed.

True, the queen of Tenton was always a bit distant and really only cared about Haden's appearance. Mother would often complain that trying to teach the princess any lessons was useless because Haden's mind couldn't handle it. But two years ago, it was as if Mother had been replaced with an entirely new woman.

Mother never struck her physically, but her venomous words were sharp enough to pierce Haden's heart.

Useless.

Fool.

Idiotic.

Worthless.

Haden pushed the words from her mind. She had always known something was different about her. How she never fit in with royal life. She also hated the cold, sterile feel of the palace. And while all the fine clothes and luxuries she had were appreciated, they never felt like her, who she really was.

It wasn't until Mother made an offhand comment about Haden's appearance that Haden realized she wasn't really the monarch she was bred to be.

"Princess?" Miguel asked, pulling Haden from her thoughts. "Follow me, please."

Amir led them out of the building and across the street to a two-story home nestled between two larger homes. Warm, red-brown clay comprised the exterior with sheer white curtains flowing through the open windows. Haden took in the pleasing sight. She could definitely get used to it.

"Will this be okay for a princess?" Amir whispered to Miguel and Haden realized they didn't know she understood Kadeshian.

Though she wasn't the best princess, Haden knew when to be polite and when to be forward. This was a time to be polite and let the men believe she was ignorant of their conversation.

As Haden kept her gaze on the building, Miguel switched back to Tentonian and asked, "We know you're accustomed to a more lavish residence, but will this be suitable for now?"

Haden grabbed the strap of her bag, almost giddy to explore the humble home. "Oh, this is perfectly delightful. Thank you." She smiled at Amir who looked away bashfully.

Miguel spoke to Amir once more before the man took off.

Opening the door, Miguel glanced over his shoulder and said, "Come, we have much to discuss."

Once Haden entered the home, Miguel made sure to lock the door behind her. She wasn't much of a fighter—as proven when she was given to the Kadeshians before the battle of Edo—but Haden kept a knife in her bag, just in case. Subtly, she placed her hand in the bag, ready to strike if she needed to.

Please let him be who I think he is, Haden prayed to Tunri, but she didn't release the handle of the knife.

Beautiful tapestries of red and gold hung on the walls. Equally bright rugs laid across the floor. A long settee rested against the back wall, covered in the plumpest pillows Haden had ever seen.

"What is this place?" she asked, overwhelmed yet loving all the color around her.

Miguel pulled his turban off his head, unveiling a mess of curly brown hair. Haden glanced back at him. She still clutched the knife hidden in her bag but found her fingers loosening from the hilt. He seemed younger than what she thought, but if she figured out the math correctly—there was a possibility she hadn't—he was almost fifty summers. Although his barely graying hair kept his appearance young, Haden could see the age in his eyes. What had this man seen—endured—to flee his home country and live with his enemies for almost twenty years?

"This is a welcoming house for all dignitaries and diplomats who visit Kadesh," Miguel replied, trying to subtly rub a wrinkle out of his tunic.

Fear struck Haden to the core. "What?" she cried, ready to yank out the knife.

She didn't come all this way for Miguel to rat her out to the Kadeshian government. She knew Mother and Father weren't looking for her. She had known that when they used her as bait to lure Kadesh closer to Tenton soil. That's why she was so stunned when the Seer, Devora, came to rescue her.

"Not to worry, princess," Miguel said as he moved the lush pillows out of the way and took a seat. "There haven't been any dignitaries or diplomats from Tenton to Kadesh in a long time. Amir is the owner of this house as well as many others in the city of Renta. We are here with his permission."

Haden relaxed but screeched when four quick knocks came to the door.

Unfazed, Miguel stood. "Ah, that would be Amir. He can't help but be a hospitable host."

Haden frowned at the remark, remembering how rude he had been when she first tried to enter the gaming den.

But, true to Miguel's word, Amir hurried in holding two trays: one with a metal pitcher and two cups, the other with an assortment of cheeses, breads, and fruits. Haden's mouth watered at the sight, and she found herself fully releasing the knife in her bag.

Thankfully, she had been smart enough to bring a sack of coin with her for her passage to Kadesh. But she had been careful not to spend it all so quickly, which meant getting just enough food to stave off hunger and nothing more. Mother always thought she was horrible at math, but really, Haden just needed a little more time to figure out the numbers. She had proven over the last few weeks that she could do calculations correctly when her livelihood depended on it.

Amir placed the trays down on the table before the settee. With a bow, he exited the room, closing the door behind him. Miguel locked the door behind the man then sat again.

Upon noticing Haden still standing, he gave her a warm smile. "Come, sit and eat. I'm sure you have quite a story to tell."

Not needing any further convincing, Haden strode forward and sat next to Miguel. The little home felt safe, safer than the palace ever did, and Haden enjoyed the comforting feeling of it.

Taking a hunk of bread and a piece of cheese, she took a healthy bite. The warm flat bread was the perfect texture against the cold cheese and Haden was already reaching for more when her scarf slid off the top of her head.

Before she could set it back in place, her shoulder-length, now black hair was revealed.

Haden wasn't sure what his reaction would be, but so far in the short time she'd known Miguel, he'd surprised her. And his next response did just that again.

With a warm smile, he commented, "It's amazing how much you look like your mother. Though I expected your hair to be lighter."

Haden blinked at the man then set the piece of flat bread down. "Ah, it was." She chuckled. "I thought dyeing it may help me blend in better." Before she could stop them, her mind flitted back to Mal, his delicious accent and his perfect grin. Where was he now?

Haden shook her head, banishing all memories of the strange man she had met in the market. "That's actually how I figured out my life was a lie," she added.

Miguel's bushy brows rose. "I'm intrigued to hear more."

Haden took a breath then pulled the first scroll from her bag. She'd been so fearful the night she snuck into Maldove Palace's library. She swore at every corner she turned, Mother would be there, waiting to stuff Haden back in her cage.

But Mother never appeared, and Haden was able to find the genealogy scroll and take it. It took her days to figure out all the names and put the pieces of her lost history together, but she had done it. She accomplished such a difficult task, and she was so proud of herself. But could tell no one. And just a few days after she discovered where she really belonged, Haden was thrown at the mercy of Kadeshian general, General Sage.

"Mother—Queen Leza," Haden corrected, for now she knew Queen Leza was not her real mother, "said the same thing."

Miguel's eyes widened as Haden continued the story.

Mother was primping her to be paraded around another duke to potentially marry.

"Dear, it's what you were bred for. And your beauty is the only thing that shines about you," Queen Leza said before instructing the seamstress to tighten the dress further, striking every last breath from Haden's lungs.

Haden learned long ago not to respond when Mother insulted her. When she did, Haden ended up in the cage far longer than she was meant to be. No, it was always better to stay silent and take the verbal beatings rather than try to deflect them.

The queen strode up to Haden, threading a strand of her white-blonde hair through her thin fingers. She sighed.

"You're fortunate you look so much like your mother."

After barking at the maid in the room to fix her a drink, Queen Leza left Haden and the seamstress alone. Although the queen assumed nothing happened in Haden's mind, she was wrong. Just because Haden couldn't read or write as well as others didn't mean she didn't have her own thoughts—her own ideas. And right then, her mind was spinning like a whirlwind.

*As Haden grew up and was prized for her beauty, she real-
ized she didn't look like either of her parents. She didn't have
her father's light-brown hair or extremely fair complexion.
She didn't share her mother's striking dark eyes or silky black
locks. Haden was the piece of the puzzle that didn't fit, and
Mother just confirmed it.*

*Waiting until she was sure Mother was gone from the room,
Haden whispered to the seamstress working on her hem.
"Madeline."*

*Haden knew all the servants feared Mother and were in
the queen's presence as little as possible. But when they were
just with Haden, they relaxed slightly.*

"Yes, Princess?" Madeline asked, her teeth full of pins.

*"If I were to seek my family's records, where would I find
them?"*

*Madeline's fingers paused on the hem of the dress. Haden
wondered if the seamstress would question her or try to deter
her from the idea. Many of the servants tried to get in the
Queen's good graces by treating Haden like a small child
instead of the young woman she had become.*

*But Madeline was different. She was quiet and reserved,
but she always answered Haden's questions. In fact, Madeline was the reason Haden learned to read and write as well
as she did.*

*"I would have to say the library where the genealogy
scrolls are located would be the best place to look, Princess."
Haden began to thank the seamstress when Madeline continued, "I also heard that the queen will be traveling to Grenly
to buy a new crown for your upcoming birthday, so she will
not be available to show you until she returns. In five days."
Madeline coughed and focused back on the hem.*

*"I see," Haden replied as her plan started forming. She
always knew she liked Madeline. "That is quite unfortunate."*

"Yes, Princess, unfortunate indeed."

That night, when the palace was asleep, Haden flew out of her room toward the library. Thankfully, a white mustached librarian guided her to where the scrolls were kept and assisted her in finding which ones she was looking for.

The scrolls were heavy, but Haden managed to get them back to her room and pored over them every day until Mother returned home. By then, Haden had discovered the devastating secrets of her past, but it was already too late. Before she could confront the queen, Haden was transformed early, stuffed in her cage and given to Kadesh like a pig led to slaughter.

She never did understand why the Kadeshians didn't kill her outright. She assumed they had made some sort of deal with Mother. But it wasn't until Haden saw the Seer that she started to realize her mother's nefarious plans.

Chapter Three

Haden, Renta, Kadesh

Haden bit her lip. While she knew she didn't belong to the king and queen biologically, it was another man with white hair and a mustache in Maldove Palace's library who had given her the genealogy scroll leading her to Miguel. The odd man also gave her the clue to further investigate Mother's personal collection of scrolls. At the time she assumed he was a librarian, but now she wasn't so sure. Was Miguel a member of her true family like Haden hoped he was?

"Did she think you wouldn't pick up on the comment?" Miguel asked once Haden finished recounting the tale. Haden must have looked confused because Miguel explained, "The comment that you looked like your mother. You obviously look nothing like the queen. Well, when your hair is the right color, I suppose. I'm surprised she would have been so careless with the comment due to the great lengths she went through to take you."

Haden chewed on her bottom lip, surprised at Miguel's forwardness. For the past eighteen years of her life, everyone had been so guarded around her. She could tell when the servants or other members of nobility carefully chose their words, fearful of saying the wrong thing and evoking the queen's wrath. And then there were the others that saw her as only a foolish child. Haden despised those people the most.

Taking a breath, Haden replied, "She doesn't believe I'm very smart."

Miguel's eyebrows furrowed as he wiped his hands on a cloth napkin. "And why is that?"

Haden held her breath.

Keep quiet and look pretty, that's all you're good for.

That was the truth, right? She was only a pretty face, nothing more. But there was something about the statement that always felt wrong to her. Why couldn't she be more?

When Devora saved her from General Sage's camp, Haden couldn't believe a woman who was also a Seer had saved her. *And* Devora was beautiful. If the Seer could be all those things, why couldn't Haden?

But the truth of her skills still sat raw in her heart: she didn't have any. She couldn't read well, she couldn't write well, and once Haden's tinkering gift didn't appear, Mother gave up on her, never spending any time trying to find something else Haden enjoyed doing. So, the princess had no practice developing any other skill.

"I can't read or write very well, and I have no gift from Tunri," she eventually replied.

And once again, Miguel surprised Haden by laughing outright. Ashamed, Haden turned her head and already started chastising herself for believing this man would help her.

Miguel wiped a tear from his eye with a finishing chuckle. "I apologize, princess. I'm not laughing at you, but at your queen."

Haden crossed her arms over her chest, quirking her brow at Miguel.

Before explaining, the man stood and peeked out the window. The chattering of the Kadeshian people hurrying about their afternoon business was still underway. After he peered out the window for what seemed like forever, Miguel faced Haden.

"Tunri rarely blesses two people in the same family with the same gift."

Haden frowned. "What are you talking about?"

"You found the real genealogy of your family, yes? That's the only way you could've found me and where I was."

Yes," she confessed. "Though I did have some help from a stranger." Haden recalled the mustached man. Even though librarians could be bulky and muscular, she had never seen any quite as large as the man with the white mustache.

Miguel harrumphed as he sat next to her. "Your father is one of the greatest Tinkers I have ever known. But—"Miguel held up his finger, stopping Haden from speaking—"his first born was not blessed with the gift of tinkering. And when the queen came to Yekel, searching for a child, your parents told her this, but she wouldn't listen. Before your mother or father could put up a fight, the queen wiped their memories clean of you and whisked you away." A saddened look came to Miguel's face. "I returned from my rotation a few days later, horrified that you were nowhere to be found. I tried to convince them that they had another child, that we had to save you, but they didn't believe me. The only one who seemed to remember was your older sister, but she was only two at the time."

Haden gasped. "I have a sister?" She wasn't entirely sure how to read the genealogy scroll correctly and a lot of the names had been marked out, which she assumed meant they were deceased.

Actually, Haden had no idea how she made it to Kadesh unscathed to find her uncle, her *real* uncle. It must have been by Tunri's hand.

When she was a young child, she desired to learn to read. At the time, Mother still believed Haden would be useful to her, so she hired the best tutors. But when they deemed Haden as unable to understand written Tentonian, Mother replied, "She has no need for such things, for her beauty is all she needs."

But that didn't satisfy Haden. Before the tutors fled, Haden snatched a teaching scroll out of one of their bags and hid it until she knew they were gone. When she was all alone, Haden studied the learning scroll until she could make out the first line.

Tunri will guide your path.

Haden kept this up until one night Madeline caught her. Haden was so scared the maid would tell Mother, she almost fainted. But Madeline didn't. Instead, she worked with Haden, showing her the different Tentonian symbols and rewriting them in a script that was easier for Haden to read. Madeline patiently taught Haden how to recognize them, even if they twisted around in her mind. With time, Madeline had taught Haden how to read through all the prayer scrolls, learning much about Tunri and His goodness.

So, it had to be Tunri who protected her and gotten her to Miguel safely.

"I was heartbroken the day I had to leave the family again and serve in Tenton's army at the battlefront," Miguel continued, pulling Haden back to the present where she was no longer in Maldove Palace hiding from Mother, but in Kadesh with her newly found uncle. "But when I intercepted a note from the king, ordering my commander to make sure I didn't return from battle, I knew the queen discovered that I still remembered her actions and I remembered you. Who you really were—are," he amended.

Haden scooted to the edge of her seat, transfixed by the story. So many emotions filled her heart, she didn't know which one to feel first. Joy at finding a member of her true family, sadness that the rest of her family had no idea who she was, or elation that she had a sister. Haden had felt so lonely for so long; the thought of having a sibling made her almost giddy. Did they look alike? Enjoy the same things? Would they ever get to meet?

Haden shook her head. *One thing at a time.* First, she needed to know if Miguel would help her with her plan to take down Mother.

"So, you fled to Kadesh once you intercepted the note? Wouldn't that make you a deserter?"

Miguel shrugged. "I was one man, a lowly scrag in the army, against the King and Queen of Tenton. Who would you have listened to? I took my chances."

Haden pursed her lips but knew Miguel was right. The king's and queen's word were law and anyone who defied them was killed.

Haden shuddered, thankful that Mother *did* shield her from that part of the monarchy.

Miguel ran a hand through his curly hair, wrinkles crinkling around his eyes as he smiled. "So that leads me to my next question, Princess. Why did you come all this way to find a deserter of His Majesty's Army?"

Haden tapped her long fingers on her knees. Why, indeed. She hatched this plan over many late nights while caged away. But she never in a million years thought she would get this far. Now that she was here, doubt weighed on her. She couldn't actually do this, right? She couldn't *actually* expose the queen's secrets and bring down the tyrannical monarchy that had ruled for twenty years. Haden was just one girl. A small, insignificant girl who could barely write her own name properly. Yet the second scroll in her bag, the one she discovered in Mother's desk, felt like it would burn a hole through the leather. She needed to get it into the right hands and fast.

"Well—" she started, painfully aware her plan wasn't completely concrete as she pulled out the scroll. Handing it to Miguel, she said, "You should take a look at this."

Miguel's gaze was suspicious but curious as he took the scroll. Yet as he unrolled it, the look shifted to horror.

"This is here?" he whispered, his tone laced with disbelief.

Haden squeezed her fingers over her knees. "I believe so. As soon as I found out who you were, I thought you could help me get it into the right hands."

Miguel's brows furrowed in concentration as he studied the scroll. "When I first came to Kadesh, I was able to procure a job at the palace as a guard. I may be able to reach out to some old contacts and get this information to the crown prince."

Haden frowned. "The crown prince? Why not the king?" Haden hadn't heard much about the crown prince of Kadesh, only horrible stories about his father, King Redore IV. He was ruthless in every sense of the word and just the mere thought of sneaking into his country sent Haden's nerves in a fright.

"The king is—" Miguel started when a loud knock banged on the door.

His eyes immediately shot to the door, a look of panic covering his face. "Did you tell anyone who you were?" he whispered to Haden.

Haden's lips parted in shock, as she remembered her brief time in the market. The merchant, Lazaar, and the handsome stranger, Mal, were the only people who could have seen her white-blonde hair long enough to recognize her. But would either of them know who she was to report her to the monarchy? Haden shook her head violently. There was no way either of those men could have known who she was.

"We have a direct order from King Redore IV. It has been issued for every household in Renta," the booming voice on the other side of the door said.

Miguel released a sigh of relief then turned back to Haden. "Cover your head and keep your eyes down, just in case. Your hair is dark, but if anyone was looking for you, they could easily recognize your features." Rewrapping his own head in a turban, Miguel squared his shoulders. "This shouldn't take too long. The king releases orders on a weekly basis."

Haden nodded fervently, her hands shaking as she wrapped her cerulean scarf around her hair and neck before keeping her eyes glued to the swirling pattern of the carpet on the floor.

Please don't let them find me, Haden prayed, squeezing her eyes shut. She had come so far; she didn't want to be caged again.

Miguel sucked in a breath before opening the door. "Good day, my good man. What does our fine king wish for us to know?"

The guard snorted. "King Redore IV has decided to host a pageant to find a wife for his son, the crown prince of Kadesh. Every Kadeshian woman, sixteen summers to twenty-two summers must report to the palace in two days' time."

Haden's eyes shot up. A pageant to find a wife? She had never heard of such a ridiculous thing. Although, if she had been able to host a pageant to find a husband, it probably would've made finding one a lot easier. Haden shoved the thought aside. No, promenading *anyone* around like they were prized cattle was a horrible thing to do. There were more to people than how they looked.

Miguel extended his hands. "I do love a good wedding! It's been years since we've had one. I thank you, my good sir, for the information. And if I happen to see any lovely young women, I will be sure to let them know."

Haden's heart palpitated in her chest. Had the guard seen her? She did her best to hide from the door's line of sight.

Miguel bowed and began to close the door when the guard placed his foot in the doorway.

Haden's heart jumped to her throat as the door smashed against the soldier's boot. She wasn't sure whether to try to hide or stay put. Mother always told her to obey no matter what. And Miguel told her to stay where she was. Yet a voice inside her was telling her to run and hide. But whenever she listened to the voice before and went against Mother's wishes, Haden would always be punished.

Paralyzed in her indecision, Haden sat like a statue as the guard pushed the door back open.

"There was a rumor at the gaming hall that a beautiful young woman was searching for a Miguel Salvar. You are Miguel, correct?" The soldier asked as he stepped into the small house.

Haden wished she could shrink in on herself as the bronze Kadeshian armor came into view. She still had nightmares of when the soldiers captured her, poking and prodding her when she was in her transformed state, laughing at her inability to do anything.

Haden kept her head down, praying not to be seen, but knowing it was already too late.

"Yes, that is my name," Miguel replied, defeat in his voice.

"Well, now who is this?" the guard demanded, and Haden knew he had finally seen her. "A pretty bride for the prince?"

Rough footsteps stalked toward her and before she knew it, her chin was being jerked upward. Her eyes widened as she stared at the soldier before her. Tanned skin and dark hair covered his face and while he exuded a mean persona, Haden saw a depth of sadness lurking in his brown eyes.

As the guard took in Haden's bright-green eyes, his grip on her chin softened. "You are quite a sight," he whispered then stopped as if realizing what words escaped his lips. Clearing his throat, the soldier turned to Miguel. "If you hand her over willingly, I will look past your lie earlier. The king is rewarding every family who offers a woman with a handsome sum." The soldier pulled out a large sack of coins from his belt and jingled it before Miguel's face.

But while the guard and Miguel were conversing, Haden's mind was already forming a new plan. A bride for the prince? If anyone had enough power to stop Mother, surely the crown prince of Kadesh could, or at least convince his father to help. While Haden didn't have the courage to meet the ruthless Kadeshian king head on, maybe his son would be able to offer the aid both their countries needed to save them. And Mother always said she was only good for marrying off anyway. So maybe, just this once, her beauty would help her, and she could do good.

It was a crazy plan. It was a chaotic plan. But something in her soul told her that it just might work.

Finding her courage, Haden stood. "I will go with you."

Chapter Four

Matthias, The Fortress, Tenton

"The validity of this plan is shaky, at best, Tristan," General Matthias Blake told his younger and too enthusiastic brother as he followed him to Level Five of the Fortress.

"Relax, brother," Tristan replied, waving Matthias off. "This plan is foolproof!"

Matthias pinched the bridge of his nose and refrained from showing his exasperation before descending the final stairwell to Level Five. A pair of silent footsteps followed behind. Matthias glanced back at his friend, Ben, also known as One Shot. It was a name given to him when he was sentenced to time in the Fortress for killing four men in only one shot.

"What do you think?" he asked the giant-like man.

One Shot gave a wary glance at Tristan, who was merrily whistling while heading down the stairwell. "I don't like him, but I think he may be on to something."

Matthias quirked a brow. "Really?"

One Shot nodded. "He got us in and out of the Dark Market unseen. If he has an idea how to get us into Kadesh, I'm willing to listen."

Matthias studied the back of his younger brother. Could Tristan conceive a workable plan to help them find Devora and Mother?

Matthias still wasn't completely confident in his gambling-addicted, lying younger brother, but he was desperate. Ever since he'd seen Devora leave with General Beta, Kadesh's third and final general leading the war against Tenton, he couldn't rest. Sleep wouldn't visit his eyes, and although food held no flavor, he made himself eat, knowing he couldn't allow himself to lose strength until Devora and his mother were safe.

What was most surprising of all was that General Beta, who had been undercover as the headmistress of Vlacklear Academy for the last fifteen years, was also a Seer. Matthias couldn't believe the news when Ida, Rae, and Nadia told him. How could Tunri bestow such a gift on someone from such an evil nation?

But was Kadesh truly an evil nation? Because Matthias had also learned that Ida Shabawn was Kadeshian and she was practically kindness incarnate. Was it just to judge an entire group of people because of their poor leadership?

Matthias rubbed his head and pushed the thoughts from his mind as he descended the final step leading to Level Five. He didn't have the mental energy to philosophize now. With hardly any rest, his inner wolf was clawing to be released and wreak havoc. The memory of the paralyzing liquid Queen Leza injected into his neck at Ida's trial flooded his brain. Since that event, the wolf had been more stir-crazy than normal. And what was worse, when Matthias tried to shift on his own, he couldn't. The queen had somehow changed the rules of his curse, and Matthias was leery to find out what the new ones were.

Tristan led the trio through the dank hall of Level Five. The prisoners were eerily quiet, and Matthias wasn't sure whether it was a good or bad thing. Finally, they arrived at the cell at the end of the hall. It was the largest cell the Fortress had, save for the Behemoth's—Vinn's—cell. Matthias hadn't heard anything about the giant magical elk-like creature in ages and he prayed it had done a better job of finding Devora and his mother than he had.

"Gentlemen," Tristan said, facing Matthias and One Shot with a wide grin. "I give you our ticket back into Kadesh." Tristan bowed with more flair than necessary as he pointed to the cell holding the giant, Babshee the Horrid.

Matthias narrowed his gaze, his confidence in his brother's plan decreasing by the second. Babshee had been arrested the day Devora and the others came to the Fortress. According to Sir Conan, Babshee attacked Devora's caravan heading out of Grenly on the day of the Categorization Call a few months ago. The giant had been restrained in the Fortress ever since.

"I'm not helping ye get anywhere," Babshee growled, spitting at Tristan.

Tristan barely dodged the giant wad as it sprayed through the iron bars. He crinkled his nose before facing Matthias and One Shot with a glittering grin. "Well? A great plan, right?"

Matthias sighed, not knowing where to begin his criticism. He heard One Shot shift his crossbow around then ask, "What's the plan? All you're showing us is an angry giant."

Sometimes Matthias was thankful he wasn't the only one with a brain.

Tristan laughed. "Of course! All giants want to go to Kadesh, right? Because the king promised them jewels if they joined the army."

Matthias could see where Tristan's idea was going, and while it wasn't a horrible plan, it left Matthias uncomfortable with giving so much trust to a criminal giant.

Matthias stalked up to the giant. The large man sat hunched, his shoulders grazing the ceiling of the cell. Long red hair splayed across his broad shoulders in a mess of tangles. A pang of guilt pierced Matthias' heart at the poor conditions, but he shoved it away. Now wasn't the time to get soft. Babshee had attacked a caravan of students and killed knights of the Fortress.

"What der ye want, *General?*" the giant replied with mock respect.

Matthias paused, trying to decide which approach to take. After a few moments, he asked, "That's what I wish to know. What do *you* want?"

Babshee gave Matthias a suspicious glance, the green in his eyes twinkling against the torches lining the stone walls around his cell.

After a moment, the giant answered, "Is this a trick?"

Matthias sighed and took a step closer. "No trick. As much as it pains me to admit, I am out of options for saving my mother and the woman I love."

Babshee shifted position so he fully faced Matthias. "That young Seer I almost clobbered?"

One Shot coughed while Tristan looked confused. Matthias bowed his head. Yet another one of his mistakes he was trying to forget. When Devora and the rest of the new recruits came to the Fortress, Matthias decided to use Babshee to test the new recruits' fighting skills. Looking back, Matthias wanted more to scare the new recruits at the reality that awaited them on the battlefield so they would take his training seriously. But he was the one who was frightened the most when Babshee almost killed Devora with his earth manipulation power.

"Yes, the same one," Matthias replied, realizing he hadn't been as secret with his feelings for Devora as he originally thought.

"Hmm," Babshee replied. "What's in it for me?"

"Ah," Tristan said, springing to life like a daisy. "That's where I come in." Tristan pushed Matthias out of the way, then dramatically straightened his tunic. "You see, Babshee, while I was in Yekel, I heard that the king of Kadesh is set to host a beauty pageant to find his son a wife."

"I'm not wife material," Babshee deadpanned.

Before Matthias could react, a deep laugh erupted from One Shot. The sound was so startling that the three men turned toward him in surprise.

After regaining his composure, One Shot wiped his eye. "I apologize. Please continue."

Tristan scoffed at One Shot. "As I was saying, the king is looking for women all over the country to win his son's heart. So, first"—Tristan ticked off on his fingers—"as a giant, the Kadeshians will welcome you with open arms and second, when you offer them two lovely potential brides for the prince, the rest of us can sneak in as well."

"Who are these other brides?" Matthias questioned, trying to find some fault in Tristan's plan.

Kadesh *did* love giants and wouldn't bat an eye at another one desiring to enter the country for treasure. But this was the first Matthias had ever heard of a beauty pageant to find a wife for the crown prince.

A ripple of fear suddenly pierced his heart. Was General Beta going to force Devora into this pageant? Was she going to have to marry the prince of Kadesh and have her powers used against Tenton?

Questions layered upon one another in his mind until Tristan shrugged and said, "I assumed Ida and Rae would—" Before he could finish the sentence, One Shot grabbed Tristan by the collar and slammed him against the wall. All laughter from the tall man's face was gone.

"Rae is not going anywhere near Kadesh."

Matthias was about to interject when another voice sounded from the end of the hall.

"And why not? If I choose to go to Kadesh to find Devora, then that's my decision," Rae said, coming into the light. Her arms were crossed, and her glare fierce. Matthias was glad for once he wasn't at the receiving end of it.

Behind Rae stood Ida, Jacques, Nadia, and the Sandje twins, Hestia and Reese.

Matthias rubbed his eyes, exhausted. He specifically told Tristan to only tell *him* any ideas or plans. Apparently, his brother still had a blabbing mouth after all these years.

"Matthias, why weren't you going to tell the rest of us about this plan?" Jacques started.

At the same time, Rae stalked up to One Shot and said, "Put him down, Ben."

Sheepishly, One Shot placed Tristan down and was immediately scolded by Rae for making decisions without her.

Nadia suddenly burst into explanation about a contraption that could sneak all of them into Kadesh without the need of potentially marrying anyone off.

On top of all that chatter, Hestia demanded why she and Reese weren't good enough to be a part of the pageant. Reese bluntly reminded her sister that she was already married to Jacques' younger cousin, Charles, and legally couldn't be married again. As the group argued with one another, Matthias stormed away.

Turning the corner, he pressed his forehead against the cool Fortress stone and squeezed his eyes shut. This was madness. He had led battalions of soldiers, thousands of men, into battle and he couldn't even get a group of his "comrades" to work together.

"General?" a cool voice said from beside him.

Matthias reluctantly opened his eyes to find Reese and Ida standing next to him. They seemed to be the only two who thought first before they spoke.

"If I may, sir," Reese said, holding up her abacus.

Matthias eyed the tool. Reese Sandje had a brilliant mind and was known for her spot-on probabilities about any event. She was the reason all of Matthias' previous ideas to save Devora had been thrown out. With no more than a ten to twenty percent probability of success, Matthias wasn't willing to risk anyone else's life.

"Go ahead, Reese."

The twin pushed three metal beads to the left. "If what Tristan says is true and *if* Babshee is willing to help, this will be the plan with the highest probability of success, so far."

"And that is?"

Reese moved a few more beads around. "Fifty-two-point-six percent."

Matthias ran his hands through his hair, trying to drown out the bickering behind him. "That's better than the others, but putting lives on the line for only half a chance of success?"

"With all due respect, sir," Reese interjected. "We *want* to put our lives on the line for Devora. Whether we have a one hundred percent chance of success or only a two percent chance. It's our choice."

Something new awoke inside Matthias at Reese's statement. His soul had been burdened and cursed for so long. For the first time in ages, he felt the warmth of hope. "Thank you, Reese. Even a commander needs someone willing to speak truth to them sometimes."

"Sir?" Ida said before Matthias turned away.

Matthias glanced down at the petite woman. She was the exact opposite of the tall woman beside her. With her shining ebony ringlets and cocoa-colored skin, Ida would have no problem returning to her country of birth.

"I would like to confirm that what Tristan said is true. It has been a long time since there was a beauty pageant in Kadesh to find the current prince a bride, but it has happened in the past. The last one was a little over twenty years ago."

Matthias frowned. Something about the timeline of the pageants and the start of the war between Tenton and Kadesh niggled at his thoughts, but he didn't have time to dwell on that now.

Ida continued, "At the orphanage where I lived, we always dreamed there would be a pageant when we were old enough and we would be taken and doted upon by the king's servants." Ida lifted her shoulders with a small smile. "As someone with nothing, it would be a dream to be chosen and become a princess."

Matthias couldn't help but smile. "Well, I don't think you've done too horribly, future Duchess Delequa."

Ida blushed at her title, the giant diamond on her finger winking as she clasped her hands in front of her. "I don't think Jacques will be happy to know I agree with Tristan's plan and am willing to go, but I know this is the path Tunri wishes me to take." Ida smiled up at Matthias. "Maybe this is why I was saved all those years ago."

"Perhaps," Matthias agreed. He was thankful he'd been able to save Ida's life after she was accused of being a spy for Kadesh. And Jacques got himself a fiancée, as well.

Some guys have all the luck.

Faced with the arguing group before him, Matthias glanced back at Ida and Reese. "Thank you both for keeping calm and logical throughout these trying times. I need soldiers like that."

Both women saluted.

"We are always here to help, General," Reese replied.

"Yes," Ida agreed.

With a nod, Matthias stalked back to the crowd. Raising his voice, he bellowed, "If you all are quite finished, I believe we have a plan."

Chapter Five

Rae, The Fortress, Tenton

As Rae watched Ben almost choke Tristan for his suggestion of her being a part of the plan to save Devora, boiling fury took over. She knew she should've kept her head and stayed in the shadows to hear the rest of the plan, but the anger inside of her that she had tried so hard to keep under control spewed out.

"Put him down, Ben!" she practically screamed, causing Ben to jump in surprise before he hastily lowered Tristan to the ground.

An eruption of chatter sounded behind her, but Rae could only focus on Ben. "Why would you try to make that choice for me?" she barked.

Ben rubbed the back of his neck. "Rae, I—"

Rae cut him off. "You know I won't be controlled or have anyone else making decisions for me. You know this, yet you were going to do it anyway."

"Rae," Ben tried again, his voice as cool and calm as ever.

But Rae wasn't done. Tears gathered in her eyes. "After everything we've been through, everything I've told you, I thought you would understand."

Before she could continue, Ben reached out and gently cupped her face. "Rae, stop. Just listen, please."

Rae tried to blink back the tears, but it was too late. They rolled down her cheeks only to be brushed away by Ben's thumbs.

"Don't cry," he whispered gently, banishing the anger she held. "Tristan has hatched crazy plans before. I didn't want him to see you as an expendable object to make his plan a success."

Rae sniffed, suddenly ashamed of her outburst. "Really?"

Ben nodded. "I probably shouldn't have said you're not going to Kadesh, but sometimes words slip out. I'm sorry."

Rae grabbed his forearms. "No, I'm sorry. I responded harshly. I'm just so jittery being cooped up here, not knowing what's going to happen next, if Mami is okay or not." Rae closed her eyes.

Right before Devora left with General Beta, the general told Rae it was her skeleton key that had unlocked the Temple doors to free all the enslaved women inside. But what Rae didn't realize was that using the key came with a price and that price was the life of her mother.

Rae didn't know what to do but prayed that if she could find the key again and destroy it, Mami would be well again. But it was a far-fetched hope.

Guilt was also raking Rae from the inside out for letting Devora go into the enemy's hands. If Rae had tried harder, been stronger, she could've saved Devora and brought her home.

"Do you want to go to Kadesh to try to save Devora?" Ben asked.

Rae opened her eyes to see his concerned gaze sweeping over her. The past few days had been a whirlwind in trying to figure out a plan to save Devora and Kanna but also not get the rest of them killed. Everyone had come up with different strategies and ideas, but none seemed to work.

Though, from what Rae had heard of Tristan's plan, it sounded concrete. When she worked in the market in Yekel, she had seen many giants pass through on their way to Kadesh. The beauty pageant was new, but Rae wasn't surprised. The Kadeshians often spoke of their prince and when he would find a suitable bride. To Rae, it seemed that the Kadeshians were ready for a new ruler.

"I think, if any of us were to be able to blend in with the Kadeshian people best, it would be me. I lived among them for years. I know their language and customs fairly well," Rae finally answered. "I think Tristan is right in this case."

Ben searched her eyes once more before he laid his forehead against hers. "Okay."

Rae's brows rose. "Okay?"

Ben nodded before standing to his full height. Taking Rae's hand, the two of them turned to face the others who had been waiting for them to finish their conversation.

Hot embarrassment crept up Rae's neck. *How long has everyone been listening?*

Thankfully, Matthias diverted the attention toward him. "Although I gave strict instructions for you all to stay upstairs, it seems this impromptu meeting has proven providential. Reese has informed me that Tristan's plan is the best one we've come up with so far." As Matthias gestured to Reese, Rae watched Tristan give a small fist pump in the air. Nadia smiled and patted him a few times on the shoulder. It may have been a trick of the light flickering off the torches, but Rae swore she caught a slight blush come to Tristan's cheeks.

Yet, there was still something about Matthias' younger brother that concerned Rae, but she couldn't quite put her finger on it. He'd seemed reluctant to help her in Yekel, yet now he was ready to be a team player? Rae eyed the man, unsure if she was ready to trust him or not. And she definitely did *not* like the way he looked at Nadia. If he made one move toward her, Rae would be ready to protect Nadia at all costs.

"First things first," Matthias continued as he strode back to the giant in the cell. "Babshee, you've been surprisingly quiet through all the bickering. What are your thoughts?"

Even though the structure was fairly large, Rae hated how squished the giant was in the cell. She wasn't sure of the crime the large man committed, but it still pained her to see him in such awful conditions.

"I couldn't get a word in with all the yapping," the giant replied, causing Rae to hold back a snort. "But if ye promise to let me go free after I get ye through to Kadesh, I will follow your plan."

Matthias eyed the giant. "I need a bit more than your word, Babshee. Swear on your power that you will follow orders and no harm will come to those who travel with you to Kadesh."

Rae was impressed with the general's thoroughness. *How many times has he been double-crossed to be so wary of trusting another person?* But then Rae realized she had acted the same way. Ben had given her every reason in the world to trust him and still she held back trusting him fully.

Squeezing his hand, she leaned into Ben's side as the giant made an oath upon his earth manipulation power to obey Matthias' orders. Rae didn't know a lot about a giant's powers, but she had heard if they swear upon them and break the oath, they will lose every ounce of power they possess.

Satisfied, Matthias gave Babshee a nod then turned to Rae. "You heard the plan. What do you think?"

Rae still couldn't get over the cold steel-gray of the general's eyes. They were eyes that haunted her for years. Even after she discovered Matthias saved her father instead of forcing him to work for King Atol, she still almost flinched at the sight of them.

Ben gently nudged Rae, snapping her out of her daze, and she replied, "I think Tristan's plan is the best option we have. I've lived among the Kadeshians for long enough that I should be able to pass through fine. I'm not sure about this beauty pageant, but once I'm in Kadesh, I'll be able to find out more."

"We're," Ben amended, adjusting his crossbow strap across his chest.

Rae quirked a brow at him. "'We're' what?"

"Once *we're* in Kadesh."

Rae stared at the tall man in shock. "You're not coming."

Ben took a steady breath before gazing down at her. "You don't want me to make decisions for you and I respect that. But you also can't tell me what I can and can't do." His dark eyes gleamed with a soft stubbornness, and Rae knew she wouldn't be able to convince him to stay in Tenton.

"Matthias," Ben said, bowing his head to the general. "As we all know, I have always been mistaken for part-giant. I would like to offer my services in assuring that Babshee and Rae get to where they need to go."

Matthias nodded readily and Rae couldn't believe Ben had turned her own words against her. "I think that's wise," Matthias conceded before turning to Ida.

"What are you doing?" Rae whispered to Ben as Matthias, Ida and Jacques talked among themselves.

"I'm coming with you," he said. "You can put your life on the line all you want, but you can't stop me from coming beside you. I will protect you with everything I have." A small smirk came to his lips. "Plus, Devora is my friend too. I'd like to see her back home again."

Rae's heart thundered so hard in her chest; she didn't know what to do. As the days ticked on, her feelings grew stronger and stronger for Ben, and it frightened her. She wanted to fall for him, to be fully trusting, but she just couldn't. Not yet.

However, that didn't stop her from reaching up, grabbing his neck and pulling his lips down to hers. Ben stumbled forward in surprise but reciprocated the kiss.

A groan from Tristan broke them apart. "First my angry brother," he scoffed, "and now the brooding giant finds love? What is the matter with women these days? Does no one see excellence when I walk by anymore?"

Rae glared but her rebuttal was superseded when Babshee, surprisingly, spoke instead. "Not all brooding giants find love."

Tristan faced the large man. "Ah, you're unlucky with the ladies as well, my friend?"

Babshee nodded, and Rae rolled her eyes.

"Rae," Ben breathed. "What was that for?"

Rae bit her lip. "I don't know how to tell you how I feel, so I showed you instead."

Ben grinned. Leaning down he kissed her on the forehead. "You can show me anytime you'd like."

"All right," Matthias said, drawing their attention back to him. "If this plan is going to work, we all must be one hundred percent committed to our missions. Understood?"

The group blinked at Matthias, and he hung his head, releasing a frustrated breath. Rubbing his neck, Matthias composed himself and said, "Okay, we're going to go around and say what our missions are. Babshee, you start."

The giant suddenly looked nervous at everyone staring at him. Clearing his throat, he replied, "I'm to get the young ladies into Kadesh and not hurt anyone in the process."

Matthias waved his hand in the air. "Good enough. Rae? One Shot?"

"We're to travel with Babshee to Kadesh. Once we get there, we'll find out more about the pageant and any leads on where Devora could be," Rae answered. Ben nodded in agreement.

"Good," Matthias said. "Ida?"

"I will travel with Babshee, One Shot and Rae to Kadesh. Once there, we will do as Rae said." Ida looked to Rae. "I have been reading more in the Book of Ages and I think once we cross into Kadesh more will be revealed."

"Very good." Matthias turned to Jacques, Hestia, and Reese.

Rae noticed the forlorn look on Jacques' face, and she assumed that he was not traveling to Kadesh with his betrothed.

The blond knight spoke. "As the new head of Delequa Iron, I am going to try to undo the deceptive deals my father has made over these past years. So, when weapons are needed to hopefully end this war, they will be ready."

"Thank you, Jacques." Matthias nodded. "Reese? Hestia?"

"We also have a lot of snakes to vanquish from Sandje Textiles," Reese replied, moving her abacus beads back and forth. "However, we'll start working on how the headmistress—General Beta—was able to be undetected all these years."

"I love a good mystery," Hestia added with a grin.

"I believe I'm most useful in Totem, sir," Nadia piped in. She rolled her charcoal stick around her fingers. "My gift as a Tinker can be used anywhere, but I believe my skills will be most beneficial to our group and Tenton working on Lucas' machine."

Rae caught Nadia's eyes and smiled. They had talked through much since leaving Yekel, and Rae was thankful their relationship was solid once again. Rae didn't feel one ounce of jealousy toward Nadia and she was grateful. And Nadia was right. Papi would need her help. The device he created was unlike anything Rae had seen and if it could really nullify the effects of imperial opal, it would be their secret weapon in defeating whoever was stealing souls in Yekel.

"Spoken like a true soldier," the general replied. "I will make sure accommodations are in place for each of you to get where you need to go."

"Um, brother?" Tristan questioned from the corner. "What about me?"

Rae turned toward Tristan, having completely forgotten this was all his plan in the first place.

"I thought you were going with the others to Kadesh," Matthias deadpanned, clearly having spent too much time with his sibling.

Tristan smoothed out his tunic. "Well, yes, but I didn't get to announce it to the group like the others." He gave them all a winning smile causing Matthias to rub his eyes in exasperation.

"Fine. Go ahead."

Puffing out his chest, Tristan declared, "And I will lead my group to victory in not only finding my once betrothed but also my beloved mother, who I dearly miss. Together we will vanquish the enemy and bring peace to our land."

Hestia and Nadia clapped after Tristan's anecdote, causing the man to take a bow.

"Enough," Matthias said, waving his hand at Tristan. "Are there any questions?"

"No sir," the group replied in unison.

Rae squeezed Ben's hand, realizing she was thankful for his stubbornness and that he would be by her side. Ben squeezed her hand back, assuring her that he would always be there.

Matthias assessed the group. "Good. Then let's go."

Chapter Six

Ida, The Fortress, Tenton

Ida stood in her cell in the Fortress for what she assumed would be the last time. She had never dreamed of traveling back to Kadesh after all these years, but she meant what she said to the general. Ever since the Book of Ages revealed the lost prophecy to her, she knew she would have a part in saving Devora. At the time, she didn't know how, but as soon as she heard Tristan's plan, it was as if Tunri pressed the mission on her heart.

Sighing, Ida sat on her cot, looking at the different ribbons she'd hung on the walls before she had been sent to Vlacklear Academy. To be honest, she was thankful she wouldn't have to return to the corrupt school. After it was discovered that the headmistress was a spy for Kadesh, Queen Leza instated a new headmistress and the school continued on like nothing had ever happened.

Ida frowned at the thought as she smoothed a wrinkle in the coarse fabric of the sheets. There were too many confusing circumstances, none of which she could figure out. Where did General Beta take Devora? What happened to Sergio, General Beta's nephew? Who was really behind everything happening in Tenton?

Ida ran a hand over her tight curls. Her most important mission was to find Devora. Being Kadeshian, Ida would easily blend in with the crowd. But what concerned her wasn't what was ahead, but what she was leaving behind.

"A coin for your thoughts?" Jacques' voice came from outside of the cell.

Ida's heart skipped as she turned toward him. Handsome as always, he leaned against the dark gray stone. He smiled, but Ida knew he wasn't happy about the plan ahead.

"You'd need a whole sack of coins to get them all," Ida replied with a giggle. She motioned him inside where he promptly took a seat beside her.

Ida breathed in his honey scent, missing the happiness they experienced for only a few moments when General Blake announced them as officially betrothed. How was their wedding going to happen now?

Jacques nudged her shoulder. "What's going on in that mind of yours? I can see your wheels churning. Don't keep me in the dark."

"Sorry," Ida said with a sigh. "There's just a lot that's happened in a short amount of time."

Jacques laced his fingers through hers. "That seems to be the case with us lately, hm?" He picked up her hand and kissed the back of it, sending thrills down her arm. "You do need to promise me one thing," Jacques continued, stroking the back of her hand with his thumb.

"What's that?" Ida whispered.

His deep hazel eyes gazed into hers, a tornado of emotions swirling within them. "Promise me you'll come back before the month is up." Tilting his head to the side, he added, "I can't plan a wedding all by myself. I know nothing about flowers."

Tears gathered in Ida's eyes as she wrapped her arms around his neck, pulling him close. She knew Tunri wanted her to travel to Kadesh to find Devora, but why did it have to be so hard to listen?

Jacques' long arms wrapped around Ida's back, and they held the embrace for longer than necessary. Eventually, they broke apart with Ida wiping her eyes and Jacques doing the same.

"No more tears," he said, gently tapping her nose, a soft smile playing on his lips. "It'll be okay."

"Will you be okay?" Ida asked, reaching out to stroke his cheek. He leaned into her palm, his eyes closing.

"I'll have to be," Jacques responded. "You know that Father only has a week left, at best."

Ida nodded. After the chaos of the battle with Kadesh, Jacques received word from his father's servant that Lord Delequa's sickness had gotten severely worse. As Ida and the others made a formal plan to save Devora, Jacques planned to travel straight to Delequa Manor.

"Is Charles going with you?"

Charles, Jacques' younger cousin, was the only reason Jacques and Ida were able to become betrothed. While Ida had been locked in the Tower by Sergio and the headmistress of Vlacklear, Charles and Hestia were married; thus, fulfilling the marriage contract between the Sandje and Delequa families. Jacques no longer had to marry Hestia and was free to marry whoever his heart desired. Which, still to Ida's surprise, was her. Sadly, she was only able to live her fairytale for a moment before Kadesh attacked Tenton right after her trial.

Jacques ran a hand through his hair. "I'm not sure. While I would love his help and opinion on things, I know he will probably stay by Hestia's side." A forlorn look came over Jacques' face and Ida hooked her arm through his.

"It's not your fault. You didn't know he was at the Fortress, and he didn't want you to know."

Jacques had been berating himself ever since he found out his younger cousin had categorized for the Fortress but didn't make himself known.

"But that's what bothers me the most," Jacques replied, wrapping his arm around Ida's shoulders. "Why didn't he want me to know? And then he goes off and gets married without telling anyone!"

Ida giggled. "Well, at least we know Hestia loves him and because of him, we can be together."

Jacques turned to her, a glimmer of mischief in his eyes. "True. I do have him to thank for that."

Then, before Ida could say anything further, Jacques cupped her neck and brought his lips down to hers. Ida melted into the kiss, desiring nothing more than to stay there until eternity. But that was an unattainable dream and they both knew it.

As soon as the kiss ended, Jacques stroked Ida's cheek one last time and stood.

Holding his hand out to her, he said, "Shall we get you ready for departure, my lady?"

Lacing her fingers through his, Ida stood and strode out of the cell, praying Tunri would not take away the beautiful future He'd promised her.

⸻

Ida gawked at the lavish carriage with Rae. The last time she had been in a carriage she was sneaking into the masquerade ball to find the Book of Ages and to stop Jacques from marrying one of her best friends. Ida shook her head. Only with Tunri's guidance she was able to accomplish both tasks. Standing next to the carriage on the other side was Babshee. To Ida's surprise, the giant had no manacles around his wrists and hadn't deserted the plan. Maybe everything would work out.

A light-green colored scarf came into view. Ida turned to see Rae holding the fine fabric out to her.

"I know that many Kadeshian women enjoy wearing colorful scarves and since this will be your new family's color, I thought you would like it." A tint of pink came to Rae's cheeks, almost as if she were embarrassed by the gesture.

Ida couldn't imagine the fierce female being shy about anything. Well, other than One Shot. She had seen how the two looked at each other and it warmed Ida's heart to no longer see so much pain in One Shot's gaze.

Grinning, Ida took the scarf, loving how the shining green contrasted with her dark skin. "It's beautiful, Rae. Thank you so much for thinking of me." Reaching out, Ida took Rae's hands and squeezed them. "What will you wear?"

Rae pulled out a deep cerulean scarf and wrapped it around her short white-blonde hair. "I've realized that I enjoy blue a lot more than red."

"And it looks great on you," One Shot commented as he strode by.

Rae blushed again before Tristan stalked beside One Shot, rolling his eyes. "None of this mushy stuff," he grunted, flicking his wrists toward Rae and One Shot. "We have a job to do."

"Matthias, I believe you're rubbing off on your brother," Jacques said as he walked up to Ida. He laid his hand on the small of her back before lightly kissing her temple.

Ida nuzzled closer to him, trying to soak up her last moments with him. It wouldn't be forever. They would be reunited again soon. All would be well. She hoped.

"That would be the best thing that ever happened to him," General Blake replied with a stiff laugh.

Ida noticed that the general tried to step closer to the group standing outside of the Fortress, but it was as if something was holding him back.

Scoffing, Tristan stomped to the front of the carriage and climbed up. Tristan had offered to drive, and One Shot sat up front with him, sure to vanquish any threats that arose.

"General," Ida said softly, bringing everyone's attention back to Matthias. "Are you seeing us to the border?"

Matthias had instructed them to head to Yekel where Sir Tocha, one of his most trusted knights, was currently overseeing the rebuilding of the city. The general had sent a coded message ahead of them to the knight about their plans and how to assist the group.

A thick vein pulsed in Matthias' neck and Ida couldn't help but notice he looked the same way he did at the end of her trial. Like something, or someone, was controlling him.

"I—I don't believe—" Matthias' voice was cut off by a loud howl.

Ida jumped with fright, a squeak escaping her lips.

"What the—" Rae cried, her head whipping around to stare at Matthias.

Jacques hurried Ida and Rae toward the carriage, fear in his voice. "Get in the carriage. Now. Go!"

Ida's eyes widened as she watched, Matthias, her commander, change into a creature.

"Jacques!" she cried. "What's happening to him?"

"Ida, go! He can't control himself in this state," Jacques yelled. "I know how to handle him. Please leave!" Desperation and fear swirled in Jacques' eyes as he reached for the nearest weapon he could find.

"Hurry, Ida," Rae said, pulling Ida into the carriage.

As soon as Ida and Rae were in the carriage, Tristan had them off like a shot with Babshee racing behind. The carriage jostled back and forth, throwing her and Rae around like they were nothing but rag dolls. But Ida couldn't focus on anything else beside the memory of fear in her betrothed's eyes and the piercing howls echoing behind them.

Chapter Seven

Haden, Renta, Kadesh

Maldove Palace was incredibly lavish and filled with opulence. But that was nothing compared to the Kadeshian palace Haden was currently standing in. Warm yellows, oranges, and reds swirled on tapestries around her, while cool blues and purples lined the rugs below her severely scuffed boots. It was a direct contrast to the sterile whites and beiges of Maldove Palace and Haden couldn't be happier. After so many years of monotonous isolation, it was as if she were finally seeing color and its beauty for the first time.

But the lovely moment only lasted until she was led down a different hall into a less extravagant room with a plethora of other young women. Haden couldn't help but notice she was a good four inches above all the others, making it easier for her to realize how much she stood out, literally. Many of the women in the room had beautifully bronzed or dark skin. Even with Haden's sun-kissed skin from her journey, she still was lighter than the rest. She was thankful the hair dye was black instead of brown, but her flat limp hair was nothing compared to the voluminous curls twisting in all different ways on the heads around her. Though, she did notice there were a good number of women with red-dyed hair. Apparently, the merchant, Lazaar, was more convincing than she realized. Maybe the crown prince really did have a thing for redheads.

Yet, compared to how she looked a few weeks ago, Haden could pass for a citizen of Kadesh. As long as no one looked at her too closely and definitely didn't look at her lighter eyes. If she kept her head down and didn't make a fuss, she prayed she could at least gain a meeting with the prince of Kadesh so she could show him the second scroll from Mother's desk.

Once the palace guards exited the room of chatting females, Haden relaxed a bit more. An array of small sandwiches and cakes lined the walls, and Haden couldn't help but be drawn to their exotic coloring and beautiful designs. As she wove through the crowd toward the delicacies, she noticed that there were a few other women who didn't look Kadeshian. One woman, wearing a beautiful blue headscarf almost the same shade as her own, caught Haden's eye. Familiarity tugged at her mind and Haden tried to search her thoughts when someone stepped on her foot.

"Ow," she gasped and tore her gaze away from the woman and down to her foot.

Her poor boots had fared well but could endure no longer. Peeking through the top of the well-worn leather was her toe.

"Apologies," a deep voice, rich with the Kadeshian accent replied.

Haden's stomach flopped involuntarily at the voice, recognizing it as the same one she had heard two days ago in the marketplace. The same thought fluttered through her mind then as it did now. She had never heard a tone so warm and soothing and felt herself blush as she noticed the gaze of a young man carrying a tray of cups. It was him: the handsome stranger, Mal.

Did he follow me here? She wondered before pushing her hope away. Why would he follow her? They didn't even know each other.

Yet she couldn't tear her gaze away from the beautifully dark skin and warm caramel eyes smiling back at her. In fact, she stared at the man with her mouth open like a fish out of water.

"It's good to see you again. I see the hair dye was a bit darker than what you wanted ," he nodded to her dark strands, yet his smile stayed on his face.

"Yes," she agreed, pulling the blue scarf farther over her forehead.

"Not that it looks bad," Mal hurried to add.

"Yes," Haden repeated like a bumbling fool before she realized the attractive man was no longer staring at her but at her toe sticking through the top of her boot. Haden rushed to cover her toe with her other foot. Lifting her eyes, she laughed nervously.

"It seems I owe you a new pair of shoes," Mal replied, laughter dancing in his eyes. Taking a cup off his tray, he handed it to her. "Alas, I am fresh out of shoes at the moment, but maybe you will take this instead. After all, you helped make it."

Haden reached for the cup, still mesmerized by the beautiful cadence of Mal's voice. It wasn't until a few moments of silence passed that she realized she hadn't said anything intelligent—or anything at all, for that matter.

"Oh," Haden quickly rushed, hoping the cup in her hand was actually warm, and it wasn't her embarrassment flooding her entire body. "What do you mean I helped make it?"

"The green bottle you got for me held the spices I needed to make *sheta* for the crown prince's pageant." He leaned forward, so close that Haden could smell his alluring cardamom scent. "Sayidi Tamor will argue that his recipe is best, but really, I make the best *sheta* in the whole palace."

Haden blinked before glancing down into the light-brown liquid in her cup. It was the same beverage that General Sage had drank every night she was captured with the Kadeshians. Cautiously, she raised the hot liquid to her lips and took a sip. An explosion of spices rolled down her throat and Haden couldn't help but take a larger gulp.

"It is quite hot," Mal stated, a touch of concern layering his voice.

The *sheta* was refreshing but cozy at the same time and Haden loved it. "It's amazing," she breathed, closing her eyes as she lifted the cup to her face. The warm steam tickled her nose and cheeks.

"I'm glad you like it," Mal replied. "Hopefully I will be able to make you more in the near future."

Haden's eyes shot open at the statement, but she found that Mal had disappeared within the crowd of women. She wasn't sure what she felt when Mal was near, but she needed to stay focused and not be distracted by attractive servant boys who made amazing tea.

At that thought, Haden peered down at the brown liquid again, the scent of cinnamon and cardamom enveloping her in a warm hug. In a matter of minutes, the delicious drink was at her lips and her cup empty within a few sips. The elegant spices warmed her insides, and Haden wished that Mal would return so she could have another cup. And maybe she could look at him some more.

Taking another glance around the room, Haden realized more women had been packed inside during her conversation with Mal. She didn't know how many more people could fit in the space, because it was starting to become cramped.

Just then, the trill of a flute sounded at the entrance of the room, immediately silencing the females gathered.

"Welcome and congratulations," a deep voice announced. It wasn't as soothing and warm as Mal's, but commanding, demanding respect and attention. "It is a great honor to be here to participate in *Sundarata Taashama*. Only one of you will be chosen to become the crown prince's wife and future queen of Kadesh."

The man speaking was tall, with bulging muscles ready to strike down any enemy. While Mal had soft tight ebony curls, this man had no hair at all. Or he had shaved it all off for his head was shining like the sun at midday. A simple white tunic with brown pants and boots covered the rest of the man's tall, muscular features. However, it was the giant sword, sheathed in an ornate blue and gold sheath, that made Haden nervous.

Whispers waved over the crowd of females in reaction to what the man said about the prince. There had to be at least a few hundred women in the room, so the whispers weren't as quiet as intended.

How am I going to be able to see the prince against so many others?

She had been told for as long as she could remember that she had a pretty face. But as she glanced around, there were stunning women with far more striking features than her own. *And they probably have plenty of skills and can read properly too,* Haden surmised. What prince would choose a future queen who needed a few moments to read some lines on a page?

As the harsh reality descended upon her, Haden's hasty plan to become part of the marriage beauty pageant for the prince was suddenly seeming like a very bad idea. Swallowing, she turned back toward the man speaking.

"Each of you will have seven days of beauty treatments then seven days of testing before you are allowed to be in the prince's presence. Once there, the prince will decide what he wants to do with you."

A series of scoffs mixed with excited giggles responded to the statement. Haden gripped the cup in her hands, wondering what she had gotten herself into. She glanced around the room again. There was no way she could escape now. If Tunri had gotten her this far, He would help her succeed enough to see the prince and gain his assistance. Hopefully.

"Every lady will have a guard that will accompany them to their treatments and other activities while here at the palace," the man continued. "Your guard is non-negotiable and if you try to venture around the palace without your guard, you will be disqualified from the contest and banished from the palace."

At that, the room hushed. Only the steady rippling of the fountain in the courtyard outside could be heard through the open windows.

The man glared at the room of women with hard, dark eyes. "There are rumors of Tentonian spies in Kadesh and we will not hesitate to execute anyone who acts suspicious."

Haden's throat went dry as she tried to look anywhere but at the man's piercing gaze.

Is he looking at me? Why did she suddenly feel like the room was getting warmer? Was it getting smaller? That man definitely knew she was from Tenton, and he was going to kill her on sight.

"Now then," the man said, a look of satisfaction on his face at the women's fear. He pulled out a large scroll. "When I call your name, step forward and you will be assigned a guard."

For what felt like the hundredth time since Haden entered Kadesh, she panicked. What if they recognized her name? Were there many women named Haden in Kadesh? Would they kill her right here with all these people?

Before she could spiral deeper, Haden saw the familiar woman from earlier. The woman with the blue scarf was called up front. Haden couldn't see her face, but she knew she recognized her guard. A tall, pale man with dark shaggy hair was assigned to guard the woman with the blue scarf. But Haden remembered the tall man because he was the one who guarded Haden and the Seer, Devora, after the Battle of Edo at the oasis. His name was something odd and had to do with an arrow or something. Maybe a bow?

Then Haden's brows rose. Were the tall man and the scarfed woman the Tentonian spies the angry man was referring to? Another idea sent a spike of fear into her heart. Were they spies for Mother? Haden didn't want to find out and made a note to stay away from them.

Thankfully, the pair exited the room without glancing at Haden once and the next woman was called up. She had to be Kadeshian for her coloring matched most of the other young women in the room. Yet as the petite woman turned and scanned the room, her eyes landed on Haden. Haden stood frozen, wishing she could blend into the crowd better or at least shrink a few inches. There was something familiar in the Kadeshian woman's gaze as she gave Haden a knowing smile then followed her guard, a tall man with sandy-blond hair, out of the room.

Chills raced down Haden's spine, and she shivered. It seemed like that woman knew who she was. *Is she a spy for Tenton?* How many Tentonian spies were in Kadesh?

Before Haden could ponder any further, her name was called.

"Haden Riveria," the bulky, bald man called.

Thankfully she had changed her surname, but her first name was still the one given to her at birth. If she had thought quicker, she would've come up with a better alias.

Thinking isn't your strong suit, my dear, Mother's voice chimed in Haden's mind. *Just smile and look pretty. It's what you do best.*

Not knowing what else to do, Haden did just that. Straightening her hunched stance, Haden made sure to look confident as she strode forward. All her lessons in posture and balance came to mind as the other women parted for her to walk through.

While Haden hadn't been around many people outside of the palace, she recognized malicious glares easily enough. As if a new toy on display, the other women's eyes scrutinized her as she gracefully took each step. There weren't any whispers, like she had heard many times before when Mother and Father held court and she was forced to attend. But the judgment in the surrounding women's eyes was enough.

"She's too tall."

"She's too thin."

"Why do men fall at her feet?"

"The portraits make her seem more stunning than she is in person."

Haden pushed the comments she had heard in the past aside. All those nobles were nothing but two-faced politicians that would do anything to get in the king's and queen's good graces. Even spout insults about the princess behind their hands and then compliment her on how beautiful she looked a moment later.

Haden didn't make eye contact with the women mentally critiquing her appearance, but she did wonder whether they would lie to her face, like the nobles in Tenton, or tell her the truth. The latter may hurt more initially, but it would be refreshing.

Once she reached the front of the room, the bulky, bald man was glaring at her. Apparently, she had taken too long walking from the back of the room to the front. Haden dipped her head in apology, which the bald man waved off.

He then motioned to the guard standing to his left. "Your guard's job is to follow you to all your treatments and protect you should any ill predicaments come your way. Do not try to evade him. He is under strict orders to do anything within his power to keep you confined within the palace walls."

Haden's brows rose with surprise, but she nodded. She was used to being confined to a cage, so this didn't seem much different. However, it worried her on how adamant the bulky, bald man had been about keeping the participants of the pageant enclosed within the palace. Was there something the women would find out that King Redore IV didn't desire the rest of Kadesh to know?

"Off you go," the bulky, bald man said, moving Haden to the side as he called the next name.

Haden stumbled over a few steps before she bumped into the chest of her new guard.

Shaking her head, Haden glanced up. "Oh, it's you!" she said aloud when she found herself clenching Mal's biceps.

A tittering of snickers echoed behind her and Haden wanted nothing more than to transform and fly away. Embarrassment crept up her cheeks as she forced herself to look anywhere but at the attractive young man who had given her the delicious drink only minutes ago.

"We must stop meeting like this," Mal said with a playful grin. "Though I am pleased you haven't forgotten me so soon, my lady," he replied with low bow.

Haden couldn't help but enjoy his playful banter. "Oh yes," Haden replied hastily, rocking back and forth on her feet. "My memory isn't that bad."

Mal chuckled again before righting himself and motioning Haden to follow him out of the room. Haden obeyed without question, and it wasn't until they were halfway down the outside corridor that she realized she should be a little more guarded. Here she was, the runaway princess of the enemy nation, and she was flirting with a palace guard.

Well, trying to flirt, she admitted to herself.

She had never been successful at talking to any boy her age. And if they were nice to her, she knew it was only because she was the princess, and they wanted to be in her favor so she could give them what they desired. That's all it had ever been like since she was a child. Any friend she made eventually wanted something from her. Presents, money, invitations to balls. Would anyone ever like her for just being her?

"If you talk any less, I'll be worried you can't speak at all and that just won't do," Mal chuckled, and Haden realized they were no longer in the outdoor corridor but another section of the palace entirely.

Haden inwardly groaned. She was doing a horrible job at being undercover. She should've been taking notes of her surroundings and trying to memorize the layout of the palace. Instead, she was wallowing in self-pity.

"I apologize," she said quickly, trying to focus her mind on the direction they were heading instead of letting it wander off in multiple directions like it usually did. "A lot has happened, and I'm trying to process it all."

Haden's eyes raked over the interior of the palace. Warm yellow, orange, and brown tones coated the walls while tapestries of bright blues hung on golden rods. A thin light-brown carpet with dark-green swirls ran beneath their feet. Trying to ignore the hole in her boot as she walked, Haden's eyes followed each of the paths of the swirls as she strode beside her guard, imagining them as pathways to an intricate maze.

Focus, Haden! She scolded herself once she realized she was lost in her imagination again.

When she turned toward Mal, she realized he was watching her with very keen eyes.

"I like the carpet," she blurted before she could stop herself.

Mal tried to keep a stern face but failed and let out a laugh. For the second time that day, embarrassment heated Haden's face. How was she ever going to impress the prince when she couldn't even stop a guard from laughing at her?

"It's a very nice carpet, I agree," Mal replied, surprising Haden. His tone was neither conceited nor condescending, but it wasn't overly agreeable either.

"My home doesn't have so much color," Haden confessed. "It's nice to see so much of it here."

Mal nodded, taking in the space around them as they turned another corner. "I, once again, agree. Colors are a beautiful thing given to us by our Creator and should be displayed whenever possible."

Something warm came over Haden's heart at Mal's comment. But she didn't have a chance to decipher it before he continued.

"I'm Mal, by the way. I'm not sure if you remember my name from when we first met. And Sayidi Tamor failed to mention it to you." A mild irritation laid in the statement.

Haden frowned at the name. "Sayidi Tamor?"

Mal smiled and Haden noticed how beautifully white and straight his teeth were. "The big, bald guy with enormous muscles and no humor," Mal added, and Haden snorted before she let out a laugh.

Horrified, Haden slapped her hands over her mouth, recalling another one of Mother's chastisements: *Princesses don't snort or laugh out loud. If you find something humorous you smile daintily and comment on the humor instead of showing your enjoyment of it.*

Haden shook her head. Eighteen years of etiquette lessons and Haden still couldn't get it right.

She turned to find Mal watching her again with interest. Clearing her throat, Haden replied, "I did remember your name. It's nice to meet you again, Mal. I'm Haden."

"I know," he said with a grin that made Haden blush and look away.

Not knowing how to respond, Haden studied the new hallway they were in and mentally slapped herself *again* for not noting how she got there. However, within a few more steps, Mal stopped before a cerulean-shaded wooden door. Detailed designs of swirls and dots lined the border of the door, and Haden forced herself not to become entranced by the pattern.

"This will be your room while you're here," Mal explained. "Unfortunately, you'll have two other roommates, since the king underestimated the number of ladies who desired to become a princess."

Mal tried to make the comment light, but Haden could sense an undertone of annoyance to his words.

"The two guards for the other participants and I will decide on who will guard you ladies each evening, however we will all be here tomorrow morning to take you to your first beauty treatment."

"I see," Haden nodded then her stomach grumbled. She wished she could crawl in on herself at the loud roar coming from her gut. But in her stomach's defense, she had lived off rations for weeks now and barely was able to enjoy the food with Miguel before she came here.

Miguel!

Haden had been so wrapped up in trying to devise a plan to see the prince and stop Mother she had completely forgotten about him.

"Are we allowed to have visitors?" Haden asked Mal before she thought better of it.

"Why? Do you have a suitor you wish to see?"

Haden blinked at Mal's frankness, but replied, "Why would I have a suitor if I was here to marry the prince?"

Now Mal looked surprised at her response. "So, that's a no?"

"Of course it's a no."

Mal grinned. "Good. And if you wish to have visitors while you're here it will have to be approved by Sayidi Tamor."

Haden nodded and decided she would try to seek out Sayidi Tamor tomorrow.

A bell chimed in the distance and Mal let out a sigh. "I will bid you goodnight, Haden. I have other duties to attend to. Sleep and eat, for tomorrow will be an interesting day." Mal gave her a deep bow and started down the hall.

Before Haden could stop herself, she cried, "Wait!" Mal stopped and turned, watching her with interest. Haden fiddled with the ends of the scarf now around her neck rather than over her dark hair. "I wanted to apologize for how I acted at the market. You were trying to help me with buying the dye and I was horribly rude."

Mal grinned wide and took a step toward her. "I was impressed with your willingness to stand on your own rather than take my offer. However, I will accept your apology, as long as you agree to have another cup of *sheta* with me soon."

Haden couldn't believe how bold Mal was for a guard, but she enjoyed someone not tiptoeing around her for once. And it was nice that he didn't find her awkward or foolish.

"I would like that," she replied quietly.

Mal gave her another stunning grin before bowing once more and retreating down the hall.

As Haden watched his broad shoulders disappear, she wasn't sure what to think about the overly friendly guard, but she did know she needed to rest and try to start thinking of a plan of how to see Miguel. Hopefully, he could help her with finding a way to get the information about Mother to the prince.

Sighing, Haden rubbed her eyes, suddenly realizing how exhausted she was. Mal said she would have other roommates, but Haden didn't care who was in her room. All she hoped to do was sleep.

But as she turned the knob of the door and strode into the room, Haden froze. All thoughts of sleep fled from her mind because seated before a table of delicious treats were the spies from Tenton.

Chapter Eight

Matthias, Maldove Palace, Juro – A few days after Tristan and the others left for Kadesh

Slicing pain ripped through Matthias' back as he reverted from his wolf form. Cool sweat covered his brow, hunger gnawed at his stomach. Prickles of hay poked into his bare body and Matthias groaned. So, he was back in the stables with the warden's other wolves again. Wiping the sweat from his brow, his gaze landed on a pair of black trousers slung over a bale of hay.

Standing, he winced as his muscles strained with each movement. As he pulled on the trousers, Matthias tried to recollect what had happened before he shifted into wolf form.

He was standing outside the Fortress, seeing off the group that was heading to Yekel. But when he tried to walk toward the carriage, an invisible string tightened around his neck, like a leash. And when he tried to fight it, his curse took over, forcing him to transform.

A low growl rumbled in Matthias' throat, knowing that whatever happened to him was Queen Leza's doing. He had been able to control his curse for years; he couldn't remember the last time he had transformed unwillingly. But there was something about the liquid the queen injected into his neck at Ida's trial that now ruled over him. The thought scared him to no end. But what frightened him more was the fact that he couldn't leave the Fortress grounds. He had always been able to travel around Tenton freely, especially to do the king's bidding in disposing threats to the crown. But being confined to only the Fortress left a bad taste in his mouth. How would he be able to find Devora and his mother if he couldn't leave the prison?

The door to the stables creaked open and Matthias readied himself to face whoever was on the other side.

"Stand down, sir, it's only me," Jacques said, entering the stables.

Relief coursed through his bones, and he relaxed. "Jacques, what happened?"

Jacques handed Matthias a black tunic and boots before he replied, "When you tried to follow Ida and Rae to the carriage, you transformed. Only this time it was as if the wolf overtook you entirely. You were rabid, trying to chase after them to do only Tunri knows what. Thankfully, I was able to lure you to the stables and lock you in until you transformed back."

Matthias pulled the tunic over his head before placing his feet in each boot and lacing them around his calves. His mind whirled over Jacques' recounting. The last time the wolf had fully taken over him was when he had first been cursed as a young knight. It took Matthias months to control the wolf, but he had done it. But apparently, that was no longer true.

Glancing up at Jacques, he asked, "How long was I gone?"

The knight thinned his lips. "About four days, sir."

Matthias cursed under his breath. Four days lost because of one false step. How would he be able to aid his team if he didn't know how far he could walk? "Did I harm anyone, Jacques?"

"Don't do that to yourself, Matthias. You know you're not yourself when you're in that form."

Matthias clenched his fists, noticing the white bandages around his friend's wrist. "Is it a bad wound?"

Jacques clasped his hands behind his back. "Nothing I can't handle, sir."

Standing, Matthias ran his hands through his hair. "I apologize. Like you said, I wasn't aware of my actions."

"No apology necessary, sir."

Matthias placed his hand on Jacques' shoulder. "You're a good friend, Jacques. I don't deserve your friendship."

Jacques nodded. "Yet you have it all the same, sir."

Matthias smirked then headed out into the snowy landscape of the Fortress. His steps were cautious, not knowing what perimeter the queen had given him. But after he made it inside the stone building without any harm, he breathed a little easier.

It wasn't until he and Jacques made it to the upper levels of the prison that he asked, "Any word from the others?"

Jacques nodded, keeping his voice low. "I received word from Ida late last night that they arrived in Yekel and were hoping to cross into Kadesh early today. I've had no news since then but I'm praying that means they were successful."

Matthias could hear the concern in his friend's voice. He couldn't imagine knowing his betrothed was walking into enemy territory with no more than a hope and a somewhat solid plan at best. But then again, the love of his life willingly offered herself up to the enemy. So maybe he could relate.

"She's a smart woman," Matthias offered. "From what I've learned, Ida has survived many trials. She will prevail through this, as well."

"Thank you, sir," Jacques replied, stopping before Warden Hazor's office. "I believe the same."

Matthias stared at the warden's door. How many times had he stood before it, dreading whatever news awaited him? He knew this time would be no different but would have to face it head on, just like the other times.

"Unfortunately, we probably will not hear any word from them until they cross back into Tenton."

Matthias was careful not to use "if." He had to believe with every fiber of his being that his team would return to Tenton unharmed and with his mother and Devora. Because if they didn't, he didn't know what he would do.

"Yes sir," Jacques replied. The knight glanced at the door to the warden's office. "Good luck, sir."

Matthias nodded. "Thank you, Jacques." Before the knight turned to depart, Matthias asked, "Any news on your father?"

Jacques sighed. "I'm taking leave to visit Delequa Manor in Tinwa as we speak. I wanted to make sure you were back to normal first."

Matthias strode forward and did something he never thought he would do. He embraced Jacques in a hug. Jacques, obviously surprised, stilled with shock. Matthias quickly released Jacques and cleared his throat.

"Thank you for your concern, Jacques, but I fear I will never be normal. You may have your leave without worry. Please keep me posted on anything that may assist our efforts."

Jacques laughed and saluted Matthias before heading down the hall.

Matthias prayed that with Jacques named as the new heir of Delequa Iron they would have access to resources to help them end the war with Kadesh, once and for all.

As Jacques rounded the corner, Matthias faced the warden's door once more. Steeling his nerves, he knocked twice and waited.

"Enter," Warden Hazor replied.

Matthias placed his hand on the knob and turned.

The warden's office looked the same as it always had since Matthias first entered it four years ago. Various maps of Tenton and Kadesh, weathered with age, were nailed across three of the four walls. While some held no markings, others were coated in blots of ink. A single wooden chair sat before the warden's desk, one which Matthias had occupied many times. Beyond the lonely chair stood the solid, oak desk. Though the warden seemed haphazard in his rules and insane tournaments, his desk was pristine. A tall, clay pot neatly held rolled scrolls. Next to it sat a clean bottle of ink with three quills to the side, all lined up like perfect soldiers.

Matthias forced his steps forward, continuing to study the warden's office instead of thinking why Warden Hazor wished to speak with him. Whenever he was summoned by the warden, it was usually bad news. The only good news he had received from the warden was when he heard nobility was coming to the Fortress, which had meant Devora. But, at the time, he had considered it bad news.

Taking a breath, Matthias cleared his throat and said, "You requested my presence, sir."

Warden Hazor lowered the scroll he was reading. Piercing dark eyes peered at Matthias. Even after all these years, Matthias still couldn't decipher what was lurking beyond the penetrating gaze.

"I see you've gained control again," the warden commented as he rolled up the scroll.

Matthias nodded once. If it hadn't been for the warden's grace when Matthias was first cursed, Matthias would've probably been shot long ago. Most villages don't take kindly to a wolf harming their people.

"I thought you'd learned to control the beast already."

"I had, sir," Matthias replied. "Something's changed."

The warden blinked once. "Has it anything to do with the queen at the trial?"

Matthias' brows rose. He had gone over the moment in his mind again and again and knew no one else had seen what the queen had done to him. He didn't realize that the warden was at the trial at all, and Matthias said as much.

"You were at the trial, sir? Why did you not make yourself known?"

At the question, Warden Hazor did something he rarely did. He grinned. "You know as well as I do that the monarchy de-spises me, Blake. Atol tolerated me, but with the crown on a different head, well..." The warden paused. "My days may be numbered."

"What?" Matthias gaped. "Have you received a threat?" Who would dare threaten the warden of the Fortress?

"Not in words," the warden gruffed. "But that's not why you're here."

"Unfortunately, I have a guess as to why I am," Matthias grumbled.

"The queen wishes to see you as soon as possible."

Matthias resisted the urge to roll his eyes. "If she desired to see me so badly, why did she make it so I couldn't leave the Fortress grounds?"

Warden Hazor leaned back in his chair, crossing his thick arms over his chest. "Do you know how far your boundary goes?"

Matthias shook his head.

"Interesting," the warden commented, stroking his mustache. "My guess is you'll be able to get to the palace without harm, but beyond that, who knows."

Matthias deduced as much as well, but the memory of the consequence of taking one step too far made him uneasy.

"Thank you, sir. Shall I transform into a horrid beast that kills without a thought, you will be the first to know."

Warden Hazor chuckled. "Fortunate for you, I've had personal experience with many beasts of that kind." He then turned serious and added, "Keep your eyes open, Blake. A dangerous game is being played and I'm not confident in the rules anymore."

Matthias saluted the warden then exited the office, equally unsure of the trap he was walking into.

Though Matthias flinched with every step his horse, Atir, took on the ride to Maldove Palace, he arrived at the castle, thankfully as a man and not a wolf. After dismounting Atir and handing his reigns to the stable boy, Matthias peered up at the white marble structure before him. Just like the warden's office, the palace hadn't changed at all. But instead of the opulence and grandeur Matthias once thought it held, he now knew it was all lies. Yet, being a farm boy from the countryside, he had to give himself grace. He was as naïve as they came, and the king and queen had taken full advantage of that. But he was naïve no more.

Taking the steps two at a time, Matthias reached the landing where a knight stood guarding the entrance.

"Miss me, Blake?" Sir Conan asked with a smirk.

This time Matthias did roll his eyes. "Of course, but to ease my pain of your absence, I conquered an entire city, reunited our kingdom, and became a general. What have you done in my absence besides become a latrine for birds?"

Matthias motioned to the fresh white spot on Conan's shoulder, placed there only moments ago from a sparrow flying by.

"Ugh," Conan said, trying to wipe the bird feces from his armor. But he only made it worse by streaking it farther down his arm.

"As much as I love our banter, I must see the queen."

But as Matthias took a step forward, Sir Conan held out his arm. "Wait, Blake. I know I told you before, but I'll tell you again. There's something amiss in there. I haven't seen a servant, or anyone leave for days at a time. I don't know what's happening, but I don't dare leave my post."

Matthias' attitude turned somber. "Understood. Thank you, Conan. Unfortunately, this is something I cannot hide from."

Sir Conan lowered his arm and motioned Matthias forward. "Tunri be with you, Blake."

Matthias nodded, praying the God that he only paid minor attention to would protect him from whatever the queen had in store.

He wished the next few steps were miles away. Unfortunately, it was only moments before Matthias was standing before Queen Leza's meeting chambers. He despised the hand-carved doors and their exquisite designs featuring Tenton's seal—two antlers coming forth from a crown. How much harm had he done under that seal? How many horrible deeds, how many lives taken, and all for the crown?

Matthias didn't know when his curse would break, or if it would ever break, but once he was free of it, he would make sure the queen paid for what she had done to him.

Pushing ideas and plans of revenge from his mind, Matthias knocked on the door.

"Enter," the queen's delicate voice replied.

Matthias had been fooled by the queen's dainty appearance, believing her to be merciful and loving of her people. His naivety once again was diminished.

"Welcome back, General," Queen Leza said with a knowing smile. "I expected you to be out of commission for far longer than only a few days." She took a small sip from her porcelain teacup, laughter shining in her eyes.

Matthias was not a man who showed emotions often. But this woman was able to pull out the absolute worst in him. Still, he was able to keep his tongue under control, but only just.

"I would've appreciated it if you had explained the boundaries of my curse at the trial, my queen," he replied coldly.

The queen placed her teacup back on its saucer on the table. "Now why would I do that? You work for me, remember, General?"

Oh, he remembered. There was hardly a day he forgot about his penance to the king and queen of Tenton. But, seeing how the queen was trying to goad him, Matthias decided to enter the battle.

"Of course, my queen. Although the king always allowed me to complete his tasks with the freedom to travel anywhere in Tenton."

As Queen Leza pursed her lips, Matthias knew he had struck a nerve. The death of the king was known to him, but it seemed the queen had yet to make a formal announcement to the rest of Tenton on the state of their king.

After a moment, Queen Leza slipped on her conniving persona once more. "Unfortunately, my poor husband was found dead in one of the lower chambers of the castle."

"A shame," Matthias rebutted without pause. "Murder, perhaps? A lovers' quarrel?" He knew the queen had disposed of her husband; he just didn't know how. Unfortunately for Matthias, the queen was a labyrinth of secrets.

Queen Leza narrowed her eyes. "Careful, General. People may assume you're accusing your queen in a falsehood, which we all know screams treason."

"Apologies, my queen," Matthias replied with a bow. "I only care for your emotional state after such a loss." He straightened, ready to seal his fate with his next comment. "With the princess still lost and the Seer's location unknown, I feared that your husband's death would unravel you completely." As soon as Matthias finished his statement, the chain around his next tightened until he couldn't breathe.

"Feeling confident today, aren't we, General?" the queen mused, still seated in her plush chair. She watched with amusement as Matthias struggled to remove the chain from his neck. "Squirm all you want; you will never remove the leash I have placed on you."

Matthias wheezed, his lungs constricting. He knew he was goading the queen. He knew it was a possibility that she would kill him. But he didn't fear death. He only regretted not seeing Devora and his mother one last time.

"Unfortunately—" The queen snapped her fingers, and the chain instantly loosened.

Matthias fell to the floor, his hands sinking into the thick carpet as he coughed, gasping for breath.

"I still need you, Blake. But don't worry, your time with me is coming to an end."

Standing, the queen strode over to Matthias and placed her cool hand on the back of his neck. Matthias forced himself not to yelp as her nails pierced the pressure points on either side.

"Three corrections for you, General. First, those nasty Kadeshians killed my beloved husband, or that is what all Tenton will know tomorrow when I hold his funeral service. Second, my poor daughter was found slaughtered in the siege." The queen sighed dramatically. "Such a waste of a pretty face, but she will be mourned at the funeral, as well."

Black spots were forming on the edges of Matthias' vision. Queen Leza's hold was firm around his neck and there was nothing he could do about it.

"And third, I know exactly where the Seer's location. She's right where I want her; with your mother."

Chapter Nine

Rae, Renta, Kadesh – Before Tristan and the others arrive in Kadesh

Rae couldn't believe that Tristan's crazy plan had worked. While it was odd returning to Yekel, Rae was relieved to find she no longer felt any animosity toward her former home. She even had the opportunity to see Master Monham and visit him for an evening. But it wasn't until they found Matthias' soldier, Sir Tocha, and were being smuggled into Kadesh that Rae's nerves settled down slightly.

The boundary into Kadesh was just on the other side of the Edo desert. While Rae feared the trek into the desert would be harsh, it didn't take nearly as long as she anticipated.

"The southern edge of the desert is the narrowest," Tristan had commented when Rae explained her worries to Ben on their last stop before they reached the Kadeshian border. There was a small freshwater stream where they decided to rest and replenish their water supply before entering enemy territory. "It's why Kadesh seized Yekel, it's the easiest way to get in and out of both countries without too much effort."

"Stop eavesdropping," Ben retorted.

"Ben, stop," Rae replied. "Thank you, Tristan. That was surprisingly helpful."

She noticed the looks Nadia and Tristan had given each other and the few words they exchanged before Nadia departed back to Totem. Though she didn't like it, Rae wasn't about to tell

Nadia who she could and couldn't admire. It was best to keep an open mind about Tristan. Maybe he would surprise them all.

Tristan snorted as he placed the cap on his waterskin. "My brother may be a strategic genius or whatever, but I'm not a complete idiot."

"Could've fooled me," Ben muttered under his breath.

"Be nice," Rae scolded him, then kissed him on the cheek.

Ida giggled at the interaction. It was the first acknowledgement she made toward any of them since they left the Fortress a few days ago. She had been quiet in the carriage, keeping her nose buried in the giant book she always held. Rae tried to engage her in some conversation but failed. Ida did have to leave her future husband behind. If their positions were switched, Rae would've been heartbroken if she had to leave Ben, and they weren't even betrothed.

The idea of marrying Ben and being with him forever brought a funny feeling to Rae's stomach. It wasn't that she didn't want to be with Ben but forever was a long time. Wouldn't he get tired of her? What about when they argued or were unkind to one another? Could they continuously mend their relationship again and again?

Rae pushed the questions from her mind. Ben had never spoken one word of forever to her and was content with where they were right now. And Rae would do her best to keep her thoughts and heart in the present as well.

"Have you found anything interesting in there?" Rae nodded to the giant book in Ida's hands as she filled up her waterskin, trying to focus on something else.

"Oh yes," Ida replied, smiling at the large tome. "There are so many extraordinary stories in here. The one I'm currently trying to understand is about a spirit guardian."

"That sounds creepy," Tristan commented from where he stood next to the carriage.

"I've never heard of that before," Rae replied, ignoring Tristan. She turned to Ben. "Have you?"

Before Ben could reply, Babshee spoke up, surprising the group. He, too, had been surprisingly silent as they trekked across the desert. "A spirit guardian protects something important but not ye gold and jewels. Something unseen."

"Like I said, 'creepy,'" Tristan repeated.

Ida turned to Babshee. "What do you mean 'unseen'?"

Babshee shook his head, his red hair flopping around his face. "Something unseen. A spirit of something, a person, a place. There are many tales of them throughout my peoples' history. But since ye blasted king took over, all my people fled, leaving no one to continue the tales."

"But how?" Rae asked, not sure she understood. How could something "unseen" be guarded? Why would a spirit need to be guarded?

Babshee scratched his backside. "Not all gifts need to make sense to everyone."

"Hmm," Ida said before flipping her book open again. "Thank you, Babshee."

As the group piled back in the carriage and headed toward the border of Kadesh, Rae's mind couldn't help but wander back to what Babshee said about gifts. Maybe the spirit guardian's gift didn't make sense, but all the other gifts she had witnessed made perfect sense to her. Papi and Nadia could make amazing things with their Tinker gifts. Devora could See and interpret prophetic visions directly from Tunri with her Seeing gift. Ben never missed a shot with his Marksmen gift. And Ida could understand any language with her Translator gift. So, once again, Rae was left without a gift. Well, she supposed Tristan didn't have a gift either, but she didn't want to be lumped in a group with him.

Sighing, Rae leaned her head against the side of the rolling carriage and closed her eyes. Maybe not having a gift was a good thing. The kingdom didn't wish to kill her. She paused. Actually, the kingdom did want to kill her, just not her specifically. They destroyed her home in Yekel and allowed their Kadeshian enemies to invade. Those same enemies she was willing to meet head on.

Too tired to think about it any longer, Rae decided to try to sleep before they arrived in Kadesh where they may be killed on sight.

After what only felt like moments of blissful rest, Rae felt a hand on her cheek.

"Rae, wake up, we're here," Ben's soft voice said in her ear.

Rae groaned but sat up, trying to rub the sleep from her eyes. Once she opened them, Ben's face greeted her with a smile.

"Sorry to wake you, but we need to make our disguise convincing. Apparently, Tristan is now our new owner."

"What?" Rae sat up. "When did that happen?"

Ben rolled his eyes. "When we found out that his word is the only one that holds weight in Kadesh."

Rae glanced to Ben then to Ida who whispered a few words before the giant book in her lap shimmered from sight. Rae blinked in surprise then shook her head and asked, "What do you mean? What's going on, Ida?"

Ida sighed. "We're women, Babshee is a giant, and One Shot looks more giant than not." She shrugged. "Sorry, One Shot, I don't mean to be rude."

"Stating facts isn't rude, Ida," Ben replied with a kind smile, then turned to Rae. "But she's right. Once we get in the city, we'll use the original plan. But unfortunately, we have to rely on Tristan a little longer. He did do a good job in getting me and Devora in and out of the Dark Market unnoticed."

Rae grunted but nodded. She remembered the first time she met Ben when she was disguised under her alias, the Crimson Cord. The ruse that Tristan created then certainly worked in the Dark Market, so she had to trust that his plan would work again now. And though Rae would never forget how the Kadeshian soldiers treated the women in the Temple, she would play the part again, but only until they were in Renta.

As Ben exited the carriage, Rae secured her blue scarf around the strands of her white-blonde hair. It was a few inches long now and Rae loved that it was growing back steadily.

"How do I look?" Ida asked, trying to secure the light-green scarf around her voluptuous curls. Though Ida had tried her best, strands of hair sprung out in every direction from the scarf.

Rae chuckled. "Let's just smooth it out a bit here and here—" Rae gently tucked the curls in and laid the scarf over them before securing the rest of the fabric around Ida's neck and shoulders. "There."

Ida smiled up at Rae. "Thank you, Rae. I'm glad you're here."

Rae paused at the comment. She hardly knew the people Ben called friends from the Fortress, but they had been nothing but welcoming to her. It was odd for her to be accepted so easily when, for the past few years of her life, she had to scrape for everything she desired.

Before Rae could respond to Ida, Tristan's annoyed face appeared in the carriage window. "Come on, ladies, we don't have all day."

Rae narrowed her gaze and quickly opened the door, causing Tristan to flail back until he fell to the ground. Rae helped Ida out of the carriage then looked down at Tristan. "Don't get too comfortable in the part you're playing, Tristan. I can still take you out in one hit."

Rae expected Tristan to reply sardonically, but instead he stood and brushed off his legs. He glanced at her with a humbled expression, and Rae felt her irritation dissipating.

"Apologies, I may not show it, but I'm a bundle of nerves. I'll be better when we're within Kadesh's borders. Hopefully with all our heads." Tristan tugged at the collar of his tunic with a nervous laugh.

"It's all right," she replied. "We'll all be okay."

"I pray you're right," Tristan replied before spinning around and striding away to speak with Babshee.

Frowning, Rae turned around to find a thick, stone wall just beyond the edge of the Edo desert. It was a strong, sturdy wall not unlike the one that had protected Yekel for years until King Atol destroyed it and allowed Kadesh the perfect opportunity to seize the citadel. Thankfully, General Blake had reseized Yekel, and Tenton was whole once again. Even so, the horrors of Yekel had left their mark and Rae still couldn't forget about Mami's sick form in Totem. Somehow, Rae had to find General Beta's key and destroy it.

As Rae started to follow Tristan, she felt Ben's large hand slide into hers. "It'll be okay," he said, squeezing her hand.

"I'm just worried about Mami," Rae replied. "How are we going to find the key?"

From her periphery, Rae watched Tristan pause at her words, acting as if he wasn't eavesdropping, but Rae knew he was.

"We'll find it," Ben reassured her. "Tunri will help us," he added. "I know you can take care of yourself, but I'm not going to let anything happen to you."

Warmth tugged around Rae's heart as she squeezed Ben's hand back. When Kadesh destroyed her home, she was left to her own devices to survive. And survive, she did. But Rae wasn't sure if she would ever be free from the scars during that time. At least for right now, she didn't have to go through life alone and she was so grateful for that.

"I won't let anything happen to you, either." Rae grinned at him. "We'll stay together. And if we're separated, we'll find each other."

"Always," Ben replied before leaning down and brushing her lips with his.

Butterflies soared through her stomach at the kiss. Since their first one, Ben had become increasingly greedy with stealing kisses, and Rae didn't mind in the least.

"All right, all right, enough of that," Tristan sighed, coming up to them.

Ben reluctantly pulled away. "When this is all over can I use him for target practice?"

Rae giggled. "Not unless the general allows it, which he might." *Nadia may not be so agreeable about it, though.*

Ben chuckled and kissed Rae on the forehead before they both faced Tristan. He had been efficient in the few moments Rae wasn't paying attention. Babshee already had a rope tied around his wrists. Ida stood next to him looking incredibly small. Thankfully, Tristan did not take his story so far as to bind her as well.

"As soon as we get in, I have a contact that will help us locate where General Beta is and we can continue our plan from there," Tristan explained. "If anyone asks about you two"—he motioned to Rae and Ida—"explain that you are here for the beauty pageant. If you're somewhere in the city they don't like, tell them you're lost and give them a dazzling smile. I know that always works on me with attractive females."

Rae found herself nodding along then paused at Tristan's last statement. Had he been slighted by a female before? Something tugged at the back of her mind about hearing Tristan and Devora being betrothed but she couldn't remember the details. Before she could think any further, their group was heading toward the wall.

Ben gave Rae one more kiss before taking his spot in line. Though Ben was tall, he looked like a child next to Babshee.

Ben glanced up and muttered a few words before handing the giant his crossbow, which looked like a toy in Babshee's hands. The giant stuffed it in his pocket with a nod, and the two continued on.

Rae hurried to catch up with Ida, who looked poised and confident as she strode behind Tristan. Huffing, Rae gave her a smile and took a few deep breaths to calm her racing heart before they reached the gate. As Rae took in the thick stone wall, she suddenly wondered how Tristan was able to have a contact in the enemy country. She remembered that Ben told her Tristan knew the ins and outs of the Dark Market, as well. So how did the pretty boy from Vlacklear know all of this?

Yet before Rae could ask about her suspicions, they were at the gate. A line of Kadeshian soldiers stood at the top, crossbows and bow and arrows in hand. One false move and they would be skewered. However, all the soldiers were at ease, thankfully not seeing them as a threat. Yet.

"Greetings, my friends," Tristan said in perfect Kadeshian. He opened his arms wide and bowed.

Well, he certainly knows how to play the part, Rae thought, impressed with how well Tristan could speak the foreign tongue.

"I bring gifts from Tenton and seek entrance into your prosperous land."

The gate before them opened just enough for a soldier to march out. Rae forced herself not to cringe at the bronze armor with the Kadeshian seal. Every time she saw it, she was brought back to General Yada and the torment he put her through.

No, that's in the past, she told herself. *I'm not that girl anymore. Tunri is with me.*

A cool peace overcame Rae's heart, and she relaxed slightly, knowing that even now Tunri was with them, guiding their steps. But though she trusted Tunri, she still wished she could reach out to Ben, knowing he was doing his best not to grab his crossbow Babshee had hidden for him. Sucking in a breath, Rae prayed no one would find out she and Ben witnessed the death of the general.

"Papers," the soldier gruffed, extending his armored hand.

Rae wished she could see the soldier's face and if she recognized him from Yekel. But he kept his helmet firmly in place.

"Ah yes," Tristan replied, handing a scroll to the guard.

Thankfully, Sir Tocha, General Blake's right-hand man who oversaw the rebuilding of Yekel, had assisted in drawing up the necessary paperwork so the group could enter the foreign land. But Rae still held her breath, knowing that one false move could end their lives here and now.

The guard carefully scrutinized the papers before waving to the soldiers above. Rae couldn't believe it when the solid iron gate started to open.

"Release the giant and take him to the treasury to get his payment," the guard ordered.

Three soldiers hurried before Babshee. The giant gave Tristan a nod of thanks before he stomped behind the soldiers.

"Take the ladies to the palace where they will be entered into the pageant. The prince may like exotic women from Tenton," jeered one of the guards, and the soldiers standing upon the wall gave a few chuckles.

Rae held her tongue, desiring nothing more than to smash all the soldiers' heads together.

"Yes, of course," Tristan said, bowing again. "I would be happy to escort them there."

But as Tristan started toward the gate, the guard drew his sword. "*My* soldiers will take them there. You and that small giant over there will stay here until I call General Beta."

Fear pierced Rae's heart as the soldiers came near her and Ida. She couldn't be separated from Ben, especially since she knew the soldiers meant Ben and Tristan harm. She saw Ben twitch in the corner of her eye, and she knew he was ready to react as well.

"I appreciate your efforts, my good sir," Tristan continued, pausing Rae's steps. "I am thoroughly impressed with how efficient the Kadeshian military is. Well done!" He gave the soldier a small punch in the shoulder and smiled. The soldier didn't seem as amused by the gesture. "However, I've already made an appointment with the general. There's no need for you to bring her all the way out here."

It was then that Tristan produced another scroll, this one with the Kadeshian seal on it. As the guard read the scroll, Rae started to wonder whose side Tristan was really on.

The guard grunted. "Very well, I will take you to General Beta, myself." The soldier whistled and two more soldiers appeared. "Take the ladies and the small giant to the palace. Sayidi Tamor can decide what to do with them."

As she strode forward, Rae released only half a sigh of relief before she felt a small hand in her own. Glancing over, Rae found Ida staring at the large city beyond the wall. Rae was so caught up in her own fears, she never thought about how Ida would feel returning to her home country.

"Are you okay?" she whispered to the petite woman.

Ida nodded once and swallowed. "I will be."

Before they could see any of the city, the girls were swept into the back of a carriage with Ben instructed to sit up front with the driver. Before Ben climbed up, Rae noticed he swiped something that was leaning against the wall and threw it into the carriage. A few moments later, his crossbow landed in her lap.

"Keep it safe for me," he said then closed the carriage door.

Rae and Ida didn't speak much before they were brought to the palace. It was beautiful and grand, full of color and warmth. When they exited the carriage, Rae quickly handed the crossbow to Ben who promptly strapped it to his back. The Kadeshian soldier who was instructed to lead them to Sayidi Tamor, whoever that was, left them by the steps of the palace and drove the carriage away.

Efficient military, indeed, Rae mused remembering Tristan's false compliment.

"So, what now?" Rae asked, watching the carriage disappear into the distance.

"I don't know," Ida confessed.

"I knew Tristan was shady," Ben muttered. "But I didn't think he'd disappear as soon as we entered the city." He sighed and rubbed the back of his neck, peering around. "At least we got in without being killed."

"Hello there," a voice called from the left.

The trio turned to find a tall man about their age, waving at them with a big smile. His skin was dark like Ida's, but his eyes were a light shade of copper.

"Welcome to Kadesh, are you ladies here for the pageant?"

Rae blinked at the man. The guards had been so gruff, something she was used to. But this man seemed unusually kind, and she wasn't sure how to react.

"Yes," Ida replied, slipping into the Kadeshian tongue with ease. "My friend and I have traveled quite some distance so that we may participate in the prince's pageant."

Rae knew that Ida had a gift for translating languages but couldn't believe how beautiful Kadeshian sounded coming from her mouth.

"Yes, of course," the man said, but there was something else in his gaze and Rae wondered if he knew more about them than he was letting on. He turned to Ben, a look of relief on his face.

"I pray you are another guard because there are far too many ladies for the number of soldiers the palace has."

"This is my friend's guard," Ida explained quickly with a nervous laugh. "He is required to stay with her throughout the duration of the pageant."

Rae wished she could hug Ida. The guard readily agreed and told them to follow him.

Soon, the three were taken into the palace and into a room where Ida was assigned a guard that looked disturbingly similar to Jacques. Rae wasn't sure who that first man they met was, but he had somehow convinced a very large, very angry looking man named Sayidi Tamor to allow Rae and Ida to be roommates as well.

Thank Tunri, Rae thought. But what surprised her the most was when Princess Haden, the crown princess of Tenton, opened the door to their room.

Chapter Ten

Haden, Radaa Kingdom, Kadesh

Haden's mouth dropped open as she stared at the two women from Tenton. Of course, her terrible luck would have her be roommates with the two spies. They would probably report back to her mother the instant Haden wasn't around.

Haden's mind was already deep into a daydream where she was being led back to Tenton in shackles when she realized the two women hadn't said a word. If they were truly spies for Tenton, wouldn't they have tried to arrest her? Or maybe they wished to befriend her first, then she would trust them and *then* they would arrest her.

Though Haden didn't like being so paranoid, she would fight them as hard as she could. She would not be sent back to Mother. Not when she had made it this far.

Narrowing her eyes at the pair, Haden asked, "Who are you?"

The young woman with oddly similar hair to Haden's natural color quirked her brow, but it was the petite dark-skinned woman who spoke. "I'm Ida, and this is Rae."

Her smile was warm and inviting. Haden found herself already hoping to be her friend. But after she had let Mal almost sweep her off her feet, and the possibility that these two women may be spies for Mother, she had to stay on her guard.

"What are you doing here?" Haden questioned, trying to sound authoritative and commanding like the princess Mother wanted her to be.

Ida shared a look with Rae then said, "I believe we're going to be rooming together while we're here. For the beauty pageant." She tilted her head to the side and studied Haden.

Haden cringed at the look. She had seen that look far too many times in her life from the servants and members of the court. It was a look that said, "Is the princess okay? Why can't she pay attention? Why can't she understand faster?"

Haden hated that look of pity and wouldn't stand it from a stranger.

"Of course," Haden said with a chuckle, straightening her stance. She would have to do better in thinking before speaking.

The two women gave Haden strange looks before Ida said, "So, what's your name?"

Haden blinked. Did these women not know who she was? Were they really not from Tenton? But she knew she recognized the tall man with Rae. Maybe Rae had no idea who he was either. Haden wasn't sure how to proceed. She could make her alias name now. But then she remembered she had already told Mal her real name and Sayidi Tamor had already read her name aloud to the entire room of women.

I should've started thinking before speaking a lot sooner than now. I might as well stick with the truth.

Hoping the truth didn't come back to haunt her, she answered, "I'm Haden."

The women glanced at each other again, and Haden wished she could be a part of their silent language.

Haden watched Ida nod before the other woman, Rae, asked, "As in Princess Haden of Tenton?"

"Shh!" Haden cried, slamming the door behind her. "How did you know?"

Rae snorted and folded her arms across her chest. "Anyone who takes one step into Tenton has seen your face plastered somewhere."

Heat crawled up Haden's neck. Unfortunately, Miguel had been correct. Even though her skin was slightly darker and her hair a lot darker, her face was still her face. And she hated that Mother had "plastered" it everywhere. Haden never understood the reasoning behind it, but she would never defy Mother's wishes. Not after that first time and look where that got her. In a cage, every night since.

Panic suddenly struck Haden's core. She never had roommates before. What would she do when she transformed tonight? She assumed when she fled the palace her transformation would end, but it still happened every night since.

Haden pulled herself from her thoughts and found Rae and Ida whispering to one another.

"Should we notify the general that she's here?" Rae murmured.

Ida shook her head. "Even if we could get word to him, what could we do about it?"

Irritation rose in Haden's heart at their interaction. She hated it when people talked about her like she wasn't in the room. Since she was a child, she was meant to be seen and not heard. But that ended now.

"I can hear you, you know," she said, lifting her chin, trying to hide how nervous she felt at standing up for herself to two people who may potentially have her sent back to Tenton.

"Right, sorry," Rae said, unfazed by Haden's boldness. "We weren't sure when you were going to come out of..." Rae gestured to Haden. "Whatever you were doing."

"What Rae means," Ida interjected. "Is that we know some people who have been looking for you for some time now."

"Aha!" Haden cried, pointing at the two women. And before she could stop herself, she blurted, "I knew you were spies for Mother. Well, you can't take me back. I'll fight both of you if I must." Haden lifted her fists, ready to defend herself.

Rae took one look at her stance and barked out a laugh. "Even if we were sent to spy for the queen, you would never defeat us with that stance."

Ida gave Haden a sympathetic smile. "We're not spies for the queen. But we work with someone you may remember, Captain Blake. He and our friend, Devora, saved you in the Battle of Edo and brought you back to the palace."

"General," Rae corrected as she took a bundle of fabrics from a sack and began folding them in a neat pile.

"Right, General Blake," Ida amended.

Haden lowered her fists, embarrassed once again. "General? When did that happen?"

"Only recently," Ida said with a sigh.

Haden waited for Ida to explain more, but the woman stayed silent. Apparently, a lot had happened since Haden ran away.

The air between the three women grew hot with tension, or maybe Haden was the only one who felt it. Rae seemed content folding her scarves, and Ida was watching Haden with a small smile.

Haden never had people wait for her to respond. She was always told what to do, where to go, what to wear, and what to say. Now that she was free to do what she liked, she panicked.

"Well, I have important business to attend while I'm here," Haden explained, backtracking toward the door. "So, I better be going."

She didn't know how to react or what to say. It was better to flee when she could. Before either of the women could reply, Haden rushed out of the door and bumped straight into the chest of a very tall man. Glancing up, Haden realized it was the same man she had seen with Captain—General—Blake after the Battle of Edo.

"It's you!" she cried. "I knew I had seen you earlier."

The tall man scanned the corridor before he bowed deeply. "Hello again, Princess. What are you doing in Kadesh?"

Haden crossed her hands over her chest. "I could ask you the same question."

The tall man smirked. "I'm merely following orders."

Haden opened her mouth to reply when Mal turned the corner. "Ah, Haden, I see you've met one of the other ladies' guards."

Haden glanced at the tall man who cocked his head to the side, as if asking her if she would rat him out or not. Haden didn't know why a soldier from General Blake's battalion was in Kadesh, but she also didn't want anyone else to know who she really was either.

"Yes, um—"

"Ben."

Haden nodded. "Yes, Ben here was doing a fantastic job guarding our door." Lifting her hand, Haden gave Ben a pat on the arm. "I feel safer already."

As soon as the words slipped from her lips, Haden wished she could've sewn them shut.

Why are you such a nuisance? She could hear Mother demanding in her ear.

But when she looked at Mal, she didn't see contempt or mock flattery in his eyes. Instead, he gazed at her as if he thought she were an adorable kitten. Haden wasn't sure how she felt about that.

"I'm glad Ben is doing an astute job on his first day," Mal commented with a grin. He then pulled a piece of parchment from his belt. "But I actually came here to find you. If you wouldn't mind taking a walk with me. There's something I want to show you."

Haden glanced at Ben, but he had already returned to his post by their door.

"Uh, sure."

Haden walked in stride with Mal until they were halfway into the courtyard. A beautiful bubbling fountain spurted water into its circular basin below. A variety of colorful flowers Haden had only seen in books decorated the space around the fountain, filling it with a fresh and alluring scent. Northern Tenton was cool and gray; hardly any beautiful flowers grew there. And Haden was grateful she didn't need to read the descriptions of the flowers in the books to enjoy their beauty.

Four stone benches sat around the fountain so admirers of the courtyard could sit and enjoy its tranquility as long as they wished.

Mal strode before her and plunked down on the bench. He patted the space next to him. Haden hesitantly sat down, unsure of the forwardness of her guard. Thankfully, she still had her bag with her knife. She may not be a soldier, but she would use it in self-defense if needed.

"I went to ask Sayidi Tamor about the visitor policy. I didn't mention your name, but he gave me this." Mal handed Haden the scroll.

Sweat beaded on Haden's brow as she took the scroll. She wasn't ready for Mal, or anyone in Kadesh for that matter, to discover her poor reading skills. How would she be able to win the heart of the prince of Kadesh—or at least talk to him—if he thought she was a fool?

Unfortunately, it wouldn't be the first time. Haden frowned, remembering all the suitors who had politely but firmly reneged their offers of marriage once they discovered Haden's difficulty with reading.

Sucking in a breath, she made a show of unrolling the scroll and making her eyes run back and forth, a ploy she often did during her learning lessons so her tutors would leave her alone. Of course, she would always complete her lessons by the next day but would work on them all throughout the evening when she could take her time to decipher each phrase in peace.

As Haden glanced at the scroll, she knew she was in trouble because the Kadeshian tongue glared up at her in harsh black strokes. She studied it as best she could, but it always took her a bit longer to decipher the slanting symbols. Haden parted her lips to say this when she bit her tongue. If she didn't know how to read Kadeshian, that would expose her lie and Mal would know she wasn't from Kadesh.

Lost in her thoughts, Haden didn't realize that Mal was watching her. She wasn't sure if he suspected her or not, but he offered, "Would you like me to read it to you?"

"That would be lovely," Haden replied a bit too quickly. "I'm just so drained from the events of today." Haden winced at the added dramatic flair, but a girl had to do what was necessary to not be arrested and possibly hanged.

Mal nodded with understanding, but his eyes said that he noticed more. Clearing his throat, he read, "Any visitor of the palace must gain approval from King Redore IV to have additional guests."

Haden's heart sank. She would never be able to see the king and get approval and speak with Miguel. Just when she had found a member of her true family, she had lost him again. Haden's shoulders slumped. "Oh, well, thank you for asking."

Mal rerolled the scroll. "If there is a way I can get the king's approval for you, I will let you know. Who is it you wish to see?"

"My uncle," Haden replied, the title feeling foreign on her lips. She had never known any family outside of Mother and Father. And now that she knew they weren't her real family, she felt even more lost than usual.

The setting sun in the distance reminded Haden of the long day she'd had and the even longer day she would experience tomorrow when the beauty pageant treatments officially began.

Standing, she glanced at Mal. "Thank you again, Mal, for your kindness and welcoming me to the palace. I truly do appreciate you finding out about the visitors for me."

As Haden stood and started forward, Mal said, "My sister has difficulty reading. It takes her twice as long as me and she has hated it since we were children. I try to encourage her and say our greatest weaknesses can become our strengths."

Haden paused, keeping her back to Mal, hating that he had seen right through her charade. "And how does she reply?"

"She punches me in the arm and tells me to *shetza con*," he chuckled.

Haden couldn't help but giggle. She could only imagine what kind of insult that was.

Standing, Mal took a step toward her. "If you ever need help, please ask me first." Haden tried to find the deceit in his copper-colored eyes, but there was nothing but honesty within them.

"I'll be sure to remember that," Haden replied, her voice barely a whisper.

With her heart thumping, Haden hurried out of the courtyard. She knew she should wait for Mal to escort her back to the room, but she didn't like the way he made her feel so many emotions at once.

Though, when she heard his steady gait following her, she knew he was making sure she returned to her room unharmed. She couldn't help but feel relieved knowing that he was there, making sure she was safe.

Thankfully, she had remembered where her room was, but when she reached the wooden door, she found it was no longer Ben guarding it, but another guard with yellow-blond hair.

"Can I help you?" he asked, his eyes a penetrating shade of blue.

"Um," Haden started, taking a step back. "This is my room. Mal is my guard." She pointed over her shoulder, hoping that Mal had almost caught up to her.

But, before she could say another word, the door cracked open and Ida peered out. "It's okay, Raphael. She's with us."

The stern guard gave Haden a once-over before nodding and moving to the side. Once the door closed behind Haden, she breathed a sigh of relief. "Is that your guard? He's terrifying."

Ida laughed. "I've met far scarier guards than him."

Although Haden still didn't know whether the girls were going to send her back to Mother or not, she felt a sense of peace blanket over her as she entered the room. It was as if Tunri was telling her to trust these two women and she would be okay. Tunri had gotten her here safely, and Ida and Rae had yet to make any threats to send her back to Tenton. She would continue to do her best to trust Tunri.

Relaxing, Haden took a moment to study the room. She had been so frightened earlier she never had the chance to examine where she would be staying. The space was divided into three sections: Ida and Rae had taken the first two slots on the left, leaving the far right to her. A large bed with a flowing white canopy sat in the center of each space. Next to each bed stood a table with a bouquet of fresh blue and orange flowers from the courtyard outside. Haden couldn't wait to curl up on the plush bed, hoping to figure out what to do next.

It was then that Haden noticed Rae was gone. "Where's Rae?"

"She needed some fresh air," Ida replied simply as she sat on her bed with an enormous book that Haden wouldn't dare try to read.

Haden nodded, understanding when to not ask any further questions, and decided she had had enough excitement for one day. Without even taking off her ratty boots, Haden bid Ida good night and jumped into the farthest bed, praying tomorrow would bring her some answers.

Chapter Eleven

Haden, Radaa Kingdom, Kadesh

The sunlight streamed through the canopy surrounding Haden's bed, waking her from a deep slumber. As Haden blinked open her eyes and stretched, she realized tomorrow had come and she still had no answers on how to proceed with her plan in winning the pageant to see the prince of Kadesh.

When everyone told Haden to be silent, she realized not speaking was a power of its own. For if she was silent, then she could listen. And that's how she discovered Mother's treacherous deeds. Mother had been able to bamboozle the entire kingdom, but not Haden, for she knew why Mother wished to end Seers all those years ago. And she had to tell the prince of Kadesh.

Haden wasn't sure if Mother had found out that Haden knew the details of the queen's plan because after her sixteenth birthday, everything changed. Before Haden turned sixteen summers, Mother had treated Haden with love and kindness. But as soon as her birthday came and went, Mother's attitude toward Haden turned on its head. No longer was she sweet, kind, and loving. Instead, she was harsh, rude, and cruel. Haden didn't understand until she overheard Mother talking to Father.

"She was supposed to show signs of the gift two years ago, Atol," Queen Leza snarled. *"And nothing has happened. She's just as useless as before."*

"Now, now, my queen, there's still time," King Atol consoled. *"You don't wish for all your plans to be for naught, do you?*

Let's give her until her eighteenth birthday in a few months, then decide what to do with her."

"If she hasn't developed the Tinker gift by now, she never will," the queen replied. "I'm taking care of this problem now."

Haden shuddered, remembering overhearing the conversation after she had decided to try locating the genealogy scroll Madeline had told her about. Thankfully, the white-mustached librarian had assisted her, and Haden was able to store the scroll in a safe place, for it was later that night when she transformed that Haden was taken from her home and given to the enemy. At first, Haden wanted to believe what she heard her parents discussing was all lies. That maybe, for whatever reason, they were putting up a front. But when General Blake had returned her to the palace after the Battle of Edo, and mother locked her in her room without so much as a welcome home, Haden knew all the words were truth.

As Haden sat up in her bed, her fingers brushed a few blue-tipped feathers. She winced, realizing she was so exhausted she had made no plans on how to hide her transformation from her new roommates. Peering over to the other two women, Haden found them still sleeping soundly in their beds. It seemed yesterday was a trying day for all of them. And she assumed that if Ida and Rae had found her as a sparrow instead of a young woman, an alarm would've been sound.

Sighing, Haden tried to comb out the knots in her hair. There were so many things she had to think through, how was she going to figure them all out on her own? She glanced down at her hands and released a gasp at the black tint of her fingertips. The dark dye she had used to cover her bright hair was starting to wear off. Whatever she needed to do, she had to do it fast. If the Kadeshian monarchy discovered the Tentonian princess had snuck into their kingdom unnoticed, it would amplify the war without a doubt. And Haden was here to stop the war, not make it worse.

Trying to rub the dye off her fingers, Haden started toward the wash basin at the front of the room. As she hurried by, Ida and Rae started to stir. Haden concentrated on washing her hands clean, but her mind was still whirring. Could she consider them friends? She still hadn't confirmed whether they were spies for her mother or not, but it would be so nice to have friends to share her burdens with. While she wasn't sure about Rae, Ida seemed very kind.

A knock sounded at the door and Rae sprang from her sheets, scaring Haden half to death. Water from the basin sloshed all over Haden's tan dress and the floor around her.

"Who's there?" Rae demanded; her short hair spiked in various places.

Ida groaned drowsily and pulled the sheets over her head.

"It's me," a deep voice replied. "With breakfast."

Rae immediately attempted to smooth out her hair before she hurried to the door. Haden watched the exchange between the tall guard, Ben, and Rae. Her brows rose, and she smirked as Ben caressed Rae's hand as he handed her a tray.

If they are spies, they're spies in love, Haden mused as she bent down and started cleaning the water off the floor.

She knew she would never find love. Though she had tried, many of the nobles didn't wish to marry their eligible sons off to Haden. Not that Haden minded. They were either too young, too old, too boring, or too adventurous. None of the suitors felt right, so Haden decided she would be happy with a life of solitude. It was all she was used to anyway.

Rae noticed Haden watching and took the tray from Ben, slamming the door in his face.

Haden winced at the action.

"Did I make you do that?" Rae asked, placing the tray down before grabbing a towel.

"Oh, don't worry about it," Haden replied, trying to swab the water faster.

Rae crouched down next to her and started wiping up the rest of the spilled water. "There. Now that that's done, we can all eat."

"Thank you," Haden replied, curious at the transformation from the unsure and distant Rae of yesterday to the peppy, happy one of today. Maybe she was more of a morning person and was grumpy in the evenings.

"No worries," Rae replied, sitting at the small circular table where she had set the tray. "Come eat."

Haden shuffled over and sat across from Rae. An array of succulent fruits and nuts sat atop one another. Ben obviously had a good eye for picking out delicious food. Haden couldn't wait to try each one.

As she reached for a plump red cherry, she commented, "He seems nice."

Rae's cheeks were dotted with pink as she poured some water into a glass and handed it to Haden. "Who? Oh, my guard? He is. I mean, I only just met him yesterday." She laughed nervously, and Haden felt a strange familiarity to her.

"I think we need to be honest," Ida grumbled from beneath the sheets of her bed.

Haden popped the cherry into her mouth, thankful that its pit had already been taken out. Grabbing a handful more, she inquired, "Honest about what?"

She had barely placed another cherry in her mouth when another knock sounded at the door.

"We're certainly popular this morning," Rae commented as she stood to open the door.

But this time it wasn't Ben, but the blond guard who wasn't going to let Haden into the room last night.

"It's time for your first treatment." His tone was cold and hard.

Haden couldn't imagine having him as a guard when Mal had been nothing but kind to her.

"Where's Ida?" the guard asked, his cool eyes darting around the room.

"I'm right here," Ida said, rolling from her bed, her hair a mess of curls atop her head. "I thought the first treatment wasn't until midmorning."

"There are too many ladies to complete everyone's treatments at once," Ben replied, stepping through the door around the stern guard. "Your groups are being staggered."

Haden glanced at the two guards and then wondered where Mal was. Wasn't he supposed to escort her everywhere so that she wouldn't run away, or so Sayidi Tamor had said?

The angry blond guard turned to her. "We will escort you to your treatment until Mal returns. Don't get any ideas of deserting." He spun around and marched out the door.

Haden blinked, unsure of how to respond.

"Don't worry about him," Ida said, walking up next to Haden. "His bark is worse than his bite."

"Did you know him before you came here?" Haden asked, eyeing Rae and Ben whispering to each other by the doorway.

Ida smiled. "No, but I know his family. Come on, let's see what this first beauty treatment is." Ida batted her eyelashes and Haden giggled.

It was hard to believe the prince thought all the beautiful women she had seen needed to become even *more* beautiful for him. Though Haden already didn't like the vanity of the prince, she had to do her best to impress him because he and his kingdom were the only ones who could stop Mother.

Haden, Ida, Rae and their guards strode through a series of corridors until they reached a large room with six pools of water. Cerulean blue tiles, painted gold, white, and orange, lined the walls and floors. A comforting humidity bloomed from the space and Haden wondered what their first treatment would be.

"We will be waiting outside," Ida's guard said and turned without a second glance.

Ben nodded at the three ladies, his gaze lingering a bit longer on Rae before he too exited the space.

Haden studied the swirling lines on the tiles, wondering where Mal was again until another few groups of women joined them.

"Welcome future princesses of Kadesh," a voice from the back of the room called.

Haden glanced up to see a stunning woman with voluptuous curves striding toward them. A bright, bold teal dress wrapped around her frame, accentuating her features in all the right places. As she approached, Haden noticed shimmers of gold sparkling from the woman's braided hair, like stars in the night sky. Her dark skin was flawless, and Haden had never been more envious of someone else's beauty before.

"I am Sayida Erza, but you can call me Erza." Her plump pink lips separated into a stunning smile before she extended her arms and continued, "These are the purification pools of Kadesh. The minerals within their waters will cleanse and exfoliate your skin of any impurities so that you will shine like the sun for the crown prince."

Many of the ladies giggled at the statement.

Erza then clasped her hands in front of her, her dark eyes bright with excitement as she surveyed the group. Haden suddenly felt someone shoving her forward and it took all her balance to not ram into the woman standing in front of her. When Haden glanced over her shoulder, she saw Ida hiding behind her.

"What are you doing?" she whispered down to Ida as Erza started directing a group of women to the furthest pool.

"Oh, uh, I think I dropped something," Ida said with a shaky laugh.

Even though Haden didn't always catch on to things quite as quickly as others, she knew Ida was lying and trying to hide. But from what?

"You two, the beautiful blonde and the elegant tall one," Erza said pointing to Rae and Haden. "You will go to the front pool. Head to the back room and change into your special swimwear." Sayida Erza glanced at Haden's hair with an arched brow. "There are wraps for your hair, if you wish it to not get wet, as well."

Haden was thankful Sayida Erza probably assumed she had dyed her hair to gain the prince's attention, rather than hide her identity. She nodded in acknowledgment and started following Rae when she felt Ida grab onto the fabric of her dress.

Haden didn't understand why Ida was latching onto her like a child looking for her mother. Maybe she didn't want to be left alone in a strange place. The thought softened Haden's heart. "I'm sure Sayida Erza won't mind if you come with us," Haden started to say before Erza hurried toward her.

"Please come along," she clucked, clapping her hands twice. "We have many ladies who need to bathe!"

But when Erza reached Haden's side, her eyes darted to Ida—who was still trying to hide behind Haden—and she gasped. "Ida?" the woman cried. "Is that really you?"

But Ida didn't answer. Instead, she ran out of the room, sobbing. Haden started to follow her, when she felt a hand on her shoulder.

"I'll go after her," Rae said. "Go ahead and enjoy the pool."

Haden suddenly felt very alone as she watched Rae hurry after Ida. She had only just met the two women, but she already enjoyed having them around.

Sighing, Haden turned back to Erza to find her gaze still searching for where Ida went.

"Is everything okay?" Haden asked, snapping Erza out of whatever daze she was in.

Erza shook her head and plastered her smile back on her face. "Yes, of course. Let's get you into the pool."

Haden quickly changed into the special swimwear, which was odder than anything she had ever worn. Tan fabric wrapped around each of her limbs and her torso. On top of that was a billowing skirt made of the same material. Haden didn't understand why this outfit was any different than the one she was wearing, but she didn't want to make a fuss. Erza was still shaken over seeing Ida, and Haden was curious as to why. Taking another piece of tan fabric, Haden wrapped it around her head, praying the black dye would do its job for just a little longer.

As Haden lowered herself into the pool, rippling warm water covered her legs, relaxing her tense muscles. She easily sank into the clear waves, enjoying how soothing the mineral water felt.

Leaning her head back, Haden stared at the tiled ceiling, trying to think of a way to see Miguel. He had said he may have contacts from when he worked at the palace. But that was probably years ago. Would his contact still work here? Of course, Haden could just wait until she earned a spot in the pageant and the prince requested her presence, but seeing the stiff competition of beautiful ladies did not encourage her in that plan.

Could she have Mal ask the king to allow her to see Miguel? But Mal was only a guard. At Maldove Palace, guards were just one step above a servant. The rules in Radaa Kingdom may be different, but Haden doubted it. Mal wouldn't have the authority to speak with the king whenever he wished, or even be in the king's presence without special approval.

Sighing, Haden sat up and started rubbing the water onto her arms when a bright-yellow turban caught her eye. Craning her neck, Haden peered out the open doorway to see a man who looked distinctly like Miguel pacing outside the courtyard of the palace.

Haden wished she had prayed more to Tunri since arriving in Kadesh because He was clearly taking care of her. Breathing a prayer of thanks, Haden started climbing out of the pool.

"Your treatment is not complete," Erza chided behind Haden. "You need to stay in the pool at least until midday. If it is refreshment you need, I can have your guard bring you something to keep you relaxed."

Haden shivered as the cool air outside of the warm pool chilled her skin. "Midday? But I'll be shriveled like a prune by then."

Erza furrowed her elegant brow. "A what?"

"I mean," Haden coughed as she stood. She wasn't taller than Erza, thank goodness, but she still had to muster all her confidence to keep eye contact with the suspicious woman. "I need to take care of something personal."

Before Erza could protest, Haden darted out of the room. A cool wind wrapped around Haden's wet limbs, but she hurried as quickly as she could to the exterior wall of the courtyard.

"Miguel," Haden whispered, although loud enough for him to hear.

The yellow turban whipped around, and her uncle hurried forward. "Haden," he cried. "You're okay."

Haden was astounded by the genuine concern and care in Miguel's eyes. She had only met this man once and he already held more concern for her than her false mother of eighteen years.

"What are you doing here?" she asked, the mineral water of the purification pool dripping from her arms onto the ground below as she gripped the iron-wrought fence caging in the courtyard. Miguel had somehow gotten past the outer gate to have gotten this far, and Haden was impressed. She assumed Miguel would leave her to Kadesh's mercy after she was taken for the beauty pageant and enjoy the large sum the king had provided.

"I came to find you. I needed to make sure you were well, and I also heard some horrid news."

Haden felt her eyes widen. "What news?"

Miguel glanced around to make sure they were alone. "The queen of Tenton has scheduled a funeral procession for the king and princess."

Blood fled from Haden's face. "What?"

Mother had declared her *and* Father dead? What had happened to Father?

But before Haden could ask any further questions, blood-curdling shrieks and cries came from the purification pools.

Haden whipped her head around to see a series of guards rushing toward the pools, the cries of the young women inside growing louder.

"Go!" Miguel urged her. "It will look suspicious if you are not there. Meet me in three days' time at midnight. I will tell you more of what I've heard."

Haden nodded quickly before rushing back toward the pools.

"Haden, Haden!" a voice called and through the crowd came Mal.

"Mal," Haden breathed as she reached his side, water still dripping from her swimwear down to her bare feet. "Where were you?"

"Where were *you?*" he asked, his eyes wide and panicked as more guards pushed past them.

Sayidi Tamor came into view and Mal quickly took Haden's arm, pulling her away from the crowd. Haden glanced over her shoulder. Three of the women that had been assigned to one of the pools were being carried out by several guards. Their swimwear was in tatters, hanging in shreds around their limbs. But what horrified Haden the most were the red splotches covering their skin.

"I thought the waters were supposed to purify, not burn," Haden whispered once her and Mal were far enough away.

"They are," Mal said, frustration lacing his words. "I don't know how this could've happened."

"Attention all participants of *Sundarata Taashama*," Sayidi Tamor's voice boomed over the courtyard.

Haden turned to face the large man when she noticed Mal's hand had moved from her arm to around her waist, holding her close. She felt awful at the excitement his touch brought to her, especially considering three women had been terribly burned by the purification pools.

"A horrible act has occurred," Sayidi Tamor boomed. "Three of our participants have been burned by poisoned water placed in the purification pools. While this is a competition, I will not tolerate any acts of sabotage. Each of you will be personally questioned by the crown prince to discover who committed this crime. Whoever it was will be hanged."

Hanged? If that were the punishment for committing a crime, what would they do to the Tentonian princess hiding in their midst?

Fear seized Haden's heart as Mal pulled her closer, as if protecting her. But protecting her from what? It wasn't as if the poison was meant for her, right?

"Come on," Mal said, releasing her waist and grabbing her hand. "Let's get you out of here."

Haden nodded mechanically, unable to erase the image of the women's burned bodies from her mind.

Yet as Mal led her past the purification pools, dread sat like a rock in her stomach. The pool that had been poisoned was the same one she had sat in only moments before.

Chapter Twelve

Ida, Radaa Kingdom, Kadesh

"Ida, wait!" Rae's voice called from behind.

But Ida didn't wait. She needed to get out of the room and as far away as possible from that woman.

When Ida volunteered to travel to Kadesh, she anticipated battles and hardships along the way. But she never expected to come face to face with Josef's mother. The same woman who looked at her and treated her like trash when she was an orphan in Renta years ago.

Ida sucked back the tears that were begging to fall. She couldn't crumble here. She had to be strong. Tunri led her here, didn't He? He had provided her with the Book of Ages and allowed her to learn so much about the history of Tenton and how the land could heal from the evil that had plagued it for too long. And Tunri had blessed her with Jacques. Wonderful, amazing, incredible Jacques. If not for herself, she had to see this through for him. So that they could be together forever.

But in one moment, she was brought back to the poor, unwanted unloved, and undesirable little girl she had been. How could she ever face Erza again?

Ida finally ceased her running when she came upon another one of the palace's gardens. Her guard, Raphael, had explained there were several surrounding the palace, each one holding unique flowers. Apparently, the former queen loved exotic plants from all over Kadesh.

"Wow," Rae said, huffing for breath as she stopped in front of Ida. "You're a lot faster than I thought."

"I'm sorry," Ida replied, her tears starting to fall. "I didn't mean to run so far. I just had to get away." Ida turned from Rae. She couldn't let the strong woman see her in such a state. Rae had been through so much and was still able to persevere. While Ida thought she had gotten stronger since leaving Vlacklear Academy, she was still just as frail as when she entered the terrible school.

"What happened?" Rae asked, motioning to one of the stone benches nearby. "Do you want to talk about it?"

Ida plunked down; happy Rae had chosen a bench surrounded by lilies. They reminded her of her desert lily she had grown back in Vlacklear and the beautiful lily dress she had worn to the masquerade ball when she proposed to Jacques.

Ida's secrets about being Kadeshian and a Translator had been explained to the group back at the Fortress, but she had never had a conversation about it one on one with Rae.

"Before I was saved and brought to Tenton, I lived here, in Renta," Ida began.

Rae's eyes grew wide. "You lived in the palace?"

Ida shook her head with a sad smile. "No, unfortunately, I was an orphan. But I did have one friend who always came by to see me." Her smile wavered at the mention of Josef. Even though she loved Jacques and couldn't wait to marry him, her heart was still pained by the death of her childhood friend. So many things left unsaid.

"Are they still here? Is that who that woman was?"

Ida was impressed at how perceptive Rae was. "Sayida Erza was Josef's mother, and she did not like her son befriending an orphan when his father was the weapons master to one of King Redore IV's top generals."

Rae's lips formed a line. "Ah, I see." She paused for a moment before adding, "When I first met Devora and Ben, I had a hard time believing they would see me as anything other than a former Priestess of the Temple."

Ida nodded, remembering she had first met Rae after the battle at Maldove Palace when General Blake insisted they all share who they were. Ida couldn't believe how much hardship Rae had gone through after losing her father to King Atol and then her mother to the Temple. Then being forced to serve General Yada as a slave in his awful brothel.

"But they never saw me as less," Rae continued, tucking a short piece of white-blonde hair behind her ear. "Through their kindness and love, I have been able to heal from the false labels that were placed on me."

Rae reached out and squeezed Ida's hand, surprising Ida. Rae always tried to stay away from physical contact as much as possible and Ida understood completely.

"'The actions of others do not define who you are. Only you decide who you want to be.' Kanna Blake told me that and I remind myself of it whenever I start to have doubts," Rae explained. "I don't know what Sayida Erza said or did in the past, but the past is done. What matters now is that you're a talented Translator who is betrothed to a wonderful man who just so happens to be the next duke to a very large company *and* is smitten by you."

Ida giggled at Rae's description of Jacques, her heartwarming at the thought of him. How she wished he was here with her. All she could do was pray Tunri would keep him safe.

"Thank you, Rae," Ida said, squeezing her hand back. "I know you've only just met me, but I already consider you a part of our team and a good friend."

Rae grinned. "I'm just glad there were more of you that were not like Tristan." They both laughed. "Speaking of Tristan, what happened to him?" Rae added.

But before Ida could reply, a series of shrieking screams echoed from the purification pools.

Rae darted off before Ida could blink. Rising from the bench, Ida followed as quickly as she could. By the time she reached the purification pools, a crowd of guards and participants in the pageant had gathered around. Ida stood next to Rae, trying to figure out what happened.

"Rae!" Ben's frantic voice called through the crowd. The dark hair of the tall man wove in and out of people scattering this way and that.

"Ben!" Rae called, waving her hands in the air. In seconds, he found her and scooped her up in his arms.

Ida blushed, unsure whether she should leave them to their tender moment or not.

"Where were you?" he gasped, holding her close. "I heard what happened and was so afraid when I couldn't find you."

"I'm right here," Rae whispered in his ear, wrapping her arms around his neck.

Ida cleared her throat. "I'm sorry, One Shot. Rae came after me."

One Shot lifted his gaze. "I'm so glad you're okay, Ida. Raphael is not happy with you."

As if hearing his name mentioned, the blond guard barreled through the crowd. There was a fire in his usually cold stare.

"You are not meant to go wandering around the palace without me," Raphael scolded. "What if something happened to you? What would I tell Jacques?"

"What?" Rae and One Shot said simultaneously, still holding on to each other.

"I know, I'm sorry," Ida said, placing a hand on her forehead. "I was caught up in the moment." Ida then turned to Rae and One Shot. She knew she would have to tell them sometime who her guard was. It was a surprise to her at first too.

Raphael pulled the trio away from the growing crowd. "My brother was able to get word to me about your mission before you left Tenton. I haven't been home in years, but I would do anything for Jacques. And when I heard he was betrothed—" Raphael shook his head. "I realized I'd been away for far too long."

"Raphael explained all this to me when he was first assigned as my guard," Ida added.

"Well, that's good to know," Rae mumbled, still casting a suspicious gaze at Raphael. "I can see the family resemblance. Although Jacques—" She paused.

"Jacques is far kinder and more personable than I am," Raphael finished for her. "Yes, it has always been that way. I wish I didn't leave the weight of the family on his shoulders, but I had to get out from under my father's grip. So, when he commanded me to bring weapons to Kadesh's troops, I deserted the cause and have been here ever since."

"Are you able to reach Jacques?" One Shot asked, finally releasing Rae from his tight grip.

Raphael shrugged. "It depends on who's smuggling messages. Some people are loyal, some are not."

Ida sighed, knowing they needed to get word back to General Blake about Tristan's disappearance and that they had found Princess Haden, as well. Though they hadn't figured out why the princess was here alone.

As the group began to discuss some sort of message, their conversation was disrupted by Sayidi Tamor's declaration of sabotage of the purification pools.

Ida gasped at the sight of the three women, suddenly thankful she had run out of the pools. What if that had been her and Rae? Tunri had always protected her, even when she wasn't thinking about it. Ida then gasped again and turned to Rae.

"The princess," she whispered. "Where's Haden?" Haden stayed in the pools while Ida had fled. Ida would never forgive herself if something had happened to the princess.

Rae's brows shot to the top of her forehead before she whispered up to One Shot. The tall man scanned the crowd.

"I see her," he said, bringing Ida immense relief. "She's with Mal. She's okay."

"Thank goodness," Ida breathed, placing a hand over her frantic heart.

Once Sayidi Tamor ordered everyone back to their rooms for the time being, Ida and Rae hurried back with One Shot and Raphael not far behind. When they reached their room, Ida felt a gentle hand on her shoulder.

She spun around to face Raphael, his face downcast. "What's the matter?"

The serious man sighed. "I was never a good brother to Jacques, or our cousin, Charles. It wasn't that I didn't want to be. I just had to deflect Father's greed on me so it wouldn't poison them. I'm sorry for leaving them behind. And now that I've been away for so long, I don't think I can return."

Ida's heart softened at the words. Even though Raphael had a hard exterior, his heart still loved. She then realized how similar the stoic guard was to General Blake and that was probably why Jacques got along with the general so well.

"He has never once mentioned anger toward you to me," Ida replied with a smile. "And he still trusts you enough to tell you about me."

Raphael smirked. "True. I have other friends in the palace. I have started asking about anything suspicious. I will keep you and your friends updated if I find anything. I will also work on getting a message out to Jacques."

Ida smiled and bowed her head. "Thank you, Raphael."

As the two started toward Ida's room, Ida saw another figure waiting outside of the carved door.

"Why is she here?" Raphael asked, his suspicious gaze back in place.

Ida sucked in a breath at the sight of Sayida Erza. "Someone I knew when I was young," Ida explained. "I'd like to talk to her but not completely alone."

"Understood," he replied. "I'll stay right here."

Ida smiled again, enjoying seeing the same fierce loyalty in Raphael that she saw in Jacques. Hopefully the brothers would be reunited one day soon.

Raphael stood a few paces behind Ida as she gathered her courage and headed toward Sayida Erza.

The actions of others do not define you. Only you decide who you want to be, Ida encouraged herself. *Your past does not define you either, Ida,* she added for good measure.

"Ida," Erza breathed as Ida came closer. "I-I didn't expect to see you here."

Ida's mind soared back to the last time she had seen Josef's mother. It was just a few days before Tenton raided Renta and burned the capital city of Kadesh. It took Ida years to forget the screams and cries of the attack, but she would never forget how Erza looked at her like she was no greater than the dung on the side of the road.

Ida then remembered Erza probably thought she had either died in the attack or had been in Kadesh this whole time. But the woman before her had no idea that Ida had traveled all the way to Tenton, had a new family, and was now betrothed to one of the wealthiest men in Tenton. As much as Ida desired to prove her self-worth with these facts, she knew, deep down, they didn't matter to her. She would've loved Jacques even if he wasn't rich. In fact, she had fallen for Jacques before she knew he was the heir to Delequa Iron. Ida also realized, to keep up her façade and stay undercover, Erza could *not* know that she now resided in Tenton.

"Here I am," Ida said quietly.

"I thought—" Erza started then paused. The woman Ida once saw as so mighty and powerful looked almost ashamed.

Because of me? Ida couldn't believe that Sayida Erza would be ashamed about anything. Especially not Ida.

Erza took a breath then squared her shoulders, the gold beads in her braided hair glistening in the afternoon sun. "After the raid in Renta, we came back to the orphanage, Jarrick, Josef, and I. We found it destroyed. We thought you had been killed."

It may have been the midday light, but Ida could've sworn tears gathered in Erza's eyes.

"Josef was devastated. He never forgave me for taking him away from you and now—" Erza broke off again, and this time she really did burst into tears.

All the anger Ida held for the woman before her vanished in an instant. In a few steps, Ida was at Erza's side, patting her back softly.

"I heard about what happened to Josef a few years ago," Ida said softly. "I'm so sorry."

Erza sobbed into her hands, and Ida was astounded that even the proudest people could be reduced to puddles. Not that Ida ever wished harm upon Erza, but her words stung Ida more than the woman would ever know.

"I know and I am so sorry for how I treated you that day," Erza confessed, carefully wiping her eyes to not smudge the kohl lining them. "You were only a child. How awful of me to have been so cruel when you had no one to care for you. You didn't make those choices. This terrible life did."

Ida nodded, agreeing with Erza. She did have some terrible cards dealt to her, but Tunri had transformed every negative thing in her life to a positive one. And Ida was so grateful. "While that is true," Ida said, "I have learned to trust that Tunri will help me, even when things get difficult."

Erza lifted her eyes, her attempts to dry her tears proven futile as the kohl lining her eyes now dripped down her cheeks. "Tunri has been well to you, yes?"

Ida nodded, thinking of her family, friends, and soon to be husband. With a smile she said, "Yes, yes He has."

Erza wiped away the black tears haphazardly, her face stern. "Then I must know why you are here."

All of Ida's happy thoughts fled. "I'm here for *Sundarata Taashama*, like every other woman."

Erza shook her head fiercely then peered over her shoulder. Raphael was still standing guard a few feet away but other than that, they were alone. Erza turned her back to him, her voice low. "Heed my warning, Ida, there are strange things happening in the palace. The king has not been himself for quite some time. After I disposed of General Sage, Jarrick and I returned here to live a quiet life. But there have been odd edicts being passed."

Ida tried to keep up. "You did *what* to General Sage?" She vaguely remembered the name being mentioned when Devora and Nadia had gone to the battle of Edo. "What edicts? What's happening here?"

Fear swirled in Ida's mind, twisting every thought into a horrible one. Did the edict have to do with Devora? What about Kanna Blake, Matthias' and Tristan's mother?

Erza shushed her. "I cannot say more. But be wary of your meeting with the prince. The monarchy is searching for someone powerful. Anyone who gets in the way of their search will be killed."

Ida gasped. That was the second time in only a few hours that the lives of the pageant contestants had been threatened.

"Be safe, Ida. I don't know who they want but don't trust anyone in this palace." Erza reached out and hugged Ida close, catching Ida completely off guard, before she hurried off.

As she watched Erza rush by Raphael and round the corner, Ida wondered who the monarchy was looking for and why she had a suspicion that it was Devora.

Chapter Thirteen

Haden, Radaa Kingdom, Kadesh

Haden kept biting her nails as she and Mal stood outside of the throne room a few days later, waiting for her interrogation by the crown prince of Kadesh. Apparently, there were so many interrogations to be made, the crown prince could only handle a certain number a day. And while Rae and Ida had passed their interrogations, Haden had been beyond stressed about hers. Thankfully, she hadn't found feathers in her bed last night. Was she finally far enough from Mother to break her curse?

"You're going to have nubs left if you keep that up," Mal chuckled.

Haden immediately lowered her hands, knowing that it was a habit Mother hated. "I can't help it. What's happening in there?" She rose to her tiptoes, trying to see over the heads of the other women and their guards. Some women had come out pleased and others looked as white as ghosts. Was the prince that awful?

Haden absentmindedly brought her fingers back to her mouth then thought better and fiddled with the fringes on her cerulean scarf. Although the circumstances for meeting the crown prince were less than ideal, she was hoping she could share what she knew about Mother's plans. She had tucked the second scroll she had stolen inside of the tunic beneath her dress. It was the only proof she had to show she wasn't lying and that she wasn't a spy for Tenton. Even though her confession would completely blow her cover, Haden knew that if what Miguel had said was true and Mother had killed Father, the queen of Tenton would strike Kadesh soon.

When she was a child, Father always tried to divert Mother's attention from Haden when Mother decided to go on one of her tirades about her not learning fast enough. Haden knew the king wasn't her real father, yet she was still thankful that he had protected her in those moments. She couldn't help but feel sadness that he would no longer be around if Haden returned home. But Haden had realized from a young age that there was space for only one person on the throne and it was Queen Leza.

Haden shook her memories of the queen and king from her mind and focused back on her interrogation with the crown prince. Would she be able to ask the prince if she could meet with Miguel? It would make life a lot easier to speak with her uncle freely instead of sneaking around. Although Haden had made it to Kadesh undetected, that didn't mean her luck would last forever. And frankly, she was tired of lying and hiding.

Haden glanced over at Mal, still wondering where he had been the morning of the crime in the purification pools. Her mind had drifted over the idea that he was the culprit, but she couldn't believe it. Mal had looked frightened when he couldn't find her in the crowd. If he wanted her dead, would he have been so relieved to have found her unharmed?

Haden soon became too lost in her thoughts that she chomped down on her pointer finger not realizing she had begun chewing her nails again. "Ow!"

"Told you." Mal smirked before he took her finger and examined it. "Are you okay?"

Butterflies took flight in Haden's stomach at his touch. Mal was awfully forward for a guard. The guards in Maldove Palace would never hold her hand without her permission. Or wrap their arm around her like Mal had after the accident at the pools. Haden's cheeks flushed with the memory of it. But even if the guards at Maldove Palace had her permission to hold her hand or escort her somewhere, none of them wanted to.

"Guards need to know their place," Mother always said. *"Which is far beneath royalty."*

Yet, as much as Haden tried, she could not be cruel to the guards at Maldove Palace, and she certainly couldn't be cruel to Mal.

Without thinking, Haden blurted, "Mal, do you know the prince?"

Mal's fingers stilled, warm atop hers. "Of course. I'm a guard in the palace."

Haden blushed at the obvious answer. "Yes, I mean, have you ever talked to him?"

Releasing her hand, he replied, "A few times. He's not a man of many words." Mal motioned to her hand. "Looks like you'll keep all ten fingers."

Haden laughed quickly then continued, "If you had, let's say, incriminating evidence against someone, would the prince be the person to tell?"

The laughter left Mal's eyes, his grin shifting into a hard line. "Haden, what are you talking about? Do you know who poisoned the water?"

Haden shook her head, realizing her mistake. "No, nothing like that. I was just wondering if the crown prince was a trustworthy person."

Mal studied her. "From what I know he's made his mistakes, but he desires what's best for his kingdom."

Haden averted her gaze from Mal's perceptive eyes as the next woman exited the throne room bawling her eyes out. "And what of the king?" Haden asked. "Why is he not doing the interrogations instead of the prince?"

Mal sighed and turned his gaze forward once more. "I don't know the details, but the king hasn't been himself for quite some time."

Haden started to ask another question when the line moved forward. She had been so focused on asking questions and wondering about the prince and king, she hadn't realized it was time for her interrogation.

Haden's knees shook as she peered up at Sayidi Tamor. Though she had just seen the man, she had already forgotten how frightening he looked. His tall stature and thick muscles demanded respect, along with his penetrating gaze that seemed to bore into Haden's soul.

"You will only speak to the crown prince when you are spoken to," Sayidi Tamor commanded, his dark eyes glaring daggers into Haden. "Ask no questions, only give answers. Understood?"

Haden swallowed her fear and nodded, too frightened to answer the intimidating man as she wrung the ends of her scarf between her hands.

At least Mal will be with me, she thought, and her fear fled for a moment.

But as she strode forward and Mal tried to follow, Sayidi Tamor held out his arm, blocking Mal.

"Only the contestants are allowed to enter. Guards must wait outside."

Haden's face blanched and when she peered over her shoulder, Mal's face was almost the same shade of white. Thankfully, he regained composure quicker than her.

Mal flashed a winning smile at the stoic man. "What is this rule, Sayidi Tamor? I thought we were supposed to accompany our participants everywhere they went."

Though Mal certainly could convince Haden, or any other female for that matter, with that smile, Sayidi Tamor was unmoved. "Only the contestant," he repeated, a threat lacing his words.

Mal stood a little taller. "What if something happens to my contestant in there?"

Haden's steps faltered. *Why is Mal trying to defy Sayidi Tamor? The man looks like he could eat Mal for breakfast.* Chills ran down Haden's back as she witnessed the terrifying glare Sayidi Tamor gave Mal. When Sayidi Tamor raised his arm, Haden winced, believing he would smack Mal in the face. But when he only moved Mal to the side, she was both relieved and confused. Mother had struck guards and servants for far less than what Mal had done. Maybe the rules regarding servants and guards were different in Kadesh.

"The king's guards are in the throne room. Should anything be a threat to the prince or the contestant, they will handle it. Move along, Mal. This is your final warning."

Mal glanced over at Haden with a look that she couldn't decipher before he walked away. Sayidi Tamor then turned to Haden, and she almost yelped in fright.

"Remember the rules. Enter now."

Haden rushed forward, almost slamming into the bright red doors before the guards on either side opened them. Thankfully, she didn't make a fool out of herself and entered the throne room as calmly as she could.

Haden strode forward while trying to memorize every detail of the colorful space. While Mother had made the throne room in Maldove Palace drip with luxurious gilded items, this throne room was far simpler. Exquisite tapestries, woven with fine colored threads, hung on either wall, each depicting stories of the kings' past. Square-shaped holes were carved into the ceiling, allowing just the right amount of natural light to illuminate the room. Under Haden's feet laid an azure rug, with specks of gold and orange woven in. It wasn't as plush and thick as the ones back home, but the designs on it were immaculate. Haden pulled her eyes away from the designs. Before her sat two golden thrones, one occupied by the crown prince, the other bare.

Where is the king? Haden wondered before her eyes focused on the prince.

With long, thin legs, the Prince of Kadesh sat straight on the golden throne, as if a pole had been injected into his spine. Billowing, colorful robes surrounded his frame, covering every inch of his body, save for his brown boots. But what kept Haden staring was the bright-blue mask hiding the prince's face. It was plain in design except for a few white dots lining the outer edge. Yet it still performed its duty, for she could see neither his eyes nor mouth, or any facial features for that matter.

Was the crown prince in some kind of accident that harmed his face? Why else would he cover it?

It struck Haden as odd to hide one's face, especially when hers had been shared publicly since she was a child. Royalty was meant to be seen, or so she had been taught. So why did the prince hide? The mask intrigued Haden more than expected.

"Are you a participant in the pageant for the crown prince's hand?" a voice from the far-left corner of the room asked.

When Haden turned, a skinny, squat man appeared at the prince's left side. There was something about the man's beady eyes and large nose that made her uneasy. "Uh," Haden started then stopped.

Sayidi Tamor told her only to speak when the prince spoke to her. But the prince didn't speak to her, that other man did. Why weren't the rules clearer?

The man released an annoyed sigh. "My name is Sayidi Brocaw. I speak on behalf of the prince. He does not wish his voice to be heard or known by any potential criminals."

"Oh, that's wise," Haden commented before she could stop herself. Slamming her lips shut, she curtsied. "Apologies, sir."

"Yes, yes." Sayidi Brocaw waved away her manners like they were an annoying fly. "Answer the question."

Haden had to remember the question before she answered, "Yes, I am a participant in the pageant."

"Were you in the purification pools yesterday for your first treatment?"

Haden nodded, resisting the urge to bite her fingernails again.

"Did you see any suspicious activity happening in or near the purification pools?"

Haden thought back to the reaction Ida had to Sayida Erza. It certainly was odd, but Haden couldn't believe Ida was the one who poisoned the pool, could she? She had been so kind. Now Rae on the other hand didn't seem to like Haden as much. But Haden remembered Rae being ready to change and step into the pool that had been poisoned. If Rae had poisoned the pool, surely, she wouldn't walk into it freely, right? Yet, Haden had also fled the pools to see Miguel, so she could easily be a suspect if that fact was known.

Haden realized it had been too long since she responded. Sayidi Brocaw and the masked prince stared at her, waiting. Though she couldn't see the prince's face, Sayidi Brocaw's features were lined with suspicion.

"I did not see any suspicious activity in or near the purification pools," Haden confessed almost too mechanically, her Kadeshian good enough to not raise suspicion.

She would have to be careful and make sure she didn't accidentally slip up and expose Miguel visiting the palace uninvited. She still needed to meet with him to find out more about what was happening in Tenton.

"Hmm," Sayidi Brocaw replied before he reached behind his back and pulled out a scroll. He handed the scroll off to a servant who took four steps and handed it to Haden.

Haden wanted to giggle at the ridiculousness of the action, but again, she sealed her lips shut. If she were guessing correctly, she was failing her interrogation.

"Before my next question, I want you to read the law written on the page."

"Um, okay," she muttered, her fingers shaking as she unrolled the scroll.

Why did she have to read anything? Would her inability to read well have her hanging on the gallows?

Once the scroll was open, Haden focused on the Kadeshian script. Even though she had spent her childhood learning the differences between Kadeshian and Tentonian, the symbols still twisted around each other when she tried to read them.

"Well?" Sayidi Brocaw pressured.

Haden glanced up to see the crown prince had leaned slightly forward in his chair, making her more nervous.

Clearing her throat, Haden stared down at the symbols again, praying they would stay put so she could figure out what they said.

"In...the case of...t-treason," she began, sweat dripping down her temples.

"Can you not read, girl?" Sayidi Brocaw demanded. "Or is it that you can't read Kadeshian and are really a Tenton spy sent to kill the prince?" He motioned the guards lining the room forward.

"What? No!" she exclaimed quickly, her eyes darting around. "I can read," Haden added quietly. "I just need more time than others."

Sayidi Brocaw narrowed his gaze. He was about to say more when the prince held up his hand. The guards immediately stopped in their place, and Haden breathed a sigh of relief. She wasn't sure why the prince was being gracious, but she was thankful for it.

The prince then leaned over and spoke in Sayidi Brocaw's ear.

"Are you sure, sire?"

The prince nodded.

"Very well." Sayidi Brocaw motioned to a guard on Haden's right.

For a moment, Haden thought the guard was coming for her and would take her straight to the gallows to be hung. But when the guard turned around and left the throne room, Haden was even more confused.

"The prince has a final question for you," Sayidi Brocaw said, bringing Haden's attention back to him. Although Haden was thankful not to be killed, Sayidi Brocaw did not look pleased that she was still standing there.

"Bring him in," Sayidi Brocaw called.

Furrowing her brow, Haden turned to the right. Forgetting she was meant to put up a façade, she gasped aloud. Standing next to the guard, was none other than Miguel.

Chapter Fourteen

Matthias, Maldove Palace, Tenton

Matthias loved wearing black, but this was not the occasion he wanted to wear it for. He smoothed out the dark tunic, remembering the last time he wore it at the masquerade ball with Devora. He had replayed the memory in his mind every night. It was the only way he could find some sleep among his nightmares.

After he had been told Devora went willingly with General Beta, Matthias had no idea what to think. Could the woman he loved have turned on him? Did she not feel for him the same way he felt for her? But then why would she risk her life to come to the palace, to warn him of the queen's treachery, if she didn't love him as well?

Matthias shook his head. He had been asking these same questions repeatedly and until he found Devora, they wouldn't be answered.

Unfortunately, he was no closer to finding Devora and his mother today than he was weeks ago. And with no word from the groups in Totem and Kadesh, Matthias was starting to lose hope. He even prayed he'd hear something from the Sandje twins or Jacques, but there was nothing but silence on all fronts. Silence that suffocated and choked him like the chain around his neck. Because he was confined to only the Fortress and the palace, Matthias was restless. He needed to get out, run, do something without the queen's gaze on him, but he couldn't. Just like the last few years of his life, he had to wait and plan for the appropriate time and then strike.

A knock sounded at Matthias' door, pulling him from his woes. He sighed, praying it wasn't the queen. After their last meeting he couldn't bear hearing any more depressing news from her wicked mouth. The thought that she held the two women he loved in the palm of her hand was enough to make him do anything she said. And that's exactly what she wanted. However, if he could avoid her at all costs, he would.

"Enter," he said, bracing himself for another mental attack.

Who entered wasn't the queen, but Jacques. Matthias breathed an audible sigh of relief. It felt like it had been years since he'd seen his friend.

"Jacques, what are you doing here?"

Jacques quirked a brow. "I'm paying my condolences to the slain king and princess, of course."

Matthias rolled his eyes, knowing very well that Jacques knew of the king's demise before the queen's lies. "How were you able to get to my rooms?"

Ever since Matthias' backtalk to the queen and the announcement of the king's and princess' funerals, Queen Leza had tightened his leash even further. Though he was allowed to travel to the Fortress, the queen knew his every step, where he went and who he talked to. It was maddening. So, Jacques—his closest friend, ally and confidant—being allowed to see him was surprising.

"I've been telling you since day one, sir, if you smile at people every once in a while, they will be a lot more pleasant to you." Jacques smirked and Matthias couldn't help but grin. "As the heir to Delequa Iron I have more sway than I anticipated."

"Still the heir?"

Jacques averted his gaze. "I was, until this morning. Father passed in the early hours."

Matthias placed a hand on his friend's shoulders. "My sympathies, Jacques. Losing a loved one cannot be easy."

Jacques nodded. "Fortunately for my sake, my father and I never had a close relationship. While I'm sad we could not render it, I am ready to fix the damage he'd done with his part in the war."

Matthias never wished harm upon Duke Delequa, but when he discovered Jacques was the heir, he knew his friend would be able to turn the tide of the war with Kadesh once and for all. However, only one person could get in Jacques' way.

"Does the queen know?" Matthias asked in a low voice.

Jacques shook his head. "I swore the doctor and nurse to secrecy. There are many things I can do to help, but I would prefer if the monarchy stayed out of it."

"Good man," Matthias replied as he turned back to the mirror.

Though he was in mourning clothes, he did not mourn the king, and something told him that Princess Haden was still out there. He only hoped that when the princess returned, she would help stop her tyrannical mother from ruining Tenton.

"Matthias," Jacques said, interrupting his thoughts. "Though father is gone, that is not the reason I'm here."

Matthias spun, his Thoughts whirling as a tiny seed of hope sprouted in his heart. "Did you hear from them? Have they found Devora and my mother?"

Matthias' hope wavered as his friend took in a deep breath and handed him a scroll. By the look on Jacques' face, it wasn't good news. Every possible horrific scenario flooded through Matthias' head. Had his mother and Devora been tortured? Killed? Did General Beta, the Kadeshian general who had taken Devora, desire a ransom? Matthias would pay anything to get the women he loved back.

But as Matthias unrolled the scroll, he no longer felt fear, but disappointment.

"So, Tristan turned out to be a scoundrel after all."

He kept his face a mask of calm, but his soul was overwhelmed with defeat. He had prayed Tristan had changed his ways, that his little brother had finally moved on from his tainted past. But based on what the scroll explained, Matthias was the fool for believing that someone like Tristan could change.

"At least he got them into Kadesh." Jacques shrugged, disappointment plain on his face. "My contact said Ida and the others aren't sure where he went after they were taken to the palace."

"Once a traitor, always a traitor," Matthias muttered under his breath as he tried to decipher the slanted handwriting on the scroll. Jacques had been stingy with the details regarding his contact in Kadesh, which made Matthias all the more curious.

Before Matthias could study the manuscript further, Jacques swiped it out of his hands.

"Still don't trust me with who your contact is?" Matthias smirked.

Jacques rolled up the scroll. "It's for your safety as well as Ida's and the others'. I can't let anything happen to you all because of my carelessness."

Matthias grew somber. "I understand, truly."

"There is one more thing," Jacques confessed.

Matthias sighed. "There always is."

Jacques scanned the room, as if someone were hiding behind the curtains. Leaning toward Matthias, he whispered, "Princess Haden is in Kadesh, and she is very much alive."

***

After Jacques departed, Matthias hurried down the steps of Maldove Palace, taking two at a time. Though he kept an appearance of indifference, hope soared in his chest. Princess Haden was alive and that meant there was still a living monarch to usurp the queen.

Unfortunately, Matthias didn't know much about the princess besides the short conversation they had when he returned her to the palace after the battle of Edo. She seemed distant and caged. Not unlike himself at times. There were so many times he almost deserted the military and hid, especially after he had fallen for Devora. Yet with his mother's life on the line, Matthias had to follow through. And the king and queen knew that.

But Matthias still remembered what the princess said to him in the carriage on their return journey after the Battle of Edo: *"You can't lie to someone who's been cursed by the same witch."*

He had racked his brain on how the princess would know it was the queen who had cursed him unless she'd been cursed herself. But why would the queen curse her own daughter?

Matthias shook his head. There were still so many lies in the queen's web that he had yet to untangle.

Too soon he stood before the two tall doors leading to the highest balcony of the palace. Matthias had assumed the queen would have a small funeral, only inviting each region's dignitaries. However, Queen Leza desired a large, grandiose affair to honor her husband's and daughter's deaths. But after she had made sure none of the attendees of the masquerade knew or even remembered the king, Matthias was curious as to why the queen was putting forth so much effort to make sure her late husband was honored.

Straightening his spine, Matthias slowly stepped through the doors to the balcony where Queen Leza stood. Thankfully, her back was to him, but he despised being in the presence of the woman all the same. She wore a dress so black it camouflaged her waist-length black hair. Since the king's death—or murder, as Matthias assumed—he had yet to see the queen in mourning attire. But today it seemed she decided to pull out everything she needed to convince the public she was grieving. As Matthias drew closer, he noted the queen had also decided to wear a black lace veil beneath her imperial opal crown.

"You're late," Queen Leza snipped as Matthias approached.

He ceased his steps, giving himself a wide berth. "Apologies, my queen" was all he responded. He didn't want to put any ideas in the queen's head by telling her Jacques had visited.

"Care to share the details of your meeting with the heir of Delequa Iron?"

Ice froze Matthias' spine. So, she did know. But she still called Jacques the heir, so the queen was not privy to the information that Duke Delequa had passed. And Matthias would do everything in his power to leave it that way.

"He only wished to give his condolences on your tragic losses, my queen."

The queen turned her veiled head to Matthias. While Matthias thought Queen Leza was unnerving before, the dark, bride-like veil made him severely more uneasy.

"You're a good liar, General, that's why I like you."

Matthias wasn't sure what to say in response, so he kept quiet. The statement about Jacques hadn't been the complete truth, but it wasn't a complete lie. Yet, as he had learned many times before, sometimes the best response was no response at all.

Thankfully, Queen Leza had other things on her mind. Turning back around, she stepped forward on the balcony.

Matthias had a quick vision of seizing the queen and throwing her over the railing. Could all his problems be solved so simply? It was certainly tempting, and Matthias felt himself allured by the evil idea. But something tugged at his conscience, whatever amount of conscience he had left. Or was it his soul that persuaded him to clasp his hands behind his back and let the queen wave to her subjects below?

Matthias averted his gaze from the queen, trying to banish his thoughts of attempted murder. What was the state of his soul? Devora had seen it before, back in the Fortress. Was it shattered like it felt? Was there any goodness left within it? The only goodness left, he thought was with Devora. And she, too, had been taken from him.

As the trumpets sounded and the subjects below quieted, Matthias tuned out the herald announcing the deaths of the king and princess. It was all a lie anyway. The queen had killed her husband—not the Kadeshians—and Princess Haden wasn't dead. Matthias wondered what she was doing in Kadesh, but hopefully more answers would be provided through Jacques' contact.

As the herald spouted more lies, Matthias resisted the urge to roll his eyes. It seemed that his entire life consisted of lies. When would he find truth?

As the ceremony honoring the late king and princess continued, Matthias let his mind wander. What was truth anyway? Was it words written on a page, claiming to be fact? Or stories that, because they had been passed down by so many generations, were deemed credible?

Matthias withheld a frustrated grunt. After all his years of scouring books to learn about Tenton and the various places his mother could possibly be hidden, he never once found any scholar or author who had written one ounce of truth that stirred his soul.

But there was one route of thinking he had never taken. Despite his mother's devotion and trust in Tunri, Matthias had never sought further information about the God. Should he have cried out to Tunri when his mother was taken? Probably. Why didn't he?

Matthias' attention was diverted from his thoughts and back on the queen as she began a tearful recollection of the memories she shared with her husband and daughter. This time Matthias did roll his eyes. Thankfully, the queen couldn't see his face or read his mind. If she could, he would've been killed long ago.

But, despite all the dangerous missions he had been on, Matthias was still alive. Often he wished—hoped—he would be slain on one of the king's murderous missions and be free of the leash that controlled his life. But, for some reason, he was still here. Why did he still draw breath if he was meant to only be a slave?

You are not finished.

Matthias jerked at the voice speaking. The guard to his left gave him a strange look, to which Matthias responded with a cold stare, causing the guard to face forward once more.

Who had spoken to him? Devora had visions from Tun-ri, but did He audibly speak to her? Matthias remembered Rae recounting how she'd heard voices when she was put in front of the statue of Pahga. So, was the voice who spoke to Matthias the light or dark? He couldn't dwell on his self-reflection any longer, for the crowd below the balcony was beginning to rile.

"We will not tolerate our enemies for stealing our leader and our future away from us," Queen Leza roared, her small fist pounding on the column railing lining the balcony platform.

The crowd cheered in unison, almost as in a daze. Matthias held his breath, unease crawling up his spine. This is exactly how the people acted at the masquerade ball.

"This war will end now!" the queen continued. "We will no longer wait for Kadesh to come to us, but we will bring the battle to them!"

The crowd roared in response and the blood drained from Matthias' face. What was she doing?

"All who wish to conquer Kadesh and claim its land as our own, now is your chance!" The queen removed her crown from her head before ripping off the black veil. Replacing her crown, she unsheathed a sword that had been strapped to her belt and thrust it into the air. "It's time to defeat our enemy once and for all!"

As if taken over by an unnatural force, the crowd erupted into chaos. Matthias rushed past the queen to peer over the edge.

The men and women below were in a rage. Fights and brawls broke out every few feet. It was madness.

Matthias spun to the queen. "What did you do to them?"

Though he wasn't a Seer, Matthias sensed the dark aura building around the queen as her dark eyes turned on him. Since the beginning, he had never felt warmth from the queen. But the essence seeping from her now was something entirely different. And it was dark.

Queen Leza sheathed her sword, ignoring Matthias' question as she strode past him. "Rally your knights, General. We leave for Kadesh at dawn." She snapped her fingers and the chain around Matthias' neck tightened, leaving him no choice but to obey.

Chapter Fifteen

Haden, Radaa Kingdom, Kadesh

"Do you or do you not know this man?" Sayidi Brocaw practically yelled in Haden's face when she didn't respond immediately at the sight of Miguel.

Haden's thoughts were like a flock of wild chickens in a frenzy. *Should I tell the truth that Miguel is my uncle? Or lie and say I have no idea who he is? Would it matter either way?*

Haden wasn't sure why Sayidi Brocaw disliked her so, but he seemed ready to send her to the gallows as soon as possible. She didn't want to die yet. She *couldn't* die yet. She had spent so much effort to get here to stop Mother. But she wouldn't lie. Even though she scarcely knew Miguel, she knew he had good in his heart and Haden wouldn't allow anything to happen to him.

Straightening her shoulders, Haden replied, "Yes, I know him. He's my uncle."

Miguel's face softened at the statement.

And what happened next surprised Haden the most. Sayidi Brocaw smiled. Not an evil, conniving smile, which Haden expected. But a genuine, pleased smile.

"This man has caught the perpetrator who poisoned the purification pools. He said one of his family members was a contestant in the pageant, so that was why he was near the palace. Normally, uninvited visitors are sent away, but because of your uncle's presence near the gates, he caught the criminal who attempted to sabotage the contest."

Sayidi Brocaw beamed. "The prince wished to honor not only Sayidi Miguel, but his family, as well." The man bowed. "The crown prince of Kadesh would like to invite both you and your uncle to dine with him tonight."

Haden stared, shocked. This was not where she thought this conversation was going to end but she was so glad she wasn't heading to the gallows. "Um, okay," Haden replied, her gaze darted to Miguel who gave her a firm nod. She then curtsied and amended, "We are deeply honored and accept the crown prince's invitation."

Sayidi Brocaw clapped twice, and two guards appeared. Relief swarmed Haden's heart as she saw one of them was Mal. He gave her his winning grin and a quick wink. Her pulse thumped in her veins, and she returned his smile.

It's just because you were already nervous, she tried to convince herself.

"Please take this young woman and her uncle to our finest rooms and have them prepared for tonight's feast," Sayidi Brocaw instructed the two guards who immediately bowed in obedience.

Haden frowned at the statement. Prepared? What did that mean?

But she couldn't give it a second thought before Mal was by her side, his arm extended for her to take. His presence comforted her in ways she couldn't understand, but she was glad he was by her side all the same.

The second guard approached Miguel, and within moments her uncle had the guard chuckling at something as they exited the throne room.

As Mal led Haden out the large doors, she had the feeling she was being watched. Subtly, she glanced over her shoulder to find the masked prince's gaze still on her. Lifting his hand, he gave her a wave. Though Haden couldn't see his face, she blushed and turned away.

Did the prince find something attractive about her? She didn't look like the other women in Kadesh, but maybe that was okay. Haden caught herself smiling at the thought that the prince may like her. But what about these strange feelings she had for Mal? Could anything become of it? Though she wasn't the king's and queen's real daughter, they legally adopted, her so wasn't she technically still the princess of Tenton? Could she marry a guard?

Haden pursed her lips. Mother would never allow her to be married to a guard, especially not a Kadeshian one. But Mother also wasn't here and if Haden played her cards right with the prince, hopefully, Mother would be taken care of for good.

"Well, I'm certainly glad I'm not escorting you to the gallows," Mal said, pulling Haden out of her jumble of questions.

She laughed nervously. "I'm thankful, as well. Tunri has been good to me."

"It seems He has his hand on you, yes?" Mal replied.

Haden wasn't sure how to respond. After reading the scroll she stole from Mother, she assumed all of Kadesh worshiped the Goddess Pahga. But this was the first time Mal had brought up his belief in a different God.

"Yes," Haden finally replied, not sure how to ask what Mal's faith was.

"You know what I just realized," Mal continued, changing the topic of conversation. "I still owe you a cup of my famous *sheta.* How about we swing by the kitchen on the way to your new room and we can celebrate you not going to the gallows?"

Haden couldn't help but laugh and she nodded. It wasn't until they were almost at the kitchens that Haden realized Mal said she would be going to a new room. Haden was curious to see what this new room looked like, but her heart fell at the thought of leaving Ida and Rae. They hadn't known each other long, but she enjoyed their company.

Once they entered the kitchen, Mal led her to a stool before he grabbed several bottles from a shelf, including the green bottle he had gotten the first day they met. Had it only been almost a week since then? It certainly felt like it had been weeks or months since she met Mal. But then she realized she really didn't know a lot about him.

"So," she started, tucking a piece of her not-as-black hair behind her ear. "Where are you from, Mal?"

Mal smirked at her as he started pouring liquid from the first bottle into a clay pot. "Is it time for my interrogation now?"

Haden focused on her chewed nails with a smile. "No, just curious about the man who is meant to follow me everywhere."

Mal laughed outright. "I am from here, Renta. I've lived here my whole life."

Haden watched as Mal placed the pot on top of the clay wood-fire stove. He stirred it before mashing up some brown spices in his palm and sprinkling them in. The warm aroma wrapped around Haden and soon her mouth was watering.

"Have you traveled anywhere else in Kadesh?"

Mal lifted his shoulder as he stirred. "Here and there. But when I got old enough to work, I didn't have time to travel."

Haden nodded, remembering how her only time to visit the other regions in Tenton was when Mother wanted to remind its citizens that the king and queen still ruled over them.

"All right, enough about me, what about you?"

Haden's spine went rigid. "What?"

Mal's back was turned to her as he continued stirring. He flicked the spoon to the side. "Don't I get to know more about the lovely young woman I have to follow everywhere?"

Haden found herself embarrassed by and enjoying Mal's forward comment at the same time. Though she wished to continue their banter, she would have to be careful with her answers.

"What do you want to know?"

Mal grabbed a towel and wrapped it around the clay pot before picking it up and setting it on the table in front of Haden. The sweet spices were still rotating in a mesmerizing fury.

"Let me think," he said, placing a pair of beautiful porcelain cups decorated with intricate azure and orange designs in front of Haden and himself. With a ladle, he poured the liquid into each cup until it reached the brim.

"Thank you," Haden said, already wrapping her hands around the beautiful cup. "The cup is lovely too."

Mal pulled up a stool opposite her. He lifted his glass. "Only the best for the future princess of Kadesh."

Haden's eyes went wide as she looked up at him. "What do you mean?"

Mal took a swig from his cup, not glancing her way. "The crown prince. I heard he's invited you and your uncle to dinner tonight. That's a good sign that he'll choose you to be his bride." Mal took another swig of his *sheta* and mumbled, "Congratulations."

Haden frowned. "A dinner invitation and a marriage proposal are not the same thing." Yet Mal's comment sparked a new fear in her heart all the same. *Was* the dinner invitation a marriage proposal? It was a surefire way to speak with the prince about Mother's plans, but marriage already?

Haden picked up her cup like Mal and took a long gulp.

"I have my question," Mal announced, finally meeting Haden's gaze.

Haden slowly met his eyes, surprised at the sadness and slight anger lurking behind them. "Go ahead," she whispered.

"The day I met you, you wanted to buy hair dye. My only assumption is that you wished to hide who you really were."

Haden swallowed the fear building inside of her. Her heart felt like it would burst out of her chest. Had Mal figured her out? Was he going to report her to the crown prince before dinner and actually have her escorted to the gallows?

Haden didn't respond as Mal's keen caramel eyes studied her face.

"My question is: who are you hiding from and why?"

"I—" Haden started before the door to the kitchen swung open, smacking the wall. Haden yelped in surprise, spilling the *sheta* all over the table.

"I'm so sorry," she muttered, grabbing a towel to clean up the mess. But was she apologizing for the mess or her cowardice to hide the truth?

"Mal, what are you doing in here?" Sayidi Tamor's deep voice questioned.

Haden glanced up to see the large man and Mal glaring at one another. Though she didn't know the rules for guards in Kadesh, she didn't want Mal to get in trouble.

"It's my fault, Sayidi Tamor." Haden resisted the urge to crawl into a hole when the large man focused his penetrating gaze on her.

You can do this, Haden encouraged herself.

"Mal was escorting me back to my rooms when I requested a cup of *sheta.* I remembered he had served it when I first came to the palace and begged him to make me some."

Mal's stern face softened into one of surprise then adoration.

Sayidi Tamor, on the other hand, quirked a brow before heading over to the clay pot on the table. "Is that so?" He held up the pot and sniffed. "Hmm."

Haden wrung her hands in front of her, anticipation slurking up her spine.

"Stopping for a cup of *sheta* is fine," Sayidi Tamor said then turned to Mal. "But you are to report where you are going first. Haden is supposed to be with the ladies' maids for tonight's dinner."

"My apologies," Haden said with a curtsy.

"I will escort her there right away," Mal mumbled, standing from his stool.

Sayidi Tamor shot daggers at Mal's head before he turned to Haden. "If you ever desire a *real* cup of *sheta*, let me know." He gave Haden a smirk which caused her to snort and laugh before she covered her mouth and followed Mal out of the kitchen.

Chapter Sixteen

Haden, Radaa Kingdom, Kadesh

Silence felt like a noose around Haden's neck as she and Mal exited the palace kitchen. Though she tried to not chew on her nails, her nerves won the battle, and she spent the next few hallways wrapping the fringes of her scarf around her fingertips.

Finally, Mal sighed. "You don't need to be nervous around me. That wasn't the intent of my question."

Haden glanced over at him as he kept his gaze forward, his brow stern.

"I only asked for fear you were in some kind of trouble." He slowed his pace and turned to her, sincerity in his features. "I wondered if you needed any assistance and if I could provide it."

Haden's heart melted at the sentiment, not understanding how this man came to adore her so quickly.

Taking a breath, Haden took a leap of faith and replied, "I am in trouble..." she paused, taking a breath, "but only the prince can help me."

Mal's features, which were always so open and friendly, closed. "I see." He started marching forward and Haden hurried to catch up with him.

"Wait, Mal. It's not what you think."

"Of course it's not. Why would you wish to be with a palace guard when the crown prince of Kadesh has invited you to dinner? He can give you an entire kingdom and I can't." Mal's voice wavered at the end, and Haden's heart almost shattered.

"Mal, I have enjoyed every moment we've spent together, even though there hasn't been many," Haden started, trying to control the words coming out of her mouth, but they kept coming. "And I don't want to be a princess! Why would I want to be caged to a position where everyone tells me what to do and what to wear and where to go?"

Mal eyed her with suspicion, and Haden buttoned her lips. She waited a moment before she continued, "There is something gravely important I must speak with the prince about. The only way I could think to get close to him was this pageant. I am not interested in the throne or being a princess, I promise."

And that was the truth. Haden didn't want to be a princess. She didn't wish to rule over Tenton *or* Kadesh. She just desired to be free of Mother. And the only way to be free of Mother was to get rid of her.

Mal searched her face, no doubt searching for the honesty in her words. Haden watched him, waiting for him to complete his verdict. Finally, he reached out and held her hands.

"I apologize for my words. They were unjust. It was unfair of me to make you share something so personal. As you said, we have not known each other long and don't know much about one another. However, I would like to amend that." He grinned and brought her hand to his mouth and gave it a kiss.

Pleasant chills raced up Haden's arm. Suitors had kissed her hands before, but they were often sloppy and she had to control herself from yanking her arm back immediately. But Mal's kiss sent fire coursing through her veins, and she hoped to never move from the spot.

"I would be okay with that," Haden whispered, not trusting herself to say more.

Mal grinned again, releasing her hand and offering her his arm. "I shall plan something exquisite for us, my lady."

Giggling, Haden took his arm, easing into his side. "I'm looking forward to it."

They strode arm and arm back to Haden's former room. She needed to pick up the few things before heading to her new chambers. In that short walk Haden learned Mal loved the color blue, disliked cashews and was trying to learn to play the lyre, though his father disapproved.

Haden shared that she also loved blue, was a fan of cashews *and* almonds, and would love to hear Mal play the lyre, whether his father approved or not.

In just a matter of moments, Haden felt like she had learned so much about Mal and she didn't want their conversation to end. However, as they approached Haden's former room, she noticed two figures seated on one of the benches in the courtyard. When she looked closer, Haden realized the pair were Rae and her guard, Ben. She also noticed how the two sat far closer to each other than she would've thought a potential princess and guard should. But as Haden glanced down at her arm linked with Mal's, she backtracked on the thought.

Once their footsteps were heard, Rae and Ben quickly sprung apart, but Haden had seen them holding each other's hands and she was even more curious now.

"Haden," Rae said, standing quickly, her cheeks tinted pink. "Are you all right? You left so early this morning for your interrogation, we didn't get to see you. Ida and I went by the throne room, but there were no contestants left in line. We asked Sayidi Tamor and he said there would be no more interrogations."

Haden was surprised at the look of worry in Rae's eyes. Was it for her? No, it couldn't be. Although Rae had never been cruel to Haden, she hadn't gone out of her way to befriend her either. Still, it was nice to have other people care about her well-being.

"Yes, I'm okay," Haden replied, releasing Mal's arm once she saw Rae notice their closeness. "They have caught the perpetrator that poisoned the purification pools, and it wasn't me."

Rae smirked. "Thank Tunri for that. Well, I'm glad you're okay." A sudden shyness came over the woman as she added, "Are you heading back to the room? If so—"

"Haden has been invited by the crown prince to dine with him tonight," Mal interrupted. "It's a high honor. I was only escorting her back here to gather her things."

"Things?" Rae questioned, surprise covering her features. "Are you moving rooms?"

Haden nodded, unsure how she felt about Rae's concern. "Yes, the prince wishes for me to stay in a different room, at least for tonight, to prepare for dinner." She offered a small shrug.

"I see," Rae replied, her brow furrowed.

"That's still wonderful news," Ben added. "Congratulations." He added a soft smile, and Haden could see how Rae fell for her guard.

"Oh yes," Rae said quickly, snapping out of her thoughts. "Congratulations."

Haden didn't know how to respond to the pair. *Did Rae hope to have dinner with the prince and win him over?*

Haden quickly shook that assumption from her mind as her gaze drifted to the tall guard still seated behind Rae. He had turned his gaze to the courtyard around them, but Haden knew he could still hear everything. He was a strong protector, and Haden admired that about him. Why would Rae want to have dinner with the prince when she seemed smitten with her guard? Still, the sudden change of behavior was odd. But before Haden could explain further, Mal started pulling her away.

"Haden must get ready for tonight. If the prince allows it, I will bring her back later."

Rae pursed her lips but said no more as Haden stumbled backward before righting herself.

When she was well out of earshot, she pulled her hand out of Mal's.

"Why did you pull me away from Rae? Dinner isn't for another few hours, surely, I'm not so hideous I need *that* much preparation."

The surprise look on Mal's face matched her own. She had never spoken so abruptly and forward before. If she said one word out of place, Mother would lock her in her room or force her curse to transform her form. Sometimes it would be both.

"I apologize, Haden," Mal replied, taking his hands in her own. "I just didn't want you to get mixed up with the wrong people."

"'Wrong people?'" Haden repeated, defensive of her new friends. "You don't even know them."

"Neither do you," Mal replied, raising his voice. "You are far too trusting, Haden. You need to be careful."

Haden pursed her lips. Where was this coming from? They had just started getting to know each other and Mal was already trying to control her like everyone else.

"Well then I shouldn't trust you either, because I know you even less than I know them." Spinning around, Haden stomped off.

Who was Mal to tell her who she could and couldn't talk to? He wasn't her betrothed. Even if he were, she still didn't have to listen to him. Tears stung Haden's eyes, but she blinked them back. She would find her own way to her new room.

Haden had barely taken ten steps before she heard steady footsteps behind her. Glancing over her shoulder, she saw Mal striding behind her but keeping his distance.

"Go away," she called over her shoulder. "I don't need your help." No one would tell her what to do again. This was her life. And hers alone.

She walked faster only to find Mal easily keeping a steady pace behind her.

"It's my job to protect you," he answered. "And you don't know where you're going."

Haden frowned. Unfortunately, after she had taken three lefts and a right, she ended up back at the courtyard where Ben and Rae had been sitting. She hated that Mal was right and she really didn't know where she was going. Rae and Ben had since vacated the bench, so Haden slumped down onto it. Now that her fury had dissipated, she was exhausted and desired nothing but sleep.

Burying her head in her hands, Haden wished she could fly back home and hide in her bed like she had done many times as a child. She didn't care if everything would be okay in the morning, she just wanted to run away. This place was so new and strange. The people were different and she was so confused about the prince's invitation and Mal's overprotection. It was all too much.

Sometimes, it was easier when her curse transformed her. Her thoughts became simpler, her mind not so clouded, and the world didn't require so much out of her. She could simply be a sparrow and not Princess Haden.

A shuffle sounded beside her, and Haden slid her gaze to the side. Mal stood with his side facing her as he scanned the courtyard. Haden sucked down her tears, subtly wiping her eyes.

They were quiet for a moment, listening to the water trickle from the fountain.

"I apologize," Mal said softly. "I didn't mean to upset you. Twice in one day too. I'm not doing very well to impress you, am I?"

Haden stayed quiet so Mal continued. "We take threats very seriously at the palace and the crown prince is very afraid that the rumor of spies within our walls is true." Mal paused and glanced over at Haden. "I didn't want anything to happen to you."

Haden looked back at him. He confused her greatly. He barely knew her, and he wanted to protect her like they had known each other their entire lives.

"Why?" Haden asked.

Mal quirked a brow. "Why what?"

"Why do you care so much about me? You don't know anything about me or who I am."

Mal tilted his head to the side. "Are you so sure about that, princess?"

Haden's lips parted in shock. "How did you—"

"I knew who you were the moment I spotted you in the marketplace." He smiled and motioned to her cerulean scarf around her neck. "A headscarf can only conceal so much, your highness. Though the black dye was a smart move."

"Shhhh!" Haden cried, standing and pressing her fingers against his lips. "Would you rather me be hanged by the prince than have dinner with him?"

Mal gently pulled her hand from his mouth with a laugh. "I tried to get you to tell me earlier, but you looked like I was going to skin you alive. And the prince is not going to hang you." He squeezed her hands. "Don't worry, Haden, if it's still okay to call you that. I won't tell anyone your identity. But it may be better to be honest with the crown prince sooner rather than later. Especially if you need his help with something dire." Mal frowned. "Who knows what enemies lie within the palace that would love to get their hands on the princess of Tenton?"

The fear that always consumed Haden as a child returned in a flash. Mother had constantly reminded her that anyone could kill her in an instant. It wasn't until Haden was older that she realized Mother was referring to herself.

Mal smiled down at her, his dark skin glistening in the midday sun. "May I escort you to your new room? I promise not to say anything pigheaded for now."

Haden wasn't sure how a palace guard had recognized her when no one else had, but something told her to trust Mal. Standing, she took his hand, praying to Tunri she wasn't making the wrong decision.

Before Haden knew it, she was in her new room where the woman from the purification pools, Sayida Erza, waited. With swaths of fabric at the ready, the woman wrapped Haden in beautiful cerulean silk lined with orange and gold thread. Mother had always dressed Haden in light colors and pastels and Haden despised it, thinking they made her blend in with the snow more than made her stand out. But as she studied her reflection in the mirror, Haden gasped. The deep blue was stunning against her skin and made her green eyes appear bluer rather than emerald. Haden spun around, loving the gold tassels dangling from her belt. She couldn't remember the last time she enjoyed wearing an outfit so much.

"Are you satisfied, princess?" Sayida Erza asked with a hopeful grin.

"I'm not a princess," Haden said quickly.

After Mal had recognized her so easily, she couldn't let her guard down again. Maybe she could visit that merchant and purchase more hair dye.

Erza laughed. "Not yet, dear, but if the prince has invited you for dinner, one thing leads to another and then..." Erza giggled, and Haden suddenly felt uncomfortable about going to dinner with the crown prince. Thank goodness Miguel would be there. Haden wasn't sure what she would do if she had to dine with the masked prince alone.

"I love the dress and the color, Sayida Erza, thank you," Haden replied flicking the golden tassels with a grin.

A knock sounded at the door and Erza quickly opened it. Mal stood in the opening wearing a white tunic and pants with blue, orange and gold embroidering on the edges. Haden peered down at her own outfit, confused as to why she and Mal matched.

"Cerulean and gold are the prince's favorite colors. Orange is the color of Kadesh," Erza commented upon noticing Haden's reaction. "And if you wish for a proposal by the end of the night, you must do everything you can to make yourself appealing." Erza waggled her brows.

Haden frowned at the comment but stepped toward Mal anyway. She didn't want a proposal at the end of the night. She wanted to speak with the prince about stopping her Mother from trying to take over Kadesh. Haden was never good with diplomacy, but she would have to try and convince the prince otherwise.

Pretending her beautiful blue dress was a suit of armor, Haden raised her chin and exited the room, hoping she could stop this battle before it began.

Chapter Seventeen

Rae, Radaa Kingdom, Kadesh

Rae watched Haden's guard pull her away with a frown. Every instinct she had told her to follow them, to tell Haden the crazy thought that entered Rae's mind. But she didn't. Rae stayed rooted in the courtyard, unsure of how to react.

As Rae watched Haden and her guard round the corner, the shuffle of footsteps came behind her.

"Were you going to tell her what you thought?" Ben said, laying a hand on her shoulder.

Rae reached her own hand up and squeezed his. "I wanted to. Now I'm not so sure."

Rae had seen depictions of Princess Haden since childhood. They were torn down once Kadesh invaded Yekel, but still, Rae had never noticed anything about the princess other than what everyone else had: she was beautiful.

However, now that Rae had actually seen Princess Haden in person, there was something...familiar about her. Rae decided to study the princess from afar, trying to figure out whether Haden reminded Rae of someone or if she was just remembering the various drawings she had seen of the princess throughout the years.

However, it was Ben who brought forward what Rae had been tiptoeing around. After Ben had seen Haden for the first time in the palace, he mentioned it to Rae while she was unpacking the few items she had brought with her.

"So, the princess of Tenton is here."

Rae glanced over her shoulder. "Yes, she's rooming with me and Ida. Though I don't know why she's here and how no one has noticed."

She placed the folded cerulean scarf on her bed, thankful she had brought a color the Kadeshian palace seemed to love decorating with.

"It really is strange," Ben replied.

At the uncertainty in his voice, Rae turned around. "What are you thinking?"

Ben rubbed the back of his neck, something he always did when he was unsure whether he should share his thoughts or not.

Rae walked up to him and wrapped her arms around his waist. "You can speak freely with me, Ben, you know that."

"I do," he agreed, pulling her close. "I just never noticed it before when I always saw the pictures, but I hadn't met you yet."

Rae furrowed her brows as she laid her cheek on his lower chest. "What are you talking about?"

Ben blew out a breath. "The other night, when Haden came out of the room and I saw her with the same scarf as you, I thought she was you. You two look a lot alike, almost as if you were related."

Rae leaned back and stared at Ben. She took a step back then laughed. "You can't be serious. That's nonsense. The princess is known throughout Tenton for her unrivaled beauty and I'm just—" Rae shrugged. "I'm just me."

Ben cupped her cheek. "You are beautiful inside and out, Rae."

When Ben leaned down to kiss her, Rae fully accepted it. A few kisses later, the two broke apart and continued their guise as a guard and contestant in the pageant.

But since that conversation, Rae had been watching Haden, trying to find similarities between them. And she had. The way they both swung their arms when they walked and how their toes pointed slightly out with each step. But it wasn't only similarities with her. Rae noticed a few of the gestures Haden made were scarily accurate to how Mami would talk with her hands.

Could it be?

She knew she hadn't been as open to Haden as Ida because, well, Ida was kind to everyone, and Rae couldn't help but be suspicious of new people. But after discovering these similarities, Rae's mind started to wander back to when she was a child. *If* she and Haden were related, Rae would've been no more than two when Haden was born. That was a very young age for her to remember anything about a long-lost sister.

However, there was something niggling at the back of her mind. Rae remembered Mami and Papi hoping for another child, so Rae wouldn't be alone. There were faint memories of Mami's stomach being large and a very loud little bundle, but everything was hazy.

Are these memories real? Or am I just wishing for something that's not really there? And if it is true, why would my younger sister be the princess of Tenton?

The idea consumed Rae more and more until finally she brought it back up to Ben a few days later.

"I have to ask her," Rae confessed as they sat in the courtyard. "I don't think she'll remember anything; she was just a baby. But if I feel this familiarity, maybe she does too."

"I don't think any harm can come of asking," Ben replied with a soft smile.

That was when Haden and her guard appeared in the courtyard. And just when Rae was about to ask, her guard stole her away.

"Maybe it's for the best," Rae added as she turned back to Ben. She placed her scarf over her head, blocking her eyes from the midday sun. "I mean, she's royalty and I'm not anything. It's probably just a coincidence that we have any similarities at all."

Ben gave Rae an unconvinced look but said nothing.

Then a pitter-patter of footsteps quickly came toward them, and Rae spun around.

"There you are," Ida gasped. "I've been looking for you two."

Rae peered behind Ida to find Raphael marching as straight and true as any palace guard would.

"We were just enjoying the flowers since the contest has been put on hold," Ben said with a smirk.

"You should've invited me then," Ida replied with a grin. "You know I love them."

"We should have," Rae added quickly, not wanting to burden Ida with her crazy notions about the princess. "You said you were looking for us, has something happened? Have you received word from the general or Jacques?"

"Yes," Ida replied, lowering her voice. She took a quick look around the courtyard. "Raphael has received some information from the other palace servants."

The three of them glanced up to find Raphael had made it to where they all stood. Late in the night, Ida had confided in Rae that Raphael was Jacques' older brother that had fled from Tenton years ago. Rae would've assumed the man's claim was a ruse—as she hardly trusted anyone blindly—but Ida insisted it was true. Still, Rae would keep an eye on him.

"Let's step closer to the fountain, in case anyone happens to pass by." Raphael motioned for the two women to sit.

Since the poisoning of the purification pools, Sayidi Tamor prohibited anyone from leaving the area around their rooms unless summoned by the crown prince for interrogation. Even with the rule, there were many young women and their guards wandering about, not knowing what to do in the meantime.

Rae followed Ben and she sat on the edge of the fountain. The bubbling of the current within the stone was loud enough to muffle their words to those striding past.

Once Ida settled herself next to Rae, Raphael stood to the side as if he were talking to Ben. To the passersby Ida and Rae looked to be enjoying the beauty of the courtyard with their dutiful guards by their sides.

"One of the guards overheard the chef in the kitchen complaining about a large order of meat General Beta ordered not two days ago," Raphael began. "The chef said that if the general kept ordering so much meat, there wouldn't be enough left for the crown prince's wedding."

Rae watched a group of women all with the same shade of red hair stride by. "So, what does a large order of meat have to do with Devora?"

Raphael slid his gaze to Rae. "General Beta is hardly seen at the palace and when she is here, she is not here to eat copious amounts of meat. So, who or what is she ordering the meat for?"

"Still, I've traveled with Devora and know she eats the same amount of food as any average person," Ben added causing Rae to hold back her chuckle.

Raphael rolled his eyes and huffed. "I'm not implying your friend eats as much as a giant. What I'm saying is the general is trying to feed a large number of something—whether it be hidden soldiers, giants, creatures—and I want to know what and why. But also, within the same order, General Beta ordered a pot of millroot. I don't know what it is, but the guard mentioned he'd heard that it could dull the senses."

Rae narrowed her gaze. "I'm not sure this is much to go on for finding Devora."

"I know it's not as concrete as we would like, but with Tristan gone and no other leads, I think it's worth checking out," Ida replied, trying to be the peacemaker as always.

Rae was glad Ida was there to keep a level head.

Frowning, Rae watched the same group of redheads walk in front of them again. She was still furious that Tristan had left them after she had agreed to his plan and went along with all his shenanigans. While she was thankful he hadn't betrayed them outright, who knew where he was and what he was up to.

Rae faced Ida and already felt herself buckling under Ida's big doe eyes pleading with her to agree.

"What do you think?" she asked Ben, who was fiddling with the orange scarf in his pocket. It warmed Rae's heart to think he still carried it with him from the first day they met. Well, since the first day he met her when she was herself and not disguised as a male street fighter named the Crimson Cord.

Ben sighed. "I agree with Ida. We need to start somewhere and after the pools were poisoned, I'm nervous that something worse will happen soon. For whatever reason, someone is targeting the contestants, and I feel uneasy having you two mixed in. We need to work fast."

Rae nodded, realizing Ben was right. She had no idea where to begin trying to find Devora, but some information was better than nothing at all.

"Okay," she turned toward Raphael. "Where should we start searching?"

———◆———

A crescent moon appeared in the night sky, coating the courtyard in a soft glow. Rae remembered Haden's guard saying that Haden was dining with the prince that night, so it was the best night to sneak out and search the palace.

Raphael decided they should search the palace's scroll room to find out what millroot was first and go from there. Ida, with her knowledge of plants, gently brought up that the herb may just be a sleeping tonic for the general instead of something more.

"We need to be vigilant and mark off what isn't the right course to take. What remains will be the right course," Raphael replied before they all agreed to meet back in the courtyard later that night.

As Rae slipped out of her room, with Ida right behind, she couldn't help but think Raphael reminded her of General Blake, but not in a good way. She wondered what had happened to the general after they had seen him transform into a gray wolf. Rae had seen a lot of strange things in her life, but nothing quite like that.

Ben stepped out of the shadows and met them outside their door. His crossbow was strapped across his back. Rae then realized she hadn't seen him wear it when he was on duty being her guard.

Where did he stash it during the day? she wondered.

"I didn't know you brought that." He motioned to her black Crimson Cord uniform.

Rae felt herself blush as he looked her up and down and smiled.

"I've always liked it," he added, his eyes flashing with something mischievous.

"Stop," she said, playfully swatting him on the arm.

Ida giggled and embarrassment rushed over Rae like a wave. "Sorry, Ida," Rae said, unable to look Ida in the eye.

Ben had been more forward with his thoughts and feelings when they were alone, but Rae wasn't sure she could handle his boldness in front of Ida or anyone else for that matter.

"Oh, you don't bother me," she replied as she tried to stuff her curls back into the dark scarf covering her head. "It just makes me miss Jacques more than I already do."

Rae's heart drooped. Now that she had Ben in her life, she couldn't imagine him not being there. She never stopped to think about how Ida was feeling separated from her betrothed.

"I'm sorry," Rae said again. "It must be difficult being so far."

Ida nodded, grasping her hands in front of her. "It is, but it's not forever. When I return, I get to marry him after all."

Ida smiled as her hand went to the engagement ring she hid around her neck on a chain. It was a stunning ring, and Rae couldn't help but wonder what it would be like to have one of her own. She slid her eyes to Ben who was checking the straps on his crossbow. Although he had been forward with how much he cared for her, he hadn't mentioned anything about a future together. But if he had, would Rae be ready for it?

Sighing, Rae pushed the idea from her mind. She wished she could be more like Ida. She was constantly surprised at the positive attitude the future Duchess had about everything. If only Rae wasn't so negative and suspicious all the time, maybe she could view the world as brightly.

"Is everyone ready?" Raphael asked, stepping up to their group.

They all nodded and followed him quietly down the hall. Rae was impressed with their group's silence. She assumed with four people hurrying about they would be louder. But as they crept through the palace halls, not a single step was heard.

In a matter of moments, they came across a bisection of corridors when Raphael stopped them. Turning his blond head in both directions, the guard headed left.

But when Rae and the others followed him, they found him pressing his hand against a small portrait on the wall.

Rae was about to question him when a small snap sounded and the space beside the portrait swung inward.

"A hidden door?" Ida gasped, excitement flashing in her gaze.

Rae's brows rose as Ida followed behind Raphael without question. Even though Ida trusted Raphael, Rae still wasn't sure. There seemed to be more to Jacques' brother than met the eye.

However, Rae didn't have any reason *not* to trust him, so she cautiously followed behind Ida. The space within the wall was narrow and cramped, squeezing against her shoulders. Though she wasn't the smallest woman, she definitely wasn't huge enough to feel so squished. Wasn't there a better way to get to the scroll room?

Rae glanced back, worried that Ben wouldn't fit. But when she saw him duck down into the space, relief dropped her tense stance.

"You okay?" she asked him.

"Yeah," Ben replied, his shoulders hunched as his head was practically smashed on the ceiling. "This reminds me of your house in Yekel."

Thankfully, Ben smiled after his statement and Rae reached out and grabbed his hand. They shuffled through the small space until Raphael opened another secret door that opened into the scroll room.

"I've never been through a secret tunnel before," Ida said with a grin.

"Why all the secrecy?" Rae asked Raphael with a quirked brow. "I thought the scroll room was open to everyone in the palace?"

"It is," he replied, starting to scan the shelves. "However, you all aren't supposed to leave your section of the palace, and we are supposed to guard you. I figured stealth would be more appropriate considering we would all be punished if caught. And by punished, I mean you all will be cast out of the pageant, and Ben and I will be arrested."

The blood drained from Rae's face at the statement. "That was wise," Rae admitted, kicking herself for trying to find a reason not to trust Jacques' brother. "Thank you for thinking of all of us."

Raphael gave her a firm nod before heading toward another section of scrolls. The group fanned out around the small, squared room. Iron lanterns hung from every few feet on the walls, illuminating the numerous shelves of scrolls.

"What is all this?" Rae asked aloud, running her finger along the rolled-up pieces of parchment.

"It looks like a little bit of everything," Ida replied from the row over. "Start with trying to find something to do with gardening or plants."

Rae frowned at the scrolls. She knew a fair amount of Kadeshian since living among them, but she wasn't sure how strong her understanding would be with so much information to read. However, she wasn't about to stand there uselessly, so she decided to pull out a scroll and hope something would stand out. She found a few maps of the city of Renta and studied those for a while before moving on.

After the first few scrolls held nothing remotely understandable to Rae, she took a break.

"You seem to know what you're doing," Ben said, coming up beside her.

Rae sighed. "I can speak Kadeshian fine but reading it—" Rae shook her head. "There are a handful of symbols I know and the one for 'millroot' isn't one of them."

"Well, you know more than me." Ben shrugged. "I'm much better at watching you than trying to read a foreign language myself."

Rae's cheeks felt like fire. While Rae adored the constant confirmation of his feelings for her, she didn't always know how to respond to it. Who knew the gentle giant had such a flirtatious side?

"Hmm, so I have to do all the work while you stand there and look good?"

Now it was Ben's turn to blush and Rae secretly loved it. Laughing, she faced the shelves again and pulled out a random thick scroll. While some of the parchments seemed like they hadn't been opened in years, this one easily unrolled.

Intrigued, Rae opened it farther. The scrolls she had looked at so far only had symbols, but this one also had illustrations, and to her surprise, there were drawings of different herbs.

"Ida, I think I found something," Rae called with excitement.

Ida and Raphael were at Rae's side in a flash. Knowing Ida was a Translator, Rae quickly handed the parchment to her and watched in amazement as Ida's eyes shifted from their warm brown to a glittering gold. But what Rae always loved was Ida thanked Tunri for her gift before she used it.

The room was as silent as the summer breeze as they waited for Ida to translate what the scroll said.

"Oh no," Ida finally whispered. "This isn't good."

"What does it say?" Rae asked before anyone else could.

Ida's golden eyes ran along the page. "'Millroot is an herb that can be grown quite easily if the planter knows how to create the right environment. This herb is not only able to dull the senses but can also dull the effects of certain gifts. But be warned, this herb should not be taken in great amounts, or it will poison the body leading to possible numbness, irreversible blindness, or death."

"What does that mean, Ida?" Ben asked, peering over Rae's shoulder.

Ida glanced up from the page, her eyes still shining. "Devora spoke about a dung tea her parents would make her drink every few weeks. But since Devora never had any of these side effects, I'm assuming the dose she took was minimal. Even so, if someone hoped to dull her gift or stop it for a time, they could force her to take more of this."

"But that would mean—" Rae started before Raphael interrupted.

"Your friend could very well be dead before we find her."

Chapter Eighteen

Devora stared into the black abyss. She didn't know where she was or how long she had been there, but she did know she preferred the sunlight to the dark. The figure on the far wall stirred. Thankfully, she wasn't alone. While trekking through the underground tunnels leading out of Yekel, Devora hated being alone. Especially cramped in the dark. Even though the cell she was in wasn't cramped, a candle would've been nice.

A howl sounded from down the corridor and Devora shuddered. The constant wolfish noises brought her back to the battle of Edo where the iron-armored beasts had torn through Tenton's army. She wasn't completely certain these were the same creatures, but something in her heart told her the assumption was correct.

"Did you get any rest last night?" Kanna's soft voice asked, scooting closer to Devora.

Trying to ignore the howls, Devora smiled, even though she knew Matthias' mother couldn't see it. Ever since she was thrown in the cell with Kanna, the woman had treated Devora like her own daughter. She shared her scraps of food with Devora, told her encouraging stories of when Tunri saved her from harm, and always checked on her emotional state of being.

"Some," Devora replied, trying to ignore the pain in her spine from sleeping on the cold stone floor. She would've thought she was used to sleeping in horrid places, but her muscles begged to differ. The barking and howling of the creatures didn't help either.

Though Devora had already come to love Kanna, it made the pain in her heart for her own mother cut deeper. She hadn't seen Mama or Papa since she fled the Fortress. Devora couldn't remember how long ago that was. She just prayed and prayed that Tunri would protect them and that they would be reunited again someday.

"I wish I could tell you it gets easier over time," Kanna sighed. "But it doesn't."

Devora couldn't see through the darkness, but she knew Kanna had drawn near for her voice was closer than before.

"Have you had any visions from Tunri?" Devora asked, hoping the answer would be different than the last time she asked.

Devora felt Kanna's hand take her own and she knew the answer was "no."

"Do not fear the unknown, Devora. The light will banish the shadows, it only takes time."

Devora squeezed Kanna's hand, not knowing how to respond. For the first few days, Devora was hopeful that something would happen, and she could escape the cell she was in with Kanna. But day after day came and there were no signs of anything that could possibly lead her to breaking out. And though she had prayed and cried out to Tunri, He stayed silent.

"If only we didn't have to take the awful dung tea," Devora muttered.

Kanna let out a light laugh. "Your name for it makes me laugh every time."

Devora couldn't help but smile. Even when they were shut in the dark for what seemed like weeks, or when the boy, Sergio, was late with their rations, Kanna's spirit was always bright. She reminded Devora so much of Ida and her faithful spirit. Devora still had so much to learn, not only as a Seer, but as a follower of Tunri too.

"It amused Matthias, too," Devora commented, her heart filling with more sorrow at the mention of his name.

Every night since the masquerade ball she dreamed of him. His dark, wavy hair, stormy gray eyes, and perfectly kissable lips. Even though Kanna shared stories with Devora about Matthias, Devora often kept her personal thoughts about him to herself.

"If I know anything about my son, I know that he hasn't given up yet. As far as I can remember, he was determined and stubborn. I wouldn't be surprised if he was on his way right now."

"I miss him," Devora confessed, tears brimming her eyes. "I wish we would've had more time."

"Who says you won't?" Kanna asked, her own stubbornness layering her words. "Though I cannot see you, I can hear you just fine. Breath flows in your lungs and blood through your heart. Your life has not ended, Devora."

"It certainly feels like it has."

When she first received the vision from Tunri about General Beta, a Kadeshian Seer, poisoning the mind of the king of Kadesh, Devora was confused. Why was Tunri telling her this? She wasn't Kadeshian. As far as she knew, Kadesh had incited the conflict with Tenton years ago. However, she'd learned that what she had been taught in her lessons wasn't necessarily correct. While she was disguised in Yekel, she had the opportunity to research more of Kadesh's history. A Kadeshian merchant had set up a bookshop in the marketplace and Devora could never resist browsing through different tomes. Yet as she flipped through one of the texts, she was even more confused. All her life, she was taught that Kadeshians were the cause of all the hardship and pain in Tenton. But after she read that it was a former princess of Tenton that caused the war, Devora began to understand. For the former princess was no longer a princess anymore, but a queen. A queen who would do anything to get revenge.

Devora ran a hand over her extremely frizzy hair, coming back to the present. The dripping of water sounded in the distance. The sound had accompanied her and Kanna since Devora arrived. She only assumed they were underground somewhere, possibly a cave or cavern. The thought always made her hope dwindle. How would anyone find them if they were hidden underground?

Sighing, Devora tried to control her depressing thoughts. Instead, every day she would try to riddle out why Queen Leza would want to attack Kadesh and what that had to do with General Beta, King Redore IV, and her. But each day she didn't have any answer.

The iron door leading in to wherever they were imprisoned opened. Devora recognized the grating metal sound from when she lived at the Fortress. That life seemed so long ago, when her only fear was of an angry captain saying cruel comments to her. Now the angry captain was a general and held the keys to her heart.

"Good morning, ladies," Sergio's voice chirped in a mocking tone. "I hope you slept well."

Devora held in her growl. The condescending man striding toward her reminded her too much of Tristan for her liking. And though Tristan had helped her and One Shot in Yekel, she was never completely certain about his intentions.

"Good morning, Sergio," Kanna responded in a kind voice. "Everything was as usual."

Devora wasn't sure if Sergio had put a different herb in Kanna's tea than her own, but Kanna always treated him with kindness and respect. All Devora wanted to do was throttle him and demand he release them.

"That's good to hear," Sergio replied, his voice not as mocking as before.

The clink of the tray holding their usual scrap of bread and the awful dung tea echoed as Sergio placed it before the bars of the cell. It was this moment every day in which Devora hoped something would happen. It was one of the three times a day in which a match was struck, a lantern lit, and she could see the world around her.

She had played out several scenarios in her mind. Once Sergio lit the lantern, she could try to grab his wrist and force him to release them. She had attempted it once and since then, Sergio always stood a few feet back from the bars of the cell.

Devora had also thought about feigning sickness or injury to get Sergio to open the door. But seeing how Kanna was blind, and her predicament was the same as Devora, Devora assumed the young man had no heart at all. Though, she knew that wasn't entirely true.

Devora shifted her vision to engage her soulsight. Everything was bleak and dark, but she could still see the faded light of Sergio's soul. When she first ended up here, Devora noticed Sergio's soul was gray and smokey, similar to King Atol's. But now his soul held fractals of blue. Was it possible Sergio held sorrow for the life he was leading? Or was it something else? The loss of a loved one?

Devora was able to squeeze some information from him and learned General Beta was his aunt. Apparently, his parents had been killed in a Tentonian raid when he was a child, and he lived with his aunt ever since. Devora hated to admit it, but the story did bring sympathy to her heart for Sergio.

"Are you going to drink your tea today, little Seer?" Sergio asked and Devora knew he was speaking to her.

The only liquid they received were cups of the dung tea. Although Devora had taken the tea since she was young, the amount she consumed was nowhere near as strong as the brew given to her now. She didn't know much about the tea or the herbs that created it, but she assumed that if an herb could suppress her Seeing gift, it had to have serious side effects if consumed in large amounts. Kanna had told her as much when Devora first arrived. Since she was in captivity, Kanna was forced to take the dung tea. She tried to resist at first, but after a few days with nothing to drink, Kanna knew she had to take it. And, unfortunately, she knew the side effects of the tea, as well.

But Devora, much like Matthias, was stubborn and determined. While she still needed liquid to survive, she didn't consume all the drink. Unfortunately, she hadn't received any visions from Tunri since consuming the dung tea again, but she could still use her soulsight.

"Maybe. If you tell me where I am," she replied, hoping Sergio saw the fire in her violet eyes, if they were even violet at all anymore.

She understood that Kanna had fought a long and hard battle, but Devora wasn't ready to be kind to her captors just yet. Not when she knew Matthias and the others were still out there, trying to find them.

Sergio gave a dramatic sigh and tilted his head to the side. "You know, if you would've gone to Vlacklear like you were supposed to, we probably would've been married by now. Such a shame."

Devora scrunched her nose. "I would never pick someone like you."

"Oh, really?" Sergio laughed with a quirked brow. "But you did. You just didn't know it."

At Devora's confused expression, Sergio laughed and picked up the lantern, taking away the only light Devora would see for a while.

When the iron door shut, Devora reached through the bars and felt for the tray. Once her fingertips touched the cool metal, she pulled the tray forward and grabbed the two hunks of bread.

"Here, Kanna, take this." She handed the bread to Kanna, but Kanna pushed it back.

"No, Devora, I'm okay. You need to survive to end this. I'm not sure how much fight I have left in me."

Devora scoffed and felt for Kanna's hand and wrapped her fingers around the bread. "That talk is not allowed. You have been so strong for so long. We will get out of here and you will be united with your sons again."

Devora felt Kanna's hand squeeze hers before she took the bread.

"I'm thankful one of my boys found a good woman," Kanna said after a few bites. "I've always been worried about the other one."

Devora munched on her bread, unsure about whether she should divulge to Kanna that she had been engaged to Tristan first—even as short as it was. But before she could begin that conversation, the iron door scraped open once more.

The hope that Devora thought had left her soul returned with a fury. The only person they had seen was Sergio and that was only at mealtimes. In the duration of time Devora had been imprisoned, she had never seen another person besides Kanna and Sergio.

With her mind churning, she tried to think of a plan before a bright light encased the entire space. Devora immediately shielded her eyes. How long had it been since she'd seen a light so bright?

Once her eyes adjusted, Devora scooted to the back of the cell, nearly squashing Kanna in the process.

"Have you enjoyed your time in my cell, Seer sisters?" General Beta asked.

Devora glared at the woman. Though she knew she was walking into an unknown situation, she never expected General Beta to starve her half to death and then try to poison her with the dung tea. Thankfully, Devora had enough spite to survive. But once the light had shown what Kanna really looked like, fear struck Devora's heart.

Thin, birdlike limbs were attached to the woman's already frail figure. Her light-blue dress was tattered and fraying at the edges, as if she hadn't received a new garment from the time she was captured years ago. Devora reached out and grabbed the woman's hand, afraid she would break her fingers if she squeezed too hard. And though her eyes were clouded, they still showed violet, making Devora realize how strong Kanna's gift must be to still show its presence even with the effects of the dung tea. But what encouraged Devora was the hopeful smile on Kanna's face.

Turning her gaze back to the general, Devora quickly surveyed all she could of the space surrounding them. They were locked in one of a series of cells that were similar to the ones in the Fourth Level of the Fortress. Not the worst cells in the prison, but certainly not the best. Unfortunately, Devora knew these cells weren't in the Fortress because of the coloring of the stone walls. While the Fortress was made of dark stone, these cells were comprised of red, claylike bricks.

Devora racked her brain, trying to remember where in Tenton an abundance of red clay could be found to make a structure of this kind. But, as far as she knew, one couldn't find red clay in Tenton. The only place it could be found was in...Devora's brows rose in her realization.

"That's right, Seer sister," General Beta chuckled, clutching the bright orb of light she held. "You're a long way from home."

Devora's stomach clenched. She was in Kadesh. How would Matthias ever find her when she was in the enemy country?

The vision of General Beta poisoning the king of Kadesh's mind resurfaced in her own. Was Kadesh really the enemy? Or was it General Beta?

"My nephew has been telling me of your stubbornness to take the millroot herb. But in the end, it will work in my favor." General Beta released the glowing orb in her hand, leaving it bobbing in the air.

Devora's eyes widened but she held back her gasp. She wouldn't give the general satisfaction in impressing her. She had seen that orb before, but where? As the general stalked back to the iron door, Devora stared at the glowing sphere, willing the memory to come forward.

As three sets of footsteps came toward them, it hit her like a boulder. The orb of swirling light before her was the same orb she had seen in Yekel, in the heart of the statue of the goddess, Pahga in the Temple. This time Devora did gasp.

"What?" Kanna asked, her head darting around. "What's happened, Devora?"

Devora didn't have time to explain the whole story to Kanna. "There's a floating orb. I saw the same one when I was in Yekel. It was in a giant statue of the Goddess Pahga. But it was horrible. This orb doesn't contain just light, but the stolen souls of countless young women."

"What?" Kanna repeated with a gasp. "How is that possible?"

"It's very possible, Kanna," General Beta replied, her wide grin stretching from ear to ear. "And you two will help us complete the final stages of our decades-long plan. Sergio, open the cell. We are finally ready for the Seers."

Devora wanted to scream and shout, to fight back or shove Sergio out of the way, but she couldn't. Because the third set of footsteps she heard belonged to someone she thought was on her side. But, once again, he had proven her a fool. For standing next to General Beta with a smug grin was none other than Tristan.

Chapter Nineteen

Haden, Radaa Kingdom, Kadesh

Following closely behind Mal, Haden did her best not to trip over the long train of the blue gown. Though she loved the gown and its exotic look, it was almost as difficult to walk in as a ballgown. Thankfully, it wasn't nearly as restricting so Haden could enjoy all the delicious food being set out on the table in the grand hall.

Mal stopped abruptly and Haden smashed into his back. A light chuckle came from him as he turned around.

"Still getting used to Kadeshian dress?"

"It's beautiful," she replied, examining the shining blue and sparkling gold threads. "It's unlike anything I've worn before, and I love it."

Mal's smile grew. "Blue is your color." It seemed Mal wanted to say more, but he kept his lips closed. Stepping out of the way, Mal motioned to the seat nearest to where they were standing. Haden turned and noticed there were five seats at the table, but Mal hadn't started toward any of them.

Remember he's only a guard, Haden chided herself. Mother would've never allowed a guard to dine with them. But Mal was unlike any guard Haden had ever known. Still, she didn't know much about the crown prince of Kadesh and how he would react to her being so friendly with one of his guards. It was best to keep her distance from Mal, at least during dinner, in hopes that she could gain the prince's favor and discuss what to do about the queen of Tenton.

"Thank you," Haden said quietly at the compliment and hurried toward the seat. While she repeated her words again when Mal pulled the chair out for her, Haden kept her eyes fixed on the golden goblet before her until the next guard and visitor entered the dining room.

"Miguel!" Haden shot up, forgetting all decorum and rushing toward her uncle.

"Haden, Sayidi Brocaw told me more details of what happened at the purification pools. I'm so glad you're okay," he replied, wrapping his arms around her. "I didn't realize the perpetrator's crime when I caught him sneaking around the palace."

Haden relished the hug. She could count on one hand the number of times Mother and Father had hugged her. She always desired to feel the warmth of familial love and maybe now that she knew Miguel was her real uncle, she would.

When they broke apart, Haden noticed Miguel had shaved off his long beard.

"You look so much younger!" Haden said with a laugh. A moment later she realized that she had indirectly called him old. "I apologize, I didn't mean to imply anything about your age."

Thankfully, Miguel only laughed and rubbed his smooth chin. "Not to worry. I feel younger too."

Haden relaxed at Miguel's easy demeanor as both sat at the table. Reaching for the goblet, Haden studied the interesting array of foods plated before her. Never had she seen such a variety of fruits and vegetables of all different colors. After tipping the goblet toward her mouth, she realized it was empty. Embarrassed, she placed it back, hoping no one noticed her blunder. Thank goodness no one knew she was a princess. She had been taught table etiquette since she was a child but apparently couldn't remember any of it. Placing her hands in her lap, Haden waited a moment to see if anyone else would arrive.

After a few moments with no other guests, she turned to Miguel. "So how did you catch the perpetrator that poisoned the pools?"

Miguel's eyes darted to Mal, who stood a few feet behind Haden's chair. He waited a moment for Mal to start speaking with the other guard before whispering, "I do not wish for the king's guards to know why I was near the palace wall in the first place. There's no need to put speculation on your head. However, before I spoke with you in the courtyard, I noticed a fellow lurking around the palace gates. At first, I thought he was a besotted suitor of one of the young women taken for *Sundarata Taashama*. But once I witnessed him pry open one of the grates of the waterways, I knew he had to be up to no good. I've tried hard to keep a low profile over the last twenty years, so I didn't wish to intervene if I didn't have to. Thankfully, there was an abundance of guards coming by, so I was confident they would see the open grate and investigate."

Haden leaned forward, enraptured by the story. So there really were spies trying to get into the palace and Mal's fears were warranted. She suddenly felt ashamed for being so harsh with him earlier. Because her visitation boundaries at Maldove Palace were limited, she hardly went out of the palace without a handful of guards. Even if there was a threat, Haden would be protected. But sadly, her parents never thought her wise enough to share with her any of the happenings in the kingdom. The only reason Haden knew as much as she did about the war with Kadesh was because of her own research.

"So, what did you do then?" she asked, resting her chin on her hand.

Miguel puffed his chest out. "After we spoke, I noticed the grate to the waterway was still open. I assumed the young man I saw was the reason behind the screaming we heard. But, since the grate was still open, I waited on the side of it, hoping the criminal would come out. And he did. As soon as he stepped through, I hooked my arm around his neck and subdued him fairly quickly." Miguel added a flashy grin and Haden chuckled.

"You went after him without any weapons?"

Miguel lifted his fists. "I don't need weapons when I have these. Plus, I used to be a street fighter in my younger days. I'm glad I haven't forgotten everything about my youth."

"That's so brave," Haden replied, wishing she had the courage to take down a spy. But she knew if she were ever put in that situation she would probably hide or stand there and not know what to do.

A bell chimed, causing Haden and Miguel to turn toward a door at the far back of the dining room. The first person to enter the room was Sayidi Brocaw. He had cleaned up significantly since Haden saw him earlier, donning the same type of clothing Mal and Miguel wore.

"Please rise for the crown prince of Kadesh," Sayidi Brocaw announced.

Haden and Miguel stood simultaneously and watched as the crown prince strode in behind Sayidi Brocaw. Haden tried not to frown as she saw the same blue mask on the prince's face. She was hoping since this was a private meeting, the prince would reveal his face to her. But the mask was still on.

I shouldn't have assumed I was anyone special for the prince to reveal his face to me. He's probably invited tons of girls to dinner already.

But as the prince strode by Haden, he gave her a nod of his head. Haden flushed, not knowing how else to react when she couldn't see his face.

Once the crown prince was seated with Sayidi Brocaw standing to his side, the bell chimed three more times.

"Please stay standing for the rest of the party dining with us tonight," Sayidi Brocaw explained.

Haden gave Miguel a confused look. Who else would be joining them for dinner? Thankfully, she didn't have to wait long before a tall, thin woman entered. Haden did a double take as the woman marched into the dining room. She'd recognized that birdlike nose and those thin lips anywhere.

Haden furrowed her brow. *What's Aunt Beta doing here?*

Of course, Haden now knew that the woman *she* grew up referencing as "Aunt Beta" was not her real aunt. But still, Haden was confused before fear pierced her heart. What if Aunt Beta told Mother she was here? If what Miguel had said was true, Mother already had a funeral for Haden and Father. So, if she found out that Haden was really alive, would Mother actually kill her this time?

Haden wished she could transform into a sparrow and fly away. And she almost did if it weren't for the hand she felt on her shoulder.

"Is everything okay?" Mal asked, his warm breath tickling her ear.

The hairs on the back of Haden's neck rose at his closeness. It was strange how Mal always seemed to know when Haden was distressed or ready to run away. Did she look a certain way to clue him in?

Haden nodded. "Yes, just thirsty." She reached forward and grabbed the goblet in front of her which had now been filled and downed whatever the sweet yet tangy liquid was.

"Okay," he replied, letting his hand linger on her shoulder a bit more than necessary. "I'm here if you need me. And be careful with that drink." He motioned to her goblet.

"Why? Is it poisoned?" she asked, half-jokingly.

Mal's face turned serious. "It could be."

"Oh," Haden replied. "You're right, I should be more cautious."

Mal smirked. "I already checked your goblet for poison after you tried to drink from it the first time and it's fine. I wanted to warn you that that's a very strong wine and you just drank a whole goblet in three gulps."

"Oh," Haden replied, sinking in her chair, wishing it would swallow her whole. So much for all her etiquette lessons.

Miguel's deep chuckle rumbled beside her as he took a sip from his own goblet.

The bell chimed again; this time six rings echoed throughout the dining room. Aunt Beta, Miguel and even the prince still stood as the final person who would be dining with them entered the room. Haden quickly stood from her chair, wishing Sayidi Brocaw would've said how many additional people would be joining them tonight.

Shuffling forward, King Redore IV, the king of Kadesh, crossed the threshold into the dining room. But he wasn't the strong and menacing leader Haden had been told he was. The man before her was barely a man, resembling more of a corpse. His limbs were frail and thin, as if they would snap with another step. Wild straggles of white hair sprang around his golden crown. His elegant robes of blue, orange and gold, hung over his hunched frame, dragging along the ground with each painfully slow step.

Haden did her best not to gawk at the ill appearance of the king, but it was hard not to. This was not who she pictured when she heard about Kadesh's bloodthirsty king.

It seemed as if every person in the room held their breath as the king creakily made his way to his chair at the head of the table. And though a pack of guards followed him, none offered aid.

Haden released a sigh of relief when the king finally sat. Not only because he had made it to his chair in one piece, but she didn't have to wait any longer to eat.

However, as soon as Haden sat down, Aunt Beta caught her eye and smirked. She guessed her dyed hair only did so much to hide her identity.

Haden knew the general wouldn't call her out right away. That's not how monarchy politics worked. No, Aunt Beta would wait until the opportune moment to slide the topic of Haden's presence into conversation with the king to exploit her publicly and *then* Haden would either be sent back to the woman who wanted her dead or hung on the gallows right here in Kadesh.

Now I really wish I could fly away.

"Have we caught the culprit who tried to sabotage my pageant?" King Redore IV wheezed as if he had a bucket of sand in his throat.

Sayidi Brocaw quickly rushed to the king's side. "Yes, sire. That is why we're hosting dinner in the east wing tonight. The man who caught the perpetrator is dining with us."

The king slowly turned his head toward Miguel and Haden. A cloudy film covered his eyes and Haden wondered if the king could see anything at all.

Squinting his eyes, the king addressed Miguel, "You look familiar, have you dined with us before?"

Aunt Beta snorted and interrupted, "Sire, we hardly make it a custom to invite the lower class to our table."

Haden's brows rose at the snarky remark, wondering what issue Aunt Beta had with Miguel. While Haden thought Miguel would take the blow and stay silent, he proved her wrong.

"While I haven't dined with you, your highness, I did work in the palace many years ago. Perhaps that is where you remember me."

Miguel kept his scorned gaze on Aunt Beta and Haden was even more curious as to what their relationship was now.

"And who is the lovely young lady seated next to you?" the king asked. "A participant in the pageant, perhaps?"

Haden wanted to sink into her chair. She was hoping no attention would be brought to her, but how could she avoid a direct question from the king?

Thankfully, Miguel took over for her. "She is, your grace. And she is my niece."

Haden watched Aunt Beta at the remark, knowing she knew where Haden had grown up. But the only indication that the general made was a narrowing of her eyes before she took a long sip from her goblet. Haden, avoiding eye contact with the steely-eyed woman, also took a drink, but a smaller one this time.

"I see," the king said with a weak smile. "Are you the one I'm going to wed?"

Haden spurt her wine across the table. Sayidi Brocaw gasped in horror while Haden heard the chuckling of Mal behind her.

Though she was thankful he was still there, she didn't appreciate him enjoying her embarrassment.

"Fetch someone to clean this mess up," Sayidi Brocaw ordered to a nearby guard before leaning down to the king.

"No, sire, you already had a *Sundarata Taashama* for your wife many years ago. Remember, you chose Queen Amina, Pahga rest her soul."

"Amina," the king repeated, his gaze seeming to reach into the past. "Are you sure? Was there another before her?"

Sayidi Brocaw stammered, "Well, sire, there was an incident, but you took care of that and chose Queen Amina."

The king hummed. "Amina. It has been quite some time since I heard her name. How did she pass? Did we have children?"

The whole room silenced once more as all eyes now turned to the masked prince. Sadness filled Haden's heart as the prince's shoulders drooped slightly. The king didn't remember he had a son.

"Ah, yes, sire, you have a son, the crown prince of Kadesh, who is here with us tonight," Sayidi Brocaw said, a nervous smile on his lips.

"Ah," the king replied, but he didn't sound convinced.

"Well," Sayidi Brocaw said, lifting his goblet in an attempt to salvage the meal. "Let us dine and celebrate Sayidi Miguel Salvar for catching a criminal and saving the pageant so that the prince may choose his future queen."

The rest of the table lifted their goblets then started in on the meal. But Haden couldn't concentrate on the delicious food. Everything she had been taught about Kadesh had been turned on its head.

Up until Mother had sent her into the enemy's hands as bait, Haden had been told that Kadesh's king was a cruel, evil, manipulative man. But what Haden saw before her were none of those things. In fact, the king seemed quite the opposite: definitely delusional and almost on the brink of death. So why did Mother hate him and Kadesh so?

Clearing her throat, Aunt Beta turned to the king. "Sire, now that we are gathered together, there are pressing matters we must discuss about the oncoming battle."

"Battle?" the king wheezed as he tried to skewer an olive with his fork. "What battle?"

"The battle with Tenton, my lord," Aunt Beta replied, her voice smooth as silk. "We have been at war with them for these past twenty years."

"Really?" the king questioned. A satisfied smile clung to his face as he successfully stabbed the olive. "And why is that?"

As the conversation continued, Haden became more and more horrified by the king's responses. This man had no idea what was happening outside of the food rolling on his plate much less a whole country. Haden shifted her gaze to Miguel, who looked equally horrified at the king's comments. She wished she could turn and speak to Mal, but with Aunt Beta here, knowing she would immediately report back to Mother once dinner was done, Haden didn't want to make Mal a target.

"We don't need to get into details about that, sire," Aunt Beta said with a smile and then something odd happened. A thin black string of smoke left the general's mouth straight into the king's ear. "What matters is the oncoming battle. I have finally procured the weapon we need to vanquish Tenton once and for all."

Chapter Twenty

Ida placed the Book of Ages on a stack of books as she hurried about the library. After they had discovered what millroot could do to someone with a gift from Tunri, she'd spent every free moment trying to find an antidote for it. Unfortunately, the Book of Ages didn't reveal everything to her at once, or there was nothing in there regarding millroot. So, Ida decided to research more about the herb in some less magical books.

Thankfully, this week's beauty enhancement treatment was all about training a future queen's mind to learn and think quickly. Though Ida had no intentions of marrying the prince of Kadesh, she did enjoy these lessons, hoping they would help make her a better duchess when she returned to Tenton.

If you return, she reminded herself.

Their group had yet to be caught, but she knew time was limited.

Raphael had received word from Jacques about the queen announcing the death of King Atol and Princess Haden, to which Raphael replied that Princess Haden was alive and well. Ida always hoped that there would be a separate note or something for her when Raphael received the coded messages from Jacques, but so far, there had been nothing.

He's just busy, she told herself, trying not to make an issue out of something when she couldn't speak to Jacques about it herself.

Ida knew Jacques' father was unwell and didn't have much time left. Jacques was probably tending to him and preparing to take over Delequa Iron. Ida knew it was a big responsibility for him, but still, she couldn't help but wish he had sent *some* regards or thoughts for her.

Ida glanced down at her ring finger, now bare to keep up with the ruse that she desired a chance at winning the future king's heart. Every night she would take the beautiful diamond off the chain from around her neck and wear it, praying for Tunri to keep them both safe so they could be together. But as time went by and Jacques never wrote anything for her, doubt started to creep in.

We're so young. Though we've known each other since before the Fortress, how well do we really "know" each other? Am I ready to be a wife? What if I'm not good enough?

Most of the time Ida was able to banish these thoughts, but lately it had become more difficult.

More of the contestants gathered in the library, filling every seat available. Thankfully, Rae was seated beside Ida on one side and Haden had slid into the chair on the other.

Ida was worried about the state of the princess. The dye in her hair was starting to lighten and the strands were a mess of tangles, barely concealed by the blue scarf slapped haphazardly on her head. Dark circles rimmed her eyes, and her overall posture seemed downtrodden. Rae had told Ida Haden had dinner with the prince last evening, so why was the princess' face so glum?

Ida turned toward the princess and asked, "Are you feeling okay, Haden?"

Haden lifted her tired eyes. "I'm not sure, Ida."

Ida cast a concerned glance at Rae. They had discussed the possibility of bringing Haden in on their plan to find Devora and Kanna. But since they weren't sure of the princess' intent in Kadesh, they decided against it.

Still, Ida worried for the princess. Even though Ida had always been an orphan, she knew her adoptive parents still loved her. She couldn't imagine what Haden was experiencing, her own mother pronouncing her dead.

Just as Ida was going to try to comfort Haden, Sayida Erza strode into the room. Since she was a child, Ida had admired Erza's poise and style. She was always in the finest clothes and had the most elegant hairstyles. And today wasn't any different.

Swathed in a deep teal fabric, Erza fluttered into the classroom, the tassels on the scarf covering her head shuddering with the movement.

Rae gave a soft gasp under her breath.

"What is it?" Ida whispered as Erza chatted with some of the young women seated at the front of the room.

"I knew I recognized her at the purification pools," Rae said, turning to Ida. "Sayida Erza came through Yekel when I sold scarves. She bought everything I had in that shade of teal. And that"—Rae motioned to the scarf with a hint of pride—"is one of my scarves."

Ida smiled and touched her own light-green scarf covering her curls. "You do a wonderful job, Rae. I love the one you gave me so much."

Rae blushed. "I just hope she doesn't recognize me. It's getting harder to stay quiet and blend in."

Ida nodded, feeling the same pressure. She was ready to scour the palace to try to find Devora. But Raphael said he hadn't heard anything else suspicious besides what he'd already told them about the millroot and the meat. And though the large quantities of meat did intrigue Ida, she hadn't the chance to look into it further.

"Good morning, future princesses of Kadesh," Erza called, gaining the attention of the women.

"Good morning, Sayida Erza," they called back.

Erza beamed at the response. "Since the criminal who tried to sabotage our pageant has been caught, Sayidi Tamor and the prince deemed it permissible to continue with our exercises."

Some of the girls in the front clapped while others whispered excitedly.

"Now," Erza continued, her tone serious. "This next exercise is not to be taken lightly. For it is after this week that you all will have your individual meetings with the prince."

Ida held her breath. She knew this was coming. But she hoped they would've found Devora and Kanna quickly and she would already be heading home to Tenton and Jacques before she had to lay eyes on the prince.

Home. Ida liked the sound of it. Although she had grown up in Lower Grenly and loved being with Ama and Jil, she always knew it wasn't where she was born. The Fortress had felt like the first home she had but that was only because of her friends. But where she really yearned to return to was with Jacques.

What would Ida even say to the prince when she was alone with him? "I'm sorry but I'm betrothed to another"? She still prayed something would happen before then.

Ida slid her gaze to Rae, watching her friend's fingers tap on the dark wooden table. Ida wondered if Rae dreaded the same thing. She never mentioned anything but, Ida knew Rae snuck out of their room in the evenings to see One Shot. She envied Rae who could see her loved one as much as she wanted, but Ida feared they would be caught if they weren't careful.

"Before you have your meeting with the crown prince, you must first read and memorize the Kadeshian code of matrimony. If recited perfectly, the prince will invite you to dine with him privately. There you may use whatever you deem necessary to impress him."

More giggles sounded from the room. Dread like a rock sank in Ida's stomach. She definitely did not want anything to do with a private dinner with the prince.

Ida glanced around as Sayida Erza began passing out scrolls with the Kadeshian code of matrimony written on them. While most of the young woman got to work right away on memorizing the passage, Haden stared at the rolled-up scroll as if it were a beast ready to attack her.

"Haden," Ida whispered, her worry for the princess increasing as she lightly touched Haden's hand. "What's wrong?"

Haden snapped out of her fear and plastered on a fake smile. "Nothing at all, Ida. I'm just not the best reader."

"I can help you," Rae said hastily around Ida's shoulder. "I mean, if you'd like."

"Uh, okay," Haden replied, her face unsure.

But Rae didn't seem to notice as she hurried and sat next to Haden. Ida smiled as she watched Rae coach Haden on what the symbols meant. She always knew Rae had a softer side, but the woman very rarely showed it to anyone other than One Shot.

A tied scroll was placed in front of Ida, causing her to glance up.

"Good morning, Ida," Erza said softly.

"Good morning, Sayida Erza," Ida replied, unsure in the woman's presence. Though she knew Erza chatted with all the young women participating in the pageant, Ida tried to make herself scarce when Erza was around.

But after a few moments had passed and Erza hadn't moved, Ida turned to her. "How are you today?"

"I am well, thank you," Erza replied, fidgeting with the last scroll in her hand. "And you?"

Ida furrowed her brow at Ezra's nervous tone. "I am well. Is there something you wish to speak with me about?"

Erza checked their immediate vicinity then leaned down to whisper, "I am worried for you and your friends. I cannot say more, but I wished to entrust this to you. Please be safe, Ida." Sayida Erza quickly placed the scroll that had been in her hand next to the other one in front of Ida and scurried back to the front of the library.

Ida frowned. *Does Erza know we're trying to find Devora and Kanna? Or is there something else afoot in this palace that worries her?*

Ida glanced up, wondering if Rae and Haden had noticed the odd behavior of their proctor. But after hearing Rae praise Haden for reading the symbols correctly, Ida knew she was the only one.

Staring down at the scrolls, Ida pushed away the matrimony code and carefully unrolled the other. Though the scroll was in the Kadeshian tongue, one which she easily understood and grew up speaking and reading, she still prayed to Tunri for guidance. Based on the look on Erza's face, whatever was in this scroll could get her in trouble.

Ida took one last look around the library. All the girls were focused on their scrolls, trying to memorize the matrimony code. With another breath, she began to read:

On the seventh day of the harvest season, every unmarried woman from sixteen summers to twenty-five summers must participate in the beauty pageant for Prince Redore IV. Failure to participate will result in an immediate tax increase for the eligible woman's family. Those that have daughters participating in the contest will receive a tax decrease and allowance each week their daughter continues to the next round.

Ida pursed her lips. She remembered hearing about the *Sundarata Taashamas* in the past; her and the other girls in the orphanage always dreamed of being old enough to be chosen as the future queen of Kadesh. But she never knew that there was a penalty if a family didn't send their daughter. The information was interesting, but Ida still was unsure as to why Sayida Erza wanted her to read this. But still Ida read on:

This year the competition will not only be open to women of Kadeshian nationality, but Tentonian, as well.

At this, Ida's brows rose. From what she knew, the contest was only for Kadeshian women. Why did the kingdom decide to open it to Tenton? Ida suddenly realized this was before the war had started between the two nations. She glanced up at the date to realize it was almost twenty years ago when the king had chosen his bride. So, what happened during the pageant that struck the two nations as enemies?

Ida's gaze flitted over the next section explaining when and where the eligible ladies should be dropped off. But then something snagged Ida's attention. While the beginning of the edict was written in flowing cursive, a section at the bottom had tight, straight script. Ida unrolled more of the scroll to find the section was a list of names.

Participants in the pageant?

Scanning the list, Ida stopped upon the name *Erza Rundisha.*

Erza was a part of the pageant. But how does that connect to me?

But then Ida ran across another name: *Vera Beta.*

Ida withheld her gasp. General Beta was in the pageant? She obviously wasn't chosen since she was now one of Kadesh's generals, but did she still hold scorn toward the king for not choosing her?

Ida wished Erza would come back so she could ask her these questions but didn't want to make a scene of calling her over. Sighing, Ida tried to file the questions away to ask Erza later before turning back to the scroll. As she filed through the rest of the names, Ida let out a gasp as she reached the end of the list.

Leza Santorno

A few of the girls around her glanced up from their scrolls, glaring at Ida. One even shushed her and buried her nose back in the scroll. But Ida couldn't take her eyes off the name. Queen Leza, who has been the queen of Tenton these past twenty years, was a participant of the pageant to become the queen of Kadesh.

The questions Ida formerly had now doubled. This meant that Erza, General Beta, and Queen Leza had all competed to win the heart of the former prince. Did they know each other? Were they friends or foes? And how did it all fit together with what was happening between the two nations now?

Ida was bursting to tell Rae, but her friend was still coaching Haden on the scroll. Biting her lip, Ida did her best to stand as quietly as she could. Rae looked up at her quizzically, but Ida just hurried toward Sayida Erza at the front of the library.

"Excuse me, Sayida," Ida said with a curtsy. "I have a few questions regarding the wording of the scroll." If Ida had learned anything at the Fortress and Vlacklear it was that people were always listening, even if it didn't seem like it. Thankfully, Erza understood her meaning.

"Of course, dear. Let us step over here to where the light is more prominent. My old eyes don't see as well as they used to."

Guiding Ida away from the listening ears, Erza stopped in front of a large window set in the back left of the library. Though they were still within the vicinity of the others, one would have to be close to hear their conversation.

As soon as Erza turned toward Ida, Ida exclaimed, "You knew the general and the queen when you were young?"

Erza brought a finger to her lips. "Yes, we were all participants in the pageant for Prince Redore's hand. I wasn't sure you would believe me, considering how terrible I've been, so I wanted you to have proof first."

"Sayida, I did love Josef, but I was only a child then. My heart still feels the pain of the loss of his life, but I no longer hold contempt for you," Ida replied.

Tears filled Erza's gaze as she reached out and hugged Ida. "You are a treasure, Ida. Truly set apart from the others. The prince would be lucky to have your hand marriage."

Ida reciprocated the hug. She wished she could tell Erza she was already betrothed, but she kept that detail to herself. "So, why did you want me to know this?" Ida asked. While she did find it interesting, she still couldn't connect all the dots.

Erza nodded. "As you know, I have been happily married to Josef's father, Jarrick, all these years. The prince did not choose me and for that I am grateful. The prince also did not choose General Beta. But there is one he did choose."

Ida stifled her gasp. "The queen," she whispered.

"Yes," Erza said, her voice so low, Ida could barely hear her. "Though it has been stricken from almost every history of Kadesh, the prince's first wife was Queen Leza. I felt prompting that I must tell you this knowledge."

Ida couldn't stop her jaw from dropping. But when she was about to ask another question, an eruption of screams filled the library.

Chapter Twenty-One

Jacques, Delequa Manor, Tinwa

Jacques stared at his father's record books and sighed. It was horrifying how long Duke Emmanual Delequa had been smuggling iron into Kadesh. How could he have given so much without being caught? Jacques despised that the wealth his family now held was because his father was a traitor to his country.

Running a hand through his hair, Jacques stood. It only felt like a few days ago where he had proposed to the woman he loved and had desired for years. Things were happy for but a blip before his life turned on its head again. Now his father was gone, Tenton was rallying its troops to send to Kadesh, and his betrothed was in the enemy nation with his estranged brother.

The latter bit of his circumstances made him uneasy. Though Jacques knew Raphael would protect Ida—once Jacques had informed him Ida was his future wife—he still didn't like the fact that she was in Kadesh in the first place. If Jacques hadn't had to take over the responsibilities of Delequa Iron, he could have been with her.

Glancing at himself in the mirror, Jacques noted his fairly pale skin, light eyes, and yellow-blond hair. He frowned. He would have stuck out like a sore thumb in Kadesh. Even though he knew Ida could blend in better, he still wasn't happy about it. And while he asked Raphael for word about her—how she was doing, if she mentioned him at all—he hardly heard anything back. Jacques was half tempted to sneak into the country and confront his older brother himself. He almost did one night, the night after his father's death. When the weight of the entire company fell on his shoulders. He hadn't assisted with the family business in years, but as he read through his father's parchments, the inner workings of Delequa Iron came back to him almost as if he had never left at all.

Unfortunately, the memories of how terrible his father had been to him also returned.

Your work is sloppy and insufficient, Jacques. Do better. If you're going to take the reins of this company, I expect you to be the best. Unlike your useless brother who abandoned his responsibilities and his family.

Jacques winced at the memory. If he hadn't seen the life drain from his father's eyes, he would've expected him to be right in this room, chastising him like he always had.

A knock sounded on the door. Dread wrapped around Jacques' spine. The queen had requested a meeting with the duke right when the illness took a turn for the worst. Jacques didn't give the messenger all the details, but he had bought himself enough time that no one suspected his father's death. Yet.

He knew he couldn't keep up the ruse forever, but he had to try. Once the queen knew Duke Delequa was dead and Jacques was his successor, she would focus on him, and she already had all the leverage she needed.

Not only did the queen hold his best friend under a curse, but she had also been present at the trial where Matthias allowed Ida to stay in Tenton only if they wed within the month.

Jacques paced around the room, trying to make it sound like he was hurrying in what he was doing to open the door, when really, he was panicking. As the days passed and Ida didn't return, Jacques worried more and more about whether they would actually be married in time. If it were him, he would've married her first and then she could've gone to Kadesh, just to be at ease that they would be together.

But Ida wanted to wait. And while he understood and respected her choice, once again, he didn't like it. Unfortunately, the people around him didn't seem to care what Jacques liked and disliked, and he knew the queen would be no different.

A knock sounded again, this time harder, and Jacques stopped his pacing. He would have to face the queen and her demands sooner or later.

Steeling his spine, Jacques did his best to impersonate Matthias' indifferent yet cold stare as he opened the door.

"Can I help—"

"How long were you expecting us to wait out here?" Nadia asked.

Jacques blinked as she pushed past him, shoving a heavy item covered in cloth into his hands. Jacques released the knob and held the object with both hands.

"Hello, Duke Delequa," Reese said, causing Jacques' gaze to shoot up to the tall, thin woman.

In the same trial that he was given permission to wed Ida, Reese and Hestia Sandje proved their father was avoiding taxes. His company, Sandje Textiles, was taken from him and given to his twin daughters. Jacques had seen neither of the twins nor Nadia since they had all discussed their missions with Matthias.

"I thought the queen—" he started but was interrupted again.

"Was on her way to make her demands?" Reese finished as she, too, pushed past Jacques and into his office. "She was, or at least one of her little pawns was."

"Don't worry, we took care of him for you," Hestia chimed in. She gave Jacques a wink as she came into his office uninvited as well.

"Uh," Jacques said, still holding the heavy item Nadia placed in his hands. "Is there anyone else here that I should know about? Where's Charles?"

Unbeknownst to Jacques, his younger cousin, Charles, and Hestia had been secretly married, fulfilling the marriage agreement that Reese had signed with her father, the former Duke Sandje. Jacques wished he could've attended the wedding and still hadn't scolded Charles enough about it.

"He's at our manor, making sure nothing happens to all the work we've done while we're gone," Hestia replied, sitting on the settee that butted up against the window on the far wall.

It pained Jacques to know his cousin was more comfortable at Sandje Manor than the home he grew up in, but he understood. While Duke Delequa was harsh on Jacques, he hardly ever noticed Charles. Jacques wished he could go back and mend the relationship with his cousin, but he feared he was too late. He hoped that one day, the Sandje and Delequa businesses could align and work together to restore Tenton.

"I see." Jacques strode to his desk and heaved the heavy object on it, thankful to be free of its weight. "What are you all doing here?"

"Wow, thank you, sir, we missed you too," Nadia snorted, taking a bowl of walnuts he had on his desk. Reaching into her pocket, she pulled out something that resembled a metal nutcracker and started littering his clean rug with walnut shells.

"I didn't mean that rudely," he said as he marched forward and took one of the cracked nuts out of her hand. "But I thought I was about to be obliterated by the monarchy. I'm glad to see you all."

Alive and well, he wanted to add but decided against it.

He had grown so used to worrying about Matthias' well-being that it was comforting to have some friends that weren't as flirtatious with death.

"Yes, well, we haven't had the easiest time warding off Father's odd business partners," Reese replied, taking a seat in the plush chair next to the fireplace. She slid the metal beads on her abacus back and forth, but not as wildly as she used to while in the Fortress.

Jacques stared at the empty fireplace, a heap of ashes where sturdy logs of wood should be. He had only lit it once and that was before Father passed. Now that he had guests, he wondered if he should ignite the wood to take the chill out of the room. He wished Ida was here; he never knew what to do in these situations. She was naturally hospitable, and Jacques was ready to do whatever she said.

"And by odd she means extremely shady," Hestia added, plopping down next to Nadia.

Jacques watched as Nadia offered Hestia a walnut, which Hestia happily took and munched on. How far these young women had come in such a short amount of time. From scared recruits of His Majesty's Army to powerful forces. They had overcome and conquered many trials while he was still drowning in his past, not knowing what to do next. If only he could receive a sign that pointed him in the right direction.

"As to why we're here," Reese said, straightening in her chair. "We heard about the former duke and foremost wished to give our condolences."

Jacques' face faltered. "Ah, yes, thank you. Though I wish word wasn't spreading so quickly." It would only be a matter of time now before the queen threatened him to make her weapons of war.

"The second reason why we're here is this," Reese motioned to the heavy object Jacques had placed on his desk.

He strode forward, realizing he had forgotten about the object Nadia handed him. "What is it?"

Although it was still wrapped in cloth, it was an odd shape, something Jacques couldn't identify.

Nadia popped up from the settee and dusted the rest of her walnut shells from her lap onto the floor before she strode over to Jacques' desk. "When you all went off to become the leaders of your companies, I went back to Totem where the last Tinkers are," Nadia began.

Jacques nodded, remembering Matthias telling him about Totem. It was an idea the general had right after he had become the king's and queen's attack dog. Totem was a hidden place of refuge for those who were arrested unjustly by the kingdom. Though Jacques knew Matthias could not save all who were killed unfairly, the general did his best to save as many lives as he could under the corrupt monarchy.

"While I was there, Rae's dad and I were working on this." With a proud look, Nadia pulled the cloth off the small device.

Fascinated, Jacques strode toward it. The device was unlike anything he had ever seen. Four metal bars fused together in a pyramid shape. Within them lay a series of concentric rings. Though, it looked like the metal they were made of was different than the exterior poles. It was shining and metallic, not unlike imperial opal.

"What is it?"

"This is the answer to your dilemma," Reese replied, standing from her chair. "As someone who understands the weight of the family business, I was seventy-point-six percent sure you were waffling on how to proceed after your father's death."

Jacques' lips formed a line. Was he that transparent? While he always knew Delequa Iron would be his once his father passed, Reese had to fight for her father's company. And fight she did.

"It's not an insult, sir," Hestia added in quickly. "We just understand the burden and wish to relieve some of it. Reese and I have each other to share the business with and with Ida not here, we wanted to help."

Jacques nodded. Every day Ida was gone left a bigger void in his heart. But as he glanced back at the three women, he was thankful they hadn't forgotten him.

"Plus, this will help with saving Devora and Kanna too," Nadia added.

Jacques' interest piqued. "And how is that?"

"We tested the device on several pieces of imperial opal we found in the hills of Snoken—or rather, Rae and One Shot found. And each result was the same." Then Nadia tapped the shining rings with her fingers, causing them to spin. Faster and faster, they rotated until they no longer resembled rings but an orb. A shining light sped from the orb, zinging into the far wall.

Jacques shouted, placing his hands over his head. A scorched scent filled the room and Jacques hoped Nadia didn't just start the fire that would burn his family home to the ground. But when he looked up, he saw nothing but a black mark on the wall.

"What was the result?" he asked, confused as to how this was going to help him.

"This device nullifies imperial opal," Reese filled in, coming beside him.

"What?" He gaped. Spinning to Nadia, he asked, "Is this true?"

Nadia stopped the rotating rings of the orb and nodded. "I've felt the effects of it myself. We tested it on several Tinkers in Totem, and they all felt the difference before and after the imperial opal was affected by the device."

"We're assuming that wherever Devora and Kanna have been taken, they will most likely be chained with imperial opal, just like Devora was after the Battle of Edo and Ida was in the Tower," Hestia mentioned as she admired a miniature golden statue of a horse.

Jacques winced at the memory, still hating himself for not saving Ida from Sergio's lies that led to her being imprisoned in the Tower.

"That's a good assumption, but we would have to get this device to wherever they are, which we are hoping is Kadesh, but that's not certain," he added. "And, if what I've heard about imperial opal is true, wouldn't we need something bigger than this?" He frowned at the device. As impressive as it was, if

Kadesh had anything like the statue from Yekel he had heard about, this was not going to be enough.

Jacques sighed and turned to Reese. He hated being the one with the heavy hand, but without Matthias here, someone had to do it.

"And that's where you come in," Nadia said with a grin. She ticked off her fingers as she spoke. "First, you're already the head of Delequa Iron, meaning you have access to all the metal we would need to create a bigger version of this. Second, we know that Tristan, Ida, Rae, and One Shot are there. If we can contact them, we can get the device in."

Jacques sighed. "Though Ida and the others are at the palace, Tristan left them as soon as they crossed the border."

Nadia paled. "What? What happened to him?"

Jacques shook his head. "They don't know, but they're assuming he had alternative reasons for wanting to return to Kadesh so badly."

Nadia's face fell for a moment before she clasped her hands into fists and shook it off. "No matter, this device will help. Rae mentioned to me before that the Kadeshians spoke of a statue of Pahga in Renta, the capital city of Kadesh, that was identical to the one in the Temple in Yekel. From what Rae heard, it was probably made of imperial opal, as well. The statue in Yekel was able to draw out the souls of young women because of the power of the stone. Even if the statue is not being used on Kanna and Devora, we can still save others from having their lives taken from them."

Pausing, Nadia concluded, "If you provide the iron needed to make a bigger weapon, we—as in me and the other Tinkers—will create it and get it to Kadesh."

Jacques liked the plan and the device, but there were many uncertainties. Where was Matthias? He knew the queen had the general on a short leash, especially since she declared revenge against Kadesh for "killing" the king and princess. Thankfully, it took more than a few days to prepare the troops to march on the enemy nation. But Jacques knew time was running short. Although this plan wasn't perfect, it was the only one they had.

"Okay," he said and all three of the women's faces brightened. "But because of our lack of reliable contacts in Kadesh, I have a better guise as to how we can move the device without anyone knowing what it really is."

Chapter Twenty-Two

Haden, Radaa Kingdom, Kadesh

As soon as Sayida Erza explained the next phase of the contest, Haden snapped out of her daze.

Reading? Why would the prince give a test about reading?

But after she pondered it more she assumed, as queen, his future wife would read and write edicts by his side. Haden wanted to groan but held it in.

She had tossed and turned all night after dinner with Miguel, King Redore IV, Aunt Beta and the prince. Aunt Beta had announced a horrific plan to destroy all Tentonians that passed into Renta. Apparently, she had been crafting a device that could instantly take the life of the soldiers without drawing blood or without any harm befalling the Kadeshian army. Haden expected the king to ask more questions about the device, but he continued to hum and eat his food. And the masked prince stayed silent, as usual. Aunt Beta went on to explain that the device had already been tested in Yekel before it was recaptured by Tenton, but the results were excellent.

Haden's stomach twisted more and more as Aunt Beta continued to describe the massacre that would ensue. But what horrified Haden the most was the look of delight on the general's face.

Haden shook her head, trying to focus on the scroll before her and not on everything she learned the night before. She wished someone would've said something to stop Aunt Beta, but no one said a word. And who was she, the useless princess of Tenton, to say anything? Would she too be killed when Aunt Beta used her mysterious device?

Haden didn't know what to think, but she knew she had to come up with a plan. The king was obviously useless, but she still held hope for the masked prince. Maybe, if she could read the script in front of her, he would be impressed enough to invite her to dinner alone and *then* they could come up with a plan to stop this encroaching battle. Wasn't twenty years long enough for a war? Couldn't Tenton and Kadesh find some sort of peace?

Haden heard Ida ask her something along the lines of "Are you okay?"

"Um, yeah, I'm just not the best reader."

"I can help you," Rae said immediately. She stood and walked over to Haden.

Uncertainty rolled across Haden's skin as Rae plopped down next to her.

Why does she want to help me? She hasn't been cruel to me, but I know she's been watching me and I don't know why.

"Did you learn Kadeshian at the palace?" Rae asked quietly as she unrolled her own scroll.

Haden nodded, not desiring to explain how long it had taken her to understand the symbols and what they meant.

"It took me a while, but since Kadesh invaded Yekel, it was either learn or allow people to take advantage of you." Rae shrugged. "I had to teach myself a lot. Well, I did have a good friend help me out for a little while. I still get some of the symbols confused though."

Haden froze and turned to Rae, remembering what Aunt Beta had said about Yekel at dinner. "You're from Yekel?"

Rae paused, her gaze suspicious. "Yes."

Haden held her breath, trying to decide whether she should continue or not.

"What do you know about Yekel that's frightened you?" Rae asked, lowering her voice.

Taking a quick look around, Haden ducked her head. "I'm not sure if I can say much here, but was there a device there that could take away life without drawing blood?"

Rae blanched, confirming Haden's fears. Swallowing, Rae asked, "How did you hear about that?"

Haden sunk farther behind the scroll as Ida stood and hurried to the front of the library. "Apparently Aunt—General Beta has one, another device, here. They want to use it on the Tentonians in the next battle."

Haden thought back to when she received the genealogy scroll from the mustached man in the library. He had said something about an interesting read her mother had in her desk and encouraged Haden to find it; that it may save thousands of lives.

While Haden wasn't sure whether to trust the mustached man, she decided she didn't want to be kept in the dark any longer. So, while Mother was out, Haden had snuck into her room, careful to only move around what she could easily put back. It was in the third drawer of Mother's desk where Haden found it, the driving force that brought her to Kadesh. Of course, once she read the genealogy scroll and discovered she had an uncle in Kadesh, she'd already decided to leave the palace. But what sent her into a frenzy packing her things were the horrible depictions of the statue of the Goddess Pahga on the scroll, stealing the life force out of the people below.

"There are more?" Rae cried, causing the contestants around them to send nasty glares their way. Rae rubbed her eyes. "I knew there was one more here in Renta, but you're saying there's more than one? How many?"

Haden bit her lip. Maybe she had said too much. She probably shouldn't have told Rae at all, but after hearing she was from Yekel, Haden had needed to confirm what Aunt Beta said was true. Now that she knew the truth, Haden was even more terrified.

"I have a scroll with the plans. I don't know how many exactly," Haden confessed.

"I need to tell Ben," Rae whispered under her breath.

"Your guard?"

Rae lowered her voice even more "Yes. He's my—"

"Betrothed?" Haden asked with a smirk. She had seen them very close, very often.

Rae blushed. "No, but he can help us." She glanced around the room. "Not now. Later. We need to learn this now, or at least pretend to, and we can talk later when it's safer."

Haden nodded. Though she expected to feel nervous or worried about divulging more information to Rae, she was actually excited. For years she had been put to the side, labeled as useless and not worth the time. But Rae saw her as an equal, someone of value.

"There was actually something I hoped to talk to you about too, but also, not here."

Haden's brows rose with interest, but Rae shook her head and started reading out the symbols.

Doing her best to focus, Haden concentrated on Rae's voice while reading the symbols. Having someone read out loud to her while she read was immensely more helpful than her trying to sound out the symbols alone. How she wished someone would've done this with her early on, before Madeline finally helped her. She would've been able to read more clearly in half the time it took her.

As Haden was trying to figure out why the symbol for love always looked similar to the symbol for cake, an odd smell infiltrated the air. Haden couldn't place the smell but when Rae noticed it too, Haden knew she wasn't crazy.

All of a sudden, a cloud of white dust encompassed the entire library. The toxic air stung Haden's eyes, causing them to burn and blur with tears. The other contestants of the pageant screamed, coughing and wheezing as the white cloud engulfed the library.

"Rae," Haden coughed, squinting through the cloud. "Where are you?"

A hand reached out and grabbed Haden's. Rae appeared with her scarf around her nose and mouth. Though her eyes were red and teary too, Rae was faring a lot better than the others.

She offered Haden the other side of her scarf, which Haden hastily placed up to her nose and mouth. Clasping Haden's hand tight, Rae hurried out of the library. Thankfully, many of the other contestants had broken free of the poisonous cloud as well, including Ida, who was waiting outside with Sayida Erza, Ben and Mal.

Ben had already been running toward the room when Rae and Haden appeared, scooping Rae up and carrying her to clean air. While Haden thought the moment was sweet, she wished she had someone to carry her to safety too.

"Away from the library, Haden," Mal said, grabbing her hand and hurrying her toward cleaner air. "Whatever is in there is poisonous."

Haden swooned at the sight of Mal, his furrowed brow and strong chin making her knees weak. Even though Mal didn't sweep her off her feet, she was thankful he was there all the same.

"All contestants leave the library!" Sayidi Tamor's voice boomed through the hall. "Guards, guide your contestants back to their rooms immediately. That is an order."

Sayida Erza quickly ushered all the girls out, trying to make sure all were accounted for.

"Let's go," Mal said, squeezing her hand tighter as they hurried down the hall.

Eventually, they caught up to Ida, Rae and Ben, who was just placing Rae down. Haden's heart warmed at the sight of the trio. They felt like good friends already. She decided she didn't care about the prince and his fancy room for her, she wanted to stay with Ida and Rae tonight, especially if there was another perpetrator trying to sabotage the pageant.

As Haden went to join the others, Mal spun her around. His warm hands cupped her face, his eyes searching her own.

"Are you all right? What happened in there?"

Haden found she liked Mal's hands holding her face. "I-I'm okay," she wheezed, the effects of the toxic gas still in her lungs. She chuckled at the sound. "Just a little hoarse."

"We were reading the matrimony edict when a cloud of white gas consumed the entire library," Rae answered, her voice sounding like a frog as well.

Haden realized she was still holding Rae's cerulean scarf in her hands. She studied the intricate design, realizing that the scarf she wore was identical to Rae's. Haden's brows rose, her eyes darting to Rae.

Rae watched her, a nervous look on her face. The vendor in Yekel, the one Haden had bought the scarf from, was Rae. Is that why Rae had been so standoffish with Haden? She recognized her before but didn't want to say anything?

"I thought the criminal who poisoned the pools was caught," Ben said, anger lacing his tone as he kept his arm tight around Rae. "Why was there another attack? Weren't you supposed to be watching the girls?" He shot the accusation at Mal.

Haden took a step back at the ferocity in Ben's face. She had never seen any side of him other than the loving looks he gave Rae. But Mal's reaction was the opposite of Haden's.

Releasing Haden's hand, he straightened his shoulders and took a step forward. "It was not on my watch this happened. I happen to care very much for the well-being of our girls as well."

Haden's heart skipped a beat. *Our girls.*

"Raphael had told me he would take the library watch just this morning," Mal continued, the fire in his eyes dissipating.

They all turned to Ida, who looked just as confused as every-one else. "I'm not sure where he is," she confessed, seeming to grow smaller. "He dropped me off earlier and said he'd be right outside if I needed anything."

Haden furrowed her brows. Raphael had been an astute guard to Ida ever since the pageant began. He was always right by her side. Had something happened to him for him not to be present?

"Wait," Rae said, taking a step away from Ben's protective arm. "Why weren't you guarding me?" She turned to Mal. "Where were you two?"

Haden watched the two men share a glance at each other and she knew that Rae had seen it too. They were both hiding something.

"Rae, I—"

"There has been an enormous turnout for young ladies enter-ing the pageant this year," Mal cut him off, giving Ben a warning look. "With so many young ladies, Sayidi Tamor asked me to recruit some of the other guards to watch other contestants on different shifts."

Rae's gaze narrowed and Haden recognized the same sus-picious feeling rising in herself, as well. Yet even though she was suspicious of the two men, Haden had no grounds to figure out if Mal was telling the truth. Rae, however, had no problem bringing up the issue.

Spinning to Ben, she questioned, "Is that true?"

Haden thought she would see Ben panic and dive on his knees, begging Rae for forgiveness. But he only nodded his head slowly and said, "Yes, it's true. Today was the first day we were trying out our new schedule."

"Yes," Mal added with an easy smile. "It has been quite a busy day."

"Hmm," Rae said, studying Ben's face. "Well, thankfully, I was watching mine and Haden's backs or else we could be like them."

She pointed across the large courtyard to where the palace physicians were doing their best to save the lives of those who had consumed the poison from the library. But, judging by the women's still lifeless forms on the ground, their attempts were proving futile.

"Rae," Ben said again, his shoulders sagging in defeat.

Rae held up her hand and Haden thought her face would hold anger and fury, but instead she just looked sad. "Please continue with your busy day. I am capable of protecting Haden, Ida, and myself without assistance." She spun around and stomped down the hall.

Ben sighed as he watched her go.

"Just let her cool off," Ida suggested with a smile. "Maybe she just needs some time to talk things out." She then looked at Haden. "Are you coming to our room tonight, Haden?"

Haden glanced over at Mal, who watched her with expectation. But she wasn't sure what he expected. All she knew was that she had wanted to discuss more about the statues with Rae, and Rae wished to discuss something important with her too. Those two facts were enough for Haden to make her decision.

"Yes, I'm coming."

As she started to follow Ida, Mal reached out and grabbed her hand. "Will I see you later?"

Haden looked into his pleading eyes and wasn't sure what to think. "Maybe tomorrow would be better." She gave him a weak smile.

Mal sucked in a breath. "Can I at least escort you to your shared room now? Though I would defend the other contestants if need be, you are my sole responsibility."

Haden's stomach twisted at his gentle persistence. She cast a look over her shoulder, seeing that Ben had given Rae half a hallway length of space before following her.

Hopefully all will be well between them soon.

Turning back to Mal, she replied, "Okay, that seems fair."

The two walked in silence. Though Haden wanted to know where Mal was when the attack at the library occurred, she desired to feel close to him as before. It seemed like they would start to get to know each other better, then something would always happen to push them farther apart again.

Is this Tunri's way of warning me? Should I stay away from Mal? Haden didn't know what to think.

As their steps sounded along the stone ground, Haden wondered if Mal was also quiet because of the dinner last night. He had been quick to drop her off at her room after dinner and also at the library this morning. Was it because the crown prince was potentially interested in Haden? Or was it because of Aunt Beta's horrible device? Or was it neither of those and simply that he decided he didn't enjoy Haden's company anymore?

Haden frowned at the thought. They hadn't known each other long, but she was happy Mal was her guard. Maybe something had happened in his personal life to upset him.

The door to the girls' room came into view. Ben stood just to the side of it, his gaze hard as he stared out into the courtyard. The crowd of contestants had dispersed from the other side and the physicians seemed to have taken those affected by the gas to the infirmary. All was still save for the soft burbling of the fountain in the center of the courtyard.

Haden fiddled with her fingers as she and Mal strode closer to the door. If she was going to clear the air between them, now was the time.

"Mal," Haden said, stopping once they were within three feet of the door.

"Haden—" Mal started at the same time.

They both stopped then smiled.

"You first," she offered.

He shook his head. "I wish to apologize. As much as I despised Ben's accusation, he was right. I shouldn't have left your well-being in anyone else's hands but my own." Mal reached out and brushed his fingers against hers, sending chills racing up her spine.

Haden sucked in a breath. "Promise you'll be there next time, and you're forgiven."

Mal's eyes flashed with a mischievous look before he reached for her hand and brought it to his lips. Placing a light kiss on her hand, he said, "Always, my princess."

Heat raced up her neck as she let him draw her close. She'd overheard the maids talking about moments like this, when a suitor fancies you and is about to make his confession of love. But Haden had just met Mal. He couldn't love her already, could he? And what would she do about it? She didn't even know if she loved herself, much rather love someone else.

"What was it you were going to ask me?" Mal asked, his voice husky.

"Um," Haden stammered, her thoughts fuzzy and suddenly focused on Mal's lips being so close to her own. "Oh, yes. You've been quiet since last night at dinner. Is everything all right?" There were many times in her life where Haden wished she would've kept her mouth shut and this was one of them. At the mention of the dinner with the crown prince, the soft moment between them dissolved. The desire in Mal's eyes subsided and he took a step away from Haden.

Why did I ask anything at all?

Mal looked down at her, his usually playful smile replaced with firm lips. "It is not, Haden. But there is nothing I can do about it."

"Oh, I'm sorry," she said, fidgeting with her hands, wishing she were back in his arms instead of two feet away. "Is there anything I can do to help?"

Softening, Mal smiled again. He reached out and tucked a piece of her muddy-brown hair behind her ear. "There is, but I don't wish for you to do it unless you choose to."

Haden frowned at the cryptic statement. "What does that mean?"

"Come on," he said, gently taking her arm. "I can't get you your dinner until you're secured in your room. And I bet you're hungry after not eating so much last night and earlier today." He gave her a knowing look.

Haden's cheeks heated. Even though she thought he was being distant, he was still looking out for her.

"I am a little hungry," she confessed as she walked in step with him.

Mal nodded to Ben who gave a stiff nod in return.

"Thank you for escorting me back," Haden said, wishing this moment could continue.

"Always," he replied. "I'll leave your dinner with Ben then bid you good night, my princess." With a stiff bow, Mal turned and marched down the hall.

After he rounded the corner, Ben asked, "So he knows?"

Haden shifted her gaze from Mal to Ben. He leaned against the wall with his arms crossed over his chest. An intense gaze consumed his dark eyes, and Haden wasn't sure if she wanted to engage in conversation with him. The only inviting thing about him was the orange scarf he clutched in his fist.

"He saw me before I dyed my hair," Haden confessed.

Ben grunted, keeping his eyes trained on the courtyard. "Smart guy."

Haden nodded and started for the room when she said, "Is there anything you want me to tell Rae?"

At the question, Ben darted his dark gaze to Haden's face. "She knows I'm here. I'll wait until she's ready to talk. Thank you though."

Haden nodded again and turned back to the door once more. But there was one more thing she wished to say. "For what it's worth, I know how much you care for her, and I only wish someone would care for me the same way."

Ben smirked. "I think you may already have that, princess. Good night."

"Good night, Ben."

As Haden entered the room, she released a heavy sigh. When she decided to come to Kadesh to find Miguel and expose her mother's destructive plots, she never thought about falling in love. But was that what this was? She hardly knew Mal; how could she love him? Though, she couldn't deny that she was attracted to him, and it seemed that he felt the same way.

"Are you okay?" Ida asked after Haden stayed staring at the closed door.

Turning around, Haden smoothed out her mud-colored hair. Her ruse would be up soon unless she could find more dye. "Yes, I'm okay. There's just a lot happening."

Ida nodded, her face gentle with empathy and understanding. "Why don't you come sit with us?" She patted the place beside her on her bed. "I think there's a lot that needs to be talked about."

Haden's gaze shifted to Rae, who was sitting next to Ida with a pillow squished between her arms. Her eyes were red and teary, and Haden knew it wasn't from the poisonous gas in the library.

"Is he still out there?" Rae asked, her voice hoarse.

Sitting next to Ida, Haden nodded.

Relief crossed Rae's face. "I've been on edge since before we got here, and it's just gotten worse. I'm worried I've taken too many of my hardships and placed them on him." Rae paused and squeezed the orange pillow. "I'm worried it'll be too much one day, and he'll leave," she whispered.

Ida wrapped her thin arm around Rae's shoulders, bringing her close. "I don't think that's ever going to happen. I haven't known One Shot long, but I know he would do anything to stay with you."

Rae sniffed and nodded, but tears still misted her red eyes.

One Shot? Haden thought, piecing together they were talking about Ben. *What an odd name.*

"He seems very dedicated and very much in love," Haden offered, praying she didn't make anything else worse tonight.

Rae lifted her gaze, surprise in her eyes. "Love? You think so?"

Haden furrowed her brows. Did Rae not see how Ben followed her every move? That she was his sunshine and light? How could it be so obvious to Haden and not Rae?

Taking a breath, Haden said, "If I had a man who would wait for me outside my door until I was ready to talk to him, I would never let him go."

All Haden desired was to be loved for who she was. Not who Mother wanted her to be or who Tenton wished her to be, but who *she* wanted to be. And Haden could very clearly see that Ben loved Rae wholeheartedly.

Tears ran down Rae's cheeks and Haden panicked. "Oh no, I'm sorry."

Rae shook her head and smiled. "No, you're right. He's wonderful. I just have a lot of healing left to do." She started to stand. "I need to talk to him."

Ida nodded and placed her hand on Rae's. "I agree you need to talk with him. But before you do that, because that may be a long conversation"—Ida smiled mischievously—"I think it's time we all say why we're really here. I believe we're all heading toward the same goal, but if we're not honest, we won't be able to achieve anything."

Haden swallowed. She wanted to trust the two girls but fear remained. Fear that they would turn on her, fear that they would tell Mother—if Aunt Beta hadn't already—and Haden would really become the deceased princess of Tenton.

Trust, her heart told her.

Haden never had issues following her heart over her head. She always chose her gut feeling over thinking things through, but still she hesitated.

"How about I start?" Ida offered with a kind smile.

Haden nodded as Rae sat back down, casting a longing gaze at the door.

Ida started by recounting her time at the Fortress, how she was sent there because of the switch in categories for the Categorization Call and how she met Devora, who she later found out was a Seer. Haden had met the Seer when she and Captain Blake had rescued her from the Kadeshians at the Battle of Edo. However, Haden had no idea the trials the young woman had gone through before entering battle. Haden was impressed but became angry when Ida explained that Devora was framed with the princess' capture and wanted for treason.

"Mother," Haden muttered under her breath.

She knew Mother desired individuals with gifts given by Tunri, but she never thought the queen would sink so low.

Ida finished by saying she was sent to Vlacklear shortly after Devora was sent to the battlefield.

"I come in next," Rae picked up, sniffing before she delved into her story.

If Haden had been horrified before, it was nothing compared to how she felt when Rae explained how she and Devora met. Though she danced around the details, Haden understood Rae had overcome much hardship in her past and she understood why Rae was having a difficult time fully trusting her heart to Ben.

"The statue you spoke of earlier, there was one in Yekel. I don't know how, but the imperial opal statue of Pahga was able to take the souls from young women when they were offered as a sacrifice."

Haden felt the blood from her face drain as she recounted the drawings on the scroll from Mother's desk. That had to be what Aunt Beta was planning. But how had she been able to procure such a device?

A knock sounded at the door, making Haden jump.

"That's probably our dinner," Rae said. She cast a look at Ida, as if asking for permission.

Ida's shoulders dropped in defeat. "There is more we should discuss, but I understand you can't focus with him out there."

Haden was curious as Ida clutched her necklace.

"We'll be here when you're finished," Ida added and before the sentence was out of her mouth, Rae was already hurrying toward the door.

An exchange of murmurs occurred before Rae took the tray of food and placed it inside. And before Haden could blink, Rae disappeared out the door.

Chapter Twenty-Three

Rae, Radaa Kingdom, Kadesh

"Your food is going to get cold," Ben told Rae as she stood in the doorway holding the tray.

Rae shifted her stance, not feeling this awkward and ashamed in front of Ben since he thought she had murdered the Wizard Wankle.

"Have you eaten?" she asked quietly.

Ben's eyes were hard, his face an unreadable mask. "I'll be fine. Go and eat."

Rae bit her lip. She recognized his look. He was closing himself up, rebuilding the walls around his heart that they had both worked to chip away at. And it was all her fault.

Turning around, Rae placed the tray on the table in the room and spun right back around to come outside, shutting the door behind her.

Ben's blank face turned to one of surprise, and Rae was glad she could keep him on his toes.

"Ben," she started, her voice barely above a whisper, an effect of the poison from the library earlier. But even if she hadn't been affected by it, Rae wasn't sure if she was brave enough to speak in a louder voice. "I'm sorry."

Ben studied her face, his shaggy ebony hair sweeping between his dark eyes. Taking a long sigh, he turned toward the courtyard.

With his back to her, Rae wasn't sure whether she should continue or let him be.

Now I've done it, she thought. *I reacted too harshly and he's going to leave.*

"Ben, I—" she started before he interrupted.

"Help me understand," Ben said, staring out into the evening sky. The sun was just setting beyond the horizon, painting dusk with an array of orange, pink and blue hues. It was a breathtaking backdrop to Ben's strong form, but all Rae wanted to do was cry.

"Understand what?" she squeaked out.

Ben pulled his orange marmalade scarf out of his pocket, holding it tight between his fists. It was the same one he bought the first day he'd met Rae when she was herself and not the Crimson Cord. Rae remembered enjoying their flirtatious banter and how kind Ben was to her when so many men were not.

Ben faced her, his eyes a storm of emotions. "Help me understand what I've done wrong."

Rae swallowed, not knowing how to respond. Though he had become chattier and more flirtatious, Ben was usually selective about how much he spoke. Not that he was rude, he just preferred listening rather than speaking. But even with him becoming more talkative, they very rarely had such intense conversations. And Rae was fearful of how it would end.

"You've done nothing wrong," she replied. "I reacted too harshly again. I'm sorry. I've just been so worried about everything. Me, you, Mami being sick, where Devora is, are we going to make it home? I'm just on edge." Everything Rae said was true. All those things were pressing on her mind. But there was one thing she didn't mention that was pressing on her mind the most. And that was the one Ben narrowed in on.

"No, help me understand why you don't trust me," he said, wrapping up the orange scarf and placing it in his pocket. "I've done everything I can think of to show you my affection, to show you how much I care and am willing to do for you. But Rae"—he glanced at her, tears brimming in his eyes— "Rae, every time I do, you shy away from me when people are near. Are you embarrassed of me?" He motioned to his long height and Rae's heart broke in half.

While she was worrying about hiding her affection for Ben, she had hurt him.

"No, Ben, of course not," she said, reaching out to him, but he turned away, shattering Rae's heart even more.

"I understand you went through many horrible things, and I've prayed to Tunri every night to heal your wounds so that you can find joy again, but whenever I think we're moving closer together, you run from me." Ben raked a hand through his hair, staring up at the stars appearing in the sky.

Rae's tears were freely flowing down her cheeks. "Ben, I'm sorry."

Ben shook his head. "You don't need to apologize for your heart not being ready. I just wish you would've told me before you stole mine completely." Turning around, Rae watched as a few tears streamed down Ben's face. "My heart will only be for you, Rae."

"Ben, it's not you, it's not," Rae said striding up to him, wanting to turn back time and control her wild emotions. "It's me. I have so many issues."

Ben gently laid his hand on her cheek, wiping the tears away. "I can't stand it when you cry."

Rae leaned into his touch and closed her eyes. "Please don't leave me," she whispered.

"I don't want to," he murmured, kissing her forehead. "But I don't know if my heart can handle much more. I know things are hard now, but you keep pushing me away." Ben paused, pulling Rae close. "Rae, I—I love you."

Rae's heart that once was shattered, rebuilt in an instant.

He loves me? He loves me! Why did she doubt?

Rae reveled in Ben's sweet words when she realized she hadn't reciprocated the statement. And Ben had noticed.

Rae knew she loved Ben. She had for a long time. But it wasn't until he pulled away from her, his face filled with sorrow that she felt her love for Ben. So, why couldn't she say it?

"I understand," he said, his voice low.

"Ben," she croaked, unable to say anything else.

Although she had been free from the chains from the Goddess Pahga, she still felt trapped in her insecurity. Not of Ben and his love for her, but her insecurity of herself.

He shook his head, his face downcast. Rummaging through his pocket, he pulled out a bracelet. Round azure glass beads made a pattern with bright orange ones in a perfect circle. It was absolutely breathtaking and had to have cost a fortune. How could Ben buy that when they had hardly any coin to spend? Ben laid the bracelet in his hand. It seemed so small against his large palm.

"I wasn't guarding other contestants," he said, staring at the bracelet. "Mal told me about a jeweler in the city who made custom orders. I asked him if he would cover for me so I could go. I didn't have enough coin for this one, so I worked for the merchant, hauling his goods to pay it off." He held it out to Rae. "It's a custom in Snoken to give a bracelet to the one you intend to spend the rest of your days with. Even though you don't feel the same, I want you to have it."

Rae was too stunned to move. *Spend the rest of your days? How could Ben be so sure? How could he know that he would still want to be with her in five years from now? Ten? Twenty years? How could he know?*

But Rae couldn't bring herself to ask these questions. She just stared, dumbstruck, as Ben placed the bracelet around her wrist.

"You said you liked blue now and orange reminded me of when we met. Funny, they're Kadesh's colors too." He gave her a weak smile before kissing her on the top of her head. "Good-bye, Rae."

And Rae stood in the hallway, with tears streaming down her face as she watched the love of her life walk away.

Chapter Twenty-Four

Haden, Radaa Kingdom, Kadesh

As Rae rushed out the door Ida sighed, causing Haden to glance her way. The small woman was admiring a beautiful ring secured on her necklace.

Haden admired the ring. "That's gorgeous! Is that from your betrothed?"

Ida nodded with a sad smile. "I haven't heard from him since we arrived in Kadesh. And now with Raphael gone, I have no way of contacting him at all."

Haden's heart ached for her new friends. One couldn't see how clearly she was loved and the other couldn't reach her love. "I'm so sorry, Ida. You must be so worried."

Ida took one last glance at the ring then hid it back beneath the collar of her dress. "I am, but I know that Tunri will take care of Jacques and me. He already orchestrated quite a lot to get us betrothed. I believe He will bring us back together again soon."

"You have such faith," Haden said as she stood and walked toward the tray of food Rae left. She picked up a piece of flatbread and tore off a section. "Where does it come from?"

Haden had learned to read Tunri's prayers with Madeline when she was a child. Though it had been difficult, whenever she completed a prayer, she felt such peace and satisfaction coming from the words. During her entire journey from Juro to Kadesh, Haden would whisper Tunri's prayers to herself in encouragement to continue. But even though Haden knew the prayers, she felt her faith was lacking. She believed in Tunri and His goodness but still worried about...well, everything.

Ida joined Haden at the tray and plucked a few grapes and a chunk of cheese. "My faith comes from Tunri. He restores my heart and soul and encourages me."

"I definitely need some of that now," Haden replied with a snort. It would be nice if she could siphon Ida's faith and inject it into herself.

"I can pray with you, if you'd like," Ida offered with a kind smile. "I know it always makes me feel better."

Haden tilted her head to the side, remembering Madeline praying over their reading lessons before they began. When Haden had her lessons with her tutors, she always felt agitated and angry, thus making it hard to focus on her reading and writing even more. But, when Madeline prayed, though reading was still difficult, she found the perseverance to continue through it.

"I would like that," Haden said with a grin.

Ida nodded, taking Haden's hands in her own, and then she prayed. Haden had heard many prayers over the years. The prayers from Tunri's prayer scroll, prayers recited at formal meetings Mother made her attend for appearances sake, but never had Haden heard a more beautiful prayer than Ida's. There weren't any fancy words or flowery language. It was simple, but honest and pure. And Haden was so thankful that Ida had included her in it.

When Ida finished, Haden couldn't help but reach out and hug her.

"Oh," Ida replied, surprised, but she reciprocated the hug.

"Thank you," Haden whispered. "I've been so scared with everything going on and now these attacks on the contestants are getting more serious, Raphael is gone, Ben and Rae are at odds, and I don't know how to gain a private meeting with the crown prince."

Ida released Haden and nodded. "It certainly is a lot, I agree. But may I ask why you need to see the crown prince?"

Before Haden could reply, the door to their room squeaked open. While Haden expected Rae to be doing backflips with joy in making things right with Ben, the woman looked like she had been run over by a horse.

"Rae?" Ida asked, shooting up from her seated position and rushing toward her. "Rae, what happened?"

"Ben's gone," Rae replied, her voice barely audible.

"What?" Haden and Ida replied.

"It's all my fault," Rae cried, falling into Ida's arms.

"I'm sure that's not true," Ida said, hugging Rae close before leading her to her bed. "It's been a long day. I think you just need to rest."

Rae cried more but didn't fight Ida as she placed the blanket over her.

"Is he really gone?" Haden whispered once Rae had cried herself to sleep.

She and Ida walked to the other side of the room, so they wouldn't disturb Rae.

Ida shook her head. "I don't think so. I'm hoping he only took a walk to relieve some stress. As you said, a lot has happened."

Haden nodded. A lot *had* happened, yet she didn't feel overwhelmed or anxious anymore. She felt ready to take on this task that was thrown her way and knew Tunri would guide her steps.

"We should probably get some sleep too," Ida suggested. "Who knows what awaits us future princesses tomorrow?" She batted her eyelashes, making Haden giggle.

As Ida settled into her bed, Haden tried to fall asleep. She was exhausted from the day' events, but her mind was on overload. After tossing and turning a few more times, Haden flopped to her stomach with a sigh. Well, at least if she didn't sleep, she wouldn't transform. She had pulled all-nighters as a child to test this and found it was true. But later in the day she would fall asleep somewhere anyway and transform then.

But, tonight, she wished to transform. She wanted to escape for just a moment to work through everything: the good and the bad. Because while she found good friends and peace with Tunri, Mother was still out there trying to control both Tenton and Kadesh. Haden didn't know all the details, but she had seen the destruction her Mother caused by being queen. Haden couldn't imagine how much damage Mother would do if she became *more* powerful.

Flipping to her back, Haden closed her eyes and thought of the wind gliding over her wings, the coolness of night taking all her troubles away. Maybe Mother had meant her transformation into a sparrow as a curse, and sometimes Haden felt that way. But many times, when she wasn't caged, there was freedom in being able to fly anywhere she desired.

Unfortunately, that's *why* Mother kept her caged once she transformed. On several occasions, Haden had slipped out of the palace to explore one time too many and she learned early on the consequences of her actions.

But, as far as Haden knew, Mother wasn't here, and Haden could do what she wished. And she knew Captain—or now General Blake, as Ida said—had been cursed by Mother too. She'd watched it happen, though Mother had no idea Haden was around. Sometimes Haden was *too* good at not being heard. When she had seen General Blake again at the Battle of Edo, Haden noticed he had gained control over his curse. If he could control his curse from Mother, why couldn't Haden control hers?

As Haden closed her eyes to try to transform, it felt as if Tunri pressed something onto her heart and mind. A thought that never occurred to her before: her curse wasn't actually a curse, but a gift.

Haden's eyes shot open as she sat up in her bed. Could it be that her transformations were a gift? That Mother hadn't cursed her after all? But how could Mother cause her to transform every night?

Frowning, Haden stared into the darkness, trying to puzzle out this new notion. Maybe, Mother *didn't* control her transformation. Maybe, Haden controlled it herself without knowing it and Mother manipulated the process. If that were true, she would be able to transform, right here, right now, while she was wide awake. If she were able to do it, then for the past eighteen years of her life, the queen of Tenton had been able to control her without lifting a finger. The thought shamed Haden that she was so easily used. But still, she had to see if this new idea had any weight.

Taking a deep breath, Haden banished all other notions from her mind except an image of her bird form: a small white sparrow with a tinge of blue at the tips of her wings. A wave of cool air suddenly washed over her, and Haden felt herself shrinking until she perched on her pillow. Glancing down, she saw her toes had changed into small talons shaded pale orange.

I did it! She thought and then realized she was still aware of her own mind.

Usually when she transformed, she had simpler thoughts. Though she could still decipher where she was flying—like how to travel to Kadesh—she didn't care about much else besides that. But this time, she was still Haden. Maybe that's what Mother had done to her. She had made her mind fuzzy when she transformed so Haden wouldn't realize she had the power to change whenever she liked. Anger welled in Haden's heart as she realized how she was just a pawn to the queen as well, but she wouldn't let it linger. She was a pawn no longer. It was as if a chain holding down her true power had finally broken, and she was free.

Now in her transformed state, Haden didn't spare another moment trying to figure out anything else. Flapping her wings, she took off through the open window, not caring to look back.

The cool midnight breeze soared over Haden's feathers, and she relished the feeling. The night air was freedom. Just like when Devora saved her from the Kadeshians and she rode her giant elk-like creature. Freedom was what Haden craved. Freedom to fly, freedom to live, freedom to love, freedom to be herself.

Mother never let Haden have that freedom, but now that she tasted it, Haden wasn't giving it back.

Chirping loudly, Haden soared high around the night clouds before looping in the air and diving again. She did the same move again and again, feeling her troubles wash away with each turn.

Exhilarated, Haden started back toward her room. Since she had willingly transformed into a sparrow, Haden prayed she could transform herself back. But before she reached the window leading to her chambers, she noticed a familiar figure striding across the courtyard.

Mal? What's he doing out here so late?

Curious, Haden decided to try her hand at espionage. Though she was horrible being a spy as a human, she could conceal her sparrow form much easier. Riding the air currents, Haden flew until she was a few feet behind Mal. Unfortunately, her landing was a bit rocky. But since she weighed no more than a piece of flatbread, Mal heard nothing.

Haden bounced a little farther before taking off again. This time she flew past Mal and perched on the edge of the castle's roof. Still, Mal paid her no mind and Haden wondered if she should've taken up being a bird spy years ago.

Mal continued through the courtyard until he strode into the throne room. Tweeting, Haden launched off the roof, flapping as hard as she could to make it through the threshold before the door closed. Thankfully, she squeezed in at the last minute and hurriedly perched herself on a tapestry to the right of the throne.

Haden glanced around the room. Nothing seemed different from when she was there for her interrogation with the crown prince. But why was Mal here? With Ben supposedly gone and Raphael disappeared, shouldn't Mal be guarding their room? And if Mal had business with the king or prince, why did he choose such a late time in the night to deal with them?

Patience was not Haden's strong suit, but she did her best to stay quiet and not make a single chirp.

After what seemed like hours, Haden heard a pair of footsteps enter the throne room. If she wasn't a bird, she would've gasped at who they belonged to. In strode the masked crown prince, yet Sayidi Brocaw was not at his side. Haden's interest immediately piqued. Did the prince and Mal know each other?

"Time is running out, we need to make a decision and soon," the masked prince said.

Haden wished she had chosen a better spot to spy from. Though she could hear most of what the prince said, the mask still muffled his words.

"I didn't expect the competition to be sabotaged as it has been," Mal replied, his usually carefree demeanor absent.

Haden couldn't believe how casually Mal addressed the prince. He actually didn't address the prince at all and spoke to him as an equal rather than the guard he was. If he had spoken to Mother that way, she would've had him killed on the spot.

Haden shuddered, shaking that image from her mind.

"Do you have someone in mind?" the crown prince asked. "There cannot be a new king unless the prince has a bride. This war will not be stopped until there is a new king, you know this."

Mal hung his head. "I know. I just need a little more time."

Haden was extremely confused by the exchange between Mal and the masked prince and decided it was time to get a closer vantage point.

Following her gut rather than her head, Haden soared to another tapestry. But this time she didn't make it. Instead, she felt the same cool breeze wash over her and before she knew it, she was falling to the ground. And *not* as a bird.

Thankfully, two sets of arms reached out and caught her and when she looked up, Haden met the confused look of Mal and the stoic mask of the prince.

"Uh, hi there," she said, thankful she had rolled into the tapestry before being caught by Mal. Unfortunately, when she transformed, her clothes did not transform with her.

"Haden?" Mal asked, his brows furrowed as he gazed down at her. "What are you doing here? How did you get in here?"

"It's a funny story actually," Haden started, scrambling to keep the tapestry around her. She paused a moment, hoping one of them would cut her off like they usually did. But neither the prince nor Mal said anything. "Actually, I think I'm just going to go."

She hopped out of the two men's arms and practically ran for the door before Mal caught up with her and seized her arm.

"Haden, what's going on?" Mal demanded and Haden wasn't sure she liked his tone. "How did you get out of your room? I thought Ben was guarding you."

Haden pulled her arm out of Mal's hand. Guard or not, he still could not handle her in such a way. Securing the tapestry around her form, she stuck out her chin. She didn't want to rat out Ben, so she went a different route.

"I-I snuck out myself. We've been cooped up since the poison at the library, and I needed some fresh air."

Haden held her stance, hoping her confidence would throw Mal off her trail.

Unfortunately, Mal was too keen.

Raising a brow, he asked, "You needed fresh air at the midnight hour and in such a state?" He subtly motioned to the tapestry covering her form.

Haden nodded slowly, trying to stay strong and not crawl away from embarrassment. "Yes. It's the best time."

Mal hummed, his gaze narrowing.

"Take the contestant back to her room, guard," the masked prince ordered Mal. "I will decide her fate in the morning."

Haden's confidence popped like a bubble and fear quickly took its place. Mal bowed to the prince and gently, but hurriedly guided Haden to the exit. Now she would never win the prince's favor. He would probably kill her instead.

Once they exited the throne room and were down the hall, Mal spun towards her.

"Out with it."

"Out with what?" Haden asked, walking as quickly as she could to get away from him.

Mal caught up to her in a few steps. "Haden, you can't outpace me. How did you get in there?"

"Oh, you know," she waffled, making sure the tapestry was secure.

If she weren't already embarrassed about blowing her cover, she would be more embarrassed about what she looked like in front of Mal. Unfortunately, she knew she couldn't throw Mal off her scent, as much as she wished she could. Of all times for her to be in control of her gift and it backfired.

"No, I don't know," he replied, his tense stance softening. "Enlighten me. But first—" Mal removed his outer tunic and handed it to her, his face turned away, but Haden still saw the deep blush rising up his neck.

Haden knew her face was probably even more red with embarrassment. She quickly grabbed the tunic and layered it over the tapestry.

"I'm dressed," she said.

Mal turned around, then crossed his hands over his chest. "Well? Why were you in the throne room at this hour, alone, and"—he swallowed—"not in proper attire to address the prince?"

"Ah, that," Haden replied, rocking back and forth on her feet. "I, um, I can kind of transform into a bird." She whispered the end of her statement so softly, Mal had to lean forward to hear it.

Haden thought he would laugh in her face or send her straight to the gallows Aunt Beta enjoyed so much. Instead, he studied her face, his light eyes searching her own.

Suddenly, his brows rose. "The white sparrow."

Haden's shoulders fell. Apparently, she wasn't as stealthy as she first assumed.

A huge smile spread across Mal's face. "I thought I noticed something following me, but figured it was just my imagination. But it was you! This is wonderful."

He laughed and Haden was more confused than ever.

Haden chuckled nervously as she took a step away, wondering if Mal had lost his mind. "Yeah. I should be getting back to my rooms. The prince is probably going to kill me tomorrow, so..." Haden hurriedly shuffled away. When she rounded the corner, she was surprised to see Ben's outline in the distance. Rae said he was gone, but he was clearly standing guard outside of their door. Still, Ben's and Rae's relationship was not Haden's concern right now. Now she had to figure out how she was going to explain to Ben why she was on the wrong side of the door. There was no way she could fit through the small window in her room.

Mal soon came beside her and placed her hand in the crook of his elbow. "Your secret is safe with me, princess. All your secrets." He winked, sending chills down her spine. Though Haden wasn't sure if they were the good or bad kind. "And don't fear. I don't think the crown prince will kill you tomorrow."

"I'm not so sure," Haden muttered as they approached Ben.

As soon as they got close, he whipped out a crossbow that Haden hadn't seen before.

Haden shrieked and drew closer to Mal. Thank goodness she hadn't tried to approach the tall man on her own.

"Sorry, Mal," Ben said, lowering the crossbow. "I didn't realize you were on shift tonight."

Haden's heart sagged at the sight of Ben. He looked almost as torn up as Rae, maybe even worse. His hair was tousled, his eyes drooped and distant, and a scowl that Haden had never seen marred his lips.

"I'm not tonight, however, I was escorting Haden back to her room."

Ben gave no indication of his suspicion other than the slight narrowing of his eyes. "Okay. I'm glad you're safe, Haden."

Haden nodded quickly and bid both of the guards good night before hurrying into her room.

Thank Tunri, Rae and Ida were heavy sleepers. Haden hurried across the room, threw her nightclothes back on and dashed into her bed, hiding under her covers as if she could also hide from the world.

What had turned out to be an exciting experience had brought more confusion and fear to her already swirling mind. The way Mal spoke to the prince was familiar, as if they knew each other. But how could that be? And how could he know whether the prince would kill her tomorrow or not?

Once Haden's pulse had steadied, the emotional events of the day took a toll on her and she finally succumbed to sleep.

⚔

When she awoke the next morning, Rae and Ida were already up and getting ready. Though Ida was trying to sound cheery, Rae looked as if a storm cloud were raining on her head.

I wonder if she knows Ben has been outside the door all night, Haden thought, still refraining from leaving her covers. She wanted nothing more than to stay in her bed and never leave.

"Haden, if you don't get up soon you won't have time to get ready," Ida called.

Haden grunted at Ida's too chipper voice.

"I hear the prince is starting his interviews today. Maybe you'll get to meet him and talk about what you told me," Rae's sorrowful voice added. "You'll probably make better choices than I did."

And before Haden could rise from the bed, Rae was crying again.

"Oh, Rae," Ida said, hurrying over to her like a mother hen. "It'll be okay."

Haden rose from the bed and ran her fingers through her tangled hair. Her entire hand came back black with dye. Sighing, Haden noticed that the white pillow on her bed was also black. She figured the dye would all come out eventually. Mal had already figured out she was the princess of Tenton and apparently the crown prince had too. Maybe her trial for spying would be the only way she could see the crown prince.

Standing, Haden wobbled a bit before bracing against the wall. She had never felt weak after she transformed before. Was it because she willed the transformation herself this time?

"Are you all right, Haden?" Ida asked, still holding Rae. The poor thing was a mess of tears and inaudible words.

Haden nodded and decided now was a good time to be blunt. "He's outside, Rae."

"Who?" Rae asked, her face red, voice stuffy.

"Ben. He's been there the whole night, guarding the door."

Rae pulled away from Ida. "What? How do you know?"

Haden blanched before she found her footing. She wished she could help Rae feel better and couldn't think of a lie to not expose herself.

"Well, ah—" Haden started before a harsh knock sounded at the door.

Yelping, Haden jumped, all thoughts of trying to come up with a lie fleeing her brain. She instantly remembered what the prince had said last night and worried if today would be her last day on this earth.

The knock sounded again, and Rae hurried to the door.

"Yes?" she asked before Sayidi Tamor burst through.

Ben came in behind, his eyes immediately landing on Rae then to a bracelet wrapped around her wrist. But Haden didn't have time to decipher what was happening between them because Sayidi Tamor was barreling toward her.

While Sayidi Tamor was a large man, he looked even bigger in their demure space. His hard gaze landed on Haden. "The crown prince of Kadesh has requested your presence immediately."

Chapter Twenty-Five

Matthias, The Fortress, Tenton

Rallying Tenton's troops in an orderly fashion took longer than Queen Leza anticipated and for that, Matthias was grateful. It seemed the new Duchesses of Sandje Textiles—who oversaw fashioning more uniforms for the soldiers—were more difficult to deal with than the former Duke Sandje and weren't as easily intimidated.

"It seems the new uniforms for the soldiers will take a bit more time, my queen," the plump herald, whose name escaped Matthias, said with a deep bow.

Queen Leza squeezed the quill in her hand so tightly Matthias thought it would disintegrate.

"These two little girls think they can delay the plans of their queen?" Queen Leza questioned with a snarl.

Matthias noticed how since the funeral of King Atol and Princess Haden, more of the queen's true colors were starting to show. He wasn't sure if Queen Leza was tired of putting up her façade of a genteel queen or if she hoped to show those around her how cruel she could actually be.

"Apologies, Your Majesty. But Duchess Sandje said, 'If the queen wished for Sandje Textiles to create new uniforms for the entire Tenton army, she should have notified us weeks ago.' That's not a quote from me, Your Highness, but from Duchess Sandje, herself," said the herald, who was quick to add to save his head.

Queen Leza growled. "Return with a message that says if the uniforms are not here by midday tomorrow, I will burn Sandje Textiles to the ground."

The herald's gaze shifted as he stammered, "Y-yes my queen. However, the duchess did say if there is any harm done to her family's business, you will not have any uniforms at all."

It took everything within Matthias not to bark out a laugh. He was proud that his soldiers had become amiable deterrents to the queen's plans. They had become so strong since they first entered the Fortress.

"What?" the queen roared. "Which one said that?"

The herald glanced to Matthias for help, but Matthias just stood as a statue next to the queen, keeping his face a blank slate of indifference.

"The first quote was from the duchess without the abacus. The second one was from the one with the abacus," the herald muttered.

The queen clenched her teeth then scribbled a few lines on a piece of parchment. "Send this to Sandje Textiles. When I rule both Tenton and Kadesh, I will see that both duchesses are beheaded. Go!"

The herald jumped a mile high at the queen's shout and quickly snatched the paper out of her hand before racing out of the room.

Queen Leza turned her glare on Matthias. "You had something to do with this."

Matthias kept his eyes forward. "How could I? You never let me out of your sight."

Unfortunately, what he proclaimed was true. Since the funeral, everywhere the queen went, Matthias had to go too. Thankfully, she still allowed him to sleep in his own chambers, but as soon as he was dressed for the day, the invisible leash she held him on forced him to find her and follow her every step.

The queen only growled at him in response as she scribbled furiously upon the parchment before her. Out of the corner of his eye, Matthias studied the queen. He had always seen her as well groomed and poised. But now, with strands of her ebony hair sticking up and the dark circles under her eyes, Matthias wondered if the queen's plans were starting to unravel.

"Come, dog, we are going to make a visit to a dear friend of yours."

With a smug smile, the queen stood and strode forward. Resist as he might, the chain around his neck tightened and Matthias had no choice but to follow.

An awful carriage ride later, Matthias and Queen Leza were outside Delequa Manor. Matthias knew the queen would find out about the former Duke Delequa's death sooner or later. He just prayed Jacques had a plan to divert the queen's attention long enough so she wouldn't try to blackmail him into doing something he regretted.

Matthias did his best to hold his head high and ignore the fact that Queen Leza could easily murder his best friend, and he could do nothing about it. His feelings of indifference toward others had worked for years, until Devora came along. Once her light entered his life, he couldn't contain the emotions he felt for her. Ever since the queen told him she knew where Devora and his mother were, he barely slept, hardly ate, and couldn't focus on anything else besides trying to escape. But no matter how many plans he came up with, he couldn't figure out a way to get to them without the queen knowing.

"Hurry along, General," Queen Leza chided, her tone mocking. "After my last messenger was sent away, I am anxious to see what the new Duke Delequa is hiding from me."

Matthias held back his grimace. If he could, he would take all the attention the queen had for Jacques onto himself. But he wasn't the newly appointed leader of the largest iron manufacturer in Tenton.

Matthias sent a prayer to Tunri as they strode up the steps to Delequa Manor. Though he was long past due on praying to the God, now seemed like a good start to make it a habit.

Matthias took in the grandiose building, baffled that Jacques had been raised in such an estate. Matthias' childhood home was barely a fraction of the marbled structure before him. Although Jacques had known of Matthias' humble upbringing, he had never treated him any less and had always stood by his side. Now it was Matthias' turn to do everything within his power to aid his friend in dealing with the queen.

Now that he thought about it, Matthias assumed they would meet with Jacques at the offices of Delequa Iron. But now he wondered if the queen planned to catch Jacques off guard in his weakened state after his father's passing. However, life always had a way of surprising, and just as the queen was readying to bang the solid oak front door down, it opened inward and out stepped Jacques.

"Ah, good morning, my queen, I am so happy to see you. I was just heading to fetch the stableboy to ready my horse." Jacques' features slid into an easy smile, convincing even Matthias that he was genuinely happy to see Queen Leza. For the first time Matthias realized that maybe the positivity Jacques always held was more of a façade than he originally thought.

"Were you now?" the queen asked, her voice oozing with condescension. "I was informed that my messengers had been sent away. I can try you for treason for disobeying your queen."

If Jacques' smile faltered, Matthias missed it, for his friend immediately responded, "I apologize, Your Highness, I don't recall ever seeing or hearing from one of the palace's messengers. Did you send someone you could trust? I hear there are Kadeshian spies hidden all throughout Tenton."

Matthias did his best to keep his face straight. Jacques had always been the first soldier to obey when Warden Hazor gave orders. He never questioned any request, no matter how harmful or degrading. But the man standing before Matthias was no longer the friend he made in the Fortress long ago. It seemed that Jacques had found himself and someone worth protecting, and he wasn't going to go down without a fight.

"Confident, aren't we?" Queen Leza mused, strutting around Jacques like a vulture ready to dive. "I would be careful, young duke. I have eyes and ear everywhere and have no problem finding your Kadeshian orphan and making you a widow before you're even wed."

At that, Jacques' composure broke for just a moment, but enough for the queen to be satisfied.

"I would be wary of threats, Your Majesty," Jacques started, his voice low. "You do not know what weaponry I was about to bring to the table for your victory over Kadesh. Once and for all."

The queen's brows rose, and Matthias was impressed Jacques had been able to catch the mistress of lies off guard. But a moment later, Matthias feared for his friend's life for being so bold. As he readied to come to Jacques' defense, the queen lifted her chin.

"Keep talking."

A flash of triumph sparkled across Jacques' gaze before he began. "Allow me to escort you to our business office. We just recently signed a contract for a device that should benefit us all."

Matthias quirked his brow at Jacques' careful explanation. But when Jacques gave him a quick nod before assisting the queen into her carriage, Matthias knew his friend had a plan. Matthias only hoped it would work.

The carriage was silent as the trio took the short trip to Delequa Iron. Matthias had never been to the mine and factory where the Delequa family had been mining iron ore for decades. He had heard stories of how the first Duke Delequa was originally a farmer and happened upon iron ore when he was searching for a place to call home. One thing led to another and the Delequa name rose in the aristocracy.

When Matthias first met Jacques, the chipper lad was always quick to sway the conversation away from himself and on to others. Matthias caught on to Jacques' act right away and questioned him endlessly until Jacques finally told Matthias his true origins.

Matthias could never understand why Jacques would want to give up his position as heir to Delequa Iron. He had the power to do great things, things to change the world. While Matthias had to crawl and scrape for every bit of respect he had earned and look where that got him.

He was never jealous of Jacques, but he did wish he could be in on his friend's plan. But it was probably best if he didn't know anything. He wasn't sure how far the queen's power went. Unfortunately, it was better if he stayed in the dark this time.

"Ah," Jacques said, a look of relief casting over his features. "We're finally here."

Jacques stepped out of the carriage first and offered Queen Leza his arm. Surprisingly, she took it with an excited gleam in her eyes.

That look always worried Matthias. He hoped Jacques would come out of this deal unscathed.

"Come along, General," the queen ordered, flicking her fingers.

Even though Matthias was already following behind the queen and Jacques, he knew the queen wanted to make him an example; to show Jacques what would happen to him if he disobeyed the queen's orders.

A vein bulged in Matthias' neck as the chain tightened. Lifting his chin, he strode as close as he could to the queen without stepping on the train of her dress.

The clanging of pickaxes rang throughout the grounds and Matthias was thoroughly impressed at the well-oiled machine

Delequa Iron was. He never realized how large of a business Jacques inherited.

"As you can see, our employees are hard at work with mining and siphoning the iron for Tenton's weapons," Jacques explained easily as they passed by a section of workers.

The grunts and growls of the workers was similar to the noises he was used to in the Fortress, but the men here were not burdened or weary. Instead, they laughed and joked with one another. Had Jacques already made this atmosphere a positive one?

"I'm not interested in your sweaty brutes, Duke Delequa," Queen Leza said. She turned away from the sweaty workers, her eyes dark orbs of judgment. "Take me to this weapon before my patience grows thin."

Jacques bowed, his easy smile resting upon his lips once again. "Of course, my queen. I will skip the tour. If you'll follow me."

It still baffled Matthias how easily Jacques handled the queen's barbs. On a good day, Matthias was only half angry when replying. Usually, he couldn't help but speak his mind. He always did so respectfully, but he made his thoughts heard, nonetheless.

They headed toward a large, stone building similar to that of Delequa Manor, but a smaller version. Jacques opened the dark, wooden door then motioned for the queen to enter.

Lifting her chin, she strode forward and thankfully, was too distracted to summon Matthias to follow on her heels.

Once Queen Leza was inside, Matthias stepped next to Jacques.

"I hope you have a plan," he muttered under his breath.

"I do," Jacques replied. "But it wouldn't hurt if you helped convince the queen."

Matthias sighed. Though he had primarily dealt with convincing King Atol a certain way, sometimes, Queen Leza did weigh his opinions heavier than her other pawns.

"I will do my best."

Matthias stood by Queen Leza's side, hoping she would believe he desired to be there instead of his inner desire to run as far away from her as possible.

"This is quite a business you inherited, Duke," the queen mused as she took in the extravagantly decorated interior. "Do you wish to sign it over to the kingdom?"

Her smile was sweet, but Matthias knew the queen was setting her trap for Jacques to fall into.

"If you had offered a week ago, I would've readily agreed," Jacques confessed, keeping his same easy smile. But Matthias noticed his eyes were sharp and alert. "However, with the design of this new device, I felt it was my duty to Tenton to see it crafted and use it to end this horrible war that has taken so much from our people."

Matthias had no idea why Jacques didn't enter the aristocracy sooner. He spoke with the ease and confidence all leaders needed.

The queen laughed. "Pretty words, Duke. Show me this device and I will make those decisions."

Jacques bowed. "Of course, Your Highness. Right this way."

Jacques led them down the hallway to a set of dark green doors. The Delequa insignia of two pickaxes crossed into an X with the horns of an elk protruding out of them were burned into the wood.

As they entered the office, Matthias immediately saw the device Nadia and Lucas Salvar crafted in Totem. They said it could nullify the effects of imperial opal. But how had it gotten here?

Matthias searched around the room, pretending to be bored until his eyes landed on Jacques. His friend gave him a quick nod before offering the queen his own plush chair behind the desk.

Matthias sucked in a breath. So, Jacques hoped he could convince the queen that the device before them would help her defeat Kadesh once and for all. When in reality, this device could be her undoing. Matthias' mind reeled, thinking of different arguments he could make to win the queen over. It was going to be tough, but he always liked a challenge.

"Is this it?" The queen scrunched her nose at the model of the device before her. "It doesn't seem like much."

"I thought so too, my queen," Jacques admitted, and Matthias recognized the truth behind his words. "However, this device was crafted by some of the best Tinkers in Tenton."

Queen Leza's gaze sharpened. "Tinkers? There are no Tinkers left in Tenton."

Panic laced Jacques' gaze, but before he dug himself an early grave, Matthias knew it was his turn to step in.

"Right you are, my queen. There are no *known* Tinkers left in Tenton. However, a few years ago, the late King Atol was able to find some survivors after the raid on Yekel. He employed these Tinkers in secret, not wanting Kadesh or anyone else to know of their whereabouts. He feared they would be taken by Kadesh and used for their own nefarious purposes."

The queen narrowed her eyes at Matthias as she fiddled with the rings on the device. "I don't remember hearing of any such thing."

When the queen didn't outright punish Matthias, he knew he was on the correct course. He bowed his head. "Apologies, Your Highness. I had thought the king would tell you."

"Where are these Tinkers now?"

While Matthias' story was a stretch of the truth—the Tinkers were actually taken to Totem and under his father's care instead of being worked to death by the kingdom—he would have to do something he always despised doing. He would have to act ignorant.

"Even I do not know their location, my queen. However, if I'm understanding Duke Delequa correctly, they brought this device to him, yes?" Matthias turned to Jacques, hoping his friend had calmed down enough for him to take the reins of this conversation again.

"Yes! The device was brought to me with urgency that it was needed to end the war. Apparently, they tried to bring it to my father, but he had no interest in saving Tenton. I wish to present this machine to you, my queen, as an act of goodwill to defeat Kadesh."

Matthias could see the sweat beading on Jacques' brow, but he was impressed with his friend's smooth words all the same.

The queen's eyes were slits as they shifted between Matthias and Jacques. But after a few agonizing moments, she leaned forward with bright eyes and Matthias knew they had won.

"So, what does my new weapon do?"

Matthias glanced at Jacques, praying he would say the right words to seal the deal.

Jacques strode up to the desk and lifted the device before the queen. "This device, my queen, can amplify the power and effects of imperial opal. Though only on a small scale."

Matthias had seen the wickedness of the monarchy first-hand, but nothing could prepare him for the pure evil grin that stretched across the queen's face.

"Excellent. Begin its creation immediately. And make it ten times this size."

Chapter Twenty-Six

Devora, Underground Temple, Kadesh

Though Devora was initially shocked to see Tristan standing next to General Beta, the surprise quickly dissolved into disappointment.

"Once a traitor, always a traitor," Devora sneered.

"Now now, honeybee. Don't take everything so personally," Tristan replied, though Devora noticed he couldn't meet her eyes.

In fact, Tristan wasn't even looking at them in the cell at all, but down the hall into the black abyss.

"Bind them and bring them to the statue room," General Beta ordered, flicking a hand in Devora's and Kanna's direction like they were no more than flies on a camel's backside.

"Go ahead with the general," Tristan told Sergio, who looked all too eager to follow his aunt. "I can handle them both."

Devora couldn't blame Sergio for wanting to get away. With weeks of no baths and only a single chamber pot to share, she was sure her and Kanna did not smell great.

Once Sergio was gone, his footsteps no longer within earshot, Tristan turned back to Devora. "Listen—"

"No, you listen," Devora cut him off, throwing all decorum aside. "I understand your betraying me. I did throw your engagement ring back at you and wasn't as kind as I could've been in Yekel. But what about your mother?" Devora gestured to Kanna who had stayed silent during the whole exchange. "How dare you betray her?"

Tristan ground his teeth. With a low voice he replied, "I would never betray my mother. Why do you think I'm here?" He cast his eyes over Devora's shoulder to where Kanna sat against the wall, his gaze filled with pain. "If General Beta noticed one morsel of sympathy from me to my mother, she would do far worse to her than she already has."

Devora glared, trying to decipher where the truth was hidden beneath his words. "I don't know why you're here," she answered, narrowing her gaze. "But I know your past actions speak for themselves."

Tristan rolled his eyes as he jingled the keys in his hand. "Okay, so I flunked out of Vlacklear. That wasn't part of the plan."

"Matthias has had to pay the price for all the mistakes you've made," Devora shouted, tears brimming in her eyes. She'd never forget the torment she felt in Matthias' soul, the burden of what he had endured while at the Fortress—while trying to find Kanna.

Tristan winced at her outburst then he leaned close to the iron bars. "My brother fights wars one way, and I fight them another. Give me your hand."

"No," Devora said, backing away. She wasn't going to allow him to take her anywhere willingly.

Tristan snorted. "I'm not going to tie you up. Not yet anyway. Give me your hand, please. I want to show you my side of things, to see into my soul."

Curiosity spiked in Devora's mind, but the past reminded her that Tristan was no good. However, when they needed his help in Yekel, he did come through and got them into the Dark Market.

Devora glared at him, keeping her hand within the cell. Still, she engaged her *soulsight* and was surprised by what greeted her. Tristan's soul, which had once been corrupted with gray hues when she checked it in Yekel, was now beaming a bright yellow glow.

How could that be? Devora thought.

Tristan was always the troublemaker, the rascal, the scoundrel. Yet his soul seemed to be the exact opposite of that.

Extending his arm, Tristan stretched through the bars. "You once saw something in me that was trustworthy enough for you to say yes to a proposal." He gave her his devilish grin. Devora rolled her eyes but relaxed her tense stance. "Please, trust me again. Just once more."

Sucking in a breath, Devora weighed the odds and decided to take a chance. "Just once more," she agreed, stepping closer.

Once she was at the bars, Devora reached through the iron gate and placed her hand on Tristan's soft shirt, just above his heart. She remembered doing the same thing not long ago, before her Categorization Call.

All that seems so long ago, she thought before she was pulled into Tristan's soul.

"Matthias, where's Mama?" a young Tristan with plump cheeks and unruly chestnut hair asked, rubbing his eyes.

Devora's heart shattered as she watched Matthias' younger self try to console the young Tristan.

Tristan had always had swagger and a quick quip for replies when confronted. So, Devora had never once thought of the pain and heartache he suffered when Kanna was taken.

The image of the young brothers spun. They were older now—teenagers. Tristan had a bulging bag slung over his shoulder as he stormed out of a quaint house. The door slammed behind him.

"Come back, son," a man Devora assumed was Tristan's father shouted from the porch. "We must stay together until Matthias' Categorization Call."

Matthias stood next to his father, his arms crossed over his chest.

Devora did a double take of Matthias. He looked so young, his eyes innocent of the horrors of war. Her heart strained over how much he'd endured. But when she witnessed Tristan ignore his father's pleas, Devora realized Matthias wasn't the only one whose soul was hurting.

Devora watched as Tristan made his way to Yekel, his encounter with the gang there, how they offered him assistance at a price, how they didn't like how much money he made while gambling. With each turn, Devora thought Tristan would call in and take his prize money, but he kept bidding higher and higher.

Devora's stomach twisted, knowing how the story ended. Matthias said Tristan had killed the leader of the gang in Yekel to get out of paying his debts. Yet what happened next surprised her. Tristan ended his turn on a win and collected his money.

"Here's what I owe you, Beau," Tristan said, handing a sack of coin to the leader of the gang named the Street Rats.

The leader weighed the coin in his hand. "You have a talent. How about you work for me, and we split your winnings?"

Tristan arched a brow. "Thanks, but I'll pass."

But as Tristan turned, the other members of the Street Rats were waiting for him. Devora closed her eyes as they beat him black and blue and took all his prize money.

After the men left, Tristan groaned and reached for a knife in his pocket.

Devora frowned. If he had that with him, why didn't he defend himself?

"Knights from the Fortress are on their way," Beau chuckled, jingling his bag of coins. "Too bad you'll be the only one here when they arrive."

With his last ounce of strength, Tristan sliced Beau's leg.

The gang leader laughed at the small nick then stopped. Purple splotches immediately formed on his skin and Devora gasped in horror. She had seen those splotches before. They were on the knight in the infirmary who had succumbed to the effects of gumberry poison. The knife that Tristan used must have been laced with it.

When the knights of the Fortress arrived, Tristan had passed out while Beau writhed on the floor, begging for someone to end his life.

Tristan removed Devora's hand from his chest.

"I went to Yekel to find my mother," Tristan explained. "I don't know how, but I knew she was there, somewhere. I never went into the Temple or else I would've found her." He ran a hand through his hair, much like how Matthias did. "I shouldn't have gambled or gotten involved with the Street Rats, but I needed a way into the Dark Market." Tristan shrugged. "I didn't want to kill Beau."

Devora thought over his story then frowned. "That still doesn't answer why you're working for General Beta."

Tristan fiddled with the metal keys the general had given him. "When Matthias swapped positions with me at Vlacklear—mind you I was surprised for I always assumed he hated me—a boy named Sergio approached me about a job that would pay handsomely. As I am always interested in earning coin, I listened to him. All I had to do was woo a girl from Grenly—the governor's daughter, in fact." He gave her a knowing look.

"So, everything was planned? All of it?" Devora asked, ashamed of herself for getting so wrapped up in a relationship that really meant nothing.

Tristan sighed. "I always enjoyed talking with you, but as for a romantic spark?" He shook his head. "Sorry, you're a bit too boring for me."

Devora scoffed. "And you're a liar."

"Good point," Tristan said with a wink.

"So, you found out Sergio's connection to General Beta?"

"Yes," Tristan replied as he unlocked the cell. "Eventually I found out General Beta was working with Queen Leza. And

Queen Leza had my mother. The only way to get my mother was to keep playing the game."

Blood drained from Devora's face as she remembered Matthias saying the same thing. Two brothers, locked into two different games, trying to save their mother. But what if that's what the queen wanted?

Devora didn't have time to dwell on the thought before stomping boots echoed down the hall.

"Look, I know she's pretty, Tristan, but Aunt Beta will string us both up if you don't bring her now," Sergio said, assessing how Tristan still held Devora's hand. "I'll grab the other prisoner."

Devora quickly wrenched her hand away. How could she have missed the pain and hurt Tristan had experienced? But still, what did it matter now? He was working with Kadesh, General Beta *and* Queen Leza. While she was still stuck behind bars with no plan or word from Tunri.

As Sergio hurried down the hall, Tristan whispered, "Trust me, honeybee." He gave her another wink and unlocked the cell door.

Devora gave a slight nod and decided not to kick him in the stomach when he came near. Sergio rushed past them toward Kanna, as if he couldn't stand being in the same space with prisoners. While Tristan took his time tying Devora's hands, Sergio was quick to knot up Kanna's wrists and lead her out of the cell.

As Tristan secured her hands behind her back, Devora said in a low voice, "Matthias doesn't hate you, far from it actually."

Tristan snorted and continued to knot the rope around her wrists, though not very tight.

Keeping her eyes forward, Devora continued, "Why else would he sacrifice his entire future at Vlacklear for you? He loves you more than you know."

At that, Tristan's hands paused for a moment then quickly finished the knot. "I hope you're right," he breathed in her ear before pushing her through the cell door.

Tristan turned Devora so she was behind Kanna and Sergio. Although Sergio acted like he was proud to be working with his aunt, his stature said otherwise.

With hunched shoulders and a deep sigh, he muttered, "Let's get this over with."

Devora noticed how Sergio gently nudged Kanna along. Now that she thought about it, Sergio was hardly cruel to them. Did he really wish to work with his aunt? Or had he been roped into this grand scheme like Tristan and Matthias, as well?

A sharp howl cut off Devora's thoughts and she jumped. "I hate that sound. What is it?" she asked, hitting Tristan's chest as she took a step back.

"Those are Aunt Beta's pets," Sergio replied, but not with the sneer Devora expected.

Another howl sounded, this time high-pitched and full of pain.

Devora winced. *What was General Beta doing with the poor creatures?*

Once Sergio was a few feet ahead, Tristan whispered, "Remember the iron-armored beasts from the Battle of Edo?"

Devora turned her head. "How do you know about those?"

Tristan scoffed. "You were all over the papers, Devora. Plus, other soldiers talk. Anyway, those creatures were once wolves."

Devora's eyes widened, hating her suspicions were correct. "What?"

She remembered the warden's wolves and their pups, praying General Beta hadn't somehow captured them.

Devora's blood suddenly went cold. Was there another reason why the queen cursed Matthias to transform into a wolf? Would she allow General Beta to morph him into one of those horrid beasts?

Tristan nodded. "Yes, General Beta likes to practice her sorcery on different creatures to see what they become. It's horrific really."

"Stop talking with the enemy," Sergio growled over his shoulder.

"He's just mad that the girl he was supposed to woo and distract at Vlacklear Academy ended up engaged to someone else," Tristan said, a smirk in his voice. "I do believe her fiancé is a duke." Yet after Sergio scowled in response, Tristan stopped speaking to Devora all the same.

Devora did her best not to jump as the howls grew louder, but she reacted anyway. *Please don't let them harm Matthias,* she prayed to Tunri. But since she had allowed herself to be captured by General Beta, Tunri had been silent.

Devora tried to block out the howls and focused on the echoing steps of her boots scraping along in the dimly lit tunnel. Where was Matthias? Nadia? Hestia and Reese? Ida? Jacques? Rae and One Shot? Were they still alive?

And where was Vinn? She hadn't heard or seen the giant white elk since Yekel. Had he been captured again? She wouldn't think Warden Hazor would recapture the giant elk, not after he had freed her and One Shot after the Battle of Edo.

Devora sighed. She was definitely walking on faith and faith alone. And though Tunri never failed her before, she was beginning to wonder when He would speak to her again.

A bright light shone in the distance. Devora and Kanna had never been outside of their cell, not since they were brought to wherever they were. The dark stone tunnel reminded her too much of the tunnel she traversed in Yekel. Yet this one sloped upwards, as if they were traveling from the underground prison she had been locked into the city above. Though she could "soldier on," Devora hated the enclosed space.

As they drew closer to the light ahead, Tristan said, "You said you'd trust me, yes? One last time, at least?"

Worry coiled around Devora's heart as she nodded.

"Good," he replied. "Then take my advice: try not to react. As best as you can."

Devora furrowed her brow before the bright light seared her vision. Clamping her eyes shut, she waited a moment before she gasped. An enormous octangular room lay before her, carved of the same dark stone as the tunnel. Thousands of orbs of light latched on to the walls, surrounding a giant imperial opal statue of Pahga in the center.

Tristan squeezed her wrists once as Devora's eyes traveled the length of the statue to its base. She suddenly understood the advice Tristan had given her, for at the bottom of the statue stood Queen Leza with Matthias, bound in chains.

Chapter Twenty-Seven

Rae, Radaa Kingdom, Kadesh

Rae made herself tear her eyes away from Ben when she heard what Sayidi Tamor had bellowed. The prince had requested Haden's presence.

She can tell him about the statues, Rae thought before she realized she was so wrapped up in her argument with Ben she had never spoken to Haden about her thoughts of her birth.

"You must be prepared at once to meet with the crown prince," Sayidi Tamor boomed to Haden, who looked like she wanted to crawl back into bed and hide from the large man.

Rae didn't know what the prince desired, but whether good or bad, she had to tell Haden the conclusion she had come to. If she didn't tell her now, she would regret it forever.

"Sayidi Tamor," Rae interjected, giving a curtsy for good measure. "Could we at least dine with our friend one last time before she becomes the next princess of Kadesh?" Rae added on a giggle, causing Haden to turn whiter than the sheets on her bed. Out of the corner of her eye, Rae saw Ben try to restrain the smirk that was trying to form on his lips.

It had only been one night since their argument and Rae already missed those lips. And when Ben strode through the door behind Sayidi Tamor, she couldn't believe that Haden spoke the truth. He really had guarded their door the entire night. Even when she hadn't said she loved him back, even when she had broken his heart, he was still there for her.

Rae focused her thoughts back on Haden. She needed to speak to the princess.

Sayidi Tamor glanced between the three girls before he released a sigh. "I suppose a short breakfast wouldn't hurt. I will inform the prince you will be delayed." He sent a striking glare at all of them. "I suggest you eat quickly."

Rae nodded, trying to ignore the shiver racing down her spine as Sayidi Tamor turned to Ben. "Guard, retrieve these ladies some nourishment from the kitchen then get some rest. You look like a cow sat on your face."

A snort snuck out of Haden's mouth to which she quickly slammed her hands over her lips. But amusement still shone in her eyes.

Ben sucked in a breath and bowed to Sayidi Tamor. Rae watched him go, praying he would look back at her. But as he took each step toward the door without turning to Rae, her heart sank lower and lower. Yet, as he was ready to leave the room, he glanced over his shoulder.

"I will try to grab some scones and orange rolls before they're all gone," his eyes flitted to hers, and Rae's heart almost burst out of her chest as he continued through the doorway.

When they were in Yekel, Rae shared her lunch with Ben, giving him her favorite orange blossom rolls. Later, he came to her house with his own homemade scones. Only she knew what those pastries meant to them. And she was thankful that there was still hope to mend the mess she had made.

"He better walk faster than that if he wants any pastries," Sayidi Tamor grunted as he stalked toward the door. "They're always the first things to go." Rae smirked at the large man's comment before he added, "You will get thirty minutes and no more. The prince does not like to be kept waiting."

"Understood," Rae agreed with a firm nod.

Once the burly man left the room, Rae turned to Ida and Haden who were watching her with expectation.

"I wanted to apologize," she started, as she sat down at the foot of her bed. "There was much we needed to discuss last night, and I was..." She trailed off.

"It's okay, Rae," Ida said offering a hand of comfort on Rae's shoulder. "We've all had moments like that."

Haden nodded and sat at the edge of her own bed. Rae noted how Haden's hair dye had almost fully washed out, allowing its natural white-blonde color to shine through. The same color that Rae's own short hair was starting to show; the same color they both shared with their mother.

A knock sounded at the door and Rae sprang up, knowing it was Ben. When she opened the door, he held out a golden tray with a stack of pastries and fruits.

"Thank you," Rae said, hoping she could speak with him again after Haden went to see the prince.

As she went to reach for the platter, Ben motioned to her wrist. "You're still wearing it."

Rae glanced down at the beautiful bracelet, still unable to believe Ben would go to such lengths to procure it for her. It was stunning in every sense of the word. "Of course," she replied. "I'll never take it off."

Ben tilted his head to the side and Rae couldn't help but find him adorable. It took everything within her not to pull his lips to hers, but now wasn't the time.

"I would like to talk again, if that's okay," she said, praying she wouldn't drop the tray due to her shaking hands. "After you rest, if you'd like. I know you've been up all night."

Ben gave her a soft smile. "I can wait until you're finished with breakfast. As long as you don't mind that I look like a cow sat on me."

A giggle bubbled up Rae's throat and escaped through her lips before she could stop it. She instantly did what Haden had a moment ago and slapped her hand over her mouth.

Ben's smile grew before he gently nudged her through the doorway. "You know where I am when you need me."

Rae nodded and headed inside, her heart already filled with hope.

Haden and Ida tried to act as if they hadn't heard the entire exchange, but they were very poor actresses. Still, Rae appreciated the effort and smiled as she placed the tray down between the three of them.

"Let's eat and try to discuss as much as we can before Sayidi Tamor returns," Rae suggested.

Haden's stomach released a loud roar, causing Ida and Rae to chuckle. She flushed. "I haven't eaten much since dinner with the prince. I've been unsettled about the information I discovered."

"What information?" Ida questioned.

While Haden had already told Rae about the general's evil plot, Ida was still in the dark. Once Haden finished explaining about the imperial opal statue of Pahga beneath Kadesh, a look of horror passed over Ida's face.

"Here is the scroll I found in Mother's desk," Haden said as she strode to her bed. Crouching down, she pulled a leather bag from beneath the bedframe and rummaged in it until she produced a scroll. "Maybe you can figure out something I can't." She offered it to Ida, who snatched it with uncharacteristic haste.

While Ida poured over the scroll, Rae ripped a piece of flatbread and placed it in her mouth. "I'm curious as to why General Beta shared such secret information with you in the room. She knows who you are, doesn't she?"

Haden plucked a dried date from the tray. "Unfortunately. Her and Mother—the queen, I mean—are good friends. She visited the palace all the time while I was growing up." Ida and Rae stared at Haden in shock. Haden stopped chewing. "What?"

"Didn't you think it's a little odd that a general of Kadesh, the sworn enemy of Tenton, is friends with the queen?" Rae asked, worried at how sheltered Haden must have been growing up.

"At the time, no," Haden admitted with a shrug. "I really didn't know much about Aunt Beta, and Mother kept me out of foreign affairs."

"But why?" Ida asked, her brows furrowed as she studied the scroll. "You're the successor to the throne. Shouldn't you learn by her side?"

Haden kept her gaze down as she fiddled with her fingers. "I'm not very quick. I read and write fairly slowly, and my aristocratic manners are lacking to say the least. Mother said princesses are to be seen and not heard. That I needed to rely on my beauty to get me where I should go."

Rae snorted as she crossed her hands over her chest. "A person is more than their outward appearance."

Ida nodded with agreement and Haden smiled. "Thank you, but that's the reason why I was so in the dark about everything. What I know now"—she swatted her hand in the air—"I've struggled to learn on my own."

"I'm so sorry, Haden," Ida said, laying the scroll down to squeeze Haden's hand. "We would like to help you with your mission, if you could help us with ours."

Rae nodded, hoping she could divulge the secret of her heart soon. "After Kadesh attacked Maldove Palace, Devora willingly went with General Beta. Since then, we have no idea where she is or what happened to her."

"We are also looking for Kanna Blake," Ida added. "General Blake's mother, who is also a Seer and has been captured for years."

Rae watched Haden suck in a breath, coming to the same conclusion. Only by Tunri's hand could all three of their interests align perfectly. For while Rae and Ida had been searching for their Seers, Haden had been too. Though she didn't know it, she too was trying to save them.

Haden gestured to the scroll Ida had gone back to studying. "I assumed the statue could extract a gift, based on the illustrations. But Aunt Beta's plan for the Tentonian troops confirmed it." She turned to Rae. "And it sounds like the statue in Yekel could do this, which confirms my fear that Mother has found a way to extract not just the soul of a person, but if they have a gift from Tunri, their power, as well."

Ida glanced up from the scroll, her eyes shining gold. "Yes, that's what the Book of Ages had said. The power of a gifted individual is found in their soul. That must be what the queen was trying to figure out how to do with the imperial opal."

While Rae had seen Ida's eyes glow before, Haden gawked. "A-are your eyes gold?" she stammered.

Ida blinked a few times, allowing the gold to dissipate. "Yes, I have a gift, as well. I'm a Translator and can understand, read, and speak any language."

"Sounds like something I need," Haden chuckled.

Rae pursed her lips, running through what Ida and Haden had just said. "But why?" she asked aloud, her brows furrowed. "Why does the queen want all that power? She's already the queen of Tenton."

Haden shook her head. "I don't know, but once I found out she had taken me from my family to try to use me for a gift I didn't have *and* about this horrible plan to harm others, I couldn't stay there anymore. I fled trying to find my uncle in Kadesh hoping he could help me find a way to gain an audience with the prince." Haden blushed then looked at the door. "It somehow worked out. I'm sure Sayidi Tamor will be back any moment now."

Rae paused a moment, trying to make sure she handled her next conversation properly. "So, the king and queen aren't your real parents?" she asked quietly.

Haden eyed her with suspicion and Rae didn't blame her. "No, but I'm thankful for that. Though I do wish I could find out who my real parents are. I found a genealogy scroll in the library—or rather a man with white hair gave me one—and it led me to my uncle, here, in Kadesh."

"A man with white hair," Ida repeated before her eyes went wide. "And a mustache?"

Haden nodded.

Ida shook her head with a laugh. "That's Warden Hazor, the warden of the Fortress. He always seems to be one step ahead of the rest of us."

"Your uncle," Rae continued, keeping her eyes fixated on Haden. "What's his name?"

Haden fidgeted with the slices of cheese she had put on her plate. "Uh, his name is Miguel. Miguel Salvar."

Ida gasped and looked from Haden to Rae then back to Haden. "I see it." She then turned to Rae. "Why didn't you say anything sooner?"

"What?" Haden cried, glancing all around as if a bug had landed on her shoulder. Rae did her best to hold back her laugh as the girl quickly swatted at both sides. "See what?"

Ida grinned. "The resemblance."

Haden's eyes widened as she turned toward Rae.

Rae gave her a small smile, trying to seem as non-threatening as possible.

"What—what are you saying?" Haden asked.

Rae thought Haden would look horrified, but her eyes lit with hope and excitement.

Taking a leap of faith Rae said, "Haden, I think you may be my sister."

When Sayidi Tamor banged on the door to collect Haden only a moment later, Rae wasn't ready to see her little sister go. In fact, Haden was a puddle of tears—tears of joy, that is—at the fact she and Rae were related.

"That's why you were always watching me," Haden blubbered. "I just assumed you hated me."

Rae laughed, and hugged Haden. "How could I hate you? I had just met you."

"I don't know," Haden laugh cried.

Three loud knocks boomed on the door again and Rae feared the large man would break the wood in half.

"You need to go," Rae said, wiping her own wet eyes.

"I know," Haden said with a sniff. "But the prince is going to think I look horrible. My eyes swell like grapefruits when I cry."

Rae laughed and handed Haden a handkerchief, remembering Nadia telling her the same thing. Oh, how Rae couldn't wait to have Nadia and Haden together, and to reunite with Mami and Papi and be a complete family again.

If Mami is still alive.

Rae pushed the thought from her mind. Mami would be alive. Tunri would protect her. He had to.

Standing, Rae hurried to the door and just in time. Sayidi Tamor had a key in the lock, ready to burst in.

"Apologies, sir," Rae said. "As you know us young ladies get nervous when we are about to see the one we care for." Rae shifted her gaze to Ben who was still dutifully standing outside their door, though he looked exhausted.

"Yes, well, now is not the time for nerves," Sayidi Tamor said, marching past Rae. "The prince is already irritated to have waited this long. Come along, Haden. It's time."

Rae took a step back from the door as Haden stepped forward. "There's so much more I want to tell you," she told Rae, her eyes glistening again.

Rae reached out and pulled Haden close, saying a quick prayer over her. "There will be time for that. Now don't cry again. Remember, grapefruits."

Haden sniffed and laughed, trying to hold back her tears. "I will relay all I know to the prince. Please send a prayer for me," she added.

"Of course."

"Don't forget this," Ida cried, hurrying to hand the scroll to Haden. "Good luck, Haden. Tunri is with you."

Haden squeezed both of her hands and turned back to Sayidi Tamor who was looking at all three of them with a confused look.

"From what I know, an invitation from the crown prince is a good thing, you act as if you are going to your death, Haden."

Haden sucked in a breath and smiled, but Rae saw the fear lurking behind her eyes. They all knew she was the princess of Tenton, but did the prince?

———————>

"I think I'm going to get some fresh air in the courtyard," Ida said as she hurried out of the room before Rae could stop her.

"Wait," Rae called, knowing Ida was trying to give her and Ben time alone.

But Rae had just divulged a huge area of her heart to Haden. Having a long-lost sister, someone who was a part of her but in a different body, was an incredible thing. But Rae was emotionally spent from the ordeal. Could her heart handle another deep discussion?

Rae glanced down at the shimmering bracelet. Ben loved her. And Rae loved him. And he deserved to know.

Praying that Tunri would help her find the right words to say, Rae stepped toward Ben, who was still playing the perfect guard.

"I told her," she said, leaning her back against the wall next to him.

Ben turned his head toward her. "How did she take it?"

Rae smiled, remembering Haden burst into tears of happiness at the fact she wasn't alone in this cold world. "Well, from what I can see."

"Good," Ben replied. He waited a few moments then asked, "So where does that leave us?"

Rae's heart pounded in her chest. Reaching out, she grabbed Ben's large hand.

"I have known what my heart feels for you for a long time. I've just been too scared to say it. What if you didn't feel the same? What if you got tired of me? What if my scars were too deep for both of us?"

Ben shook his head. "Never. I laid my heart bare before you." He swallowed. "I still feel the same. I don't know if I'll ever stop loving you."

Tears misted in Rae's eyes as she clutched Ben's hands. "Ben, I l—"

But before Rae could tell him how she truly felt, a high-pitched scream ricocheted through the courtyard. Ben and Rae shared a glance before they took off running in the direction Ida had gone.

"Ida!" Rae cried, as they ran toward the fountain of the courtyard.

Ben reached behind his back and pulled out his crossbow, aiming at the figure who stood above Ida's unmoving form.

"Don't take a step closer," Raphael ordered, his face filled with malice. "Or the same thing will happen to you."

Rae didn't have time to think before she was rushing toward Ida with Ben behind her. Everything happened so fast. Something hard smacked Rae in the head. Ben screamed her name, she tried to get to him as Raphael latched shining manacles on his wrists. As soon as Ben sunk to his knees, Rae knew they had to be imperial opal.

"Ben," she croaked, reaching out to him as he fell forward on the courtyard path.

"Don't worry, he'll be in good hands."

Placing his boot over Rae's extended hand, Raphael crushed Rae's fingers. She cried out in pain before something smacked her in the head again and everything turned black.

Chapter Twenty-Eight

Haden, Radaa Kingdom, Kadesh

A sister! I have a sister! Haden rejoiced in her mind as Sayidi Tamor led her to the same preparation room as before.

Haden still couldn't believe it. Her family, right in the same room. It had to be the work of Tunri. How else could she have found her birth family in the enemy nation?

Haden couldn't wait to know more. But as Sayidi Tamor opened the door to the lavish room where Sayida Erza was waiting, Haden had to forget about Rae and her mother and father for now and focus on winning the approval of the prince.

"You know how to make all the ladies shine, Sayida Erza," Sayidi Tamor said with a nod. "I know you will make her fit for the prince. But make haste. We are already late." He sent a glare at Haden then exited the room.

Haden winced at the glare before Sayida Erza closed the door behind the burly man.

"Don't listen to him, my dear," the beautiful woman said. "You hardly need my help to look breathtaking. Though," she tapped her finger on her pink lips. "Should we rid your hair of this dye once and for all? I know many of the girls like to change their hair colors these days, but it seems like yours has taken a turn for the worst." She gave Haden a sympathetic smile.

Sighing, Haden nodded. She knew the prince invited her into his presence because she was caught sneaking around last night. If he was going to try her for espionage, he may as well know who she truly was.

Sayida Erza worked efficiently and effectively as she scrubbed, washed, and combed Haden's white-blonde hair clean. The alluring scent of jasmine filled the room as Erza opened another bottle and placed a small amount of the liquid in each of her hands.

"This is my husband's favorite scent," she explained as she threaded her fingers through Haden's hair, filling it with the aroma. "He is always at my beck and call when I wear it."

Haden's eyes went wide and Sayida Erza laughed. "Not to worry, Haden. I'm just trying to give you all the favor you can gain from the prince."

As Erza continued cleaning and styling Haden's hair, Haden glanced over to the fabric lying on the bed. It was the opposite color of the dress she wore before, being mostly orange with blue and gold trim this time. But what concerned her the most was the veil lying next to it. Of course it was stunning, a shade of cream embroidered with cerulean, orange, and gold beads. But what did it mean? Was she walking into her wedding without knowing it? But why would the prince want to marry her after he caught her spying on him and Mal?

Haden's eyes landed on one of the beaded images of a sparrow depicted to be flying along the edge of the material. It *was* interesting how the symbol of Kadesh was a sparrow, and she could transform into one. Had Tunri orchestrated the whole thing? Haden would never know.

As Erza instructed her to close her eyes, Haden thought about her previous conversation with Mal. It still left her uneasy. He knew she could shift into a sparrow but was suspiciously accepting of it. *And,* for a guard, he was very friendly with the crown prince. Something didn't add up, but Haden knew there were many missing pieces to the puzzle.

"Don't furrow your brow," Sayida Erza instructed.

"Sorry," Haden mumbled as she felt Erza place something cool on her face.

Haden recollected the hugs and prayers Rae and Ida said over her before she left. She wished they were here with her, to help her get ready for whatever awaited her with her meeting with the prince. Though she had just discovered Rae was her sister, once the information was known, it felt as if a gaping hole in her heart had been filled. She wanted to know everything about Rae: her favorite color, food, did she like to rise early or stay up late? What was her relationship with Ben? Were their parents still alive?

Haden's thoughts froze. Her parents. Her *real* parents, alive. For so long she had been belittled and forgotten by Father and Mother—the king and queen of Tenton—it was surreal to think that there were two people in the world that desired her to be with them.

"Pout your lips," Erza instructed, and Haden raised a brow. Erza smirked. "Stick them out like this—" She pooched her lips in a perfect o-shape and Haden giggled.

Haden pursed her lips the same as Erza and as soon she did, the woman placed a bright red rouge on them.

"Now don't speak until it's dry or it will smear, and you'll look like the king's jester. And we do *not* want that. Funny as he may be, he is a fright to look at." Erza shivered before cleaning up her different brushes.

Haden's brows rose, but she resisted the urge to ask more about the king's jester.

Based on Sayidi Tamor's reaction to giving her thirty extra minutes with Ida and Rae, Haden thought it would take her hours to get ready for meeting the crown prince. She remembered how she hated getting ready for the balls at Maldove Palace. Though she looked beautiful at the end, her back hurt, her head felt like it had been stabbed with hundreds of pins and she couldn't feel her legs.

But Erza had her hair and face finished within less than an hour.

"Okay, before we put on your dress, take a look." Erza held up a gilded mirror.

Haden blinked a few times, surprised to see she didn't look too different than how she normally looked.

"If the prince likes your natural beauty, we keep your natural beauty," Erza replied to Haden's surprised look. "Oh, and you can peel off the rouge."

Unsure of what Erza meant, Haden reached up to her lips, peeling off the sticky red goop.

"Oh," Haden said, loving the perfectly pink tint of her lips. Now she knew how Erza looked so lovely all the time.

"Stand," Erza commanded as she came at Haden with the dress from the bed. "Arms up," she continued, once Haden was on her feet.

Haden obeyed and Erza wrapped the orange fabric with blue and gold trim around Haden several times until an intricate dress had been draped comfortably around her form.

Stepping back, Erza smiled. "Lovely, just lovely. Now for the veil."

Noticing Erza's shorter stature, Haden bent her knees so the woman could place the veil upon her head. The cream mesh flowed over Haden's shoulders and down her back. The front was cut short to her chin but still covered her face. Haden didn't understand why she had to have cosmetics at all if her face was just going to be covered, but she didn't want to question Erza's methods. Plus, the prince had already seen her at her interrogation *and* when her transformation failed her. What was the point of covering her face?

A loud knock sounded at the door and both women turned toward it.

"Just in time," Erza breathed. She quickly took Haden's hands. "You are beautiful, my dear. But remember, a queen is beautiful both inside and out. And from what I've seen and heard, you fit that very well."

Erza squeezed Haden's hands then opened the door. Outside stood Sayidi Tamor and Mal, both in pristine white outfits with azure and orange trim.

"We're almost late," Sayidi Tamor said, a growl behind his words. "The crown prince will not be pleased."

"Almost late is not the same as late," Erza chirped before gently pushing Haden forward. "Now hurry along."

Sayidi Tamor snorted at Erza but offered Haden his arm.

Haden hurriedly grabbed the scroll she brought all the way from Tenton before hooking her arm in Sayidi Tamor's large bicep. She expected Mal to say something to her, to give her one of his crooked smiles or make a quip about the long veil. But he said nothing, just kept his face forward and blank, like any good soldier would.

Haden's heart fell, realizing that once she began a relationship with the prince, she would have to break her relationship with Mal. No more *sheta* in the kitchens, or silly jokes walking from awful pageant classes. Haden let herself feel sad for a few moments as her guards led her silently down the hall but then pushed the sadness away. This was her whole reason for coming to Kadesh. Other than finding Miguel, she needed to speak with the monarchy so they could stop Mother from her horrible plan. There hadn't been any chaos in Kadesh yet, so Haden wasn't too late. Though she wished to get to know Mal more and spend time with him, the future of Tenton and Kadesh rested in her hands. And they both knew a princess and a guard could never be together.

Sayidi Tamor led Haden to the dining hall where General Beta had unveiled her evil plan.

"Good luck, Princess," Sayidi Tamor said with a deep bow, leaving her alone with Mal.

Haden turned toward Mal, slowly lifting her eyes through her veil. She found Mal already searching her face, his eyes a tornado of conflicting emotions. What was he thinking? Did he realize that after her meeting with the prince, what they shared—whatever it was—would be done? Was he as pained about it as she was?

After a few awkward moments of silence, Haden said, "Well, I guess this is it."

"I guess so," Mal said, his voice low.

Haden took in his somber face as she reflected on when she had first met him in the market. Mal had known all along she was the princess of Tenton, but didn't say anything. How different would her life be if she would've been able to keep the truth to herself. At least for a little while.

But no, she had a duty to her country and her people. She couldn't allow Mother to destroy both Tenton *and* Kadesh with her nefarious plans. Duty before all else. That's what she was taught, and that's what she would do. Even if her heart was breaking on the inside.

Haden opened her mouth to say more but couldn't find any more words to say. Instead, she closed her lips and gave Mal a nod before turning to the door to face her future. Sucking in a breath, she started forward when she was spun around.

Eyes wide, Haden faced Mal once more. Carefully, he lifted the veil from her face and cupped her cheek. The warmth from his palm seeped into her cool skin, wrapping her sorrowful heart in love and care.

"There's so much to tell you, but no time," he said quickly, and Haden couldn't help but swoon at the cadence of his voice. "But if there's anything I want you to know it's this: You captured my heart from the moment I saw you in the market. Before I figured out you were the princess of Tenton, I had to know who you were. Though the black hair was great and a good disguise, I love who you are, who you really are, who I have gotten to know over this short time. Please remember that as you meet the prince."

Haden's brows rose as Mal's words came out in a rush. Her mind tried to run over everything he said, wanting to cherish it, but her thoughts were frozen.

"One more thing. Remember this—" And before Haden could try to react, Mal leaned forward and pressed his lips to hers.

Haden's stomach did so many flips, she wasn't sure how she wasn't queasy. The kiss was soft and sweet, much like the *sheta* drink they shared in the kitchen.

When Mal broke away—far too soon for Haden's liking—he pressed his forehead against hers. "Everything is going to change after this," he whispered. "Please don't forget the Mal who was only your guard."

The statement broke Haden from the lovesick trance she was in. "What are you talking about?"

But before Mal could answer, the doors to the throne room opened. Mal quickly placed the veil back over Haden's face and turned her around.

"Ah, the princess of Tenton, here all along," Sayidi Brocaw said with a grand smile. "We are honored and hope to settle affairs with Tenton diplomatically."

Chills ran down Haden's spine at the pompous man's tone. She wasn't sure what lay beneath his smile, but she didn't like it.

"Right this way. The prince is eager to meet Your Majesty." Sayidi Brocaw spun around.

Swallowing, Haden followed Sayidi Brocaw, unsure if Mal was still behind her or not. His steps had always been silent, but now they seemed nonexistent.

Breathe, Haden told herself. Though Mother hadn't let her sit in many political meetings, Haden had been able to persuade the queen a few times. All Haden had to do was be the perfect princess she was taught to be, and everything would go well.

But that was the problem. Haden wasn't the perfect princess she was supposed to be. She was clumsy, she snorted when she laughed, she couldn't read or write well. Yet, all those things, her "faults," were what made her who she was. And, since fleeing Maldove Palace, Haden actually liked who she was. Not the princess of Tenton, not the next heir to the throne. Just Haden. And she realized that maybe this meeting didn't need the princess of Tenton. Maybe, with Tunri's grace, it needed just Haden.

Finding her confidence, Haden squared her shoulders and waited outside the room where Sayidi Brocaw entered. A few moments passed and the steward reappeared. With a sly smile on his face, he bowed deeply.

"Your prince awaits, princess."

Haden did her best not to be affected by his slimy words and leering eyes as she strode into the room. When the door shut behind her, Haden realized Mal had not entered with her.

Thank Tunri, she thought and added. *Please help me not mess this up.*

She had traveled for weeks, praying to get to this moment. Praying to meet the prince or king of Kadesh and unveil the queen's awful plot happening right beneath Kadesh's streets. She couldn't back down now.

Swirls of thick incense coated the room, smelling of jasmine and rose. Haden almost thought she was back in the garden with Mal. But Mal wasn't there.

Trying not to crumple the scroll within her palms, Haden let out a squeak when a figure arose from the back wall of the room. The prince, dressed in an outfit matching her own, stood.

Haden waited, knowing the crown prince never spoke. But with no one else here but them, he had to speak, right?

It felt as if hours went by as Haden faced the prince in his blue mask.

"Why are you here, Princess of Tenton?" the prince finally said. "To spy on us? Infiltrate our forces? Defeat us from within?"

Haden jumped at the low, commanding voice. She didn't know how she expected the prince to sound, but it wasn't with such a baritone voice.

She found herself reassessing everything Queen Leza told her. *"Just stand there and smile."* And that's all Haden wished she could do in this moment of fear, stand there and look pretty. But another feeling overtook her insecurities and fear. One of confidence and hope. She had always desired to show the world she wasn't just a pretty face. This was her time to use her voice and speak the truth. And she would.

Performing a curtsy, Haden lowered herself before the masked prince. "Your Highness, I am honored you have chosen me for a meeting in private. My deceit was not intended to infiltrate Kadesh for evil purposes, but to give aid and ask for assistance."

"Aid? What aid can the pretty princess of Tenton give Kadesh?"

Haden winced at the words and mocking tone, knowing that was her reputation across Tenton. Just a pretty face. But there was so much more to her. And she would make sure everyone knew.

Straightening, Haden lifted her chin and faced the prince.

"This pretty princess of Tenton happens to know all the information regarding Queen Leza's plan to destroy Kadesh *and* Tenton." She took a breath then decided to continue. "But if you are too proud to heed my warning, then maybe destruction is best for you." The fire in Haden's stomach faded with the last words and her own mouth dropped open.

Did I really just say all that to the prince of Kadesh? He's going to have me executed for speaking so boldly.

The minutes ticked by; the incense that Haden enjoyed only moments ago now stifled her lungs.

"What information do you wish to give me?" the prince finally asked.

Haden breathed a sigh of relief, thankful she wasn't to be executed. At least not yet.

She extended the scroll to the masked prince, who carefully took it from her fingertips. "The queen has planned to wipe out Kadesh from within," she began. "She has a power like no other: the power to take one's soul. This power has been confirmed by other witnesses who have seen it happen before in Yekel, when Kadesh was in power there. With this information, I hoped Kadesh would be able to stop her. She is working with General Beta. I believe there is at least one statue of your nation's goddess, Pahga, that can harvest the souls of every person in this kingdom. Please believe what I say is true."

Haden clamped her lips shut, knowing she had said everything that needed to be said. She watched the prince as he studied the scroll. Or at least she thought he was looking at the scroll. She hated the mask the prince wore, for she couldn't read any of the emotions on his face.

"If the queen of Tenton discovers you're here, you will be tried for treason and hanged."

Haden swallowed, knowing all along that was her fate. "Yes, I know."

"Yet you came anyway. Into a foreign land, one which hates you and your people."

"I did it to save all of our people," she replied, feeling her confidence rise again. "Our people do not deserve to lose their loved ones to this war any longer. It has gone on long enough."

The prince gave a slight nod. "Very well. I believe your information, but I need you alive. Since you have fled here, you will be under my protection. However, an alliance must be made."

Haden blinked. *An alliance?* She then remembered the matrimony law of Kadesh and her cheeks flamed with heat. Why did the gallows seem more welcoming than agreeing to a marriage alliance with the prince? She knew that an arranged marriage was in her future one way or another, but she never expected to marry the prince of her enemy.

The crown prince of Kadesh extended his palm. "Do we have an agreement?"

Haden bit her bottom lip, the taste of Mal still lingering from when he kissed her. What was he doing? Was he waiting for her? Or had he said his goodbye and fled?

Haden pushed thoughts of Mal to the side. He was a palace guard, and she was the princess. Marriage alliances were created all the time. Nothing was worse than the queen caging her every night. She would muddle through it somehow. She only prayed she wasn't fleeing one cage to be trapped in another.

Extending her arm, Haden placed her hand in the prince's, sealing the agreement. But, something felt odd about the prince's hand. His fingers were soft and thin, not unlike her own hand. It's not that the prince *couldn't* have nice skin, but she expected his hand to be more *man-like*.

Retracting her hand, Haden waited, not knowing what to do now.

"Well," the prince said, his voice rising an octave. "I'm glad we finally got that over with."

Confusion swept over Haden as the prince took off his blue mask. A long swath of dark curls tumbled out, cascading over the prince's back. But once Haden saw the small nose, kohl-lined eyes and lush lips, she realized something was wrong.

"You're not the prince of Kadesh, are you?" Haden asked, staring at the beautiful woman before her.

The woman laughed, looking to be a year or two older than Haden. "Oh goodness, no. I just play the part because the *actual* prince, my brother, has no patience for the monarchy. I'm Princess Amalia of Kadesh." The woman gave a flourishing bow. "Though most people think I am always traveling or at school." She waved her bronze hand in the air like it was nonsense.

Haden furrowed her brow. "So...who am I marrying then?"

Princess Amalia laughed again, a jovial alto. Haden knew she wasn't laughing at her, but she didn't appreciate the ruse all the same.

"Oh, Haden, don't you know? You've already met the real prince of Kadesh."

A series of footsteps sounded from behind the princess of Kadesh and it took everything in Haden's power to not gasp as Mal stepped next to his sister.

Chapter Twenty-Nine

Matthias, Delequa Iron, Tenton

It was amazing how quickly yet slowly things progressed once Queen Leza gave the go-ahead to create a large version of the weapon Lucas Salvar, Rae's father, had created. And when the queen allowed Matthias to stay at Delequa Iron to oversee its production, Matthias almost fainted. He hadn't been granted so much freedom from the queen since before he was cursed. But that didn't mean he lowered his guard. Every so often, his wolf senses spiked, and he searched around him. He always felt that, somehow, Queen Leza was still watching him.

However, there were other forces that Matthias felt were controlling the progress of the weapons. Some days, the iron was smelted perfectly and the molds for the weapon were cast on time. Yet, other days, it was as if everything in Tenton was working against them to get the weapon built. He didn't wish to go to war any sooner than the next soldier, but he knew this weapon was pivotal in defeating the queen in whatever her plans were.

On this particular day, however, Matthias was surprised to find not Jacques but Warden Hazor in Jacques' office that morning.

"Warden." Matthias stepped back with surprise.

Since Queen Leza promoted Matthias to general and the attack on Maldove Palace, Matthias couldn't remember the last time he had seen the warden. It saddened him. This was the man who had taken Matthias under his wing when Matthias was lost in the world. Though it was sometimes a hard place to be, Warden Hazor always took care of Matthias.

"To what do I owe the pleasure?" Matthias finally asked as the warden stayed silently glaring out one of the tall arched windows to the right of Jacques' desk.

"No need to act like you're happy to see me, Blake," the warden said, a chuckle layering his words.

Matthias smirked and stood beside him. "I hate to tell you, sir, but I actually am glad to see you. Things have been—"

"Insane," the warden finished, and Matthias nodded.

He wasn't sure if it was the warden's frankness or the fact that everyone feared Warden Hazor more than Matthias, but Matthias always felt more at ease with the warden around. Like the burden he bore wasn't as heavy; there was someone else there to shoulder it with him.

"I'm leaving, Blake."

Matthias turned his gaze from the metal workers pounding different rods into shape. "What do you mean?"

The warden kept his cold eyes focused below. "There is something I've been charged to do and though I've tried my best to avoid it, I must meet it head on. All the players are finally where they need to be."

Matthias narrowed his eyes, trying to figure out what the warden meant. But the burly man continued, "Have you noticed Vinn isn't around?"

"Well, yes, but I assumed he was looking for Devora," Matthias started then stopped. "You know the elk's name?"

Warden Hazor turned toward him, his cool stare sending a chill down Matthias' spine. "I know many things, Blake. You should know that by now." The warden stroked his mustache and started toward the exit. "Until Kanna and Devora are free, I am to care for Vinn. I'm leaving to find him. But know that the delays happening to the weapon are not mistakes. Do not fight any obstacle. You will be thankful for the extra time."

Matthias blinked at the warden, unsure of what to say. Usually, he could decipher the cryptic messages but this time he was at a loss. "Sir, I don't understand," Matthias finally admitted.

The warden smiled. "I remember a time when you would never dare say that to my face. You've done well, Blake. This is not a goodbye. Not yet."

Before Matthias could utter another word, Warden Hazor left the office. A loud explosion caused Matthias to run to the window. A plume of black smoke mushroomed over one of the pieces of machinery. Puzzled, Matthias watched as the workers frantically tried to wave the smoke away.

"What are you up to, warden?" Matthias muttered under his breath, his mind reeling over all the possible solutions to the warden's curious statements.

The door to Jacques' office slammed open, Jacques himself flying in with a flurry of scrolls in his hands.

"What in the blazes is happening now? At this rate we'll never get the machine finished," Jacques said, then continued to babble about his stress while trying to run a company and plan a wedding. He then said something about how he couldn't decide between roses or lilies for his upcoming nuptials. But to Matthias it was all static as he continued to attempt to decipher the warden's words.

"Matthias? Matthias?" Jacques said snapping his fingers in front of Matthias' nose.

Blinking, Matthias shook his head and focused on Jacques. "Apologies, Jacques. I didn't realize you were here."

Jacques gave him a flat look. It was then Matthias noticed the dark circles lining his friend's eyes. How many sleepless nights had Jacques endured since inheriting his father's company? Matthias couldn't imagine the daily work Jacques had to deal with, especially after he discovered the former Duke Delequa had been secretly selling iron to Kadesh for their weapons and armor.

"I don't know why everything is such a mess," Jacques continued, running a hand through his already-disheveled hair. "I feel like every time I try to take a step forward, I'm pushed back four."

Matthias nodded. "You're trying to make right what your father did wrong for years. Things are not going to change overnight."

Jacques frowned at him and then sighed, slumping into the chair before his desk. "You're right. Maybe I should just give the company over to someone else who could run it better." He glanced over at Matthias.

Matthias gave him a cold glare. "Don't even think about it. I have enough I need to fix."

Jacques cradled his head in his hands as a knock sounded at the door.

The two men glanced at each other, both reading each other's mind. Was it the queen?

The knock sounded again.

"It's your office," Matthias said, but when Jacques wouldn't budge from his chair Matthias rolled his eyes and stomped to the door. "Yes?" he said.

A young boy, maybe twelve summers, stood before Matthias with a leather pouch at his side filled with pieces of parchment. His boots were caked with mud and sand, but the rest of him was fairly clean. A mess of unruly black curls was stuffed into a tan cap, a few strands escaping as the boy rummaged through the pack on his side.

Matthias waited as the boy dug through the pack.

"A message for Duke Delequa," the boy said, handing Matthias a neatly rolled scroll. How it remained so tidy in the mess of papers the boy had, Matthias didn't know. But as he gave the boy a coin and started to close the door, the boy put his hand out.

"Wait," the boy cried then lowered his voice. "I have two more notes. But these are secret."

Matthias quirked a brow but then immediately thought of Devora. Had she somehow escaped? Were her and his mother free? His heart thundered in his ears as the boy pulled out two crumpled pieces of paper.

"You didn't get this from me, sir," the boy said so softly, Matthias almost missed it. He then tipped his head and said "good day" before scurrying away.

"Thank goodness it wasn't that wretched woman or one of her lackeys," Jacques said as Matthias closed the door, his eyes still on the crumpled papers. "What have you got there?"

"This is for you." Matthias handed Jacques the scroll.

Jacques practically leapt across the desk to get to the paper.

Matthias broke his gaze from the parchments. "News from your beloved?"

Jacques ignored the sarcasm in Matthias' voice. "I hope so."

As Jacques scanned the contents of the scroll, Matthias walked toward the window once more. The crew below seemed to have fixed whatever had happened to the machinery and were back at work smelting the iron ore.

Glancing down, Matthias stared at the first paper. Crumpled and ripped at the edges, the secret note resembled how he felt. But why was he so hesitant to open it? If it was from Devora, he should be overjoyed she was safe. But somehow, he knew it wasn't from her. What he feared was that it was news that he was too late. His mother and Devora were gone.

Swallowing, Matthias prayed he was wrong and opened the paper.

When the time comes, you need to trust me.

Matthias sucked in a breath. He knew that sloppy, slanted handwriting. It wasn't Devora's handwriting, but Tristan's.

What was his no-good brother up to now?

Matthias opened the other note and frowned. He didn't recognize the handwriting at all, but the information on it was baffling.

"Matthias," Jacques exclaimed, jumping up from his chair. "It seems the prince of Kadesh has found himself a future queen."

Matthias folded the paper and placed it in his pocket. If the information on it was true, he may have just gained the winning strike against Kadesh and the queen of Tenton. His gaze then darted to Jacques. "Is this public knowledge?"

"I don't think so, but we better work fast."

Matthias nodded. He had been studying the laws and history of Kadesh for years. He knew that when the young prince found a wife, he would become the next king of Kadesh. A new king meant a new willpower to fight, a new force who thought differently than the force they had been fighting for twenty years. If Matthias hoped to end this war and find his mother and Devora, he had to get to Kadesh as soon as possible.

Quickly, he opened the next note, and his jaw dropped. "Jacques, you need to see this."

Jacques ran to Matthias' side and as soon as he read the contents of the second parchment the blood fled from his face.

"Whatever we need to do, we need to do it fast."

———————

However, for the next week or so, everything worked against Matthias' hurried state. More machinery broke, a slew of workers became sick and couldn't assist in creating the device or any additional weapons for soldiers. Then, once the machine was finally complete, there were mishaps at Sandje Textiles with the uniforms for the soldiers.

With every obstacle Matthias faced, he thought back to what Warden Hazor said: "You'll be thankful for the extra time."

But Matthias still didn't understand what he meant. Thankful that with each day he was further and further from finding Devora? Thankful that his soul was dragged through the dirt with every moment wasted?

Matthias was frustrated and wanted to scream. The only positive thing about all the mishaps was that the queen stayed far away from Delequa Iron. After the first day, she made clear she disliked the smell of burning metal and trusted Matthias to take care of everything.

Yet, just when Matthias was beginning to think the queen had forgotten him—and he wished she would—an unexpected visitor arrived at Delequa Iron. Interestingly enough, it was the same day in which Matthias had finalized the nullifying weapon, the armor and additional weapons for the soldiers and their uniforms. He did not have the chance to even breathe before the queen was there, ready and waiting to send the troops into battle.

"My queen," Matthias said, bowing. It had been a bit since he had to use aristocratic formalities, and he was reminded how much he hated them.

"You're looking well, General," Queen Leza crooned, her blood-red dress spilling behind her as she strode to Jacques' desk and sat in his chair.

Once Jacques had caught wind of the queen's visit, he was scarce. Matthias hated him for it, but also understood. Jacques had a future, a wife. He couldn't bet his happiness if he said the wrong thing to the queen. While Matthias had only a small hope of a future, if he even still had that at all.

"Thank you, my queen," he said. He knew he had to tell her everything was ready. He didn't know how she knew today was the day everything would come together. Yet he learned long ago that telling the queen what she already knew was the correct course to take. "You came on the perfect day, Your Highness. We have just finalized everything for battle. The troops can leave on the morrow with your blessing."

Queen Leza laid her hands on top of each other then rested her chin on them. "It seems I'm short a commander. I've looked everywhere but can't seem to find Warden Hazor anywhere. Any ideas?"

Matthias blinked, knowing that if he paused too long, the queen would do something horrid to get him to reveal what little he knew.

"I have been working here day and night, my queen. I have not heard from Warden Hazor in some time." The half-truth slid across his tongue so easily, Matthias almost believed himself. In fact, there were many times he even questioned if the warden had come to see him at all.

Queen Leza frowned then stood. "I suppose we have no choice but to go on without him."

Matthias nodded. "Very well, my queen."

"Come, General. Your soldiers await."

The chain—the invisible leash—that Matthias so desperately tried to forget, tightened around his neck and he had no choice but to obey.

⸺⊱➤⸺

The last time Matthias donned his armor, he was a hero for recapturing Yekel and uniting Tenton. He'd felt proud and accomplished that day.

But as Tocha, who had just returned from Yekel a few days ago, helped him into his breastplate, the only thing he felt was dread. He had never led a group of soldiers this large and definitely not into Kadesh. At least Warden Hazor had experience in that area. Matthias knew nothing about a full-frontal attack on an enemy. He only prayed Tunri would guide him to do what was right when he needed to.

Matthias slid his gauntlets into place. He knew there were innocents in Kadesh just like in Tenton. People who only wished to lead their quiet lives and wanted nothing to do with war. It was always the wicked and power hungry who disrupted the lives of the innocent.

Matthias sighed as he grabbed his helmet and thanked Tocha. He had no idea how to prevent this siege. Judging by the queen's plans, she desired a full slaughter of anyone who stood in Tenton's way. He shuddered as he remembered the second note smuggled to him. Matthias knew he wouldn't be able to live with himself if her plan succeeded. He only hoped they could get Lucas' machine to where the imperial opal statue was in time.

As Matthias stepped into the early dawn, the sun just rising against the horizon, another knight clad in his armor rode up to him on a striking white steed.

The insignia of the Delequa family crest was etched into the knight's armor as they dismounted.

"What are you doing here, Jacques? I thought you needed to stay at Delequa Iron."

Jacques removed his helmet and grinned. "And let you have all the fun? I don't think so. Reese, Hestia and Charles said they would watch over things until I return."

Matthias lifted his brows.

"I haven't heard any word from Ida, only from my brother. There's something not right. I can feel it. I am going to find her and bring her home."

Matthias had gotten used to Jacques' positive and happy-go-lucky attitude; he had forgotten that Jacques was just as skilled a soldier and would not be swayed when he had a goal in sight. Matthias extended his hand and Jacques grasped it. "I wouldn't wish to fight side by side with anyone else."

Jacques nodded. "Good, I was coming whether you allowed it or not."

Matthias laughed, a shred of hope coming back into his heart. "Also, I'd pick both."

Jacques gave him a confused look. "Both of what?"

"Both types of flowers: roses and lilies. It's meant to be the best day of your life, right? Pick both."

Jacques smiled and nodded. "I think I will."

Placing his helmet back on his head, Matthias mounted his horse and headed to lead his soldiers into battle, praying it wasn't his last.

Chapter Thirty

Haden, Radaa Kingdom, Kadesh

"Mal?" Haden questioned, trying to figure out how Princess Amalia, the masked prince and Mal were all the same person. Or trying to be the same person. "You're the prince of Kadesh?"

Mal's face softened. "I'm afraid so."

Haden's eyes searched his as she remembered what he said before entering the throne room: *I love who you are, who you really are. Please remember that as you meet the prince.* Because he knew the moment she discovered he was the prince, she would think he only desired her for political gain and her beauty. Just like everyone else. And though Haden wanted to believe Mal—the crown prince—loved her, how could she be sure?

"I know this is sudden, but you had a plan to come here and win Kadesh to your side and defeat the queen of Tenton." Mal extended his hand to her. "This is the only way I know how to gain the council's influence quickly. Without a queen, by Kadeshian law, I am a prince with no future. But with your help, we can end this war. I do not ask for anything more in this marriage than your friendship and aid in saving both of our people."

Haden swallowed, her mind unable to move beyond the fact that she was about to—had to—agree to this arrangement. Was it wrong that she wanted to marry Mal and *didn't* want to marry him at the same time? She barely knew Mal—if that was his true name. Were the personalities of the crown prince and the guard she came to care for the same?

Still, she knew Queen Leza was ready to attack Kadesh as soon as she possibly could and then begin her tyrannical reign over both nations. Haden never knew why the queen hated the Kadeshians so, but since Haden's childhood, she knew Queen Leza would do anything to destroy Kadesh.

Reaching out, Haden placed her hand in Mal's, hoping she was gambling correctly. There was always the thought in the back of her mind that if the marriage did go sour, she could always transform into a sparrow and fly away in the night.

Unless Mal caged her too, like the queen had.

Fear suddenly took over Haden's heart and she pulled her hand away. "I-I can't. I only wanted to share the news with the war council, not get married. I only snuck into the contest so I could get closer to the monarchy."

Hurt flashed across Mal's face as he slowly retracted his hand.

"You succeeded in getting *real* close," Princess Amalia snorted from the corner, where she had taken off all the princely attire and was wearing a similar styled dress like Haden's. "Unfortunately, as a woman and a single one at that, you are not even allowed *near* the war council, much less to talk to them. Trust me, I've tried." Amalia rolled her eyes as she flipped her long, shining hair over her shoulder. "Why do you think I agreed to Amal's crazy plan in pretending to be him? To have a voice is a great thing."

Amal. So that's his real name.

"But even if we marry," Haden shifted her gaze from Amalia to Mal. "I am still a woman. By Kadeshian law, I still don't have a voice." Haden blinked away the tears building in her eyes. She had come all this way to be told the same thing Queen Leza told her at Maldove Palace: stay quiet and look pretty. People don't care about your thoughts or what you have to say. Just smile. *That's what you're good at.*

"If you become my wife," Mal said slowly as he took a step toward her. "You will always have a voice. I will make sure of it."

Haden took a breath and whispered, "You must promise not to cage me. Ever. I am free to leave whenever I wish."

She knew it was a high expectation, but she would not willingly bind herself to Mal if he was going to play her captor. Never again would she be controlled in such a way.

Mal nodded slowly, understanding her reference to her transformation into the white sparrow. "I would never cage you. Your wings will never be clipped."

Haden's heart pounded in her chest as she reached out toward him. Emotions of fear and love tangled in her soul, but she stepped closer all the same. "Then I will agree to be your wife and end this horrific war."

Mal took her hand in his and brought it to his lips. His kiss was soft and gentle, hopefully a foreshadowing of the Mal he really was.

"Excellent," Amalia clapped from the side, making Haden and Mal jump. "And I am your witness so let's hurry it up to the war council before your crazy mother kills us all!"

Before Haden knew it, she was dragged to the two double wooden doors. The same doors where she stood up for her uncle and her identity was revealed to the prince and princess of Kadesh. What would lie behind them this time?

A soft caress brushed against her hand as Mal laced his fingers with hers.

"I know this is all happening so fast, but I meant what I said before you knew who I was. When I saw you that day in the marketplace, I had to know you more. Not just because of your beauty. I was drawn to *you*." He breathed then added, "I do apologize for lying to you. But I knew you wouldn't be as open to me if you knew I was the prince."

"It seems we have the trait in common," Haden replied, remembering how she hid her identity from him and everyone else as well.

Mal smiled and it warmed Haden's heart. But there was still something niggling in her mind. "If you've always been the prince, why were you acting like a guard? Didn't you have other responsibilities?"

Mal grinned. "Why do you think I set up a rotation with Ben and Raphael? I couldn't be everywhere at once, but I always tried to be with you when I could."

Haden's heart fluttered before Mal added, "And I also wanted to check out what pretty girls had come to try to win my heart. Thankfully, you had already stolen it before I saw the others."

Haden scoffed before Mal kissed her hand again and faced the doors. "When we enter, we're a team. A united force, just like how we hope our countries will be one day."

Haden nodded, desiring the same thing. The war had taken too much from both nations. If her sacrifice could save the lives of thousands of people, she would do it.

Mal faced the door once more, readying to knock, but paused his hand. Turning back to Haden once more, he took both of her hands in his. "Haden, if this meeting doesn't go as we planned, I want you to know that whether the war ends or not, I will annul our marriage."

Haden gasped. "What? You would do that?"

Mal squeezed her hands. "I will not cage you. If you wish to be free of me, I will not make you stay."

"Thank you," Haden whispered, trying to control her tears. But she wasn't sure whether she wished to be free of Mal just yet.

Nodding firmly, Mal faced the doors once more. "I have never been allowed to speak in a war council either, so this will be a new experience for both of us." He gave her one last grin and squeezed her hand before letting it go. Straightening his shoulders, he knocked on the door.

Haden's heart pounded between her ears as the seconds ticked by. What seemed like hours finally ended when King Redore IV's voice said, "Enter."

"Here we go," Mal breathed. "You and me."

Haden nodded. "Me and you." She straightened her stance as well and did her best to look every bit the princess she was meant to be.

As the pair strode into the room, Haden almost crumpled under the weight of their stares. With her hair dye washed out and her skin scrubbed clean, she stood out like a palm tree in a snowstorm. But still, she knew she wasn't alone. Mal strode confidently beside her. He didn't walk ahead like the king and queen of Tenton always did, leaving her in the shadows. He made sure it was clear that they were equals and Haden couldn't have cared for him more at that moment.

And Tunri was always with her. She could feel His peaceful presence calming her thundering heart.

"Ah, my son, finally revealing your face?" the king croaked. "It's about time your masked charade ended."

Haden lifted her brows. So, the king didn't realize that Mal and Amalia were switching places? She then remembered the black smoke coming from Aunt Beta's mouth and entering the king's ears. Had the king's memories been altered? Or was he truly oblivious?

Mal bowed before the king. "Permission to speak, Father?" he asked, his voice firm.

The king waved his hand at Mal, like he was of little importance. Haden's heart hurt to see the war council looking at Mal the same way. Like he was a nuisance, a little boy with nothing to contribute. She never realized they did have a lot in common. But why did the war council and the king view him as such? He wasn't really just a palace guard. He was the crown prince, the heir to the throne of Kadesh.

It was then Haden realized someone was absent from the war council. Aunt—General Beta—was nowhere to be seen.

That's odd, Haden thought, knowing that all Tenton's generals were always present for the war council meetings she would occasionally listen in on when no one was watching.

Mal turned to Haden and handed her the scroll she had shown Amalia just moments ago. "The council is yours, my queen."

He bowed, then stepped behind her. Not in the shadows but being the silent strength she

needed to continue.

Haden took a breath. *Help me, Tunri.*

For it was by Tunri's hand she was guided here and to Mal. By His hand, she wasn't captured or harmed. She only prayed that she had gotten to the council in time.

"I am Princess Haden of Tenton and I come bearing grave news."

Haden expected the council to be outraged that she was speaking. She expected them to riot and demand her to leave the room. But what she didn't expect was for them to fully ignore her presence. It was as if a dome had been placed over the council, and they could neither hear nor see her.

Pulse racing, Haden glanced back at Mal, not realizing how much she needed his strength and courage.

"You are no longer a princess," he encouraged gently. "You are a future queen, my betrothed. Demand their respect."

A fusion of courage seeped into her being. Mal was right. She was no longer the scared princess from Tenton who only smiled from afar. She was so much more. And she would make them all see her.

Lifting her chin, Haden strode to the front of the council, where Mal's empty chair sat. He could've left her at any time to take his place at the table, to show his position and her lack of one, but he didn't. Even now he followed her and supported her decision.

"I am Haden Salvar, princess of Tenton and future queen of Kadesh and you will listen to what I have to say."

At that, the men of the war council's eyes focused on her. It was as if a spell had been broken and their reactions came one after another.

"A new queen?"

"When did this happen?"

"I don't remember any announcement."

"Or a wedding?"

As the men yammered amongst themselves, another voice spoke up, "I have witnessed the unification of Princess Haden and Prince Amal. If anyone wishes to question the word of the Princess of Kadesh, do so now," Amalia said, striding into the room. She was no longer in the same robes as Haden but covered head to toe in shining bronze armor.

Haden couldn't help but be envious of the powerful woman. Her gait was strong, her head held high. Her gaze dared any of the war council to defy her.

The men of the council glanced at one another with confusion and surprise.

"The princess of Kadesh?" a councilman questioned.

"Oh yes," another with a shining red robe said, his gaze becoming clear. "Queen Amina gave birth to twins."

"Why am I just now remembering?" A councilman with a green turban shook his head.

Then, Sayidi Brocaw, who Haden always thought despised her, stood and said, "Please proceed, my queen."

Haden didn't need to turn around to know Mal was there. She felt his strength.

The time is now, Tunri whispered to her heart.

"I have traveled across Tenton and Kadesh under a guise to get this message to you. Queen Leza has created a horrible weapon that will steal the soul of any person nearby and it is right here in Kadesh." She unrolled the scroll with the horrible depictions of the plans for the statue. The council murmured amongst themselves, but after a moment waited for Haden to continue.

"She is planning on leading Tenton's army to Kadesh to distract you from her real plan. She desires to reign over not just Tenton, but your nation as well. If you hope to stop her, you must act now. Evacuate your citizens to safety then search the palace, search underground, search everywhere if you want any life in Kadesh left."

Once again, the war council stared at her. She almost thought she had only spoken her words in her thoughts, before the councilman in the green turban stood.

"Yes, my queen."

He called over his guard and instructed him on how to begin evacuating the people of Renta. The other council members started to follow suit and Haden felt hope blossom in her chest before an eerie cackle came from her right.

Chills ran down Haden's arms as she turned toward the king. His sunken yellow eyes slowly met hers. "You think you're clever, don't you, little princess."

Ice froze Haden's spine as the king's voice shifted from his own vibrato to that of Aunt Beta's.

"Did you really think you could have the war council on your side with one little speech?"

Haden stepped back from the king and into Mal's embrace. The two of them stared in horror as the king of Kadesh shifted from his sickly state into that of General Beta.

"Though," General Beta said, her grin wicked. "I am impressed you actually went to such lengths to defy your mother. Marrying the prince of Kadesh?" She clucked her tongue. "Even I wouldn't betray the queen that far."

"Where's my father?" Mal demanded, shifting Haden behind him.

A moment ago, Haden felt so powerful and strong. Now fear consumed her like a viper and she didn't know what to do.

"He's still alive, prince, for now. Until I have no further use for him." General Beta sighed. "However, I heard a coronation is coming soon, due to our prince's upcoming nuptials." She grinned wickedly. "It seems the former king's clock is ticking either way."

"You won't get away with this." Mal started toward General Beta. But before Haden could stop him, General Beta snapped her fingers, and he froze.

From the corner of her eye, Haden saw Amalia reaching for something by her side. Haden assumed it was a weapon and realized, like a fool, she had none. All she could do was turn into a tiny, worthless, little bird.

But I will protect you even then, Tunri whispered to her and the confidence Haden held before suddenly returned. She didn't need to rely on herself, but on Tunri. He would give her the strength she needed to do what was right.

Placing a finger on her temple, the general sighed. "Men are so difficult to deal with, aren't they, Haden?"

Haden knew Amalia was waiting for an opportunity to attack. If Haden could keep the general's attention on her, then the princess of Kadesh could act.

"At times, yes," Haden agreed, remembering all the leering looks and comments she had endured over the years.

"Did you know they are why this war started? What your poor mother had to endure? Thank goodness someone had the idea to give these egotistical men what they deserve."

Haden's eyes widened. Did mother—the queen—have something to do with the start of the war twenty years ago?

"Ah, well," General Beta said waving her hand. "I'll just let her tell you herself. She's missed you so."

All the blood ran from Haden's face. "Mo—the queen is here? Already?"

General Beta slowly pulled her sword from its sheath. "Not yet, princess, but soon. I will make sure you are ready to meet her when she arrives."

General Beta lunged at Haden, and thank goodness, Amalia reacted before Haden did and pushed her out of the way.

"Get out of here!" Amalia cried, pushing the general away. "Go, warn the people! Fly!"

Haden snapped out of her daze and realized what she always thought was her weakness was her greatest strength.

As General Beta lunged for her again, Haden closed her eyes and transformed into her sparrow form. She was small and fast, too fast for the general as she flew out of the council room and through the palace.

Haden thought about what Amalia said, but how could she warn the people? She was just one person. One person who was now a bird. She then had an idea and flew to her room, where she hoped Rae, Ida, and Ben would be waiting. Together, they could find Miguel and start to evacuate the people.

Haden pumped her wings as fast as she could to return to her room. But when she rounded the familiar corner, expecting to see Ben standing guard outside, the door to their room was wide open. Fear struck Haden's heart as she fluttered inside. It looked as if a giant had broken in and had a party. Their beds were a mess, the tables turned over.

What happened?

Haden then heard a muffled sound in the back of the room behind Rae's bed. Hurrying she flew over there and was horrified to find both Ida and Rae bound and gagged with Ida's guard, Raphael, standing before them with a sword, ready to strike.

Without thinking, Haden flew toward Raphael, pecking at his ears, eyes, his whole face to get him away from her friends. The guard shrieked, not prepared for an attack from a bird. But that was all Rae needed to swipe his feet out from beneath him. The guard fell with a thud and within moments, Rae was untied, and Raphael was unconscious.

As Rae helped Ida out of her bonds, Haden transformed back into her human form. She quickly grabbed a sheet and wrapped it around herself. A few bruises marred Rae's and Ida's faces and hands, but other than that, they seemed unharmed. Rae was quick to tie Raphael's hands and feet together and Haden was impressed.

"I'm not sure what happened or why he's suddenly evil," Haden pointed to Raphael's now bound form on the floor. "But I need your help."

Rae and Ida blinked at Haden before rushing toward her. They both embraced her tightly and Haden never felt so at home.

"We were so worried," Rae said, tightening her embrace.

"Yes," Ida agreed.

The two women stepped back, both wiping tears from their eyes before they shifted gears.

"Since when have you been able to transform into a bird?" Rae asked.

Haden gave a light chuckle. "Since before I can remember. I always thought Mo—the queen had cursed me, but actually she had only taken control of the gift Tunri already gave me. I think I have finally taken the control back from her."

Rae gave Haden a smile and hugged her again.

"Transformers were believed to have been vanquished as well as Marksmen," Ida added. "And here was one right in the palace all along."

Haden giggled again before her eyes landed on Raphael's unconscious form. "So, what's going on here?"

"Raphael attacked me in the courtyard," Ida explained quick-ly. "I can only assume he has been our enemy this entire time and he is the one behind one of the attacks during the pageant."

"Ben and I heard Ida scream, and we tried to help," Rae started before tears welled in her eyes. "Haden, he took Ben. I don't know where, but I have to find him." She held back a sob. "I can't lose him."

Haden's heart wrenched in two, not knowing what had happened to Mal after she left the throne room. She prayed Tunri would protect him. "We'll find Ben. I have a feeling General Beta knew how we were connected all along. If we work together, I think we can save everyone."

The two women nodded readily.

"What do you need us to do?" Ida asked as Rae rid her eyes of tears.

Impressed with the soldiers before her, Haden quickly explained everything that happened with the war council. Both girls lifted their brows at her mention of marriage to Mal but then refocused.

"I will go into the city and find your uncle," Ida said, already wrapping a scarf around her voluminous curls. "How can I convince him we are friends?"

Haden reached for Raphael's sword that almost killed her friend and sister. Raising it, she sliced off a small chunk of her white-blonde hair. "That should convince him."

Ida nodded, then gave both girls another hug before hurrying out the door.

Haden turned to Rae. "I don't know what Raphael would've done with Ben, but if he is connected with the queen—which I'm sure he is—he would've taken Ben somewhere she could use him as bait to lure you out."

Haden didn't know how much Rae remembered when Haden was stolen from their family and she now realized this was one of the reasons why the pageant was sabotaged. The queen didn't want anyone to realize she had stolen a child she hoped had a Tinkering gift. If Rae remembered anything, the queen wanted her dead.

"You were in Yekel, you saw the statue there," Haden continued, her mind on fire with trying to find solutions to all the problems. "If the same statue is here, where would it be?"

Rae closed her eyes, and Haden could see her thoughts rifling. Her eyes then shot open. "I know where to look first."

Haden embraced her sister once more. "Go. Find him. I will see you again."

Rae nodded, gratefulness written all over her face. "We will. Sister."

Haden grinned, her heart full.

As Rae sprinted out of the room, Haden transformed back into a sparrow. Though she wished she could go back and save Mal, General Beta and the queen were far too powerful for her to face alone. Soaring out of the room, Haden rose above the clouds and headed west, knowing that Tenton's army was on its way. And, if she was correct, Haden also knew the only man to stop an entire army from laying siege upon the Kadeshians would be the one in charge: General Matthias Blake.

Chapter Thirty-One

Matthias, Edo Desert, Tenton

The desert was hot and dry, just like it had been when Matthias and Devora led Tenton's troops to battle in the Edo not too long ago. Though, it felt like decades had passed since then.

Queen Leza was eager to have the soldiers march to Kadesh and lay siege to the city as soon as possible. Matthias half expected her to be in the front of the battalions with him and Jacques. However, upon him mentioning it, the queen decided to stay toward the back of the unit with her entourage of personal knights protecting her.

Matthias breathed a sigh of relief at the queen's decision. Although he knew she still held the leash around his neck, he was thankful there was more length to it than there had been in the past few days.

"Pre-battle jitters, sir?" Jacques asked, a sly smirk on his face.

"Unfortunately, those fled long ago, Jacques," Matthias replied, keeping his eyes glued to the sandy horizon.

It wasn't the upcoming battle that kept his eyes firm on the path ahead. It was what waited for him there. He knew Queen Leza was too keen to let him waltz into battle, alone and unsupervised. He didn't know how long of a leash she had given him, but the queen's power had to have a limit. If he could break away from her while the battle commenced, he could find that limit. And once he was no longer under Queen Leza's thumb, he could begin his search for his mother and Devora.

However, as Matthias thought before, the queen had to have a plan up her sleeve. She wouldn't let him out of her sight the past couple of days and now she was allowing him to lead the troops without her by his side. It was odd.

Upon realizing Matthias wouldn't say any more, Jacques kept his eyes forward and mouth closed, thankfully allowing Matthias to think.

He still didn't understand what Warden Hazor meant and what he was planning to do. Matthias always kept his senses alert for Vinn, the giant white elk that his mother and Devora had befriended. But as each day passed and there was no Vinn, Matthias' hope dwindled. The warden always had a plan. Somehow, he was always one step ahead of Matthias—one step ahead of everyone—and Matthias had to believe that when the time was right, Warden Hazor would return.

The blistering sun scorched Matthias' body beneath his armor. It wasn't wise to move the troops through the desert during the day, especially in their full armor. It was like baking them alive. But the queen demanded they move as fast as possible, and Matthias was not in a position to disobey.

Wiping the drops of sweat from his brow, Matthias reached for his waterskin swinging from Atir's, his black steed's, saddle. Uncapping the skin, Matthias took a heavy gulp. The refreshing liquid soothed his scratchy throat, and he couldn't help but take another. Unfortunately, Matthias had no knowledge of how long the siege would take and whether they would be able to resupply their resources soon. So, he regretfully capped the waterskin.

Upon lowering the skin back into its place, a sparkle of light glittered in the distance. Furrowing his brow, Matthias paused his movements, only allowing Atir to continue forward as he sat as still as a statue. The light glinted again, and Matthias knew he wasn't delusional due to the wrath of the sun.

"Jacques, did you—"

"I saw it," Jacques replied before Matthias could finish.

Matthias turned to see his friend's eyes locked on to the shimmering object coming toward them.

Jacques lowered his voice. "Do you remember what Rae said, right after Kadesh attacked the palace and Devora went with the general?"

Matthias swallowed and nodded, returning his gaze forward. How could he forget? He had been running Rae's words over and over again in his mind, trying to figure out what Devora meant when she said, "I'll see you again when the sparrow flies."

"Sir," Jacques continued, his voice so low, Matthias could barely hear him. "I believe that is a sparrow flying toward us."

Matthias' eyes widened to see Jacques' suspicions correct. A small, white sparrow was fluttering as fast as it could toward them. But why?

Just then, Matthias felt the leash around his neck tighten. He knew his time of freedom was coming to an end. Matthias didn't know where he was going, but in his gut he knew the queen was taking him away from the battle ahead.

"Jacques," Matthias squeezed out, his throat constricting. "Whatever you do, follow that sparrow."

"Sir, where are you—"

But Matthias never heard what Jacques was going to ask for the next moment, Jacques had dissipated before his eyes. In another blink, Matthias found himself bound and thrown upon a hard stone floor. He winced as his armor dug into his skin at the impact but wouldn't allow himself to cry out. So, the queen was finally making her move. And if his assumptions about Devora's prophecy and warning were correct...

Matthias shifted his body as best he could to see the woman he loved, the woman he had been trying to find for months, standing only a few feet away, with tears streaming down her face at the sight of him. Though the circumstances weren't ideal, Matthias was thankful that after everything he had done, she still cared.

Tears brimmed Matthias' eyes at the sight of Devora, but they didn't roll onto his cheeks until his gaze shifted and he saw his mother. "Mother," Matthias tried to say, but found he had been gagged as well.

He tried to say everything his soul yearned to say with one look in her direction, but when Kanna didn't look his way, Matthias realized a white haze veiled his mother's once beautiful violet eyes.

A rage like no other overtook Matthias and he found the wolf within him waiting and ready to burst forth.

"Ah ah ah," Queen Leza's condescending voice said from behind him.

Matthias didn't dare look at the woman. He knew this day would come. The day when he would be reunited with his mother would be the day his life ended. And after all the years of planning and preparing, he still found himself at a loss. Should he try to free his mother first? Devora? Himself? Only Tunri knew the outcome of the next moments as they ticked by with agony.

"I see we have a new volunteer," another woman's voice said.

A swirl of dark smoke appeared before Matthias and he immediately recognized General Beta, the woman Devora had willingly gone with after the Kadeshian attack on Maldove Palace.

"Where's the prince?" Queen Leza snapped at the general.

General Beta snapped her fingers, and another bound young man appeared next to Matthias. Matthias studied the writhing young man. The general and Queen Leza shifted their conversation to Kadeshian, trying to conceal their plan from his listening ears.

Fortunately, he had studied the Kadeshian language enough to understand that this young man was the prince of Kadesh. But why had General Beta and Queen Leza captured the crown prince? Why had they captured Matthias when he was already bound to the queen? Nothing made sense.

All Matthias wanted was break free of his bonds, save his mother and Devora and never look back. He had always pressed on, no matter the consequences. But now he wished for nothing else than to retreat and run as far away from here as possible.

"It's finally time," Queen Leza said, switching back to Tentonian.

Matthias could do nothing but take his eyes off his mother, Devora, and the traitor he just realized was standing between them.

If Matthias' eyes could shoot daggers, he would send them straight into his little brother's heart. He knew Tristan sent the note to gain his trust once more. Had he sent the second one, as well? But how could Matthias trust his little brother when Tristan was standing by while Devora and his mother were bound as prisoners? How long had his brother been planning this? Since Matthias took his place at the Fortress? Or ever since Mother had been taken by the king and queen?

"General Beta, please bring Prince Amal forward."

Matthias finally tore his eyes away from his family and toward the struggling prince. He didn't know much about the prince of Kadesh. Though he had tried to find information about him for years, Radaa Kingdom kept a tight grip to prevent any information leaking about an heir to the throne. Still, Matthias felt sorry for the man.

"Your reign will bring nothing but the same pain and prejudice as your father's," Queen Leza said, piercing the prince's neck in a similar fashion as she did to Matthias at Ida's trial.

Matthias watched in horror as the prince screamed in pain before his body elongated into a large black wolf. Is that how he sounded each time he transformed? How horrible for Jacques to have witnessed it so many times. And how incredibly thankful

Matthias was to have found such a loyal friend to see him through his pain.

Matthias wished he could've stopped the queen from ruining another life. But with his arms and legs tied up like a beast, he was powerless to do anything at all.

General Beta tied a rope around the prince's neck and lead him to where Matthias still lay on the ground.

"Look, General," General Beta said, her tone mocking. "Now you have a friend."

Matthias didn't give her the satisfaction of a glance, but when a swift kick in the ribs caught him off guard, he shifted his gaze toward the evil woman.

"Ah," she sneered. "Now I have your attention."

"Beta, do not harm my pets before I am done with them," Queen Leza said nonchalantly. "I still need him."

"Apologies, my queen," General Beta said with a bow.

"Why are you doing this?" Devora finally said.

Matthias' soul filled with hope at the sound of her voice. It seemed she had been able to remove her gag, or it had been removed for her. Matthias shifted his gaze to Tristan. His face was unreadable, a mask of stone. But Matthias caught the discarded gag hidden up his brother's sleeve. Tristan caught his eye and gave him a slight nod, before focusing back on Queen Leza. The hope in Matthias' soul rose. Maybe his brother wasn't as crooked as Matthias originally thought.

"Why?" Queen Leza repeated the question, her voice caked with malice and fury. "After all this time, you finally want to know why?"

Devora took a step forward, and Matthias wished she would just take his mother and run away as fast as she could. But he knew she wouldn't. Devora never ran away from finding the truth. It was something he loved and hated about her.

"Yes," Devora replied, taking another step. "Help me to understand why you've caused so much destruction. So much pain."

Queen Leza rolled her eyes. "You're not worth my words, little Seer."

With a flick of her fingers, Leza threw Devora back against the wall. A crack resounded in the space and Devora screamed. Matthias started to inch his way forward but was halted by a boot on his spine.

"I wouldn't go any further if I were you," General Beta growled.

Then his mother took a step forward. While Matthias was distraught at her frail form, her stance was nothing but confident. Her faith and strength radiated from her straight shoulders and lifted chin. Matthias could not be prouder to be called her son.

"You may not wish to tell them," Kanna spoke up. "But the time is finally right, and I will."

"If you wish for death, Kanna, proceed," Queen Leza warned.

"Death is only a new journey," Kanna replied.

Before Matthias could comprehend what was happening, a flood of memories entered his mind.

"You must enter, Kanna," a young feminine voice said. "Father demands it."

A younger version of Queen Leza, maybe eighteen summers, stood before Matthias. He was shocked by how innocent and kind she appeared. The weight of the crown and evil she pursued had not yet tainted her soul. But—Matthias focused on the younger version of his mother—why was Mother with Queen Leza? And why were they in a room that looked scarily the same as the queen's drawing room in Maldove Palace?

"I don't care what Father demands," Kanna replied as she rolled up a dress and shoved it into a large chest. "I will not be a prize for the prince of Kadesh. I have already found love, and I don't intend to give it up."

Leza rolled her eyes and Matthias shuddered at the similar gesture he had just seen in the present. The realness of this memory was eerie.

"Love doesn't last, Kanna. You know this. Look at what Father did to Mother."

Kanna's hand paused on the next dress in her wardrobe. She then shook her head and grabbed the yellow frock. "No, Liam isn't like Father. He's a good man."

Leza balled her hands into fists. "You'll do it then? You'll renounce your title, give up the throne? All for some farm boy?"

Kanna nodded, her violet eyes shining. "I've never wanted the throne, Leza. You have. And now is your chance. Win the competition, marry the prince, and unite Tenton and Kadesh for good. You have always been the one Tunri chose for this path. Bring peace to our lands."

Matthias' thoughts were working on overdrive as he watched his mother and Queen Leza embrace one last time before his mother fled Maldove Palace.

The memory dissolved in his mind, giving Matthias a moment to think. Mother and Queen Leza were sisters? Then that would mean...

The memory spun again to show Queen Leza beside a man who looked similar to the current prince of Kadesh. But if this were in the past, the man next to Queen Leza had to be the now king of Kadesh, King Redore IV. As doves flew and the crowd cheered, Matthias gathered that the two had married, thus uniting Kadesh and Tenton as one nation.

But where had it all gone wrong? The new king and queen of Kadesh looked happy at the arrangement. Matthias didn't have to wait long for his answer.

"This isn't going to work, Leza," King Redore IV said, his voice distant and hollow.

"Please," Leza cried, tears streaming from her eyes, her hands on her stomach. "I know I can produce an heir. Give me one more chance."

The king shook his head and turned away. "You must leave Kadesh. Return to Tenton. My kingdom cannot continue without heirs."

It was then Matthias saw it: the change, the anger, the bitterness and hatred, enter Leza's soul. He didn't have Devora's power of soulsight, but the aura was so strong, he couldn't have missed it.

"You will regret this day," Leza threatened before she stomped out of the room.

The next memories flashed past Matthias' eyes so fast he could barely comprehend them. The annulment of Queen Leza's marriage to the king of Kadesh. The announcement of the marriage of Queen Leza to Duke Atol Eduardwa of Kimdonea and the sudden and mysterious death of the former king of Tenton. And then the first strike of the war with Kadesh that would last twenty years.

Matthias blinked, not realizing tears had rolled down his cheeks at the memories. The woman who stood before him, who had chained him, forced him to do horrible acts, cursed him into a beast, was his aunt. His own kin, his family.

He could understand her anger at the king of Kadesh. How could she control whether she could have children or not? It was cruel of him to turn on her so harshly and dispose of her like she didn't mean anything. But why did the queen wish to harm Matthias? Up until this moment, he had no idea he had any relation to the queen.

Devora gasped and Matthias realized Mother had given her the same memories. She, too, was crying.

"I don't need tears of pity," Queen Leza snarled. "Redore easily found another wife that was able to produce twins. One of which thought he could foil my plans with his own betrothal." She motioned to the growling form of the black wolf next to Matthias. "Foolish boy, I've known where Haden would flee for weeks. I've planned this for twenty years. No one will stop me now. Unfortunately for you, the former queen of Kadesh did not make it past childbirth." Matthias thought he noted a hint of sympathy in the queen's voice. But as she continued, the same angered tone spoke. "Maybe if she had, your king wouldn't have been so easy to control." She then turned back to Devora. "The king of Kadesh did what was in his best interests. And I will do the same."

"What the king did was unjust," Devora interrupted. "But why take your wrath out on thousands of innocent people?" Devora dared look over at Matthias and his heart squeezed. "Why curse an innocent man, your nephew, who has done no wrong?"

Queen Leza barked out a laugh. "Innocent? Hardly." She pointed at Matthias. "This man has done more horrid things than you will ever know."

Matthias watched Devora's face pale and the hope that had kindled in his heart began to dwindle. *Has she finally seen the evil inside of me?*

"Leza wanted not only to harm King Redore IV, but also me," Kanna spoke up.

As she tried to take another step, the male behind her held her back. Matthias instantly recognized the worm, Sergio, who tried to have Ida arrested for being a Kadeshian spy. Now it all made sense. Ida was the one who was able to find the Book of Ages and interpret the prophecy because of her Translator gift. If she had been arrested, no one would ever know the real prophecy Kanna gave to Leza.

When Sergio tried to hold his mother back again, she shoved him with her shoulder. The worm backed off and Matthias was thankful for the strong women in his life.

"Until I received the prophecy of Leza's demise, I stayed away from the palace. My father, the former king of Tenton, wanted me to continue his reign by any means necessary. I was not willing to play his games and ruin my life, my future, for his political gain." Kanna turned her veiled eyes toward Leza. "So,

I ran away, leaving my little sister to bear the weight of Father's wrath alone."

"And bear it I did," Leza interjected, a fire in her dark eyes. "And it made me stronger." The queen turned to Matthias. "You were an easy pawn to control, nephew. All I needed to do was threaten my dear sister's life and you bent like a reed in the wind. And you—" She motioned to Tristan. "Easily bought, easily won. You wouldn't know loyalty if it slapped you in the face."

Matthias thought he saw Tristan wince at the statement.

"Unfortunately, you are both the heirs of a Seer and to the former princess of Tenton; therefore, heirs to the throne. Instead of killing you, you were more useful alive. You should be grateful I spared you both for this long."

Matthias had a choice number of words for Queen Leza and her twisted definition of what being alive meant.

"And although I have loved this trip down memory lane—thank you, Kanna—I have work to do. Beta, bring the young Seer. I need a vibrant soul for my creation. My sister's is frail and useless to me now."

Matthias tried to scream and jerk to stop General Beta from grabbing Devora. He pleaded with his eyes for Tristan to help, do something, to save the woman they both cared for. But despite Devora's fighting, General Beta grabbed her arm, and Tristan did nothing.

Chapter Thirty-Two

Ida, Renta, Kadesh

Ida raced out of the room, holding the green scarf around her head like it was her lifeline. She wasn't sure how she was going to sneak out of the palace to try to find Haden's and Rae's uncle, but she had to try.

A group of soldiers were coming toward her and Ida quickly ducked into the nearest open door.

"Hurry to the throne room," one cried.

"What's happening now?" another asked.

Then a booming voice that Ida recognized as Sayidi Tamor responded, "The crown prince has been captured by General Beta. Scour the palace, let no one leave! Go, immediately!"

Ida jumped at the man's command. As soon as the guards passed her, she raced toward the palace gates. She had to sneak out of the castle before it was too late. If only her gift made her transform into a bird like Haden and fly away. But, as Ida headed toward the gates, an idea jumped into her mind.

Please give me courage, she prayed to Tunri. *And some of Hestia's acting skills.*

"Halt!" the guards said as Ida approached.

Here we go, she thought before she forced tears to come to her eyes.

"Oh, thank goodness," she cried, huffing as she stumbled toward the guards. "It's so horrible. You must help!"

At the sight of her tears, a concerned look crossed the first guard's face. "Why? What's happened?"

Ida swallowed and said, "The prince! He has been captured!"

"What?" the second guard questioned; his face laced with more suspicion than the first. "I haven't heard such a thing."

Just then a loud bell rang in the distance.

"The warning bell," the first guard said. "Something has happened."

And before Ida could say anything else, he ran off. Unfortunately, the second guard stayed put, narrowing his eyes at Ida.

"Will you not allow me to return to my family during this hectic time?" she asked, hoping the guard would take pity on her.

"If something has happened, all persons in the palace must stay in the palace until the situation is resolved," he recited.

Ida frowned. *What do I do now?*

"Ah, my dear, I have been looking for you," a voice called out.

Confused, Ida turned back to see a man with a bright yellow turban coming towards her. He bowed deeply to the guard.

"Thank you so much, sir, for finding my ward. With all the chaos in the palace, I had lost her." The guard raised a brow before the man continued, "You see, we were invited here by the king, himself, to visit the palace and enjoy the wonders of Renta. In fact, I just came from the marketplace—"

"Yes, yes," the guard interjected, waving his hand. "Just take your ward and go."

"Many thanks," the man said, steering Ida away from the front gates.

Panic rose in Ida's thoughts as she remembered Raphael approaching her in the courtyard in a similar way. He took advantage of her kindness and used it to attack her.

"I am Haden's and Rae's uncle," the man whispered as soon as they were out of the guard's earshot. "I saw you with them before the attack at the purification pools. You are their friend, yes?"

Ida couldn't believe Tunri's providence. He had brought Miguel right to her. Ida nodded. "Yes, but what are you doing here? Haden sent me to find you."

Miguel's brows rose before he responded. "I see. Well, going through the front gates is not the best way to leave a palace under lockdown." He hurried forward, beckoning Ida to follow him as he turned the next corner.

When Ida arrived, Miguel explained, "When I first arrived in Kadesh, I worked in the palace for a little while—enough to explore different ways in and out without being seen."

Miguel placed his hand on the frame of a picture and pushed it to the side. A few feet down the hall, a section of the stone slid away.

"Another secret passage?" Ida gasped, remembering the one she and the others had traveled in to get to the library.

Miguel furrowed his brow as he started toward the opening. "You know of another one?"

Ida nodded. "Yes, it leads to the library." Ida left out the fact that her traitorous guard had led them there.

"Interesting," Miguel commented before the two hurried through the passage.

It wasn't as cramped as the first. But Ida was still thankful when they arrived outside the palace walls.

"Now that we are away from any guards or suspicion, why did Haden send you to find me?"

Ida launched into a quick summary of everything that had happened.

Miguel nodded; his brows furrowed as Ida recounted everything that happened.

"It seems to me, before we do anything, we should meet up with Tenton's army and tell them this information." He turned toward the horizon. "I don't know where this statue may be, but for it to affect so many people, it would have to be somewhere where most of the citizens are populated."

Ida followed Miguel's gaze to see dark-green flags with the Tentonian crest on the horizon. While she expected to see the white mustache of Warden Hazor or General Blake's dark hair leading the troops, that wasn't who she saw.

Her heart soared as her eyes landed upon a head of sandy-blond hair.

Jacques!

Before Miguel could stop her, Ida raced toward the soldiers. Though it had only been a few weeks, it had felt like an eternity since she'd seen him.

"Wait!" Miguel called, racing after her. He soon caught up to her and the two hurried to the outskirts of the city beyond the outer wall.

"Don't charge too fast at them," Miguel wheezed, trying to catch his breath. "From this distance, they may think you're an enemy and shoot you down."

"No." Ida shook her head, remembering the light-green scarf over her curls. "Jacques will know it's me."

I hope, she prayed as she started toward the vast number of soldiers marching toward her.

As she hurried closer, Ida noticed a shining object flitting right next to Jacques. Her thoughts were drawn back to when the same shining object burst into their room and saved her and Rae from Raphael's attack. Haden had risked her own life to meet Tenton's army and guide them.

As Ida was within shooting distance of the archers, she could almost hear their arrows notch on their bows, ready to pierce her heart through. She closed her eyes, knowing that Tunri would protect her and bring her safely to Jacques' side as He had done many times before.

Suddenly, she felt a pair of small talons lightly pierce her shoulder. Opening her eyes, Ida looked upon Haden's sparrow form.

"You're beautiful as a bird too, Haden," she said, lightly patting the sparrow on her head.

Ida faced the soldiers still advancing toward her, but she stood firm. Yet as the soldiers drew near, Ida felt panic encroaching until finally, she heard Jacques' voice.

"Hold!"

Ida held her breath as he rode his horse ahead. Once he fully recognized her, he practically leapt off the steed and raced through the sandy ground toward her.

"Ida!" he cried, pumping his legs as fast as he could.

"Jacques!" Ida hurried forward and in a matter of moments she was in his arms.

"I was so worried," he breathed in her ear before placing his hand on her cheek and kissing her solidly on the lips.

"Me too," she responded, when they finally broke apart. "When I didn't hear anything from you, I was worried something had happened."

Jacques furrowed his brow. "*I* was worried when I didn't hear anything from *you*. I sent letters to Raphael and expected you to send one back, but you never did." He pushed her curls out of her face. "I thought you had changed your mind."

Ida shook her head and pulled her engagement ring out from beneath the collar of her dress. "Never. You're stuck with me forever." At that Jacques grinned wide and went in for another kiss, before Ida stopped him. "But I have to tell you, Raphael betrayed us." As Ida explained to Jacques what happened with his older brother, Jacques' gaze held fires of fury.

"I'll skin him alive," Jacques roared as he stomped toward the outer wall of Renta.

"Wait, wait," Ida said, pulling on his shirt sleeve. "Raphael isn't our top priority right now. And Rae already tied him up. I doubt he'd be able to undo all the knots she used to bind him."

Jacques' anger dimmed a fraction as he turned back to Ida. "Matthias was taken, Ida. Right before my very eyes. I don't—"

His voice wavered before he swallowed. "I don't know what to do next."

Ida's heart broke at the desperation in Jacques' voice. She wished she could provide all the answers he needed. But she didn't know what to do next either.

Suddenly, Haden lifted from Ida's shoulder and fluttered over to Jacques before flying toward the outer wall. She landed on the shoulder of Miguel who had kept his distance from Jacques and the rest of the Tentonian army.

Ida then remembered what Miguel had said. He used to work in the palace and knew different ways in and out. "Of course!" Ida cried, grabbing Jacques' hand and following Ida.

"Ida, where are you taking me?"

"Follow the sparrow!" Ida pulled Jacques until they stood before Miguel.

"There's not much time for introductions," Miguel started. "But I'm Miguel—"

"I know who you are," Jacques interrupted, his gaze suspicious but curious.

"You do?" Ida questioned, confused.

Miguel gave a nervous laugh. "Has Phineas said such awful things?"

Jacques shook his head. "There are only a few deserters that were never accounted for. Miguel Salvar, deserter to Kadesh, was one of them. Warden Hazor would bring you up every once and a while. He was still bitter he never caught you."

Miguel's brows rose. "Once we assist my niece, you may arrest me if you like. But now we have to hurry."

Jacques looked from Miguel to Ida, unconvinced. "That's your uncle?"

"What?" Ida frowned. "No, he's Rae's and Haden's uncle."

Now it was Jacques' turn to ask, "What? As in Princess Haden? What does she have to do with Rae? And isn't the princess here, in Kadesh?"

Ida resisted the urge to throttle her betrothed. Now wasn't the time for questions. Ida pointed to the sparrow sitting quietly on Miguel's shoulder. "That's Princess Haden. She is a Transformer and can shift into a sparrow at will, though the queen allowed her to believe *she* cursed her into becoming a bird." Ida then pointed to Miguel. "This is Haden's uncle who deserted to Kadesh when the queen stole Haden from her birth family in Yekel, thinking she would develop the Tinker gift and would make the queen weapons of destruction. The queen wiped the minds of Haden's true family so they wouldn't try to find their lost daughter."

Jacques blinked, his mind trying to comprehend everything. "And her birth family in Yekel?"

"Is Rae's family," Ida finished.

Jacques' eyes widened before he gave a low whistle. "Well, that certainly was unexpected."

"It is a lot to swallow, I understand," Miguel confessed, patting the small bird on the head. "But it is the truth."

Ida nodded. "Miguel used to work in the palace and knows secret ways to get in and out. If I'm understanding Haden's thoughts correctly—" She gave a nod to the bird who chirped back. "Haden wishes for Miguel to lead us to where we believe the imperial opal statue of Pahga is located. There we will find Devora, Kanna, the crown prince of Kadesh, and probably the general."

"In order to infiltrate undetected, I can't bring more than a few soldiers," Jacques said, glancing back at his rows of troops. "And if what you're saying is true, we will need something to nullify the imperial opal of the statue."

Ida's heart sank. She hadn't thought of how to destroy the statue, just only on how to find Devora. What were they going to do now?

Jacques' fingers rested gently under her chin and lifted it. "Don't look so disheartened, my love. The Tinkers Matthias saved long ago already made such a device."

Ida's eyes grew wide as the large pyramid with orbiting rings came into view behind the rows of soldiers.

"*Ay*," Miguel whispered, staring at the machine. "It's magnificent."

"It is," Jacques agreed. "I believe it was your brother and a good friend of ours who helped design it."

"A good friend?" Ida asked, hope rising in her heart.

Just then, a head of bright blonde hair peeked out from the top of the device, waving wildly.

"Nadia!" Ida cried, tears forming in her eyes before she turned to Jacques. "But what is she doing here?"

"We needed all the help we could get," Jacques confessed as more familiar faces came into view. "I asked a few friends for their help."

Ida gasped as Governor and First Lady Medee came into view, both clad in armor with their own loyal soldiers behind them. Next to them stood a strong man with strawberry-blond hair that looked extremely similar to Victoria Headings, Ida's friend she had made at Vlacklear Academy.

"That's Governor Headings from Ballear. I remember you mentioning his daughter. As soon as I spoke of our betrothal and the assistance needed, he immediately agreed. It seems Victoria had spoken very highly of you." Ida blushed before Jacques continued, "He even was able to convince Victoria's betrothed and his family to help as well."

"Victoria's betrothed?" Ida questioned before a lanky soldier beside the Governor of Ballear lifted his faceplate and grinned.

"Patrick?" Ida gasped. Victoria and Patrick were betrothed?

Jacques squeezed her hand and smiled. "You have touched so many lives without realizing it. With your kindness, we have a great many soldiers who all desire to see the tyrannical monarchy come to an end."

Ida couldn't believe Jacques was able to rally so many people in such a short amount of time and hope bloomed in her heart once more.

"The machine is fantastic," Miguel piped in. "But we need to go now."

Nodding, Jacques lifted his hand and motioned toward the machine.

Nadia immediately jumped down and within a few moments was by Ida's side. Before Ida could react, Nadia squeezed her with both arms. "I'm so glad you're okay!"

"Me too," Ida squeaked back with a laugh.

A series of shouts and cries erupted from the city.

"We need to leave now," Miguel said again, with Haden still on his shoulder. "Choose your soldiers and follow me."

"I have someone I need to find and knock some sense into," Nadia said as she started after Miguel. "So, I'm going whether you like it or not."

Jacques didn't even try to argue before he turned back to Ida. "I want you to stay here."

"What?" Ida cried, thinking of Devora as a prisoner. "But I want to help."

Jacques cupped her cheek with his hand. "I need you to be my eyes. You have always been able to see the big picture better than me anyway. If what I've learned about the statue of Pahga is true, the queen will have to unveil it to steal the souls for power. As soon as you see it, blast it with the device."

"But I don't know how to use it," Ida cried, not wanting to be separated from Jacques now that she was reunited with him.

Jacques rested his forehead on hers. "You are the smartest, kindest, and most beautiful woman I know. I am so glad you're mine." He kissed her forehead. "Governor and First Lady Medee will show you." Jacques paused once more before saying, "I love you, Ida. All will be well soon."

Tears streamed down Ida's face as she wrapped her arms around Jacques' neck and kissed him. Jacques reciprocated the kiss then pulled away.

"More of that after all this. Especially after our wedding." He waggled his brows and Ida's cheeks flushed.

Jacques called three more soldiers to follow him and with one last kiss to Ida, he was barreling after Miguel.

Keep him safe, she prayed to Tunri. *Please return him to me.*

A cooling peace came over Ida's frantic heart and she knew without a doubt that Jacques would be okay.

Chapter Thirty-Three

Devora couldn't believe Matthias was the queen's nephew. She couldn't believe Kanna and Queen Leza were sisters. So many questions were answered in such a short amount of time and at the end of Kanna's memories, Devora didn't feel hatred toward the queen, but sorrow. A deep sorrow for this woman who had been scorned so cruelly for something that was out of her control. Even though the queen was treated unfairly, her actions after the matter were not to be condoned. Devora's heart yearned to see the good in Leza's soul. But as she engaged her soulsight, she saw nothing but a black void where the queen's soul should be. Whatever good was there before was long gone, replaced by bitterness and hate.

Devora had tasted those emotions before. They were addictive and easy to consume, but Tunri always helped her fight them. He always helped her see the hope—the light—instead of the darkness. It was so easy to bend to evil, to charge after her desires. But Tunri gave her the strength to resist. And as General Beta dragged Devora toward the queen, causing her already injured arm to burn in agony, she prayed for that strength all the more. The one positive thing she thought of was that she was able to see Matthias one last time. Tunri had given her a vision of this moment. She had known she would end up here, but she didn't know Matthias would be here, as well.

General Beta dropped Devora on the ground, ricocheting pain through the arm that broke when Queen Leza slammed her against the wall. Devora cried out and curled on her side. Once the pain subsided slightly, she realized she was inches from Matthias. He had contorted his body in a way so his head could be right next to hers.

"Matthias," she croaked, letting her tears flow freely. "I've missed you."

She couldn't understand his words because of the gag, but his eyes said everything. He loved her, missed her, and he was so, so sorry.

"It's not your fault," she whispered, wishing she could reach out to him.

The black wolf who had once been the prince of Kadesh, whined, as if he too felt their sorrow.

"Beta," Queen Leza beckoned. "It's time. All our planning has finally come to fruition."

As General Beta walked away, Devora scooched to a sitting position, sliding as close to Matthias as she could. She placed her hands near his cheek where she began trying to pull the gag from his mouth. Immediately, Matthias interpreted her actions and turned his head so she could work on the knot of the gag behind his head.

"You tried to stop me, dear sister. You tried to scare me with your little prophecy, but it didn't work," Queen Leza laughed.

"The prophecy was not mine, Leza, but Tunri's," Kanna corrected, her voice firm and resolute. It was then Devora could see where Matthias inherited his strength and determination from. "I wasn't trying to stop you but warn you. You were intended to unite our lands, but instead you divided them further. And punished those gifted by Tunri in the process. He will not turn a blind eye to your corruption of His will."

Leza's face shifted into something evil, and Devora's heart jolted at the sight. There was something sinister lurking beneath the queen's façade and Devora didn't know if she wanted to find out what it was.

Queen Leza quickly relaxed her features into a wicked grin. "Tunri has kept His distance so far. I only need Him to stay away for a few moments longer."

Devora held her breath as she felt the knot at the back of Matthias' gag loosen. A few more pulls and it was free. Devora carefully tugged the fabric from his mouth while he did his best not to cough loudly and draw attention to them.

Thankfully, the queen was too caught up in her banter with Kanna to notice Matthias pushing himself into a sitting position.

With his side resting against her back, he whispered in her ear, "Are you okay?"

Devora couldn't help it, but more tears sprung in her eyes and her heart leapt for joy at the sound of his voice. "I'll live," she added. "Hopefully."

"You will live, Devora," he replied in a low voice. "I will make sure of it."

"We live together, or not at all," she replied.

She felt Matthias' eyes burning into her, but she couldn't turn to face him. It wouldn't be long before the queen or general realized that she and Matthias were talking, so she had to get her words out quickly. "I don't know what's going to happen next. But whether Tunri desires us to live or die, I need you to know that you are a good man, and I love you. No one could change that."

"Devora—" Matthias' voice broke. "This isn't the end. It can't be."

More tears rolled down her face, but whether it was from the pain in her arm or the pain in her soul, she wasn't sure. "I wanted you to know, either way."

Matthias paused for a moment then replied, "I love you too, but this isn't the end. Trust me."

Devora swallowed and nodded, hoping he was right. Focusing back on the queen, Devora noticed that Kanna had been taken away to the corner of the room with additional bindings. Sergio guarded her but looked secretly pleased to be away from the center of the room.

But where was Tristan?

Devora scanned the room but couldn't find him anywhere. However, it was at that moment that Devora realized where she had been dragged.

Queen Leza lifted her hands, igniting all the lanterns in the spacious room around them. Flickers of light darted through the dark space until they landed upon the giant shimmering statue behind Devora. Lifting her eyes, Devora gaped as she stared at the imperial opal statue behind her. It was at least twice the size of the one in the Temple of Pahga in Yekel, but the carving was the same. The same curvaceous horned woman—Pahga—was carved from the powerful stone. And where her heart should be was a giant black orb, empty and ready to be filled.

Devora tried to scurry away from the statue, but the pain in her arm made her pace agonizingly slow. She could never forget the horrors of Yekel where the people willingly gave the souls of their daughters to this horrid statue. And it was all for the queen's gain. Devora still didn't know why the queen desired the power of souls, but it couldn't be anything good.

"Not to fear, little Seer," the queen chided. "The taking of your soul will be quick and painless. It is actually an honor to be the first. With the power of a Seer, I will be able to complete my transformation."

Transformation?

Devora shifted her gaze to the black wolf tied up next to the statue. It had once been a young man who General Beta referred to as the prince of Kadesh. Was that the transformation Queen Leza was talking about? But Devora didn't have time to decipher the queen's words before Matthias spoke up.

"A high honor, indeed."

The queen peered at Matthias and grinned maliciously. "Still trying to find a loophole out of my plans, dog? You're too late."

Devora watched in horror as a chain tightened around Matthias' neck. The veins in his neck bulged as he lifted his chin, straining against it. "I just wondered, why you would give such an honor to a Seer with so little experience," Matthias strained.

Devora frowned at his words. These were their last moments together and he was going to insult her seeing abilities?

But something in his words made the choking chain cease.

Queen Leza sighed. "What are you blathering about now? At least make it useful."

Matthias coughed once then sat up straight and Devora realized this was how Matthias lasted in the queen's clutches so long. He knew she valued his thoughts and opinions, and he was using that small power he had to buy them more time.

"Of course, my queen." He bowed his head. "You mentioned that it would be an honor to be the first soul given to this statue of Pahga. However, I know for a fact that there is a more experienced Seer in this room. One with years more experience than Devora *and* more power."

The queen gave Matthias a cruel smile. "Turning on mommy-dearest? How interesting what the threat of death does to our loyalties."

Matthias clenched his jaw. "You said yourself that Mother's soul is not strong enough for your—ah—transformation. I was thinking of General Beta. She is not only a powerful Seer, but a loyal friend. You know her soul would be a fantastic foundation to begin your new reign."

Devora couldn't believe it when she saw Queen Leza consider then accept Matthias' words. She wasn't sure if it was a gift from Tunri or not, but Matthias knew how to sway a conversation in his favor, and she was eternally grateful she was not to be sacrificed to the statue of Pahga just yet.

"You're right, nephew." The queen turned toward her loyal friend, General Beta. "Beta has served me for years. I would never question her loyalty. Plus, your lover is young and still weak in her power. Her soul will be consumed later. Beta—" General Beta hurried forward and knelt before the queen. "You will have the honor of being the first sacrifice to the statue of Pahga and bring about the reincarnation of our great goddess."

Reincarnation?

Devora jolted back in shock. She turned toward Matthias who looked equally surprised at the statement.

General Beta hesitated for a moment before saying, "It would be an honor, my queen, to be the first sacrifice to our Goddess Pahga."

Queen Leza grinned and snapped her fingers. The eyes and orb of the statue of Pahga glowed. Instantly, purple and black streams of General Beta's soul were pulled from her body. The general screamed and Devora winced but was unable to tear her eyes away. Queen Leza spoke of this woman's loyalty, but the queen watched on with glee as her friend's life was sucked dry.

The final threads of General Beta's soul were pulled from her body, the statue consuming them easily. Purple and black light swirled in the orb and a faint glow radiated from the statue.

Queen Leza placed her hand on the statue and breathed deeply. "Yes, I can feel the power. But I need much more."

The queen turned toward Devora, her eyes lit with danger. Not even caring that her friend's body lay lifeless before her, Queen Leza stepped over General Beta's body and grabbed Devora's good arm. The queen's sharp nails pierced her flesh and Devora cried out.

"You managed to give your love a few more moments of life before I took her soul, nephew. Well done."

Dragging Devora to the central base of the statue, the queen threw her down. "You are just like my sister. Always favored with your special gifts. Now I will use them for my own gain."

"No!" Matthias yelled, trying to stand, but the queen clenched her hand into a fist and Matthias fell back.

Horrified, Devora watched him struggle and squirm until he let out a loud howl, shifting into a large gray wolf.

"Ah, there's my good boy," the queen cooed. "You see, Devora, when my nephew is in this form, he can only obey me. Don't make me use him against you."

Devora stared at the wolf and remembered when she first saw Matthias in his wolf form back at the stables at the Fortress. She had felt a familiarity about those gray eyes. Queen Leza thought that he was nothing but a beast, but Devora knew Matthias was still in there. He had figured out how to control the beast without the queen knowing.

"This is wrong, and you know it," Devora cried, grasping at something to bide her more time.

But she didn't know what came next. Tunri only revealed so much because He wanted her to trust.

Devora blinked, realizing her own ignorance. All this time she had been trying to find a way out, trying to find her own solution to this problem. Just like she always had before the Categorization Call that changed her life. But this wasn't a problem she could fix. Only Tunri, and Tunri alone could vanquish the evil in Queen Leza's heart. She only had to have faith that He would come through for her.

"Oh, spare me your pretty words."

The queen flicked her hand at Devora, causing her limbs to feel like rods of iron. Try as she might, Devora couldn't move them.

With another snap of the queen's fingers, Devora felt the statue's energy turn on her. Streams of purple light tugged from her chest, and she screamed. It was as if she was being torn into thousands of different pieces. The howling of Matthias, the crown prince and the other wolves in cages echoed around her but nothing seemed as loud as the screams coming from her own throat.

Tunri, help me, please, she prayed. She would give her soul if she had to, but she so desperately wanted to live.

Just then, a loud crash sounded from the right and a large white streak barreled into the statue of Pahga. The light of Devora's soul receded into her body, and she released a loud gasp.

Panting, she couldn't believe her eyes as she watched Vinn slam into the statue of Pahga.

"Vinn!" Devora cried, unable to contain her joy.

It had been ages since she last saw the giant elk-like creature and she had feared the worst.

The giant creature reared back on its hind legs again and charged into the statue, much like it had to the walls of the Fortress when Devora first released him during Round Three of Regulus Protecti.

But what surprised Devora the most was the man directing Vinn's attacks. Guiding Vinn on what to do next was none other than Warden Hazor.

Chapter Thirty-Four

Devora, Underground Temple, Kadesh

"More to the right, you worthless deer," Warden Hazor called and Devora couldn't help but smile.

Vinn snorted at the warden but obeyed. As he rammed his beautiful white antlers into the statue of Pahga, a giant crack formed in the statue's orb. Hope lit in Devora's chest. Could Vinn really destroy the statue?

"Warden Hazor," Queen Leza called, unfazed by the warden's entry. "I wondered when you'd show up."

As quickly as Devora's hope came, it fled once again. For the queen waved her hand and Vinn froze. With another movement, the giant creature and Warden Hazor were thrown away from the statue to the ground. Sergio screamed at the sight and fled. Devora took the opportunity to get as far away from the statue as possible.

Queen Leza stalked toward Warden Hazor, who lay prostrate on the ground.

"Finally, I can deal with you properly." She took a step and dug her heel into his back. The warden grunted but didn't move.

"Stop!" Devora cried, rushing toward the warden, but was thrust back by another force.

"For twenty years you have been a thorn in my side," the queen raged. "With your manipulations of that fool, Atol, protecting the last Seer, and saving the Translator girl who should've died along with your daughter. You were always ruining my plans for conquest. But now—"

Queen Leza directed her power at Warden Hazor, causing him to levitate off the ground. Flicking her wrists, she slammed his body before the statue of Pahga.

Devora winced. She hadn't realized how intertwined Warden Hazor had been in the queen's nefarious plots.

"You'll pay eternally for getting in my way." The queen sneered. Then the statue of Pahga focused on Warden Hazor before the streams of his soul started to leave his body.

"No!" Devora cried, trying to run forward, but struggle as she might, she couldn't move.

"Don't, Devora," Kanna said, hurrying to her side. Since Sergio had fled, Kanna was now free. She held Devora close to her chest. "You can't change one's fate. The warden has played this game for a long time. He knew this was always the final move."

Devora cried at the warden's screams, not understanding why he had come to save them when he knew he would die.

"It was always his purpose," Kanna explained as she stroked Devora's hair. "Warden Hazor has been a guardian of Seers for a long time. His ways may not always seem correct, but he has always known the end goal."

Devora cried more, remembering how cold he was to her the first day she met him at the Fortress. But how, only a few weeks later, he helped her escape from the prison. She had so much more to say to the rugged stern man and now she would never get to.

Queen Leza's cackles interrupted Devora's thoughts as the final streams of light vacated the warden's chest. Matthias howled in his wolf form and tried to break away from the chain confining him to his spot, but he couldn't.

The queen placed her hand on the statue and breathed in deeply. Devora clung on to Kanna as she watched Queen Leza begin to morph. Her body elongated, and two spiral horns sprouted from her head. But the transformation stopped there.

"I need more," the queen bellowed, her voice deepening an octave.

Before Devora could react, the dome of the room blasted opened from the queen's power. Screams of the Kadeshian citizens poured into the chamber as the statue of Pahga was revealed. Devora clung to Kanna. Matthias and the Kadeshian prince howled in response. What were they meant to do now?

Tunri, help us! Devora cried.

White streams of light poured into the statue. Many screams were silenced by the statue's power, but more erupted as the sounds of charging horses and clanging swords filled the air.

Devora furrowed her brow. Was the Kadeshian army fighting its citizens? Or was Tenton's army here?

Devora wasn't sure what the army could do about the giant statue, or the goddess incarnate forming before her very eyes.

Queen Leza placed both hands on the statue and was absorbing as many of the souls as she could. With each intake, she turned more and more into the likeness of Goddess Pahga.

What are we going to do? How can we defeat that?

A movement caught Devora's eye, and she turned to find Vinn slowly standing.

Are you okay? Devora asked him telepathically.

The giant white elk nodded then pointed his nose toward the statue. The first time Devora had seen Vinn in the Fortress he looked a hair's breadth away from death. Once he was freed from his prison, Vinn began to heal and grow stronger again. But now that Devora was able to study the creature again, he seemed worse now than how she found him at the Fortress. Was the evil aura emanating from Queen Leza affecting Vinn?

Do you think you can destroy it?

Vinn nodded. *With your aid, I can. I am weak and need assistance.*

"I need to help Vinn," Devora shouted to Kanna above the swirling winds and screams around them.

Kanna nodded and grasped Devora's hands. "I can't do much, but I can give you what strength I have left."

"Kanna, wait—" Devora said but she was too late.

A surge of purple light streamed into Devora's being, numbing the pain in her arm and invigorating her with strength. Devora could see the life being sucked out of Kanna and she tried to wrench her hands away, but Kanna's grip was firm.

"Kanna, stop!" Devora cried and with every bit of strength she had, she yanked from Kanna's grip.

Kanna slumped to the floor and Devora feared the worst. But when she saw the steady breaths coming from the Seer's lips, relief layered over Devora. She hurriedly ripped a strip off her tunic that was already fraying and wrapped her broken arm in a sling around her neck. It wasn't great, but it would have to do.

With her new strength, Devora sprinted to Vinn and did her best to climb up his back. She hated how far his ribs stuck out and how filthy his once lush white hair was.

"We don't stop until that statue is in pieces, understand?"

Vinn nodded and Devora held on tight as he charged the statue.

Tunri, give me the strength to give to Vinn, she prayed as Vinn rammed into the statue again and again.

Devora expected the queen to stop them, but as Devora glanced over, the queen's cackles had transformed into screams. The power of the souls surged into her body at a rapid pace, Queen Leza's human form couldn't handle the supernatural effects.

"Keep going, Vinn," Devora cried, knowing time was running out fast.

Vinn slammed his antlers into the statue and pushed it with all his might. Finally, a loud crack resounded in the orb of the imperial opal.

The screams of the capital of Renta swirled around Devora, and she buried her head in Vinn's hair, lending him her strength but also trying to block out the horrible sounds.

Once more, she said to her friend. *We're almost there.*

She could feel Vinn's power draining as well as her own. If they didn't topple the statue and destroy the orb in this next blow, Devora wasn't sure what to do next.

"Okay, Vinn," she yelled. "Give it everything you've got."

Vinn reared back on his hind legs and charged at the statue, slamming into it with a force like no other. The statue of the Goddess of Pahga cracked again.

"Keep going!" Devora cried, surging what little strength she had left into Vinn's body.

The elk bellowed as it strained against the statue until finally, the stone gave. With a resounding crash, the imperial opal statue of Pahga shattered to pieces. The souls just harvested from the orb broke free of their prison and spiraled into the air. Devora prayed they returned to their owners.

Exhaustion hit Devora and Vinn like a boulder and they both crashed to the ground. Panting, Devora reached out to Vinn and patted his head.

Good job, my friend.

Vinn gave a throaty grunt in response and closed his eyes. Devora wasn't sure if it was her injuries, but she swore Vinn was beginning to turn translucent.

Devora assumed that the destruction of the statue would mean the destruction of Queen Leza. But when the queen's shrill laughter pierced her ears, Devora's blood ran cold.

"I have been planning this for twenty years you stupid, foolish little girl. Do you really think I only had one statue?"

Devora felt her exhausted body fly as the queen's power lifted her to the skies. Terror rang through the city streets as people ran, trying to escape the giant woman. They were soon met by Tenton's army and ran the other direction. But what horrified

Devora the most were the hundreds of smaller statues of Pahga littering the citadel of Renta.

Chapter Thirty-Five

Rae, Renta, Kadesh

Rae sprinted out of the palace, not looking back even when the guards tried to seize her. Thankfully, she hadn't slacked too much on her training since she left her alias, the Crimson Cord, behind.

Screams of panic and horror flooded the capital city's streets as Rae ran. Kadeshians were pointing and running. Some tripped and fell, those behind them trampling them beneath their frantic feet.

Rae pulled an elderly gentleman who reminded her of Master Monham out of the way. "Please be careful," she cried, before she ran across the crowd.

People shoved and pushed her from all sides, but she still couldn't see what the panic was about. It wasn't until she had rounded the next corner that she *felt* the evil before she saw it.

"Oh no," she whispered, remembering the terrible feeling. It was the same feeling she had when General Yada forced her in front of the statue of Pahga back in the Temple. Rae would never forget the feeling of having pieces of her soul torn from her.

But she couldn't think about that now. She had to find Ben. Though she didn't know where he was, she felt as if Tunri was guiding her steps.

Within a few more turns, Rae saw what was causing the panic. A towering statue of Pahga had appeared from under the city. Fear squeezed Rae's heart, and she almost forgot to breathe. The statue was enormous. But what made her blood freeze was the giant black orb on Pahga's chest, already stealing the Kadeshian's souls.

I have to find Ben and fast, Rae thought, pushing against the crowds of people.

While she had no gift from Tunri, Ben was a Marksman with the ability to never miss a shot. But because of that blessing, imperial opal could easily drain his power and leave him defenseless against the statue's powers.

Though Rae hadn't been out of the Kadeshian palace since arriving in Renta, she recalled seeing a scroll with a map of the city when she, Ida, Ben, and Raphael were searching for what the herb, millroot, was. It stuck out in her mind because the inner city of Yekel looked surprisingly similar to Renta. Though Rae didn't know if the Kadeshians changed Yekel to look like Renta or it was just a coincidence, she did remember the Kadeshians placing a statue of Pahga in the center of Yekel. She didn't know why, but she felt Tunri pressing in her mind that was where she would find Ben.

Doing her best to remember the winding avenues of the city, Rae raced to the central city square. Usually, the city square in Yekel was bustling with people. It was where Yekel held its marketplace and festivals. Rae assumed Renta was the same. But once the horrors of the statue of Pahga were revealed, the city square was as empty as the grave save for one poor soul tied to the statue in the center.

"Ben!" Rae cried, rushing toward his slumped form.

While the statue in Yekel had been made of bronze, the one standing before her was comprised of imperial opal. Rae had considered this being a possibility, but didn't realize how much the sight of Ben's almost lifeless form would affect her.

"Hold on, Ben," she said, pulling at the knots Raphael had used to tie him up. Fury boiled in her heart. Seeing the bruises on Ben's face made her wish she had beat Raphael to a pulp instead of just tying him up and knocking him out.

Rae swallowed down her anger as she released the last knot but felt the pull of the imperial opal as she tugged Ben away from it.

I told you I would never leave you, the Beast of Fury whispered in her ear.

"No," Rae cried, trying to back away from the statue. "No, I've changed. I'm not the same person anymore. Leave me be."

A sinister looking beast comprised of fire and smoke formed before Rae's eyes.

You will never be able to change. You will always be tainted.

"No, that's not true!" Rae screamed, smashing her hands over her ears.

It wasn't true. She knew it wasn't true. Suddenly she felt two strong arms wrap around her, pulling her into a sturdy chest.

"Don't listen to it, Rae," Ben's soft voice said in her ear.

Ben didn't care about her past. He loved her. He wanted to spend the rest of his life with her.

Do you really think he wants you? The Beast cackled.

"I love you," Ben whispered. "I will always love you."

Rae felt the soothing presence of the words and though Ben was saying it, she felt in her soul Tunri saying the same thing.

I love you, Rae. Regardless of your past, regardless of your anger, fear, envy, I will always love you.

A bright light appeared in Rae's vision and the Beast of Fury hissed at the sight. Rae felt herself starting to return to the city square when the Beast of Fury lashed out and gripped her wrist.

You will always be angry, and I will always be with you, it roared.

At its words, Rae suddenly realized that it wasn't wrong to feel anger. It was okay she was angry at the injustice of what happened to Yekel and her parents. It was okay to feel fury regarding the women who had been enslaved at the Temple. It wasn't the emotion that was the focus, it was what she did with it. And she was willing to release it.

"I may always be scarred by my past and what was done to me, but Tunri has saved me from that darkness. And I will never return to it again!"

At her declaration, the Beast's hold on her shattered, the white light consuming it in a burning fire.

The image of the Beast dissipated from Rae's mind, and she found herself clutching to Ben's black tunic, tears streaming down her face.

Blinking, she looked up at him. "Ben."

He smiled at her. "Thank you for saving me. I wasn't sure if you would."

Rae realized she had never told Ben what her heart was screaming. She was about to confess her feelings before, but that was when Raphael attacked. She wouldn't waste any more time.

Grabbing Ben's collar, she looked him in the eye and said, "Benjamin Renore, I love you. I have loved you for a long time but couldn't find the courage to say it. I accept your bracelet as a promise to live the rest of our days together. That is, if you can handle my attitude and baking at all hours of the day and night."

Rae was convinced that if Ben could smile any wider, his face would split in two. "Baking at all hours of the day and night is perfectly acceptable to me," he said and before he could continue, Rae wrapped her arms around him and smashed her lips against his.

Ben's fingers tangled in her longer hair and Rae was so glad she had decided to grow it out again.

Just then, a large zap struck the city square, twenty feet from where Ben and Rae sat.

"What was that?" Ben asked, helping Rae stand.

They both turned their gaze to see a line of soldiers bearing the dark green Tentonian flags.

"A siege?" Rae questioned.

But then another zap sounded, causing Ben and Rae to jump and run for shelter. As they crouched inside of one of the near-

by buildings, they watched, amazed as a string of golden light
slammed into the giant statue of Pahga.

Chapter Thirty-Six

Devora, Underground Temple, Kadesh

"You see, Devora?" Queen Leza asked, her half-transformed body a terrible sight to behold. "You were never going to win. I have plenty of statues to draw power from."

The queen's cackle reverberated around Devora as her body fell toward the hard stone ground.

This was it. This was her end. She had tried her best, she had given her all. This was why Tunri hadn't shown her the end of her vision. It ended with her squashed on the floor before the crumbled statue of Pahga.

She never thought about her last moments of life. She had always thought she'd live longer than almost seventeen summers. But in those few seconds a stream of memories ribboned through her mind. She and Mama laughing in the garden. Papa teaching her Tenton's history. The few memories with Nadia, Ida, Hestia and Reese at the Fortress. Laughing at Sir Jacques' corny jokes. Riding with Vinn through the desert. And Matthias. Embracing and kissing Matthias on the balcony at the ball. If she could've frozen that moment in time, she would've.

Taking all these memories, Devora kept them in the center of her thoughts as the hard ground grew nearer. Squeezing her eyes shut, Devora anticipated the impact and sudden death, but instead fell onto something rubbery and ricocheted in the air.

"I didn't expect her to fly that far!" Nadia cried as Devora's body flew off the rubber surface and into the hard, waiting arms that caught her fall.

Unsure of whether to open her eyes or not, Devora decided to crack her eyelid and figure out why she wasn't dead.

"It's so good to see you, Lady Devora," Sir Jacques said with a grin.

Tears streamed down Devora's face as she clung to Sir Jacques' armor, which had saved her life but hurt when he caught her. She was alive. And so were her friends.

As Devora tried to stand, she wobbled and fell again. Thankfully, Sir Jacques was there to grab her.

"How are you here?" she asked, her voice scratchy.

Sir Jacques smiled. "A little birdie came by."

Devora furrowed her brow to see a white sparrow sitting upon Sir Jacques' shoulder. "I don't—"

"Just...give her a moment,"

Devora frowned. *Her?*

The white sparrow flew to where Nadia was waiting with a long tunic. A flash of light permeated the space and where the white sparrow had just hopped now stood Princess Haden.

Devora's brows rose. "That was unexpected."

Sir Jacques laughed. "I said the same thing."

But Devora wasn't in a laughing mood. "Jacques the queen's statue has somehow given power to the other statues of Pahga throughout the city. Vinn and I thought there was only one and we tried to destroy it, but there are hundreds more. She's headed to the next statue now to gain more power."

Sir Jacques nodded. "Yes, I know."

Devora furrowed her brow. "You know?"

He nodded then motioned to Princess Haden who had put on the tunic and pants Nadia offered and was heading toward them.

Devora soon felt herself swept up in two arms as Nadia squeezed her tight. "I've missed you, Dev! I can't believe my rubber blanket worked! And just in time too. You were coming down fast!"

Devora chuckled as she hugged Nadia tightly. How she missed her Tinker friend.

Haden then spoke. "Queen Leza always thought I never understood anything. While I have a few difficulties with reading, I was able to decipher her plans and take them to Prince Amal of Kadesh."

Devora darted her gaze toward the black wolf still tied up next to Matthias in his wolf form.

"Oh no, is that him?" Haden cried rushing to the large black wolf.

"Rae's father created a machine that can nullify the effects of imperial opal," Nadia cut in. "When the machine targets the statue, it will no longer be able to extract souls. It will only become a piece of rock."

Sir Jacques adjusted Devora's arm around his shoulders. "After Nadia brought me a smaller version of the device, Matthias received a message about the queen's plans. Matthias and I were able to convince the queen the machine would enhance imperial opal instead of the opposite."

Devora tried to piece it all together. "Are the others okay? What about Hestia and Reese?" Devora hadn't seen the sisters in so long, she had feared the worst.

"They're holding things together in Tenton," Sir Jacques replied quickly. "Apparently the queen left a political nightmare before she left for battle, so they are doing their best to keep things in order until we return home."

Return home. Devora never thought she would hear those words.

A loud zap sounding like lightning zinged through the air, interrupting Devora's thoughts. Three streams of golden light followed, pummeling into a nearby statue of Pahga.

"Ida is just fine considering that shot," Nadia laughed. She elbowed Jacques in the ribs. "Are you sure she doesn't have another gift like One Shot?"

Jacques laughed but didn't have another chance to reply before another tunnel of light barreled through the sky.

The sound of shattering glass echoed across the city. Hundreds of white lights streamed from various statues, ridding the idols of their power. The evil aura Devora had felt in the presence of the statue of Pahga dissipated and all was silent.

In the next moment, a loud screech interrupted the solemn moment.

"Ah, it seems the queen has found out about our little plan," Sir Jacques said. "I suggest we find a place to regroup."

Devora nodded as Sir Jacques helped her hobble to the wall of the destroyed temple. Nadia quickly grabbed Kanna's unconscious form and pulled her away, as well.

Matthias howled where he was still chained with the prince of Kadesh.

"Jacques, we must save Matthias and the prince. I don't know how to change them back, but we can't leave them there."

Jacques nodded and handed Devora off to Nadia. "Take Devora and Kanna somewhere safe. Haden and I will get the general and the prince."

"Good luck, sir," Nadia said with a salute.

Nadia quickly hauled Kanna's frail form onto her rubber blanket and pulled her to the outer wall of the building as Devora limped to keep up. Once Kanna was safe, Nadia sprinted back to Devora to assist her when a large hand came down and swiped at them.

Nadia yanked Devora out of the way just in time. "What is that?" she cried.

Horror raced down Devora's spine as she stared up at the giant form of the queen. She was still half transformed into the Goddess Pahga and by the scowl on her face, she didn't look happy.

Chapter Thirty-Seven

Mother always said he had a good heart; he just wasn't a good listener, and that phrase was still true to this day. While others were fighting for justice and peace or for their own gain, Tristan just wanted this nightmare to be over.

There were many strange and nightmarish things Tristan had seen in his life, but watching his brother turn into a large gray wolf was by far the strangest. Well, that was until the queen of Tenton began growing into a large giant owl-like creature thing.

Tristan shuddered. No matter. His job wasn't complete, not yet. While the queen was monologuing, something all villains—Tristan realized—seemed to do, he slipped away. The weasel Sergio had disappeared as soon as things got a little intense. Not that Tristan was surprised. He couldn't stand Sergio and was glad the oaf was finally gone. Idiots like him gave all suave men like Tristan a bad name.

Tristan strode to the back hall of the queen's Kadeshian lair where the wolves for General Beta's experiments were caged. He had to admit he felt sorry for the creatures, but didn't think anything of them until he watched Matthias transform into one. Then he had his answer. The answer to the question he had been mulling over for months: how was he going to get out of this mess?

Since he was a child, Tristan had been asking himself that same question. And usually, Matthias was the answer. When he stole sugar cane from the fields, Matthias paid the farmer for it.

When he talked back to the wrong person, Matthias was there, apologizing profusely.

Tristan shook his head. Where would he be without his brother?

Probably dead in a ditch somewhere, he chuckled to himself.

Tristan removed the key he had snagged off General Beta the night before. He had seen the general use the key to unlock almost every door in the underground temple. It was the same key Rae had mentioned before too. There was something about paying a price to use the key, but Tristan didn't care. He knew the goodness in his soul was something that had been used up long ago. Any consequences this key had was nothing compared to things he'd already endured.

Tristan went down to the farthest end of the hall, returning to his earlier thoughts. Even when he got in trouble in Yekel with the Street Rats, Matthias was there, bailing him out. Tristan couldn't believe his brother would give up his spot at Vlacklear Academy—somewhere Matthias had always wanted to go—for his troublesome little brother.

Tristan unlocked the first cell of wolves then continued. Matthias was the ideal older brother: strong, smart, and someone he could rely on. But Tristan knew he couldn't stay under Matthias' wing forever. That's why he got himself stuck in the mess he was currently in. Matthias would always be as straight as an arrow, always playing by the rules. But sometimes, rules and regulations didn't always win. And there was nothing Tristan loved more than winning. He just prayed his brother would trust him enough to see that everything Tristan had done was to find Mother and unite their family again.

As the last cell opened, Tristan stood in the hall and waited. But none of the animals came forth. Furrowing his brows, Tristan suddenly remembered the general had a certain whistle she had trained the wolves to respond too. And if Tristan had heard it correctly, this should work. Sucking in a breath, Tristan whistled the eight-note melody. Like clockwork, the wolves padded out of their cells. It was eerie how their eyes glowed yellow in the dark. A shiver ran down his spine and he desired nothing more than to get out of the dark hall.

Whistling again, Tristan led the wolves to where the queen had returned. She didn't look pleased. Her face was deformed, half human half...something else Tristan couldn't decipher. And while Tristan had riddled out that the queen was his aunt, he still couldn't believe the lengths this woman went to for revenge.

"Stay here," Tristan whispered to the wolves, who stood behind him in the doorway leading to the once-domed room.

"What have you done?" The queen screamed and Tristan froze. Had he been found out already?

But once he realized the queen was screaming at Devora, he continued his steps forward. He'd heard the queen speaking with General Beta about a weapon that enhanced the effects of imperial opal. There was something said about hidden Tinkers and King Atol. But Tristan had been to Totem, and he had seen the machine himself. He knew the machine Lucas made didn't enhance imperial opal but nullify it.

Once Tristan realized Queen Leza believed this lie, he knew, eventually, the queen's power would drain. And that's when his plan would come into play.

His whole life Matthias had been there for him, but now, for once, Tristan would be able to save his brother.

Creeping forward, Tristan crouched to where Matthias and the prince of Kadesh's wolf forms stood, growling at the queen. Upon his approach, Matthias swung around and snapped his jaws at Tristan. While some people would let a beast like the wolf control them, Tristan knew that the only person who could control his brother was Devora.

"Thought I left again, didn't you?" Tristan patted Matthias' back. "Wow, your hair is so soft."

Matthias growled and snapped at Tristan's hands, making him chuckle. "Okay, okay, I have a plan."

Matthias tilted his wolf ear toward Tristan as he explained what they were to do next.

Tristan kept his eyes on the queen, waiting until the right moment. As she released more of her power toward Jacques, Devora, and Nadia—who Tristan prayed could distract her just for a few moments longer—his suspicions were correct. Without the constant flow of power from souls, Queen Leza couldn't hold the supernatural form of the Goddess Pahga.

Tristan watched in awe as Nadia pulled weapon after weapon out of the bag she'd brought with her. Some she handed to Jacques and Princess Haden, but most she used herself.

As she launched a string of arrows into the queen's side, Tristan let out a low whistle. "What a woman."

Matthias snorted and did the equivalent of a wolf rolling his eyes.

"What?" Tristan asked. "You already took my first betrothed, are you going to steal another woman from my grasp?" Matthias gave a low growl and Tristan smirked. "It's almost time, brother."

Matthias stood tall and waited as Tristan unlocked the chain binding his brother to the column.

The queen was almost back to normal size, but Tristan couldn't wait any longer. He wanted this nightmare to end, once and for all.

Standing tall, Tristan whistled the same tune he had heard General Beta give over these past few weeks. And like magic, the wolves responded. Barreling through the doorway, the wolves pounded their way to where Tristan stood.

"This is your new master," Tristan said, pointing to Matthias and praying the wolves understood him. "Do what he says."

The wolves blinked at Tristan, and he realized only someone like him could hope an insane plan like this would work.

"Excellent work, Tristan," the queen called, and Tristan thought his heart had stopped.

"Yes, my queen," Tristan replied, not realizing what the queen was referring to but decided playing along always kept him alive.

"General Beta's wolves," the queen panted with a grin.

Nadia's weapons had done a number on the queen's once pristine form. Gashes and cuts lined her limbs. The right half of her face had sunken due to the failed transformation. And somehow, chunks of her hair had burned off. Tristan's eyes darted around to see small flames dotting the entire room.

Probably one of Nadia's weapons. He then realized Nadia didn't know he wasn't *really* working with the queen. A flood of curses came to Tristan's mind as his eyes reached hers and he saw hurt and distrust consume her gaze.

"Yes," Tristan agreed with the queen, though he had been so wrapped up in Nadia that he hadn't realized what he was agreeing to.

Queen Leza whistled the same whistle General Beta had, but the wolves didn't move. The queen's gaze blanched as she realized what was happening.

"You see, Auntie," Tristan said, unlocking the chain that bound the prince of Kadesh's wolf form. "Wolves are pack animals, and they need one of their own kind to lead them." Tristan stood proud beside his brother, who had his eyes set on the queen. "Thankfully, you've given them a great leader to show them the way." Tristan patted Matthias on the head. "Lead on, brother."

Matthias lifted his snout to the air and released a loud howl before charging the queen. The other wolves, easily accepting their new alpha, followed suit. In the blink of an eye, the wolves surrounded the queen.

"Get back," she cried, using the last bits of her power to push the growling animals away. She then caught Tristan's eye. "You. How dare you betray me?"

Tristan leaned against the nearby wall to cover up how frightened he really was. He crossed his arms over his chest, hoping he looked more disinterested than terrified. "You betrayed me first, when you turned against *our* family."

The queen started to say more, but Tristan knew his brother was not one for tedious conversations. Matthias howled again and the wolves attacked.

Not being one for such a bloody sight, Tristan turned away. But by the sounds of it, the end of the queen of Tenton was swift.

The wolves howled in unison and by the echoing of their steps, had left the room. Tristan mustered his courage and dared to turn around. He breathed a sigh of relief at not having to see the queen's mangled body. But what he did see, however, was Matthias' human form, and it was naked.

Tristan knew this was a solemn moment. The tyrannical queen they had been vying to destroy was finally gone. But he found himself bursting with laughter all the same. Maybe it was the release of adrenaline, or it was his stiff brother's backside being shown to the world, but Tristan doubled over in laughter.

"Why don't you make yourself useful and help me?" Matthias grunted from his prostrate position.

"Sure, sure," Tristan said as he stripped off his own tunic and handed it to Matthias. Tristan was impressed by how fast Matthias covered himself.

"Um, do you happen to have another one of those?" another voice with a thick Kadeshian accent asked.

"Prince Amal, I assume?" Matthias asked and Tristan couldn't understand how his brother could keep such a straight face at the naked prince of Kadesh.

The young man nodded. "That's right," he started before a blur rushed forward.

"Mal!" Princess Haden threw herself on top of the prince and Matthias and Tristan shared a glance before turning away.

"I'm so glad you're okay. I was so—wait, are you—I'm so sorry!" Princess Haden rambled as the sound of her boots scurrying away scraped against the stone.

Matthias' hard exterior finally broke and he laughed alongside Tristan. "Jacques," Matthias called, wiping a tear from his eye. "Please find the prince something to wear."

"Of course, sir," Jacques replied. "However, I do believe Lady Devora needs some assistance."

Jacques raised his brows, and Tristan had never seen his brother move so fast to get to Devora's side.

A warmth coated Tristan's chest. It was a feeling he hadn't experienced since he was a child. Is this what joy felt like? Was there really still good left in his soul?

Just as he was getting used to the feeling a hand came out and slapped him across the face. Tristan's neck snapped back from the impact, and he stumbled a few steps.

"You lied to me," Nadia seethed. "How dare you side with the evil queen?"

"I had a plan to betray her all along," Tristan winced, gently probing his tender cheek. If there was ever a time to say the right thing, it was now. "I'm sorry for not telling you. I didn't want to put you in harm's way."

Tristan winced again as Nadia went to move, but instead of slapping his other cheek, she grabbed his neck and kissed him. Tristan had kissed more females than he'd like to admit, however the kiss Nadia gave him was unlike anything he had ever experienced before. When she released him, he felt in a daze.

"Never lie to me again, got it?" Nadia said, lifting a weapon akin to a lance to his throat.

Tristan nodded numbly, still feeling as if he were floating from the kiss as Nadia took his hand and said something about finding the others. But as Tristan followed behind her, he glanced at their hands intertwined and felt joy enter his heart once more.

Chapter Thirty-Eight

Devora, Underground Temple, Kadesh

Queen Leza's death was gruesome, but quick. And Devora was so thankful that it was finally over. It was only by Tunri's hand that they were able to fend off the queen long enough to use up the power she'd gained from the stolen souls. Thank goodness Nadia and Sir Jacques had come—and with weapons too. Of course, Nadia always had weapons and for that, Devora was eternally grateful.

She didn't know how she had the strength to assist Nadia and Sir Jacques, but she grabbed whatever weapon Nadia gave her and used it to the best of her ability. Now that it was over—finally over—a wave of exhaustion hit Devora. Every area of her body ached with pain, and she wished for nothing more than to sleep for the next three weeks.

Once the wolves had cleared out of the room, taking the remains of the queen with them, Devora slumped to the ground, unable to hold herself up any longer. If she could just rest for a few minutes, then she would get up and try to muddle through the rest of her emotions. As she started to close her eyes, a pair of bare feet entered her line of sight.

Devora tried to move when two strong arms scooped her up. The strong, steady beat of Matthias' heart rang against her ear and Devora never felt so at peace.

"I told you this wasn't the end," he whispered.

Devora said something, but it came out garbled.

Matthias placed a kiss on her head. "Rest, my love. There is much to fix when you wake." Matthias didn't need to tell her twice. Finally, within the arms of the man she loved, Devora immediately closed her eyes and fell into a deep sleep.

Chapter Thirty-Nine

Matthias, Radaa Kingdom, Kadesh—a few days later

Rebuilding after destruction was never easy, but Matthias was ready to take the challenge head on. Thankfully, his mother and Devora were safely resting at a Tentonian camp under the watchful eye of his father—who had come to assist with the war efforts—and Nadia, Rae and One Shot. Though, when Rae and One Shot stumbled out of the rubble of the city a few days prior, they looked worse for wear. However, Matthias was overjoyed that they were alive and well. Unlike the warden. Matthias' thoughts ran back to Warden Hazor and his sacrifice. He would make sure the warden was remembered valiantly.

At the request of the Kadeshian crown, Matthias scheduled a meeting with Prince Amal and Princess Haden, the future king and queen of Kadesh. Princess Amalia, the princess of Kadesh, would be joining them as well.

With Tenton's own monarchy in shambles and knowing that he was the blood-related nephew of the former queen, Matthias had volunteered to stay behind and make agreements with Kadesh on the future ahead. Jacques, loyal as always, stayed by his side. And because Jacques wouldn't allow Ida out of his sight, she came as well. Matthias thought this was an advantage, since Ida knew the Kadeshian tongue better than any of them. And, as much as he worried about his decision, Matthias invited Tristan to come along. He had proven trustworthy after all and was a blood relation to the former queen, same as Matthias.

Before they headed to the palace, Matthias watched with curiosity as Tristan handed over a black skeleton key to Rae. What surprised him even more was Rae jumping up and hugging Tristan tightly. And One Shot didn't even shoot him down.

Interesting, Matthias thought as Tristan jogged up to meet with them.

"What?" he asked, scrunching his nose like he had since he was five summers.

Matthias smiled and nudged him in the shoulder. "Nothing. We're going to be late. Come on."

Tristan snorted at the remark but stood a little taller next to Matthias.

As the group came upon the half-destroyed palace, Matthias joked to Jacques, "What about the roses and lilies?"

Jacques sighed. "As much as I'd love to marry Ida and leave this all behind, I know you'll need a second opinion on matters. And I have always been good at giving you my opinion."

Matthias chuckled. "That is very true."

"I also like both of those flowers very much," Ida piped in, her fingers laced in Jacques.

"We shall have bouquets of them everywhere," Jacques replied, causing Tristan to roll his eyes but not with as much attitude as usual.

It seemed after Nadia gave him a good wallop to the cheek, Tristan was happier. That and the evil queen that had controlled his life for years was finally gone.

Once the group strolled into the throne room, Prince Amal, Princess Haden and Princess Amalia waited for them at a wooden oval table at the center. Matthias took in as much of the room as possible. Warm colors of orange and blue were woven in every corner. Large tapestries depicting the former royal families hung on the walls between large windows with billowing gauze curtains. As Matthias studied the space, he found he enjoyed it a lot more than the stark white sterility of Maldove Palace.

"Welcome, General Blake and Sir Jacques," Prince Amal declared. He turned to Ida. "Future Duchess Delequa." And then to Tristan. "And Prince Tristan of Tenton."

Tristan grinned widely and puffed out his chest. "Now I like the sound of that."

Matthias resisted the urge to slap him in the back of the head.

The prince laughed. "Thank you for joining us today after such horrific events."

Before Matthias could get a word in, Princess Haden rushed between him and Jacques and squeezed them into a hug.

"I know it's not correct, but I can't express how thankful I am that you believed me. Thank you for putting your faith in me," she said in their ears.

Matthias stiffened while Jacques patted the princess on the back. "It wasn't us, Princess, but Tunri. He gave Lady Devora a vision that we would see her again when the sparrow flies. And that sparrow was you. So, we should be thanking you."

"Yes," Matthias confirmed with a nod. Taking a step back, he bowed to the princess, with Jacques following suit. Ida and Tristan did the same.

"I don't know about all that," Princess Haden muttered, but she smiled all the same.

"The princess is modest," Prince Amal declared, a look of admiration in his eyes. "She is a true leader, and I know she will lead her people greatly."

Princess Amalia nodded at the statement, but Matthias detected a note of sadness in the prince's tone as he said the words.

"Come," the prince continued, motioning them to sit at the table. "There is much to discuss."

As Matthias, Jacques, Ida and Tristan were treated like royalty with special Kadeshian delicacies, Prince Amal explained everything that had happened in Kadesh. When the war first began twenty years ago, General Beta had cast a spell over the current king of Kadesh. Every time she spoke to him, he would only listen to her words and her words alone. This caused a rift between King Redore IV and the prince and princess as they grew older and tried to figure out what was happening. With the former queen having passed on long ago, it was up to the prince and princess to devise a plan to save their kingdom. Through Princess Amalia playing the part of the prince, Prince Amal was able to roam freely and travel throughout Kadesh to see what the people really needed and rally support for the new prince to take the throne. It wasn't until he ran into the disguised Princess Haden in the marketplace that the prince and princess decided the time to act was now.

Prince Amal then added that after the disastrous events with General Beta taking him hostage, Princess Amalia had found King Redore IV bound at the bottom of a well in one of the palace's many courtyards. Thankfully, he was able to recover, but from what the princess said, the king's mind was very weak after being meddled with for twenty years.

"With my father's head finally cleared of General Beta's sorcery, he has decided to step down from the throne," Prince Amal explained. "And though Amalia would be a better leader than I, she has decided she would rather be an ambassador to Tenton, if our discussions end well."

Princess Amalia raised a cup in Matthias' direction before taking a deep swig.

"Prince Amal, I believe Tenton and Kadesh have been at war long enough," Matthias stated. "I think it's time we draft a peace treaty."

Prince Amal nodded and motioned to a man in the corner. "I've had my scribe working on one since I returned to the palace—and thankfully in my human state." The prince cast a glance at Princess Haden whose cheeks turned the shade of the cherries on the table.

Matthias remembered the interaction of the two back in the queen's lair and stifled a laugh. "Princess Haden, as the heir to the throne of Tenton, would you look over and sign the peace treaty for our nation?" Matthias asked.

Princess Haden cleared her throat. "I would, General Blake, however I gave up my right to the throne of Tenton."

Prince Amal's head whipped around so fast, Matthias thought it would snap off. The prince asked, "What are you saying?"

Princess Haden gave the prince a smile and grabbed his hand. "In order to give Prince Amal and myself the power we needed to send Kadesh's armies out and evacuate the Kadeshian people, we had to become betrothed."

"It's Kadeshian law for royalty," Prince Amal quickly explained, keeping his gaze on Haden. "In order to have any voice in the council they have to at least be betrothed."

"I see," Matthias replied, now understanding why the two seemed so nervous around each other.

"But I told the princess after we defeated Queen Leza, we would call off the betrothal and she would be free to rule her country as she wished."

Matthias turned to Princess Haden. "So, you're saying you wish to stay betrothed to the prince and become the queen of Kadesh instead?"

Haden squeezed Amal's hand with a smile. "I am."

Matthias leaned back in his chair, passing the peace treaty to Ida so she could read it over. "Congratulations, but that leaves us without a leader."

"Actually, it doesn't," Tristan piped in. He grabbed a handful of grapes from the table then stood. "You see, the former queen of Tenton was our biological aunt. That means that Matthias and I are the blood heirs to the throne."

Tristan gave a wide grin that made Matthias' blood go cold.

"Absolutely not. You are forbidden from stepping one foot in that throne room."

Tristan popped a grape in his mouth, chewed then swallowed. "I wasn't talking about me, brother."

A fear Matthias never felt before struck him still. Him? King? Before he could say anything, Jacques piped in.

"He is an excellent candidate. Former general, united Tenton, then led his troops to victory over the tyrannical queen. The people would adore him," Jacques gave Matthias a thumbs up and Matthias wanted to crawl under the table and hide.

Matthias saw his dream of returning to Totem and running the vineyard moving further and further from his reach. Did he really want all that power? And what about Devora? How could he have a future with her and hold the throne? Would she even desire a life like that? It didn't take him long to decide.

Taking a breath, Matthias replied, "Thank you for your consideration, but I will have to decline the offer."

"What?" Tristan and Jacques said at the same time.

"I have been working with the monarchy for far too long and have experienced things I never hope to experience again. I desire a simple life for now. However, if whoever the new ruler is would like an advisor, I would be honored to accept that position."

"So, *I'm* going to be king?" Tristan gaped. "I can't handle that responsibility."

"No, you're going to abdicate, as well," Matthias said matter-of-factly.

"So," Prince Amal cut in, watching the three of them. "Who is the next king or queen of Tenton?"

Matthias ran his hands through his hair, concentrating on the concentric pattern of the rug beneath his boots. Usually if there is no one left in the bloodline of the royal family to take the throne, the power shifted to those of royal status, typically dukes and duchesses who had a long line of nobility.

His thoughts paused before running through everything he'd learned about the succession of the crown, and he couldn't help the grin plastering on his face.

"With neither I nor Tristan having any heirs yet, the power of the throne goes to the family of nobility who has had a noble bloodline for decades. In Tenton, I believe it's the Duke of Tinwa."

Jacques spit out his drink, causing Princess Amalia to laugh heartily. Ida's concentration from the peace treaty broke as well, her eyes glistening gold while her mouth formed a small "o."

"What?" Jacques squeaked. "But *I'm* the Duke of Tinwa."

"Yes, you are," Matthias said, patting his friend on the back. "And who better? A Tentonian born and bred king with his kind and loving Kadeshian queen, a perfect mirror to the Kadeshian throne. I say it's the makings of a peaceful future and reign for each kingdom."

"Oh," was all Ida could say, her face frozen in shock.

Jacques glared at Matthias. "I don't know how you could, but it feels like you set this up."

Matthias only laughed.

"So, Duke Delequa of Tinwa," Prince Amal said, glancing between Jacques and Ida, who still looked starstruck at the notion. "Will you and your betrothed take up the throne and help me and Princess Haden bring about peace to our lands?"

Chapter Forty

The meeting with General Blake and the others went better than expected. And though Haden thought she would tell Mal she wished to stay with him in private, the general gave her the perfect platform to announce the news to everyone.

As the meeting ended and the plans for another peace treaty meeting in Tenton were scheduled, Haden excused herself and headed toward the gardens. Though, they could hardly be called that anymore. Mother had caused so much destruction to this beautiful land. Chunks of the palace were gone. Several of the beautiful fountains Haden loved to sit at were destroyed. It was a disheartening sight, but the thought that she would be able to stay here and watch this land be rebuilt gave Haden a hope she hadn't felt in a long time.

As she strode further through the crushed shrubberies, the sound of rushed footsteps came behind her.

"Did you mean it?" Mal said, trying to catch his breath.

Haden turned toward him. He looked so different from the guard she fell in love with. His white royal robes shone in the morning sun, a contrast to his flawless dark skin. The cerulean and orange embroidery glinted as the fabric rustled in the warm breeze. But though his clothes were clean, and she knew he was the future king, she still loved the Mal she met in the marketplace.

Haden tucked a piece of her white-blonde hair behind her ear. "Did I mean what?"

Mal folded his arms over his chest, his face stern. "You wish to stay here. With me."

Haden smiled and strode toward him and pulled his arms from his chest, allowing her to hold his hands. "I do. I want to stay here. With you. Forever. If you'll still have me."

Mal's stern exterior broke immediately as he wrapped his arms around Haden and lifted her off the ground. Holding her tight he spun her around. The couple laughed together until Mal finally slowed down and lowered Haden back to the ground.

Mal leaned his forehead against hers. "I can't wait to spend the rest of my life getting to know you. I knew that day I saw you in the marketplace my life would change."

Haden closed her eyes, thinking of everything they had endured together in such a short time. Though healing a nation that had been hurt for so long would be a difficult journey, Haden couldn't think of anyone she would rather face the challenge with than Mal.

"Hopefully for the better," Haden finally replied, wrapping her arms around his neck.

Mal smiled wide again before leaning down and pressing his lips against hers. Haden happily reciprocated the kiss, thanking Tunri for the blissful moment.

Chapter Forty-One

Ida, Maldove Palace, Tenton—Two weeks later

Ida sat on the plush bed in Maldove Palace. It was a temporary room until hers and Jacques' room was ready in a week's time before their wedding.

She still couldn't believe the events happening around her. A lowly orphan becoming the Queen of Tenton? Only Tunri could write a story so outlandish and wonderful. And it was *her* story. Tunri had thought *her* worthy enough to give a beautiful story and she was so incredibly grateful she found herself crying at every happy thing. The first few times her tears flowed—when they reunited with Reese, Hestia and Charles, when she saw Ama and Jil again and explained everything, when she stepped foot in Maldove Palace again, not as a spy, but as its future queen—Jacques became extremely concerned and thought Ida was still upset about the battle in Renta. But after she explained everything, he now only offered her his handkerchief and held her close when she burst into tears. Though not all her tears were tears of joy. When she'd heard of what happened to the warden she wept for days. The man who had saved her life once before had saved hers, and all of their lives, for a final time. Hopefully, Warden Hazor was finally at peace.

Unfortunately, there were already some hardships Jacques had to deal with as well and the main one was his older brother, Raphael. Prince Amal offered to try him for his crimes in Kadesh, but Jacques declined the offer. Unfortunately, once Jacques and she had their coronation, Raphael's trial would be the first aftermath of the war the new monarchy would have to endure.

Sighing, Ida tried to push that thought from her mind as she gazed at her lovely wedding gown before a knock sounded at the door.

"Ida, it's me," Jacques called, and Ida's heart skipped a beat. She quickly closed the wardrobe where her wedding dress was displayed. She had always heard it was bad luck for the groom to see the dress early. And though Ida wasn't sure if she believed in that or not, she didn't want to press any of her luck.

"Come in," she called as she sat back down on the edge of her bed.

Jacques gave her a soft smile as he came toward her and kissed her cheek. "Is everything okay?"

Ida would never know how in one look he could see all her emotions, but he always did.

Ida motioned him to sit next to her before she took his hand. She stared at their intertwined fingers, thinking of when her reality was just a dream, a prayer she had prayed so hard for. And Tunri had answered that prayer ten times over.

"I am so incredibly happy, Jacques," Ida said softly. "But do you think I can do this? Can I really be a queen?"

Jacques furrowed his brow. "I don't see why not. Not only are you kind and loving, you're incredibly smart and the people will love that you're not from a stuffy aristocratic family like me."

Ida laughed. "You aren't stuffy."

Jacques shrugged his shoulder with a smirk. "I may not be stuffy but you should know, I do snore. Or so Matthias has told me. There were many times when we were camping out on a mission where I was kicked out of the tent because my snoring was so loud."

Ida giggled and squeezed his hand. "I think I'll be able to handle it."

Jacques reached over and stroked Ida's cheek. "Good, because I'll never leave your side, for the rest of our lives."

Ida's heart soared to the moon as Jacques pulled her close and kissed her tenderly on the lips, giving an unspoken promise of the many more moments they would share in the days to come.

Chapter Forty-Two

Rae, Totem, Tenton—Two Weeks later

Rae ran her fingers over the dark skeleton key, a gesture that had become commonplace since she, Ben, Nadia, Tristan and Miguel decided to travel back to Totem to destroy it. The future king of Tenton had given Miguel a written pardon for desertion and he could return home. As soon as Jacques was officially king, he would make Miguel's pardon permanent.

While Rae was happy to have found another piece of her family, she still worried for Mami. They had tried every weapon Nadia offered to destroy the key and nothing worked. So, Nadia suggested bringing the key to Rae's father. And Rae desperately wanted to share with them the news about Haden and reunite Papi with his brother. But as they journeyed closer and closer to Totem, fear rose in Rae's heart. Though she tried to hide her greatest fear—that she was too late and Mami would be gone—Ben and Nadia always saw right through her.

"We're here for you," Ben said one evening while they were sitting around the fire of their camp for the night.

"You can always come talk to us," Nadia added, tossing in another piece of wood.

"I know we got off on the wrong foot," Tristan mentioned, taking his now constant place next to Nadia. "But I'm here too. Though I'm a lousy listener and have no good advice to offer."

Nadia playfully slapped him on the arm but laughed at his words.

Rae smirked. She didn't understand the odd couple, but they seemed happy. However, they did bicker an awful lot.

The next day they arrived in Totem and Rae was a mess of nerves. Liam, General Blake's—Matthias'—father greeted them. Thankfully, Matthias' mother was well enough to return to her home and could continue healing with her husband by her side.

As Tristan guided Nadia inside his childhood home to officially meet his mother and Miguel was given a tour of Totem, Rae and Ben headed toward the group of tents.

It felt as if two boulders were attached to Rae's legs as she forced herself toward Mami's and Papi's tent. Totem was bustling like it had been before, but a good chunk of its inhabitants had gone to help Matthias fight against the queen.

Finally, Rae was outside the tent, but she couldn't go inside.

"Are you okay?" Ben asked. His strong, steady presence had been with her the whole journey, and she was so thankful for it.

"I'm scared," she confessed, clutching the skeleton key. "What if I'm too late?"

Ben released a breath. "Either way, you need to know."

Rae ran over his words. He was right. Either way, she had to step inside.

Give me strength, she prayed to Tunri before rallying her courage and stepping into the tent.

Silence like a brick thudded against Rae's heart. Mami's figure lay on the bed, still, and covered in thick blankets. She didn't see Papi, but her fear was rising.

"Mami?" Rae whispered. "Mami, I've come back. You're going to be okay now."

There was no response from Mami and Rae's eyes filled with tears as she knelt by her mother's side.

"Mami, your other daughter, my little sister, she's alive! And she's going to be queen of Kadesh. You have to wake up. You have to see her again. Mami, please!" Rae cried, shaking her mother's arm.

Tears ran down Rae's cheeks as she sobbed, the skeleton key still gripped in her fingertips. Her worst fear had come true. She was too late.

Ben's gentle hand lay on her back, but she was thankful he didn't offer any words of comfort.

Sniffing, Rae laid her cheek on Mami's hand. "I love you, Mami. I'm so sorry."

I'm sorry, Rae prayed to Tunri, knowing she had taken the key from the hag in desperation to free the women instead of trusting in Him.

A few moments ticked by, the silence filled with Rae's cries until she felt sand in the palm of her hand. Glancing down, Rae stared amazed as the skeleton key disintegrated in dust before slipping through her fingertips.

"Wha—" she started before she heard Mami gasp for breath.

Rae jumped back, colliding with Ben.

Blinking, Mami's eyes looked around before she stretched and sat up in her bed. Facing Rae, she smiled. "Good morning, *mija.* Did you sleep well?"

Rae's jaw dropped to the floor. Her mother, who was once dead, was now alive. All by Tunri's grace.

"Thank you," she said aloud and raced into her mother's arms, but this time with tears of joy.

Mami hugged Rae back with a confused laugh. "Did I miss something?" She glanced to Ben, who was barely keeping his eyes dry.

"Sara?" Lucas Salvar burst through the tent. As soon as he saw the two women hugging, he launched his arms around them, with tears of joy.

"Someone is going to have to explain why we're all crying," Sara Salvar said as she kissed Rae's head.

"There's plenty of time for that, my dear," Lucas said. "But first, let's eat."

"Papi, wait," Rae called before he left. "I think there's someone you want to see."

As if on cue, Miguel Salvar strode through the tent.

"*Ay!*" Lucas said, his hands flying to his head in disbelief. "Miguel is that you?"

"It is, *hermano!*" Miguel laughed before picking Lucas up in a big hug.

Rae laughed and cried at the same time. They were all together again, at last. And with the nuptials of the king and queen of Kadesh coming up, Mami and Papi would finally be reunited with their lost daughter.

Mami's healing spread throughout Totem and a huge celebration was planned. Rae laughed and ate way too much before she decided to join Ben, Nadia and Tristan at the fire near Mami's and Papi's tent.

Tristan and Nadia were cuddled close to each other, whispering things Rae knew she wasn't meant to hear, so she focused on Ben. His face and hands were still cut up and bruised from the attack in Kadesh, but Rae realized she no longer felt fear of the future with him. Yet Rae couldn't decipher the look on his face as he stared into the flames. He had rejoiced in Mami's healing as well, but as the celebration continued, Ben hid among the shadows. Though Rae had told him she loved him, and they had survived the queen's rampage in Renta, he still seemed withdrawn.

Standing, she strode over and sat beside him. The blue and orange bracelet Ben had given her in Kadesh was still wrapped around her wrist. "So, per the customs of Snoken," Rae started, fiddling with the bracelet. "Am I to make a bracelet for you too?"

Ben's eyes moved from the fire onto Rae's face. With the flickering of the orange flames reflecting against their dark hue, Rae could easily get lost in them.

"Only if you accept the terms of the agreement," Ben replied, his voice low.

Rae bit her lip and focused back on the bracelet. "I see."

She then leaned over and rummaged through her bag carrying the few things she'd been able to salvage from the attack on the Kadeshian palace. Her fingers finally landed on the cool metal she was searching for. "I suppose it's a good thing I thought ahead and asked Nadia to make me one of these."

Rae pulled out the thin metal bracelet. Though she hadn't known Ben too long, she knew he was a man of little words and even less color for his attire. Rae chuckled to herself, realizing whereas Ben wore hardly any color, Rae loved wearing her colorful scarves anywhere she went. But as she held out the thin metal bracelet to Ben, she thought it suited him perfectly. "I would like to accept your terms of living the rest of our days together, but only if you accept mine."

Ben snatched the bracelet out of Rae's hand so fast, if she would've blinked, she wouldn't have seen him slide it on his wrist. "I accept," Ben said with a wide grin. Leaning forward, he kissed Rae tenderly.

"Oh great! Another wedding we have to attend?" Tristan asked, his voice shattering the sweet moment. "Do you people realize how expensive these weddings are for the guests?" He huffed.

"Who said you were invited?" Ben countered, making Tristan shut his mouth.

"Tris, I would think you'd love being invited to the royal wedding of the king and queen of Tenton *and* the king and queen of Kadesh. I'm sure the parties afterward will be great," Nadia suggested as she tapped her charcoal on her notebook.

Tristan gave her a thoughtful gaze and slung his arm around her shoulder. "That is true. I suppose we will just have to suffer together."

"There are many things we have to take care of before we even start planning a wedding," Ben continued, stoking the fire. "There will be time."

Rae's heart melted. After all this time, after everything they'd been through, Ben still didn't press her or rush her into anything she didn't want to do. And she loved him all the more for it. "There is time, but we'll make sure there's not *too* much time."

With another wide grin, he leaned down and kissed Rae with the promise of a bright future ahead.

Chapter Forty-Three

Matthias, Grenly, Tenton—Three Weeks after the attack on Kadesh

Matthias steeled himself before the large blue door. It felt like years had passed since he first stood outside of Devora's home to warn her parents about what transpired at the ball after the Battle of Edo. He shut his eyes and turned away. He still hated himself for betraying Devora, but it was in the past. Devora had forgiven him, now he just had to forgive himself.

Is that why I'm so nervous? Matthias thought to himself as he wiped his clammy palms on his pant leg for the umpteenth time since arriving in Grenly.

It had been three weeks since he had seen her. Three weeks since Queen Leza was defeated. Three weeks since he made sure Devora and Mother were safe and healing in Tenton while he worked with Jacques and the other council members to start rebuilding Tenton and Kadesh after twenty years of terror. They were far from finished and the road to peace was never an easy one. But both nations decided to pause their meetings and discussions to celebrate two very important weddings and coronations that were about to happen. And there was only one person Matthias hoped to go with to both events.

After the battle in Renta ended, and Matthias was able to sleep and eat without the threat of being turned into a wolf at any moment, his thoughts and intentions with Devora were made clear. His heart loved her entirely and desired to be with her forever. But he wanted to get to know her first. Not under the stress of the Fortress or barbaric tournaments. He wished to know her favorite food, her favorite book. Was breakfast her favorite meal or dinner? What was her favorite flower?

Matthias paused, panic ensuing. He knew he had forgotten something in his frazzled state. How could he ask Governor Grenly to court Devora if he didn't have flowers?

Rushing away from the governor's mansion, Matthias darted down the street to where a flower vendor stood. A beautiful bouquet of purple roses and white lilies stood out to him and Matthias couldn't help but laugh.

Roses and lilies, of course.

Matthias gave the vendor way too much coin, but he didn't care. If he waited another moment, his heart was going to burst.

Gathering his courage, Matthias marched back to the governor's mansion and knocked on the door. It felt like an eternity before the door opened, revealing Governor Cusha Medee.

Matthias swallowed. Had the governor always been so tall and burly? Why did Matthias suddenly feel like a small boy again in the presence of this man? But once Governor Cusha smiled, some of Matthias' panic subsided.

"Ah, General Blake, to what do we owe this honor?" A twinkle lingered in the governor's eyes and Matthias did his best not to fumble his words.

"Good morning, sir, I've come to ask your permission to court your daughter," Matthias rushed out in a single breath. He inwardly unleashed a thousand curses at himself for looking like such a fool, but at least he was truthful with his intentions.

Governor Cusha released a hearty laugh and opened the door wider. "Why don't you come inside?"

Matthias breathed a sigh of relief. "Thank you, sir."

As Matthias strode into the house, he tried to take in everything around him. This was Devora's childhood home. Yes, he had been here before but that was under entirely different circumstances. The governor's mansion was lavish and beautiful. Very different to the humble home he was raised in in Ballear.

Matthias swallowed. Though he had more than enough coin saved up, would Devora be okay with a simple life rather than one filled with extravagant things?

Matthias shook that thought from his head. One step at a time. He wasn't leading men into a battle, he was asking the woman he loved on a date. Somehow, the latter seemed far more nerve-wracking.

"General Blake," First Lady Medee's warm voice came as she hurried up to Matthias and embraced him tightly. "We are forever in your debt. You not only kept our daughter alive but saved us as well. I don't know how we'll ever repay your kindness."

"I have a few ideas," Governor Cusha replied with a smirk.

First Lady Medee elbowed him in the ribs while she kept her smile on her face.

"No payment is needed, First Lady," Matthias said, bowing his head. "And I thank you for your aid with the future queen and controlling the device that destroyed the statue of Pahga."

First Lady Medee laughed. "Ida was always a sharp girl. I'm just thankful we were there to help her hold the thing. The poor dear is so small. There was no way she could've endured its impact alone."

"You are a powerful team," Matthias said, hoping he and Devora would be just as devoted to one another as his parents and hers. After a moment he added, "I do only wish to see Devora."

The First Lady gave Matthias a knowing smile. "Of course. She's on the roof."

Matthias blinked. "The roof?"

Cusha laughed. "She says it's where she thinks the best. No walls confining her thoughts. Come, I'll show you the easiest way up."

This new information about Devora fascinated Matthias and he eagerly followed Governor Medee up the flight of stairs. As the governor opened the roof hatch, the warm jungle breeze caressed Matthias' cheeks.

"Good luck, son," the governor said, causing Matthias to panic all over again. "If it's any consolation, you had my permission to court Devora the moment you first saved her life when she entered the Fortress."

Matthias turned to Cusha. "She told you about that?"

The governor nodded. "And other things." Matthias blanched and Cusha laughed. "Devora is a much harsher judge than I. If she's forgiven you, then I can as well." With that, Governor Cusha headed back down the stairs, leaving Matthias all on his own.

Steeling his breath, Matthias climbed through the hatch, careful not to crush the flowers. Purple always reminded him of Devora, but now he wasn't sure if she even liked the color purple. He almost turned around and fled down the steps but stopped himself.

You're being ridiculous. Get yourself together, man!

Matthias locked on to Devora's seated form. She faced the jungle depths, her eyes closed. Long waves of dark hair swirled around her, no longer bound in a braid, but free to twist and tangle as they pleased. She was a picture of perfection and Matthias couldn't help but drink her in.

After he had stood there longer than necessary, he strode forward and prayed he didn't mess everything up like he had before.

Chapter Forty-Four

Devora, Grenly, Tenton

Devora breathed in the sweet scent around her. The desert lilies from her mother's garden were in full bloom and she loved their fragrance. Warm air blew against her skin, enveloping her in a tight hug that welcomed her home.

Home.

Devora never thought she would ever come back here. Many nights she dreamed of her home. Her favorite spot on the roof, her favorite mug from the cupboard. Thank goodness it didn't hold the dung tea anymore, but just a soothing chamomile.

So much had happened, and Devora still needed time to process it all. After the destruction of the statue of Pahga and Queen Leza's demise, all Devora remembered was Matthias scooping her up and running. But when she awoke, she was back home, in her bed. Mama and Papa were there, and Devora had jumped into their arms, realizing too late that hers was in a sling. After the pain subsided, she laughed and cried with her parents. She told them everything that had happened since she was sent to the Fortress. They laughed with her, cried with her. A few times Papa was ready to strangle someone, and Devora and Mama successfully talked him out of it.

After Devora purged all her emotions, she felt better. She had heard through Papa that Haden had decided to marry the prince of Kadesh. Devora didn't know the princess well, but she was happy that Tenton and Kadesh could be united as one.

But it wasn't until Ida and Jacques visited her yesterday that Devora screamed with delight. Her friends were to be the future king and queen of Tenton. Mama was overjoyed to hear the news and immediately welcomed them into their home any time they wished. Once Ida and Mama were done speaking about floral arrangements for the upcoming wedding, the new couple pulled Devora aside.

"We do have a proposition for you," Jacques had told Devora. "But not now, whenever you feel up to it."

Devora sat back on her bed. "Okay, I'm listening."

"First," Ida started, concern on her face. "Tristan told us of the tincture General Beta made you all drink. We've seen the effects of it on Kanna and were worried about you."

"I refused to drink it," Devora stated, proud of herself for resisting the Subtle Tea—the dung tea—for so long.

Jacques smiled. "I'm not surprised. However, we wanted to ask you if you would consider helping us rebuild Vlacklear Academy. Not physically of course, but the curriculum and academics of the school. I know you always dreamed of attending there and thought you would be a great help in planning its future."

Devora's brows shot to the top of her head. "You want my help? But I never attended Vlacklear."

"No," Ida said. "But you've read plenty of books and have abundant life experience executing things you've learned to be a credible source."

"There will be others too," Jacques added. "Together we will create a school for all who wish to learn."

Devora blinked at her friends, her king and queen. Tears brimmed in her eyes as she wrapped her good arm around Ida's neck and then Jacques'.

"Thank you," she whispered. "I would be honored to help."

They hugged her back and Ida said, "But not until you're fully healed, understand? You work yourself way too hard when you're focused, and I want you to get better."

"How can I refuse my queen?" Devora replied with a chuckle.

"How indeed," Jacques replied, kissing Ida on the temple while Ida blushed.

Devora refocused her thoughts from the memory, and she opened her eyes. Tunri really had brought her full circle. The last time she sat here she had wished for nothing more than to attend Vlacklear Academy. And now, He was giving her the desires of her heart. Albeit the journey had been *very* rough, and Devora probably could've done without many of the near-death experiences. But she was here, and she was alive. And she was so thankful.

The only part missing was Matthias. Papa had told her Matthias had been meeting with the king's council and the dignitaries from Kadesh to try to hash out a peace treaty everyone agreed with. Papa himself attended many of the meetings, as well. And after a few grueling weeks, Tenton and Kadesh had finally reached an agreement.

She knew he was doing great things, as he always had, but Devora still missed him. She wanted to go see him, but how? She was still weak and healing from the drain of her power against the former queen. It had taken much of her strength to even make it to the rooftop, but she was so glad to be in the open air again.

Sighing, Devora reached out for her tea and took a sip. She would see Matthias again one day. She just prayed it would be soon.

"I do hope that's not the dung tea you talked about," Matthias' voice said from behind her.

Devora was so startled she dropped her cup, splattering tea all over the rooftop. She stood as quickly as she could, which wasn't very quick at all, and faced Matthias. Her heart pounded in her chest as she took him in. Had she wished him there?

His military uniform was as pristine as ever, with the same shiny boots Devora had come to know. Clean-shaven and hair freshly cut, Devora couldn't help but notice how desirable Matthias looked. Heat immediately flooded her cheeks at the thought, and she quickly adverted her eyes. "No, thankfully. I will never take that horrible tea again. It was a lovely cup of chamomile," she replied.

"I see," Matthias said striding toward her.

Devora had seen the bouquet of flowers in his hand and her heart fluttered. Had he brought her flowers? No, she shouldn't assume they were for her. But who else would they be for?

"I wasn't sure what flower you liked, and I heard the new queen loves roses and lilies, so I guessed." Matthias handed her the flowers with a nervous smile.

Devora smiled and accepted the large bouquet. He must have paid a fortune for it, and while Devora wanted to chastise him for spending money on her, she breathed in the honey scent of the lilies instead. Bringing them closer to her face, she closed her eyes and enveloped her senses in the intoxicating aroma. She had always loved roses since her father bought her the pink rose soap from the capital. And lilies were Mama's favorite, so naturally, Devora loved them too.

Opening her eyes, Devora found Matthias studying her. "You deduced correctly, General Blake. I find this bouquet extremely satisfactory. Well done."

Matthias smirked. "Such high praise, I am nearly undone. But I must ask a favor."

Devora frowned. "What's that?"

"It seems I have spoiled a lovely cup of tea. I would not be a gentleman if I did not offer to replace it."

Devora's brows rose. *What is he asking?*

Matthias licked his lips. "Your father has already given me permission, but I desire yours. If you would have me, I would like to take you out for tea every day—any day—you wish. We can explore all the different places in Tenton and Kadesh without the threat of being arrested." Devora laughed and Matthias relaxed a bit before continuing, "I told you back in Kadesh that it wasn't the end because I could never picture my future ending without us being together. All I ask is a chance to win your heart fully, for you have already won mine."

Devora swallowed at the knot in her throat. After all this time this silly man still thought she hated him for his betrayal. Hadn't she told him before that she had forgiven him? She had already told him she loved him at the masquerade ball, for goodness' sake.

"Matthias," she started as she placed the flowers down. Resting her hand on his cheek, she continued, "My heart has been yours since we rode into battle together. When you freed me from the dungeons. Again and again, you always came for me. So, yes, you can buy me tea every day, but I require the payment upfront."

Matthias furrowed his brow. "I don't understand."

Before he could utter another word, Devora brought her lips to his and kissed him softly. Matthias immediately wrapped his arms around her and gently pulled her close. The soft tender kisses quickly turned into ones of desire and they both pulled back.

"We should probably get that tea now," Matthias coughed, stepping away.

Devora laughed and looped her good arm through his offered one. "Lead the way, sir."

Matthias gave her another peck on the cheek before helping her through the latch on the roof. As she and Matthias strode through the streets of Grenly, laughing with one another, Devora realized that though the darkness had tried to creep in and ruin her life, Tunri's light and goodness was there and would always be there to ward it away. All she had to do was have faith.

Epilogue

Six Weeks After the End of the War

The number of weddings Tristan had to attend was unreal. *Two* royal weddings in the span of a few weeks. *And* their coronations afterward. Of course, he was expected to buy gifts for each of the couples for their wedding ceremonies *and* coronations. It was absurd! Thank goodness Ben and Rae decided to hold off on their wedding for now. Did they think he was made of money?

"Well, I used to be," he muttered to himself as he checked his attire a final time in the floor-length mirror. He pushed that thought aside. He had given up his gambling ways, turned over a new leaf, as it were. At least, he was trying to. It helped that now he had someone to keep him accountable.

Though he and Matthias had abdicated the throne, His Highness, King Jacques, insisted they stay at Maldove Palace as long as they wished. And Tristan didn't mind in the slightest. However, up until a few days ago, it certainly was lonely wandering the halls by himself.

Clearing his throat, Tristan smoothed his dark-blue tunic once more, though he knew it held no wrinkles. He placed his hands in his pocket, pulling out the piece of paper he had scoured the former queen's office for.

As soon as Jacques stated he needed help reading through the former king's and queen's documents, Tristan jumped at the chance. After Nadia had told him that her parents had been taken in the raid against Tinkers years ago, Tristan made it his sole responsibility to find out what happened to them. Though Nadia put up a tough face, he knew it was a façade. He recognized the same pain and hurt he had held in his heart for many years lingering in her eyes; the fear of not knowing what happened. And if he could remedy that pain in the slightest, he would.

"Well, old boy," Tristan said to himself. "It's now or never."

The palace hall seemed to elongate as he strode toward the room Nadia and Rae were staying in before Jacques' and Ida's wedding that evening. Even though Tristan had originally traveled to Yekel with Ben, Rae, and Nadia, he knew he needed to be with Matthias and give him all the information the queen had told him over the past years.

They had just arrived yesterday, and it took everything in Tristan's power to not run straight into Nadia's arms. But it was well past the appropriate time of day to call upon her, so he had to wait until now.

His heart felt like a thousand hammers pounding as he came upon the arched wooden door. And though he willed his hand to knock, it didn't obey his command. Tristan released a frustrated breath. What was wrong with him? He had successfully wooed many women in the past. Why was he so nervous now?

Because you actually care for this one.

Tristan's throat dried at the thought. It was true. And with all the nonsensical weddings swirling around, his mind couldn't avoid picturing what his future would look like. And whether Nadia would be a part of it.

"Come on, man," Tristan growled to himself. "You can do this." Steeling his courage, Tristan lifted his hand and knocked three times on the door. A moment passed and panic tightened Tristan's throat. He knew it. Nadia had reconsidered and decided to hate him. Defeated, Tristan started to turn away.

But then the glass doorknob turned, and Tristan righted himself, donning his usual winning smile.

"Oh, Tristan," Rae said, with a soft smile. "I thought you were Ben. Nadia is just inside." She opened the door further.

Swathed in a light-blue gown trimmed with silver, Tristan couldn't believe the transformation of Rae from when he first saw her in Yekel. The girl with no hair and an angry scowl had turned into a beautiful woman.

"Ah, well I'm sure he will regret not being here to see how lovely you look," Tristan said with a bow.

Rae blushed at his statement before a set of footsteps stopped behind him.

"Luckily, I'm here now," Ben's voice said, and Tristan turned to allow the tall man through.

"You look amazing," Ben whispered, kissing Rae on the cheek.

And though Tristan wanted to scoff, he found himself happy for the couple. From what he had witnessed and heard, they had been through many hard times together. Now was their time for peace and happiness.

As Rae took Ben's arm and waved to Tristan, she left the door to their room open. Nadia still hadn't emerged.

Finding his courage once more, Tristan knocked again lightly on the door and walked into the room. The space was similar to his with fine furniture, thick curtains and a crackling fire. But what made his jaw almost hit the floor was the beautiful woman strapping a dagger to her thigh.

"You look—" Tristan's voice squeaked before he cleared his voice, embarrassed. "My dear, you are a vision."

Nadia turned toward him, and his heart stopped. Up until this moment he had only seen her in slacks and tunics. Usually, her hands and face were covered in charcoal as well, but Tristan always found it endearing. But now she wore a shimmering yellow dress that sparkled every time she moved. Could this angel before him be the same woman?

"Hey Tris," Nadia smiled, the gold lining her eyes glinting as she smiled at him. "I was worried when you didn't come see me last night."

Tristan commanded himself to speak and in a normal voice. "I wanted to but didn't think the time of day was appropriate to call upon a young lady."

Nadia scrunched her nose with a laugh. "Ben was in here as soon as he dropped his things off in his room."

Tristan frowned. "Well, yes, if someone kept him from Rae, he'd probably shoot them." As he had threatened to do to Tristan many times.

"True," Nadia agreed as she hid another three small daggers in the bodice of her dress.

Tristan did his best to keep his eyes in the appropriate places. "Do you really think you need all that?"

Nadia shrugged, sliding the last dagger in place. "I like to be prepared." Turning, she took another final look in the mirror and fluffed her hair. She had decided to keep it the same short length and Tristan loved it. When she faced him once more, he noticed the golden hoops dangling from her ears.

"Are those earrings?" he questioned, never picturing Nadia as one who liked jewelry.

"Yep," she said, coming toward him. "My favorite pair too."

"This is good information to know," Tristan said, wrapping his arms around her. "I shall have to procure you new favorites."

Nadia laughed again and Tristan loved the sound. But he knew he had to tell her what he had found before they headed downstairs.

Taking her hands in his, Tristan said, "Nadia, I have so enjoyed the time we've spent together."

At his words, Nadia's smile fell, her eyes suspicious. Tristan knew what it sounded like, but he had to press on. "There is something I must tell you," he continued. "You told me before about your parents, how they were taken by the kingdom when

Rae's father was taken. However, Lucas was able to escape to Totem, but your parents were never heard from."

Nadia furrowed her brows. "Why are you bringing this up now?"

"Please, trust me," Tristan begged as he pulled the paper from his pocket. "I worked with Matthias and Jacques filing through the documents of the former king and queen, and I found this."

He watched Nadia's cautious gaze turn to the paper he handed her. As she read the paper, she brought a hand to her mouth, tears in her eyes.

"Is this true?" she asked.

Tristan squeezed her hand. "It's true. Nadia, your parents are still alive."

Five Years Later

Five years had passed, and Matthias couldn't believe he was finally cleaning out his desk in his office at the Fortress. Though the new kings and queens of Tenton and Kadesh were accepted by most of their citizens, there were always those trying to vie for power when a new leader came into their reign. Thank goodness Jacques was a kind-hearted king, but also a just king who wouldn't allow uprisings and riots to spread throughout his kingdom. Like Jacques, King Amal had his own worries with trying to rid Kadesh of any remnants of the Goddess Pahga. It was a rocky road for the first few years, but it seemed things were finally starting to smooth out.

Matthias placed his inkwell and quills in his bag. He had told Jacques he would stay as commander and general of Tenton's army long enough to train his successor. Thankfully, Sir Tocha had proven to be an excellent study and was ready to take command of His Majesty's Army at any time.

As Matthias went to place a scroll in his bag, his fingers brushed against a small box sitting at the bottom. He smiled at the box and placed it in his pocket. Well, there was one part of his life he had already figured out.

Over these past five years, he and Devora were able to enjoy a proper courtship. While she assisted in rebuilding the curriculum at Vlacklear—while also taking her own studies—Matthias was just beyond the murky lake at the Fortress. Twenty-seven minutes and forty-five seconds was exactly how long it took for him to saddle Atir and ride to the school to join Devora for lunch because he did it almost every day. She offered for her to come to him some days, but Matthias never wanted her to enter the stone-cold Fortress again. Though, the Fortress' reputation was changing, as well.

Instead of a half-prison, half-military academy, a new military school was being built next to Vlacklear Academy, leaving the Fortress to become a complete prison once again. And he had just been offered a position as one of their professors.

Matthias closed his bag and stared at his bare office, remembering how many times he had desired to be rid of the awful prison. And now he could finally leave.

Still, these past years trying to rebuild a broken system felt lonely without Warden Hazor by his side. The man had taught him so much and Matthias never got to say thank you. However, Jacques and Ida had instilled a day of remembrance for the sacrifice of the warden and the other soldiers who gave their lives for their kingdom. A statue of the rugged man would be placed before the new military academy as soon as it was complete. Jacques knew how much the warden would've hated the statue, but Ida insisted it be built all the same.

Matthias released a heavy sigh and hauled his pack onto his shoulder. He only wished, wherever the warden's soul was now, that he knew how much Matthias appreciated everything.

As he started toward the door, the sound of paper rustled behind him. Frowning, Matthias turned around. He had checked his desk thoroughly, but perhaps he had forgotten something. Placing his pack down, he strode toward the piece of paper that had fallen from the underside of his desk.

Upon scanning the first few lines, Matthias' eyes widened in shock, recognizing the warden's bold writing.

Blake, if you're reading this, I'm probably dead. Which is unfortunate for me, but it means I finally completed my task.

It was eerie how Matthias could almost hear Warden Hazor reciting the letter.

It's finally time for me to tell you everything.

Matthias sat back in his chair, unable to believe everything the warden had written. Shortly after his wife and daughter had been killed by Kadeshians, Phineas Hazor had been given a single vision from Tunri. But in that vision, he was told everything he needed to know and do in order to save the spirit of Tenton.

By Tunri, Himself, Warden Hazor had been named the guardian of Tenton and was charged with protecting a group of specific people, for they were the ones who would change the course of Tenton's future.

Matthias rubbed his eyes in disbelief. It now all made sense why Warden Hazor was always one step ahead. He always was able to give insight or encourage all of them in a certain way.

I always knew this path would lead to my death. But once my wife and daughter were taken from me, my soul was already dead. It was you and your friends who revived my soul and gave me hope that there really is a God.

You've always been a solid soldier and an even better man, Blake, better than I could ever hope to be. I wish you and the Seer much happiness, if you ever told her how you feel.

Matthias couldn't help but laugh at the sentence with tears rolling down his cheeks. While he always thought he was so careful with his feelings, apparently everyone knew how much he cared for Devora.

Take the lessons I've taught you and use them for good. Change this nation for the better and right the wrongs of the past. Since you came to my prison in your brother's stead, I always placed my bet on you and I'm glad to know I gambled correctly.

Matthias stared at the letter, not knowing what else to think, until he realized his hands were covering the last sentence.

Don't worry about Vinn. We've been friends for many years, and he was ready to return to his spirit form. Though I acted irate when the Seer released him from the Fortress, I was glad someone was finally able to do so. He is at peace and will continue to watch over Tenton so long as it follows Tunri's ways.

Matthias stared at the corner of the room, trying to process through what he just read. His thoughts flitted back to when Queen Leza was finally defeated. Vinn's lifeless form had disappeared entirely. Once Devora had healed from the experience, she was frantic that something had happened to him. But his mother always assured her that Vinn was okay. Was this what she meant?

Matthias ran his eyes over the script again. Everything it explained made sense to him. He only wished the warden was here to deliver the news in person.

Standing, Matthias walked over to his bag he left on the floor and placed the letter inside. As a final thank you and farewell, he would make sure the warden's years-long efforts would be acknowledged.

Devora placed the brand-new purple sash across her chest, unable to believe five years had already passed since Queen Leza tried to destroy Tenton and Kadesh. Though her wounds had healed from that day, the memories would never leave her mind. Still, tonight was a celebration of the five-year union between Tenton and Kadesh, and Devora didn't want to dwell on the horrors of the past.

Picking up a silver brush Matthias had bought for her, Devora ran it through her long hair. She smiled in the mirror, remembering having to tell the man to stop buying her so many presents. Though she loved gifts, the best gift was spending time with him. Thankfully Matthias had slowed down on all the presents, but she still wasn't surprised if a bouquet of roses or a slice of cocoa cake was delivered to her while she was at Vlacklear Academy.

It had been an intense but fulfilling five years at the academy. While many of the teachers stayed on to keep the school running, there were still gaps that needed to be filled and an overhaul of many regulations the former headmistress, General Beta, enacted. After hours, Devora worked with Ida—Queen Ida—Papa, Professor Mal, and a handful of other former students and professors of the academy to rebuild it into something great.

Thankfully, King Jacques—it was so odd to call her friends such high names—gave them all the week off to celebrate the five-year anniversary. And though Devora enjoyed her work and studies at Vlacklear, she also enjoyed a break.

Smoothing out her hair, Devora pinned back one side with a silver comb with pink pearls, another gift from Matthias. He had remembered the one Nadia had made her when she first entered Regulus Protecti and always wished to get her a new one.

Devora couldn't believe Matthias remembered so many little details about her and she was so thankful to Tunri that they were able to have this time together. But she would be lying if she said she never thought about what would happen next. Would he just continue to court her forever? Or would *something* finally happen?

Sighing, Devora took in her reflection in the mirror. When her Categorization Call first happened, she was only a girl who felt confident that she was ready to take on the world. Now, she was a woman and only desired a quiet, peaceful life with the man she loved. Placing a dab of rouge on her lips, Devora spread it with her pinky then smiled. How funny it was that time changed so many things.

A knock sounded at her door and Devora turned. Ida insisted that she get ready at the palace before the celebration so they could enter the party together.

"You'll already be at Vlacklear, it's just a carriage ride away." Ida's big doe eyes grew wide, already persuading Devora to agree.

"All right," she said. "But I do need to tell Mama and—"

"Already taken care of," the queen laughed, taking Devora's hand. "Come on, I had a special dress made for you."

And a special dress it was. Devora was frightened to ask how much she owed Ida for the glittering lilac-colored gown. Even when she brought it up, Ida said Devora was not allowed to pay for any of it, for it was a gift.

Devora ran her hands along the small beads embroidered along the side of the dress. It was a masterpiece, and she thanked Ida profusely.

The knock sounded again, and Devora hurried to the door.

"You look extravagant, my lady," Jacques said, the golden crown glinting on his head.

Devora curtsied. "Thank you, Your Highness."

"Oh stop, none of that," he insisted, pulling her up. "Dear friends never need to bow to me."

Devora glanced up at her long-time friend, still unable to believe he was a king and that he had grown a rather thick beard over the past few years.

"I knew that gown would be perfect for you," Ida beamed, her hands resting on her stomach.

Though Devora hadn't been told officially yet, there were rumors a new heir may be coming in the not-so-distant future.

"I still feel I should contribute something to the cost," Devora replied as Jacques extended his arm to her.

Ida clucked her tongue, taking Jacques' other arm. "Absolutely not. Tonight, you deserve the best."

Devora furrowed her brow, wondering what the king and queen were planning when they came to the stairwell before the ballroom. A figure, clad in all black stood at the top, waiting for their arrival.

Devora's heart skipped a beat as she looked upon Matthias. He was just as handsome as when she first saw him at the Fortress, but she would never tell him she'd thought that.

Matthias turned his gray eyes on her and smiled. "You're a dream, my love."

Devora blushed at the compliment and left Jacques' arm to Matthias' proffered one. When the king and queen began talking among themselves, Matthias leaned down to her ear. "How long do we have to stay at this party?"

Devora laughed. "It hasn't even begun yet and you already want to leave?"

Matthias pulled her close. "I just don't want to have to fight off all those suitors trying to steal a dance with you."

Rolling her eyes, Devora kissed him on the cheek. "Right, because there are *so* many suitors lined up wanting to dance with me."

"I will fend them off, one by one," Matthias replied, his face serious.

"Come on," Devora said, pulling him down the stairs. "Everyone is waiting for us."

Laughing, Matthias joined her side as they met with the rest of their friends.

After the king and queen were announced, the ball officially began, and it was wonderful. Jovial music bounced through the grand hall, immaculate foods and drinks were continuously served and Devora couldn't remember the last time she had enjoyed such fun with her friends.

When she and Matthias weren't dancing, she was catching up with Ida, Hestia and Reese, Nadia, Rae and Queen Haden—who had made a special visit just for the night. Unfortunately, King Amal couldn't attend but sent his regards and several barrels of Kadeshian wine to enjoy.

"I just hope you all like the taste," the queen of Kadesh said with a smile. "I used to enjoy it, but not so much anymore." She stuck out her tongue.

"Do not fear, my queen, I shall consume the wine for you," Tristan said with a valiant bow before hurrying toward the table with filled glasses.

They all looked at Nadia, who shook her head and followed Tristan. Thankfully he only took one glass for each of them and with Nadia's help brought them back.

"So, Reese, how is Sandje Textiles?" Ida asked, choosing to have a glass of water instead of wine.

Reese swirled her glass, her abacus absent in lieu of the night's celebration. "Father's corruption ran deep through the business, but I believe we are finally on the other side." She glanced at her sister who was twirling on the dance floor with her husband, Charles, Jacques' younger cousin. "Though," Reese continued. "I don't know how much longer Hestia will desire to work with me. There is talk of beginning a family and all that." Reese took a long swig of her wine.

Devora and the others gasped before Reese shushed them. "No, no, say nothing to her!"

"Say nothing to who?" Hestia asked, pushing her way to sit in the group.

Charles gave her a kiss before joining his cousin and the others who were enjoying the hors d'oeuvres provided.

"The queen was just asking me about how my business was going," Rae interceded, causing Reese's tense shoulders to drop in relief.

"Y-yes!" Ida cried with a too wide grin. "How is everything, Rae?"

Devora smiled as she watched Rae explain her and Ben's bakery they had opened in Juro. Matthias mentioned to the king that Rae had never been honored for defeating General Yada in Yekel and deserved to be rewarded. While Rae turned down offers of grand titles and mansions, she couldn't say no when the king offered her the prime spot for a bakery of her own in the capital city. Shortly after they had the grand opening, Ben and Rae had a quiet wedding ceremony in their bakery, inviting only their close friends and family. It was a wonderful celebration filled with amazingly delicious desserts.

"Rae's bakery even provided most of the desserts for the celebration tonight," Ida chimed in, pulling Devora's focus back on the present conversation.

"I could tell with how amazing everything tastes," Hestia commented before she shoved a petit four in her mouth.

Rae laughed. "Yes, it was a lot of hard work, but we can't say no to business with the king and queen of Tenton."

"You'll have to come visit soon and share your recipes with me," Queen Haden said to her sister.

"Of course," Rae agreed, squeezing the Queen of Kadesh's hand.

"Excuse me, ladies," Matthias said, resting his hand on Devora's shoulder. "Could I steal my date for a moment?"

Devora placed her hand over his as she glanced up. But as she started to stand, she noticed all her friends giving her extra happy grins and she wasn't sure why.

Shrugging it off, Devora followed Matthias to the balcony where they had stood during the masquerade ball. A cool breeze danced over her skin, and she wrapped her arms around her stomach. The harvest season was just about to end, but it was far too early for snow to begin. One of the things Devora loved about living in the north was the cozy snowy days Matthias and her spent together.

Matthias' back faced her as he peered over the balcony. She came up beside him, resting her head against his arm.

"This brings back memories, doesn't it?" she asked.

"It does," he replied, his warm breath a cloud against the cool night air. "Though I am thankful you haven't had a vision to predict my inevitable demise." He laughed and wrapped an arm around her waist.

Devora laughed and snuggled closer to him. Her visions had still occurred throughout the last five years, but they were nowhere near as critical or life-threatening as the ones before, and for that she was thankful. Kanna had also been teaching Devora how to better control and strengthen her Seeing abilities. Devora was incredibly thankful for the lessons and had learned so much.

Matthias suddenly turned toward her, his face serious. "Devora, we have been together for five years now."

Devora placed her hands on his biceps, unsure of where this conversation was heading.

"And they have been the best five years of my life, so far," Matthias continued. "But it's not enough."

Devora looked up at him. "What do you mean?"

She watched his throat bob before he took a step back from her. For a moment, fear clenched her heart, and she thought he wished for them to each walk their separate ways.

But instead of walking away, Matthias knelt on one knee and held out a small black box. Devora gasped, struck still by the shining diamond sparkling up at her. Suddenly she realized why Ida had given her such an extravagant gown.

"The moment you arrived at the Fortress and defied the warden, I knew you were going to turn my life upside down," he said, his own eyes glistening with tears. "And you have in the very best way. Before I met you, I was a shell of a man. You have revived my cold heart that I thought would never love again."

Devora's own tears flew down her face, no doubt ruining the kohl lining her eyes.

"Would you do me the honor of becoming my wife? To be by my side forever?"

Devora didn't reply. Instead, she launched herself into Matthias' arms, knocking him flat on his back on the balcony.

Kissing him firmly, she then replied, "I have been waiting for this, sir."

Matthias brushed a strand of her hair out of her eyes with a smile. "Forgive me, my lady. I will do my best never to disappoint you again."

As he brought his lips to hers, the soft tickle of snowflakes began to fall from the moonlit sky. Devora and Matthias shared many more kisses on the balcony before watching the snow cover the land in a blanket of white.

And though Devora thought it might be a trick of the reflection of the snow, in her heart she knew she saw the form of a white elk raising its antlers to her, a reassurance that the future was beautiful and bright.

Acknowledgements

The ending of a series is always bittersweet. I love having a complete story and seeing how much my characters, and myself, have grown. But saying good-bye to characters who all hold a piece of my heart is hard. Within their stories I have tried to describe my own struggles, hardships, and difficulties whether emotional, physical, or spiritual and how I've overcome them.

I pray you've enjoyed the stories that comprised The Legacy Chapters. It has been an honor and pleasure having you along for this journey.

First, I always thank Jesus Christ, my Lord and Savior, the inspiration and foundation for all my writing.

To David and my boys, you are my whole world.

To my family, thank you for always cheering me on.

To Amber and Crystal, thank you for the constant support, love, and willingness to talk me off the cliff when I'm ready to quit writing.

To April and Quill & Flame Publishing, We did it! The story that you took a chance on and signed first is finally done! Thank you for your willingness and dedication to my stories.

And finally, to all my amazing readers, This is it, you made it to the end of the story. I hope I have made this conclusion one that you think of and enjoy for many years to come.

www.ingramcontent.com/pod-product-compliance
Lightning Source LLC
Chambersburg PA
CBHW021407310726
48971CB00005B/1230